The Lovers' Tango

"Mark Rubinstein's *The Lovers' Tango* is a sultry, elegant piece of romantic noir. It has a terrific legal backdrop that merges the tale into a steamy courtroom thriller focusing on human frailty and the limitations of what we see before us."

 —Jon Land, *USA Today* bestselling author of *Strong Darkness*

"*The Lovers' Tango* is a true work of art, precisely constructed, skillfully rendered. It's one of *those* novels. A book you'll remember for a long, long time."

 —Scott Pratt, bestselling author of the Joe Dillard series

"Mark Rubinstein is a superb storyteller. His novels tap into the deepest of human emotions."

 —Raymond Khoury, bestselling author of the Sean Reilly
  series

Mad Dog House

"I stayed up all night to read *Mad Dog House*. I didn't plan on it, but when I got into it, I couldn't put it down. It was fantastic, riveting, suspenseful, twisting, loving, horrific."

 —Martin West, film and television actor and filmmaker

"The characters in *Mad Dog House* are compellingly real. It was a great read!"

 —Ann Chernow, artist and writer

"In Mark Rubinstein's *Mad Dog House*, the characters—all well developed and dripping with authenticity—propel the novel along with style and edge-of-your-seat excitement."

 —Judith Marks-White, author of *Seducing Harry* and *Bachelor
  Degree* and columnist, "The Light Touch," *Westport (CT)
  News*

Love Gone Mad

"*Love Gone Mad* is a beautifully crafted suspense novel. The characters are people you care about; the story is fast paced and cleverly plotted."
  —Scott Pratt, bestselling author of the Joe Dillard series

"I quickly found myself caught up in *Love Gone Mad*—part love story, part *Halloween*, and part legal thriller."
  —Elissa Durwood Grodin, author of *Physics Can Be Fatal*

"Rubinstein's second foray into the fiction arena (after *Mad Dog House*) is an intense thriller that promises readers surprising twists, heart-pounding suspense, and a bird's-eye view into both the mind of a madman and a dizzyingly realistic account of how it feels to be stalked as prey."
  —*Library Journal*

Mad Dog Justice

"What price must a man pay for doing a very bad thing for a very good reason? That is the question *Mad Dog Justice* poses, and the answer is written with great skill and creaks with tension and truth."
  —Simon Toyne, author of the internationally bestselling
    Sanctus Trilogy

"*Mad Dog Justice* speeds along with more turns than a Vespa cruising through traffic. It's a smart, twisting thriller that grows into the weightier issues of friendship, vengeance, and betrayal."
  —Andrew Gross, bestselling author of *No Way Back* and
    Everything to Lose

"*Mad Dog Justice* thrums with relentless intensity and suspense. Rubinstein has created a palpable cast of characters who stay with you long after you finish the book."
  —Jessica Speart, author of *A Killing Season* and *Restless Waters*

The Lovers' TANGO
A Novel

Other Books by Mark Rubinstein

Fiction

Stone Soup, Edited with Ann Chernow
Mad Dog House
Love Gone Mad
Mad Dog Justice
The Foot Soldier, a novella
Return to Sandara, a novella

Nonfiction

The First Encounter: The Beginnings in Psychotherapy
with Dr. William Console and Dr. Richard C. Simons (Jason Aronson)

The Complete Book of Cosmetic Surgery
with Dr. Dennis P. Cirillo (Simon & Schuster)

New Choices: The Latest Options in Treating Breast Cancer
with Dr. Dennis P. Cirillo (Dodd Mead)

Heartplan: A Complete Program for Total Fitness of Heart & Mind
with Dr. David L. Copen (McGraw-Hill)

*The Growing Years: The New York Hospital-Cornell Medical Center
Guide to Your Child's Emotional Development* (Atheneum)

The Lovers' TANGO

A Novel

MARK RUBINSTEIN

Thunder Lake Press

Thunder Lake Press
25602 Alicia Parkway #512
Laguna Hills, CA 92653
www.thunderlakepress.com

Publisher's Note: This is a work of fiction. Names, characters, places, and incidents are a product of the author's imagination. Locales and public names are sometimes used for atmospheric purposes. Any resemblance to actual people, living or dead, or to businesses, companies, events, institutions, or locales is completely coincidental.

Ordering Information

Quantity sales. Special discounts are available on quantity purchases by corporations, associations, and others. For details, contact the "Special Sales Department" at the address above.

Orders by US trade bookstores and wholesalers. Please contact BCH: (800) 431-1579 or visit www.bookch.com for details.

Printed in the United States of America

Rubinstein, Mark
    The lover's tango : a novel / Mark Rubinstein. --
  First edition.
    pages cm
    LCCN 2015902831
    ISBN 978-0-9856268-2-2

    1. Novelists--Fiction. 2. Man-woman relationships--
Fiction. 3. Detective and mystery stories.
4. Psychological fiction. 5. Suspense fiction. 6. Love
stories. I. Title.
    PS3618.U3L684 2015   813'.6
    QBI15-600064
First Edition

19 18 17 16 15   10 9 8 7 6 5 4 3 2 1

Author photo: Jerriann Geller

Please, just for me, forget the steps. Hold me, feel the music, and give me your soul. Then, I can give you mine.
  —Anonymous

You must understand, ladies and gentlemen, there are no absolute certainties when we deal with human affairs.
  —Hon. J. J. Marin

For Linda, who saved my life

Preface

Tango, A Dance of Love and Death
Excerpted and edited from an article by Alexander Mead,
Denver, Colorado (2000)
http://www.well.com/~vamead/Tango_Dance_Love_Death_00.html

Milan Kundera said loving someone is not deepened by being a passive object of adoration, but by the sacrifices one makes for the beloved. We may be attracted to "perfection" but loving the imperfections, forgiving the other's weaknesses, creates the deepest attachment.

We come to tango with great imperfections. Every devotee is challenged by the dance. It's like learning a new language: a few basic moves form the vocabulary; a set of customs and grammatical rules define the moves; and whatever you express must work within the rhythm and mood of the music. And, of course, the flow and poetry of the movement comes from the partners weaving their nonverbal conversation.

Tango calls for mental, emotional, and physical cultivation. You must quiet your chattering mind, relax your nervous anticipation, and quell any fears of intimacy.

The partners' roles have some deep atavistic appeal for a man and woman. The man navigates the floor, guides the couple, and sets the pattern and musical interpretation. His goal is to make the woman look and feel beautiful, cared-for. The woman must be in tune with him, physically, emotionally, intuitively. Yet, she has freedom to decorate and embellish the rough outline set by her partner. Her task is to be beautiful and make him look beautiful.

Argentine tango emphasizes grace and intense connection. Physical positions are clearly defined to achieve the partners' most intimate connection.

The tango is not done by one's self, or for one's self, but with a partner, and with a feeling of sublimated seduction. Insecurities may be present. Self-doubt, defeat, and death are always just around the corner. The dance reminds us of these uncomfortable matters lurking just beneath a gorgeously glazed surface.

Tango music pulls us in with its sadness and beauty. It reminds us that suffering is part of life. Like blues and flamenco, tango music carries the soul of the oppressed, their love, their suffering, and their death.

Chapter 1

I realized everything would change the moment I saw her. But I could never have known the life I lived and loved would come to so disastrous an end.

It began fifteen years ago at a West Village party, when the sound system stopped John Coltrane's saxophone from crooning "You Don't Know What Love Is."

The sudden silence was odd for this maxed-out throng, gathered in an old brownstone, because this crowd—artists, actors, musicians, and writers—was always clamorous. Plenty of booze, coke, and weed made for stratospherically high spirits.

But when Coltrane's saxophone stopped midnote—leaving a wake of silence—the lights began dimming.

That was the moment my life changed.

Because that's when I saw her.

I didn't know her name. I simply saw a raven-haired, olive-skinned woman take to the dance floor. Her hair was drawn back in a bun, accentuating her strikingly high cheekbones. She had dark eyes, a sloping nose with flared nostrils, and luscious lips. Her crimson-red pencil skirt was slit high on one thigh, and she was so very Latin-looking, so sensuous.

The crowd edged to the periphery. I sensed many people knew her. A low-level voltage pervaded the room. This incredible-looking woman—Nora, I later learned—stood theatrically poised as a svelte Latin-looking guy slipped an arm around her waist.

She held this conquistador's eyes hungrily, yet there was remoteness, too. I felt my pulse quicken. My knees weakened. She reminded me of Carmen in Bizet's opera.

Suddenly, voluptuous tango music swelled through the sound system.

The dance began.

She moved with intense feline grace. I was riveted by the arch of her back, by its lithe muscularity, by her toned, bare arms, exquisite legs, and the sheen of her bronzed skin. As they tangoed, her head-snaps were at one with the music, as she turned, swirled, and dipped.

I was consumed by the power of the dance. It was a dialogue of passion, a promise of something to come—the prologue of a love story.

Heat rose in my face, and my scalp prickled deliciously. I could have been watching a habanera at a lantern-lit café in Buenos Aires. My writer's imagination was working overtime.

Applause rocked the room when the lighting returned. As the woman disappeared into the crowd, I stood in a state of stunned silence, certain she was unattainable.

"Unbelievable, isn't she?"

A woman about my age—thirty, or so—looked up at me. She, too, had that Latin look—sensuous, pulsing with life. Yet, she looked partly Eastern European, too, maybe Polish or Russian. Her features were less delicate, more Slavic than Nora's. But there was that same black hair and dark, laughing eyes.

"What do you think?" she asked with a nod toward the dance floor.

"She's the most beautiful woman I've ever seen. And . . . expressive . . ."

"She's my sister, Nora."

"Yes, there's a resemblance."

"That's the best compliment I've heard in years," she said, extending her hand. "I'm Lee. Lee Walsh."

"Bill Shaw."

"Would you like to meet her?"

Was this a hallucination? A surge of excitement ramped through me.

"Of course. But I . . ."

"The only *but* is that she'll eat you alive."

"I'll take my chances," I said, wondering if perhaps I was dreaming. Yes, I'd had luck with women, but this seemed beyond possibility.

"I'll be right back," she said, and melted into the throng.

It occurred to me, despite all the women I'd known, I felt like a callow high school kid—uncertain, nervous. I belted down the rest of my scotch, feeling its warmth spread through my cheeks.

When the sisters approached, I was actually quivering with anticipation. I momentarily felt light-headed.

In her stiletto heels, Nora was my height. Close up, her eyes— large, dark, and liquid—roamed over me. I felt I could lose myself in the depth of her gaze.

"Nora Reyes, this is Bill Shaw," Lee said.

As I grasped Nora's hand, tingling coursed through me. Her hair glistened in the overhead light. Her nose swept down to those flaring nostrils. And her chin was full, with a plump underbelly— soft and inviting. Her skin appeared moist; I inhaled deeply, her essence filling my nostrils.

Her eyes moved brazenly over me. I felt exposed, vulnerable. Yes, Lee was right: I was being devoured by this gorgeous woman.

"I'll leave you two alone," Lee said, and was gone.

Coltrane's sax sang "All or Nothing at All." A delicious yearn- ing seeped through me, and I knew I'd always remember that night.

"Tell me, Bill," Nora said. "Have I made a mistake all these years, avoiding these West Village get-togethers?"

"You've done the right thing."

"And, tonight? Coming here?"

"The right thing, again."

She laughed. "I suspect so."

"Hopefully, your suspicions will be realized."

She laughed with an open mouth. Her teeth were perfect. Her lips were sensuous, bow-shaped, pliant, and moist-looking. I felt an insane urge to press my lips to hers, to taste the wetness of her tongue, to feel her flesh against mine. It was a craving so intense, I thought for a moment I would clutch her in my arms, press her to me, and feel her heat.

"That was a beautiful tango. Argentine, right?" I said.

"Yes. There are different types."

"Just a guess," I offered, staring into her bottomless eyes.

"A very good one," she said, as her finger brushed my cheek. My face burned.

"I could teach the tango to you."

"I'd like that." My body thrummed "Are you a professional dancer?"

"No, an actor."

"Have I seen you in anything?"

"Not unless you watch the soaps. I'm in *The Burning World*. But tell me what *you* do, Bill." She moved closer.

"I'm a writer," I said, hoping not to sound like every fool at this gathering.

"Really? You look like a . . . a cop."

I laughed self-consciously. I'd been told this so often, I felt I should have an honorary badge.

"Yes. You're tall and well built. You have a strong face. And those eyes. Such a deep blue. You look very . . . rugged. I like that in a man. And a writer—brains *and* brawn," she said, canting her head.

"You're embarrassing me." My face felt flushed.

"No, I'm not. You love it," she replied, poking a finger into my chest. "Have I read anything you've written?"

"Only if you read crime fiction." My God, did I sound like I was bragging? "I wrote *Fire and Ice*."

"*Fire and Ice?* Isn't that a movie?"

"Yes."

"About a serial killer?"

"Yes. It was adapted from the novel."

"Now I'll have to read the book. I'm an avid reader. You wouldn't be looking for an editor, would you?"

"I've never thought about it, but that could be arranged."

"Bill, we can arrange anything we want," she whispered in my ear.

"How about we arrange to go to dinner?" *God, where did that come from?* It had slipped out. My legs were turning to liquid.

"Where will we go?"

"There's a lovely Spanish restaurant on Charles Street . . . El Charro," I said, afraid she might think I was patronizing her.

"That sounds great. And then what?"

"Then . . ." I was at a loss for words. My throat tightened.

"I'll bet you live near the restaurant," she said with laughing eyes.

"I live on Charles Street, a garden apartment in a brownstone."

"Right near the restaurant?"

I nodded.

"That would be wonderful," she said, grabbing my arm.

That night was the beginning of the end of everything.

Chapter 2

It would be another night of booze-soaked gloom since Nora's funeral.

A goddamned funeral, only fifteen years after that magical night in the West Village. Feeling depleted, I was sipping more Johnnie Walker when the intercom's buzzing jangled in a burst of static-like sound. My heart seized. Then coldness seeped through my chest. Wondering who'd bother to visit so late in the evening, only a few days after Nora was buried, I plodded unsteadily to the foyer.

When I picked up the receiver, the doorman announced, "Mr. Shaw, some policemen are here to see you."

A shiver slithered through me. Had they come because of what Nora said before she died? Her last whispered words ran silently through my head.

As I recalled those words at that moment, a hollow sensation leaked its way through me.

"Send them up," I heard myself say. My stomach somersaulting.

I made my way into the kitchen and dumped the rest of the scotch into the sink. My hands felt weak.

Why are the cops here? This can't be good. Something's terribly wrong.

A short while later, murmuring came from the hallway. Then, the sound of feet on the carpet.

A brief pause.

The doorbell rang.

Opening the door, I saw a middle-aged guy with broad shoulders, a wide face, and a flattened nose. A younger man stood behind him. "William Shaw? I'm Detective Phil Kaufman, NYPD," the older one said, flashing his badge. "This is Detective Don Cirillo. May we come in?"

Do I have a choice? When cops ask permission, they're donning a mask of civility, but it's bullshit.

In the living room, I plopped down in a love seat opposite the sofa where the detectives sat. Cirillo, a tall, angular guy, peered at the framed ink etchings on the wall—stuff Nora loved and bought in various SoHo galleries. Kaufman took a small pad from his breast pocket, flipped open the pages, and eyeballed me.

"Mr. Shaw, we need to wrap up the investigation into your wife's death."

Investigation? What in hell is this about?

"Look, guys, I told the doctors everything."

The room swayed. My head felt fuzzy, as though I would faint. *My wife's death . . .* It still seemed unimaginable, beyond belief.

"There are still some questions," Kaufman said.

"Questions? What questions? Nora died from MS and her blood thinner, the warfarin. The doctors said—"

"We know what the doctors said, Mr. Shaw. But we need to clear up a few things."

Cirillo stared at a framed, glossy, black-and-white photo of Nora from her acting days. Was he ogling her? Was he aroused by her? I felt like slamming a fist into his gut.

"Mr. Shaw?" Kaufman said.

I turned to him.

He said nothing, just stared at me.

"I'd be happy to help, Detectives," I said, focusing on Kaufman. "But I'm exhausted. How 'bout we talk tomorrow morning and—"

"I suggest we go to the precinct now, Mr. Shaw."

"Why not here?" I glanced at the clock on the credenza: 10:04. My bones ached and my head throbbed. Not the time to talk to cops.

"I'll explain at the precinct, sir."

Cirillo scanned the bookshelves, the Kashan rugs, the furnishings; his gaze rested again on Nora's photo. My chest tightened at the hungry look in this young punk's eyes. I nearly choked on fumes of anger.

"I'm not sure I want to do this." My voice sounded weak in my ears.

"It's your right, sir. But it would be better to go now."

There was a vague yet discernible hint of threat in Kaufman's tone. Or was my mind playing tricks on me? I hadn't slept for days and was half in Johnnie Black's booze bag. Despite my scotch-addled brain, I sensed danger. Was I imagining something ominous?

About to refuse Kaufman's strong suggestion to go to the station house, I realized if I sent them away, I'd cogitate endlessly, far into the morning. I'd be left with a knifelike level of worry—even fear—about what the cops were after, and the night would brim with tension and turmoil. And, I'd be alone with my emptiness. I'd just guzzle more Johnnie Black. And still, sleep would evade me. My thoughts would swirl in a never-ending spiral of doubt and rumination—wondering if things could have been different. If only I'd been able to keep Nora alive for even a few more months.

But it was too late. It was all over.

The days of hope were gone.

With Nora dead, was there any purpose to my existence? I was forty-five years old, yet felt like I was dying a slow, tortured death.

And maybe that would be best: to die—just as my beloved Nora did.

Chapter 3

I hadn't been in Manhattan's 19th Precinct since interviewing Detective Ed Hanson for my last crime novel, written five years earlier. It might as well have been a century ago.

Even with concessions to modernity, an interrogation room still looked the same. When the door closed, the air seemed sucked out of the enclosure, as though it was a vacuum-sealed box. Soundproof cork covered three walls. Words sounded dull, stifled, as though my ears were clogged. The one wall not cork-lined was cinder block, painted a bilious green. The room had an odd smell—of sweat, damp cement, and cork, all melded with fear. A recessed fluorescent light cast a sickly yellowish aura onto a laminated tabletop. A small camera was perched high on a wall. No one-way mirror like in the old days.

When I was a crime reporter, I'd watched interrogations, but I'd never been the one being questioned. My body pulsed with anxious anticipation—and a gnawing sense of dread seized me.

I sat in a gray metal chair as Kaufman perched his considerable bulk in front of me. Cirillo sat behind the oak-laminated table to my right. Inhaling Cirillo's cloyingly pungent cologne, I wondered if the detectives could smell scotch on my breath. How could they miss it?

For the first time, despite my booze-addled daze, I noticed Kaufman's tweed sport jacket, gray slacks, and cloth tie. He projected a hard-boiled streetwise look—the guy was maybe fifty, had a shaved head, was wide shouldered and bull necked, and had the flattened face of a barroom brawler.

Cirillo was tall and thin, in his midthirties, obviously the junior partner. He wore a tapered blue suit—expensive looking—and a pastel-blue shirt with a red silk tie. His dress was sharp in a calculated sort of way. He had dark, slicked-back hair and the ferret-faced look of a young punk. He was pure Brooklyn—Bensonhurst or Bay Ridge. Reminded me of Christopher from *The Sopranos*. I'd met his type a million times back in the day.

"We brought you here, Mr. Shaw," said Kaufman, "because of a procedural change. We now video everyone we question."

"I don't have to talk to you," I said, wanting to establish I knew the game. Years of crime reporting and writing crime novels taught me plenty about the criminal justice system. It was heavily loaded against the suspect, no matter what the Constitution said.

But was I a suspect? If so, of having done what?

"You can leave if you'd prefer," Kaufman said.

"This is an interrogation, isn't it?"

"If you wanna call it that," Kaufman said. "The recording's for your protection and ours. So if you have no objection, we'll proceed."

"Go ahead, Detective," I said, knowing I could walk out in a heartbeat. But my legs ached and I felt so beaten, it was just easier to get it over with.

Kaufman pressed a button on a console. "This is Detective Philip Kaufman of the NYPD Homicide Division, 19th Precinct."

Homicide Division? A bolt of fear nearly threw me back in the chair. My hands clenched involuntarily.

Noting the date and time, Kaufman continued, "I'm here with Detective Donald Cirillo and Mr. William Shaw, husband of the decedent, Nora Shaw. We're recording this interview. Are you aware of that, Mr. Shaw?"

"Yes."

"Mr. Shaw, we're questioning everyone . . . you, the doctors, your wife's sister, the home health aide, Nora's friends. You aren't obligated to answer any questions, and you can have an attorney present if you want."

"Are you reading me my Miranda rights?"

"No. I'm just making sure you're fully informed."

"Am I under arrest?" My mouth was parched and my eyelids began drooping. Far too much booze mixed with a deadening sense of despair, not ideal for a police interview.

"No, you're not under arrest. You know that, sir. You've written scenes like this."

I closed my eyes, just for a moment.

"By the way, I've read your stuff. Very authentic, and gritty, too. In fact, I know you talked with Detective Ed Hanson for your last novel. He's gonna retire, cash in his chips, and move to South Carolina," Kaufman added with a half smile.

Was Kaufman trying to establish some crap-ass rapport, tickling me with some friendly banter—trying to open me up a bit? All with the recording going, nonstop, taking it all in.

Detective Tactics 101.

"Mr. Shaw, technically, your wife didn't die of natural causes. The autopsy showed a very high level of the blood thinner warfarin in her system."

Jesus, is this why they hauled me in?

A pang of panic shot through me. The room tilted. Suddenly and drastically. Yes, Nora's level of blood thinner was high when she died—it often spiked for no reason over the years of her illness.

"Nora was bedridden, right?" Kaufman said.

"Yes," I heard a thin voice reply.

"Had an irregular heartbeat, right?"

"That's right."

"And you gave Nora her warfarin by an IV setup each

morning, correct?"

"Yes."

"Because she couldn't swallow pills, right?"

"She couldn't swallow anything."

"Because of the MS, right? She was paralyzed?"

"That's right." My throat constricted. I thought I'd choke. I was assaulted by the image of Nora lying—shrunken and withered—in the hospital bed in our living room.

"And she was taking prednisone for the MS, right?"

"Yes."

"And prednisone mixed with the warfarin made her bleed even more easily, yes?"

"We all knew it . . . Dr. Radin and—"

"And you prepared the IV warfarin, yes?" Kaufman asked. His eyes crawled over me.

Cirillo sat like a sphinx.

"Yes. Like Dr. Radin instructed me to."

Jesus, I sound so defensive.

"That would be Dr. *Daniel* Radin, her internist?"

"Yes."

"And when did you give Nora the warfarin?"

"At six every morning."

"You're sure of that . . . six a.m.?"

"Yes. Absolutely."

"Now, you went to Starbucks that morning, right?"

"Yes."

"At around seven?"

"Yes."

"And you did that every morning?"

"Pretty much."

"Why so early in the morning?"

"Because I'd begun another novel . . . on my laptop."

"Why not write at home?"

"Because Nora's aide would get in at seven. She'd rattle around in the kitchen, turn on the radio. So I'd work at Starbucks until the library on 79th Street opened; then I'd go there."

"So you'd leave Nora with Roberta, the aide?"

"Yes." My heart fluttered. A dull pain bored through my chest.

"Did you meet anyone at Starbucks in the mornings?"

"At Starbucks? No." My legs flinched involuntarily beneath the chair.

"Mr. Shaw, are you seeing anyone?"

"Seeing anyone? What do you mean?"

My head shook back and forth. I squinted at Kaufman.

"What do I mean? Romantically is what I mean."

"No. Not at all."

"You sure about that?"

"*Yes*, of course."

My stomach eddied.

"Mr. Shaw, the tox report showed excess warfarin in Nora's system. Forgive me, but we know she was a burden for you, so we—"

"A *burden*? How fucking dare you!" My blood felt like it was bubbling in my veins.

"Are you saying she wasn't?"

Heat rose to my face.

"What the hell are you taking about, Detective?"

"The cost of her upkeep, the home health aide, the doctor visits, the medicines . . . and you had no insurance coverage. That wasn't a burden?"

"I don't like what you're implying, Detective."

"What am I implying, sir?"

Blood pulsed like a piston behind my eyes.

There was a long silence. The overhead fluorescent buzzed.

"You're writing a new novel, aren't you?"

Sudden change of subject. Basic interrogation tactics. Throw the suspect off balance. Suspect? Me?

Kaufman's lips formed a thin, bloodless line.

"Care to give us a little summary, Mr. Shaw?"

"Summary?"

"Of the novel?"

"Not really."

Where was this bullshit going? *Assassin's Lullaby* was a story about a hit man hired to kill a woman. Nora asked me to write something, anything—as a present to her. It was a gift.

"Been writing it on your laptop?"

"Yes."

Kaufman jotted something in his notebook, looked up, and said, "Mr. Shaw, have you deleted anything from your laptop?"

"No."

"Don't delete a thing. We need to examine it."

"You'll have to get a search warrant, Detective."

He nodded and jotted down something else.

I felt my chin quivering. My God, it wouldn't stop.

I felt light-headed. My heart began a stampede in my chest.

"Mr. Shaw, is there anything you're not telling us?" Cirillo piped up.

"I don't believe this bullshit."

I reached into my pocket and whipped out my cell phone.

"We're through talking," I said, pressing a speed-dial number.

Chapter 4

The buzzing fluorescent light in the interrogation room cast a yellowish glow on everything. My eyes stung, so I closed them. I was blighted, completely enervated. I felt like dropping off to sleep. I heard chairs scraping, smelled Cirillo's cologne, and knew the detectives were leaving the interrogation room. I sat in a fog, knowing they'd be watching me on CCTV and recording everything. My ass ached from the metal chair, but I wasn't going to budge. I was beyond caring.

As I sat in a haze, my thoughts drifted back to a day when Nora and I had been married for two years. I sat beneath the ailanthus tree in the back patio of our town house apartment— the one I'd been renting when we first met. Nora emerged through the French doors. Her face was pale and drawn.

"What did Dr. Buckman say?"

"I have endometriosis," she murmured. "You know what that means?"

"Not exactly."

I stood and took her in my arms. She was shuddering.

"It means I probably can't get pregnant," she whispered, burying her face in my chest. "It's been two years now. Dr. Buckman didn't sound optimistic." Her tears soaked my shirt.

I had to admit, I felt a secret swell of relief. Though we'd been trying for two years, having a child would change our lives. Most of all, I'd be forced to share Nora with another being. As much as

I tried shoving it away, I felt an undercurrent of jealousy.

"But we want children," she whispered.

"Nora, we didn't get married just to have children. We want to *be* together. Not having a baby doesn't lessen us." I pressed my face to her hair. Her fragrance filled my nostrils. "Sweetheart, what we *have* counts, not what we *might* have."

"Oh, Bill, your writing keeps you going."

"No, Nora. *You* keep me going. And you have your acting."

"And I learned something else this morning," she said. Her voice quavered. "They're writing my part out of the soap." She began trembling.

I was stunned. They were writing her out of the soap? And learning she couldn't get pregnant? Two major blows in one day. My thoughts raced for something to say. How could I lessen her pain, assuage her losses?

"Honey, you've had plenty of other offers."

"Lee says I should go to LA, try to get some film work."

"So, we'll go. I can write anywhere."

I tried picturing a life in the Hollywood Hills, Bel Air, or Santa Monica—where the so-called beautiful people lived. Where we'd be surrounded by wealthy, influential men: movie magnates, producers, fat-cat moguls, movers and shakers, the power elite. There'd be handsome actors and charismatic directors who'd be drawn to Nora like iron filings to a magnet. My possessiveness and nascent jealousy were never very far from the surface. Could I deal with the avalanche of challenges a Hollywood lifestyle would bring?

"But I love our life here," Nora murmured, "the theater, our friends, my sister, your brother, Charlie, and your mother's such a darling. And I'd miss this little apartment. I love coming home and finding you banging away on your laptop."

"Honey, there's plenty for you in New York—television, theater companies, and you love the workshop."

She shook her head as tears funneled down her cheeks.

I guided her to the bedroom where we lay down on the bed. I held her in my arms, kissing her cheeks and eyelids as she cried softly. I caressed her back and shoulders, tried to comfort her, told her how much I loved her, and tried conveying how my world orbited around her and nothing else. I whispered to her, saying I'd do anything to make her happy.

We lay there for hours, holding each other.

I kept repeating, "Nora, you're all I ever wanted in this life."

The cozy three-room Charles Street apartment was our street-level version of heaven. With its chestnut beams, stucco ceilings, and stone fireplace, it was perfect. The walls were covered with bookshelves and knickknacks. We'd furnished the place with eighteenth-century Federal and Georgian-style pieces. The kitchen had an exposed brick wall and a window looking onto Charles Street.

On spring and summer days, the patio with its shade-giving ailanthus tree was our private paradise. I'd write at a bridge table with my laptop and the day would flash by.

I'd finished the first draft of *Wolf at the Door*. Nora had begun editing my manuscripts.

"Remember when I offered to be your editor?" she asked.

"Of course I do. It was the night we met."

She was a fabulous editor. She could streamline my prose, improve the novel's pacing, find inconsistencies in the story—and her actor's ear for dialogue was uncanny.

"So what do you think?" I said, as she finished reading the manuscript.

"Truthfully, the dialogue isn't how people really talk." She propped her elbows on the table. "Bill, I have an idea. Why don't we act out the dialogue, see how it sounds."

"You'll turn me into an actor," I said, laughing.

"And you're turning me into an editor."

"You know what's happening here?"

Her eyebrows rose. Those Spanish nostrils flared.

"The scripts are becoming as much yours as mine."

I got up and circled the table, feeling closer to Nora than ever before.

She stood and we embraced. The feel and fragrance of her skin was deliciously overwhelming.

"Let's tango," she whispered.

"Yes. It makes me feel so close to you."

So close, I could never imagine being without her.

Chapter 5

The interrogation room door exploded open, blasting against the wall.

My heart nearly stopped and then kicked like a stallion. Every nerve in my body fired and I bolted upright.

Ben Abrams—all 240 pounds of him—loomed in the doorway. Kaufman and Cirillo followed behind.

At that moment, I nearly sobbed with relief at the sight of Ben in his dark suit and white shirt open at the collar.

His face was crimson; his nostrils flared and his neck veins bulged like thick, pulsing cords.

Once in the interrogation room, Ben turned and eyed Kaufman and Cirillo with a raw, menacing look, one step away from violence.

"What the fuck're you doin'?" Ben snarled at Kaufman.

"We're just talking here . . ."

"Well, your talk's *over.*" Ben slapped a thick hand on my shoulder. "You all right?" he asked.

I nodded.

"These douche bags abuse you, Bill? They try to fuck you up?"

"Not really," I said, wanting to bolt from the room. The walls were closing in.

"They ask you loaded questions?" Ben asked, scanning my face.

"They implied things."

"It's all on the video," said Kaufman.

"*All* of it?"

"Everything's there."

"And you *talked* to these pricks?" Ben asked, peering into my eyes.

I nodded, feeling chastised.

Ben shook his head. "Jesus, Bill. You of all people know the drill. You *never* talk to cops."

"Ben, I haven't slept for days. Besides, I have nothing to hide."

"They just wanna make a case." Ben turned and glared at Kaufman. "Shame on you, Detective. The guy just lost his wife and you're bustin' his ass. I want a copy of that tape—un-*fucking*-edited. And which ADA's on this goddamned charade?"

"That's none of your business," Cirillo spat.

"Who's *this* scumbag?" Ben pointed a thumb at Cirillo.

The junior detective blanched.

"Tell this snot-bag *anything* concerning Bill Shaw's my god-damned business."

Cirillo's face reddened.

Ben turned back to Kaufman, "So who's the ADA on this?"

"Guy named Sean Olson."

"Another young snot?"

"We're all just doin' our jobs."

"Yeah, sure. Olson. Fuckin' Olson. Never heard of him. Just another punk tryin' to make his bones. I know this game like the back of my hand. Fuck you both."

Ben slipped his hand under my arm and said, "Let's get outta this toilet."

Ben turned to Kaufman as his eyes narrowed. "If you're gonna arrest him, gimme a call first." He tossed his card on the table.

"Who said anyone's gettin' arrested?" Kaufman replied.

"Hey, Kaufman, the last time I was fucked, at least I got kissed, too."

He pulled me out through the still-open door.

Chapter 6

L ying on the living room sofa, I couldn't fall asleep. Thoughts of Kaufman, Cirillo, and the interrogation room swirled through my mind. I could still smell the place.

Kaufman, Cirillo, Ben, that boxlike room, an interrogation. Nora—a burden?

My heartbeat thumped through the cushion as my thoughts swept back to when Nora's troubles began. It was ten years earlier. Ironically, we were at a gathering thrown by Ben and Elaine Abrams, at their apartment in a white-glove, 1920s co-op building on Park Avenue. A hundred people sipped Veuve Clicquot champagne and nibbled on crudités. The place was filled with New York luminaries, including former mayor Rudy Giuliani, Alec Baldwin, Sarah Jessica Parker, Matthew Broderick, Pete Hamill, and Mario Batali.

Once *Fire and Ice* became a best seller, my career took off. I'd learned to live with what I labeled—for better or worse—the *New York life*. Despite the old saw that writers enjoy a certain anonymity, that didn't seem to pertain to me. Not after *Fire and Ice* became a movie. And my privacy really evaporated once Nora and I were married. Her visibility was soaring with her soap opera role and after she began doing national commercials for a cosmetics company.

Nora's sister, Lee, was at the party. She was earning big money brokering high-end Manhattan real estate. Lee got us a great deal on a five-room, 3rd Avenue high-rise co-op. We hated giving up the Charles Street apartment, but the building had been sold and the new landlord wanted our garden apartment.

After refilling our champagne flutes, Nora and I talked with my literary agent, Cindy Armor, in Ben and Elaine's den.

"*Wolf at the Door* will be a great movie," Cindy said, lighting a cigarette. "Nora, since you've been editing Bill's scripts, you can *hear* the characters' voices, which is why it's so easy to get the film people interested."

"That's Nora's doing," I said.

Twenty minutes later, I watched a seventy-five-year-old retired judge—he'd left the bench after a bribery scandal—flirt relentlessly with Nora. My wife had always been a man magnet. The scenario was played out time and time again, no matter where we went. There was the guy's casual glance at Nora's ring finger, the flirter's intense eye contact, his furtive glances at her breasts and long legs, and the lust-driven sweat sheen on his cheeks.

That's the price I pay for having a wife with traffic-stopping looks.

And Nora was head-turning gorgeous that night in a black, strapless cocktail dress. Her perfectly toned shoulders and arms were a complete turn-on. Her silken hair was pulled back in a dramatic updo; it was that barebacked tango look I adored—sultry, filled with sexuality and promise.

But it wasn't merely Nora's looks; she possessed some irresistible social genius.

The ex-judge—a carnal old fart—laughed uproariously at something Nora said. Amid salvos of conversation and the crowd's din, the lecher's maw moved like an out-of-control jackhammer. And his bloodshot eyes told the story: he was ruing his age, his withered marriage, and the depressing rut into which his life had sunk. Above all, he felt an intense sexual awakening—a rampaging surge of desire for Nora.

She was indulging this septuagenarian skirt chaser. And she was playing her part—the unattainable seductress, even as she cast a knowing glance in my direction.

I was insanely jealous, even of this limp-dicked lecher. I wanted to grab Nora, clutch her in my arms—kiss her, and thrust my tongue deep inside her mouth.

And I knew she would respond hungrily.

That's the way it was between us—some strange, erotic sizzle was nurtured by our mutual jealousy. Other men wanting Nora made her ever more desirable to me. And the same held true for her. At restaurants, when other women, recognizing me from my photo on book covers, cast furtive glances my way, Nora would snare my arm and plant a kiss on my lips—a clear signal of possession. Or she'd brush her lips along my neck so I'd feel a twinge of arousal, that pulse of desire.

That's just the way it was.

Suddenly, with the judge's hand touching her bare shoulder—his version of a cheap feel—Nora's face blanched and then slackened. Her eyes rolled upward and her knees buckled.

I lunged desperately toward her as a primal sense of fear surged through me. I caught her before she hit the floor. She felt like dead weight in my arms. I lowered her to the carpet as my heart thrashed in my chest.

"Oh my God!" cried a woman.

"What happened?" someone yelled.

Nora lay on the carpet, unmoving. Her pulse was rapid, thready, and strangely irregular. My thoughts raced frantically amid the press of the crowd.

"Call an ambulance!"

Reeling from fear and disbelief, amid swirling darkness, I felt my world coming to an end.

The intern at Lenox Hill Hospital was a pink-cheeked young man with long, dark hair. "The cardiogram's diagnostic. Mrs. Shaw," he said, "you have atrial fibrillation. We call it A-fib. Millions of people have it."

"What's that?" Nora asked.

She was awake, but her face was pale.

"The heart is basically an electric pump," the intern said. "It beats steadily and pumps blood. With A-fib, the heart's rhythm can go haywire. You fainted because not enough blood was getting to your brain."

"How's it treated?" I asked.

"To avoid the heart throwing blood clots to the brain, we thin the blood with a medication called warfarin."

"Warfarin?" Nora asked.

"Yes. You'll have to take it for the rest of your life."

A feeling of unease crept through me.

Chapter 7

"William Shaw, you're under arrest for the murder of Nora Shaw," Kaufman intoned. He and Cirillo flashed their badges in my doorway.

Kaufman nodded at Ben, who stood at my side. As promised, Kaufman had called him an hour earlier. Cirillo hung back, his eyes avoiding Ben's stare.

Disbelief washed over me. It felt like a scene right out of my novels. They were in my apartment, the one Nora and I shared for years, and they were arresting me for her murder.

"They'll take you for booking and arraignment," Ben had said only a few minutes before the doorbell rang.

The cuffs snapped on. My hands shook. It didn't matter how many times I'd written scenes like this: shivers rippled through me, spreading over my skin. Gooseflesh crawled over my arms, and my fingertips tingled. Cops, steel bracelets biting into my wrists, being led from my home—losing my freedom. Being arrested for the murder of my wife? Unbelievable.

"Remember, Bill. It's *no comment* to anyone," Ben whispered.

Cirillo recited the words, "You have the right to remain silent. Anything you say can be held against you in a court of law . . . " The whole Miranda thing, just like on a TV show or in one of my novels, only it was happening to me, not some character I'd created.

My life was circling the proverbial drain: Nora was dead, and

I was under arrest for the murder of my love, my soul mate and partner in life.

My thoughts flashed back to the day before, when detectives appeared at my door with a search warrant. The paper shook in my hands. They entered the apartment and combed through everything: dresser drawers, bookshelves, the kitchen, and medicine cabinets. They hauled away the medical supplies and vials of pills. Another guy—a civilian—inserted a little device into a port of my laptop, extracting its contents.

With cuffs on my wrists, sweat seeped out my pores as I thought of Nora, mute, paralyzed, and dying in the hospital bed that had been in our living room.

Leaving the apartment, Ben grabbed a camel-colored trench coat from the hall closet. He draped it over my cuffed wrists. It was the Burberry Nora brought home one day, telling me it was about time I wore something with a bit of class. A trench coat costing $1,800. Now it hid handcuffs.

As the elevator began its descent, the whirr of the ceiling fan roared in my ears. My wrists felt cold, shackled in the steel. We rode in silence. At the third floor, the elevator stopped.

The door slid open. Jack Becker, a neighbor, stood and stared, wide-eyed. "Are you okay?" he asked, as he saw the detectives' badges dangling from their jacket pockets. "I'll wait for the next one," he mumbled, stepping away.

The doors slid closed and we continued downward.

In the lobby, I heard the buzz.

"William Shaw? The author?"

"What did he do?"

"Didn't his wife just die?"

People always congregated in the lobby, especially at this time of day, when the mail had just been delivered.

I kept my head down. As we stepped onto 3rd Avenue, I was blinded by the glare of the whitish morning sky.

Brilliant light reflected from car bumpers and windshields. A pall of fumes hung in the air as midmorning traffic streaked uptown in a honking rush.

A glut of reporters appeared. Microphones were thrust in my face.

"Mr. Shaw, did you kill your wife?" called a reporter.

"Mr. Shaw, what can you tell us?"

It was the classic perp walk—a perverse spectacle. That's how it's planned. I'd learned years ago from Detective Hanson. "That's the strategy," he said. "We take the perp's freedom away. We notify the press. We rip away his dignity with the perp walk. It's a warm-up, gets the gears in motion—the start of the criminal justice process. It's pure intimidation."

"I'll see you at the station," Ben said, flagging down a taxi.

Kaufman pushed my head down as we slipped into the detectives' sedan—the same gray vehicle from a few nights earlier. Jesus, I'd seen this a million times—on cop shows, news broadcasts. I'd written scenes about it in novels and TV scripts. It was everyday cop stuff, but not when it was happening to me.

Cirillo pulled away from the curb; Kaufman sat in the front passenger's seat. We headed downtown on Lexington, the streets passing in a blurred rush. The sedan had a new-car smell mixed with the odor of stale cigarette smoke.

The 19th Precinct was a brick and sandstone building on East 67th Street. In a claustrophobic room smelling of vinyl and camphor, I was photographed: a frontal view, then profile. I was fingerprinted: a cop rolled my fingers through purple ink, then onto paper. Then, a computer keyboard began clicking away. I was being digitized, processed like baggage at an airline terminal.

Arraignment was in a cavernous room in the Criminal Court building. It was mobbed: lawyers in dark suits whispered to their clients. Defendants spoke in a polyglot—English, Spanish,

Senegalese, Arabic, and Urdu. An oceanic murmur coursed through the place. Reminded me of the evening rush at Grand Central Terminal. The funk of body odor hung in the air. Uniformed cops with holstered Glocks stood around; clerks scurried about in white shirts and ties. Telephones rang, cell phones trilled, overhead fans whirled as names were called. ADAs, investigators, and family members were everywhere. I could smell the fear. It seemed like some version of hell.

My ass ached from sitting on the wooden bench. Ben sat beside me.

"I know this judge," Ben said. "He's okay."

Judge Clarence Hogan sat behind a sky-high desk. An obese, triple-chinned Buddha-like figure, he stifled a yawn as he processed perps and paperwork. He was Charon, the ferryman at the gates of hell.

"William Shaw," boomed a court officer.

Hearing my name made me shudder. It seemed so unreal, so nightmarish.

Standing with Ben, I looked up; the judge's bench loomed above us. I tried to keep myself from shaking.

"What have we got here?" the judge asked, peering at papers.

"Ann Pierce for the People," said the junior ADA, a lithe blonde, maybe thirty years old. She wore dark slacks, a white blouse, and a blue jacket. She was taut-faced, all business, doing her job.

My pulse pounded through me, resounding in my skull.

"Ben Abrams for the defendant," Ben called.

The judge plucked his glasses from his nose. He raised his head, saw Ben, and smiled. "Mr. Abrams, I haven't seen you for years. Not since you left the DA's office."

"I wish I could say it's a pleasure to see you, Your Honor. But under the circumstances . . ."

"I understand, Mr. Abrams."

"Your Honor," said Pierce, "the defendant, William Shaw, is accused of murder in the second degree."

Murder in the second degree? Unbelievable. This is a Hieronymus Bosch painting of the damned, descending into hell.

"William Shaw? The *writer?*" asked the judge. His eyebrows rose as he cast a glance in my direction.

"Yes, Your Honor," Ben said.

"How does the defendant plead?"

"*Not* guilty, Your Honor," Ben answered.

The judge turned to Pierce. "*What,* may I ask, are the handcuffs for?"

"Standard procedure, Your Honor."

"Is this man about to flee?"

"I don't think so, Your Honor."

"Has he demonstrated a propensity for violence?"

"I don't think—well, no, Your Honor."

"Is he a danger to the community?"

"No, Your Honor."

"Have those handcuffs removed, Ms. Pierce."

"Yes, Your Honor," she warbled. She glanced at the court officer.

He inserted a key; there was a ratcheting sound; the cuffs came off.

Pierce was about to speak when Hogan raised his hand. He peered down at the papers, obviously reading the charges. His eyes met Pierce's and his eyebrows rose.

"Your Honor, this is a murder case," Pierce said. "We ask for a substantial bail."

"Your Honor, if I may," Ben said.

"Go ahead, Mr. Abrams."

"My client stands unjustly accused. It's his first time in court—ever—and though as a matter of protocol, the People must demand bail, I ask Your Honor to consider that Mr. Shaw has deep roots in the community. He's not a flight risk; nor is he a threat to anyone."

"Ms. Pierce . . ." Hogan turned to the ADA.

"Your Honor, we believe Mr. Shaw could access the financial means to flee the jurisdiction, even the country."

"Mr. Abrams," said the judge, "you'll arrange for your client's passport to be surrendered."

"Expeditiously, Your Honor."

"Excellent. Murder in the second degree . . . minimum bail, one hundred thousand dollars."

"It'll be taken care of immediately, Your Honor," said Ben.

"And Mr. Shaw will be released on his own recognizance," the judge said. He scribbled something on a piece of paper. "It's settled. ROR, bail is set . . . and the grand jury will convene soon, correct?"

"The case is calendared for two days from now, Your Honor," Pierce said.

"Then we're through here," said the judge, looking at me. "I've enjoyed your books, Mr. Shaw," he added; then he turned away.

"My client thanks you, Your Honor," Ben said, grabbing my arm.

My thoughts drifted to Nora: I recalled her charged energy— whether teaching me to tango or acting out our scripts—her infectious love of life, now gone forever. The funeral, when was it? A week earlier? Ten days before? I couldn't remember. Everything seemed jumbled, upended. My world was spinning out of control, and I was in this perverse place—feeling empty, frozen, doomed.

Chapter 8

When the grand jury convened, Sean Olson, the ADA, stood before the panel. He was in his midthirties, tall, and patrician-looking with regular features, light brown hair, and a high forehead. Ann Pierce, the junior ADA, was beside him.

The room was oak paneled with elaborate wainscoting and crown moldings. It smelled musty and stale. The jurors seemed a mass of formless faces.

Ann Pierce read the charges. "Mr. Shaw is accused of knowingly giving a lethal dose of a blood thinner called warfarin to his wife, Nora Shaw, who was paralyzed by multiple sclerosis. She couldn't move or talk, and Mr. Shaw willfully injected her intravenously, resulting in Mrs. Shaw's death."

The grand jury was a conscripted sea of humanity: twenty-three Manhattanites with faces of many colors. Forty-six eyes stared; forty-six ears listened.

There was no judge: it was a typical grand jury setting. A warden stood off to the side as Pierce read the charges. A court stenographer recorded every word.

Pierce then said, "The People call Dr. Billings of the medical examiner's office."

Billings never looked at Pierce as she questioned him. He held the autopsy report in front of him.

"What was the cause of death, Dr. Billings?" Pierce asked.

"Severe hemorrhage from the spleen, kidneys, liver, and other organs," Billings said. He described the autopsy done the day after Nora's death.

A swell of bile rose in my gullet, followed immediately by nausea.

The death certificate and autopsy findings were passed around. Each juror, somber-faced, regarded the documents.

"And was a toxicology screen done on Mrs. Shaw?"

"Yes."

"And what did it show?"

"An excessive level of warfarin was in her bloodstream."

"And did the warfarin cause the hemorrhaging you described?"

"Yes, it did."

The toxicology report went from juror to juror. I knew Ben was pacing in the hallway. Grand jury rules allowed no legal representation. The prosecution would present its case. That was it. No cross-examination of any witness. As many times as I'd written about it, I finally understood the terror of it all.

Is this America? Is this really happening? To me?

"Mr. Shaw, will you please take the stand?" Ann Pierce said.

From the witness chair, I looked out at the jurors. A stocky Hispanic man in the front row was poker-faced. An older white woman wearing rimless bifocals scowled. A matronly woman peered questioningly at me. I felt like a specimen being examined.

Pierce asked me about the warfarin: how it was given, the dose, the timing of the infusion. The questions were closed-ended—could be answered only yes or no. No explanations. No excuses. No clarifications. I was boxed in, trapped like a mouse in a cage.

There were questions about Nora's illness: how it affected her, what medications she took. I was vaguely aware of tears ribboning down my cheeks. The edges of the room darkened. With the bare-bones facts of the case, and no cross-examination of the witnesses, indictment was a certainty.

Pierce conferred with Olson. He nodded and whispered in her ear.

"You may step down, Mr. Shaw," Pierce said.

As I left the stand, a sea-sway sensation filled my head. My legs felt like liquid.

"Ladies and gentlemen," Pierce said, "you've been instructed about your duty as grand jurors. We ask you to indict Mr. Shaw on a charge of murder in the second degree. Please remember that an indictment is *not* a finding of guilt. It simply means there's evidence that a crime may have been committed. A formal trial will determine Mr. Shaw's guilt or innocence.

"Now remember: only twelve of you must find sufficient evidence to proceed to trial."

The jurors nodded in unison. A sinking sensation overtook me.

A half hour later, Ben and I were handed a document by the court clerk.

I'd been indicted for second-degree murder.

Homicide.

The People would take me to trial for the murder of the love of my life.

The paper trembled in my hands. Sweat formed a film over me, soaking my shirt.

No matter how a trial would conclude, this piece of paper—this processed wood pulp with black print—would brand me for life.

Bill Shaw, former journalist and now a crime novelist, was indicted for the murder of his wife, Nora Reyes Shaw.

Chapter 9

Lee was repulsed by that smarmy ADA, Sean Olson. He comported himself like he was the scion of some filthy-rich, blue-blooded family. It was obvious: he thought he was too damned good for everyone. Lee knew the type: Phillips Exeter Academy, Yale, then Harvard Law School. All the accoutrements of wealth and privilege. That snobbish, pin-striped, double-breasted popinjay told her she'd most likely be called as a witness against Bill. Lee trembled at the thought of saying anything that might hurt her brother-in-law. By God, he'd been so good to Nora.

It seemed ages ago when her sister was alive—*really* alive—as her beautiful, vivacious self. God, Nora was so talented. She could act, dance, sing, and speak three languages, and she had such an infectiously joyful way in the world.

Of course, that was before she got so sick.

Funny thing though, Nora always had a premonition of terrible things lurking in her future.

How had Nora put it?

I've been marked.

Lee was certain Nora's sense of a foreshortened future was because Mama was a Holocaust survivor whose entire family perished in wartime Poland. Lee recalled reading how survivors never truly recovered from the trauma. They carried with them a bequest of sadness, of loss—a keen awareness of life's fragility. And they somehow bestowed it on their children. Papa, born and raised in Argentina, was very different, but loved Mama, and understood her bleak outlook on life. Yes, Nora bore Mama's scars, and was deeply affected by the deaths of their parents when she was so young.

Lee was seventeen and Nora fifteen when it happened. It was a humid August day when they were at their summer cottage near Lake Champlain. Papa stayed behind to chop wood, while Lee, Nora, and Mama went shopping in Plattsburgh. An afternoon thunderstorm erupted; rain roared down in sheets.

When the downpour was over, they drove back to the cottage. It was eerily silent; there was no tango or bolero music coming from inside. Something was wrong.

"Ernesto," Mama called.

Silence.

Mama called again.

No answer.

Lee searched out back, at the tool shed and the wood pile.

Remnants of rainwater dripped from the trees. Dark clouds rolled eastward in a clearing sky. A fresh, floral scent hung in the air, and wet grass glistened like morning dew. But something was wrong, terribly wrong, and Papa's silence was ominous.

Then Lee saw it—a sight that has haunted her every day of her life.

Papa was lying on the ground, next to a charred linden tree. The pungent odor of singed hair, flesh, and bark filled the air.

Lee rushed to him, trying frantically to rouse him. His face was frozen-looking, ghoulish. His eyes were clouded over, whitish.

Shocked and trembling, Lee screamed. Mama and Nora rushed from the house. Mama shrieked and then collapsed. Nora stood stock-still, frozen in place, horrified.

Volunteer firemen arrived—men in yellow slickers—followed by the county coroner.

"Your father was hit by lightning," the coroner said. "His heart stopped."

It was such a random death, so unforeseen. It was impossible to accept that nature . . . fate . . . God . . . could be so cruel. It was Lee's first taste of what Mama had known for so long: life was very cruel and could end in a moment of nature's indifference.

It was a tender age for Nora to lose her father. And in such a brutal way. Lee always thought Nora was drawn to acting because she wanted to live in a fantasy world—become someone else, live a different life.

Months later, Mama discovered a lump in her breast.

Soon after the diagnosis was made, the cancer spread everywhere.

There was the day, a year and a half later, when Lee sat at the edge of the bed and stroked Mama's hair. She'd been such a beautiful woman, but her eyes were sunken; her face was gaunt and looked waxy.

"Lee, my darling," Mama said in her Polish-accented English. "You know that Papa worked very hard and the world was kind to him."

"Yes, it was. It gave him you . . ."

"Shh. We are talking about you and Nora. There is money, enough to take care of you both. You know the lawyer. The papers are signed."

"Oh, Mama."

"Lee, Nora is only seventeen. We have no other family, and you must be in charge. Nora is a romantic. But you, my darling Lee, you have a *practical* mind. You must take care of her."

Four weeks later, Mama died.

They were alone in the world. And Nora was scarred, forever believing she was marked.

The sisters lived together while Nora went to the Romanoff School of Acting. An agent got her some off-Broadway roles. Eventually, Nora joined the cast of *The Burning World*.

Maybe acting could lead Nora to cast off her belief that she had been cursed; but no, she still felt she was marked for tragedy.

There was her affair with Zachary—an actor. They were together until Nora discovered he was bisexual. It sent her reeling.

Two years later, there was Jason, another actor. Passed over for a role in *Les Miserables*, he flung himself from a subway platform into the path of an oncoming train. It was the third horrific death for Nora: first lightning, then cancer, and finally, the number 6 train.

Jason's death cemented Nora's belief she was doomed.

But meeting Bill changed everything for Nora.

"Bill's given me life again" is what Nora said.

And now Bill indicted for Nora's *murder*? It was insane. Bill was a caretaker, an unselfish giver. God, how he and Nora adored each other. Bill was as devoted to Nora as a man could ever be.

From the window of her 5th Avenue apartment, Lee looked across the expanse of Central Park. How could the world hold such beauty, yet feel so indifferent, so ugly?

Lee recalled the last day of Nora's life. She'd visited her sister at seven thirty that morning. Nora slept peacefully while Roberta, the home health aide, went about her chores. Bill was at Starbucks and would be going to the library when it opened at ten.

And now, Nora was dead. In a way it was a relief. Lee wasn't ashamed to acknowledge her feelings. For as long as she could remember, all the attention had been lavished on Nora, the romantic, sensitive dreamer. When their parents were gone, everything fell on Lee's shoulders. Nobody seemed to remember, or even care, that she suffered, too.

Lee thought about the turns in her own life.

Here I am, closing in on fifty, financially successful, but divorced and alone. My twenty-three-year-old son, Aaron, lives in Redmond, Washington, where he works for Microsoft, and never calls. I have no one I'm really close to anymore. And what am I doing? Selling apartments to wealthy clients who just want to one-up each other. How meaningless can it get?

Maybe she should call a psychiatrist—Dr. Russell, the one who met with Nora and Bill when they were having problems.

It might be time for an antidepressant.

And now, Bill—Nora's devoted husband of fifteen years—indicted for her murder. It was brutally unjust. Nora was so lucky to have had a husband like Bill, a man who loved her so completely. Lee never had anything like that in her life, not even for a few months.

And Sean Olson, smugness personified, would call her as a witness against Bill.

She reached for the telephone.

Chapter 10

I woke with a start. As consciousness returned, dread slithered through me.

I thought I'd been dreaming, but whatever was trekking through my half-sleeping brain dissolved in a web of apprehension. My throat was so dry I could barely swallow. The living room was rinsed in light. It was afternoon. When had I fallen asleep? An hour ago, or maybe three hours earlier? A fluttering sensation in my chest reminded me of Nora—her irregular heartbeat, the warfarin thinning her blood, causing it to leak, so she bled everywhere. Had I been dreaming?

I hadn't slept in the bed—*our* bed—since Nora died. I couldn't stand the thought of it: the mattress, those linens, the pillows where we'd shared so much—our bodies, everything. Since the funeral, I'd been plagued—day and night—by images of the cemetery with its endless rows of headstones, the clot of mourners, the long-stemmed rosebuds tossed onto the coffin as it was lowered into the hole on that somber day.

The medical supply company had removed the hospital bed, wheelchair, mist machine, oxygen tank, IV stand, plastic tubing, needles, and syringes. The police had seized everything else. And, Roberta Morgan, the home health aide, was gone. I would no longer have to shop, buy medicines, or take care of the million things I did when Nora's MS dragged our lives into a pit. Even those sad tasks were links to the living Nora.

Now there was nothing to do, even less to anticipate.

Except a trial for second-degree murder.

Each day would bring fear of the future, of the unknown. And the nights would bring images of Nora's illness trampling through my thoughts, infesting my dreams.

And writing? I'd be lucky if I could write a check.

I could no longer look at the framed eight-by-ten glossies from Nora's acting days—the ones that young punk Cirillo ogled. I'd taken them down and stuffed them in a box in the bedroom closet. Yesterday, when I picked up Nora's hairbrush, I noticed strands of her beautiful hair in the bristles. I felt sick to my stomach. And I smelled the shampoo Roberta used to wash Nora's hair. Pangs of sadness stabbed me.

Rolling off the couch, I got to my feet. Feeling light-headed, I made my way to the kitchen, grabbed a glass, and tried guzzling tap water. Its metallic taste made me choke. My mouth was Sahara-dry. Had I eaten breakfast this morning?

I had to eat something. Otherwise, I'd wither away—as Nora did. I rummaged around in the refrigerator. Nothing there; just a loaf of mold-ridden bread, eggs that were at least two months old, a Tupperware container of desiccated vegetables, three cans of Coors light, and a bottle of ketchup. I decided to head down to the Korean deli to pick up something to go with my one friend—Johnnie Walker.

In the elevator, I thought of the call from Dave Sheffield, the co-op president.

"Bill, I'm calling about the situation downstairs."

"You mean the reporters?"

"It's creating a disturbance. We realize there's nothing you can do, but—"

"But what, Dave?"

"Bill, you may have to make other arrangements until this

blows over."

"You mean move out?"

"Temporarily."

"I'll think about it."

Jesus. I'd just lost my wife and was now facing a murder trial. What was I supposed to do? Uproot myself? Move in with my brother, Charlie, and his family in Scarsdale? That wouldn't work. They had no room, and once the trial began, I'd be too far away from Ben.

The elevator dinged, stopped, and the door slid open.

A neighbor stepped in. I never knew the guy's name, but we'd usually exchange a little off-the-cuff banter—typical apartment-building chitchat. Before the arrest there was the usual elevator bullshit, a few neighborly words about nothing in particular. Now, there was only cringe-worthy silence. The guy didn't even glance in my direction, just peered at the numbers above the elevator door.

Each time I passed through the lobby, I was reminded of the arrest, of how I'd been on display like meat in a butcher shop. As I neared the outer door, the doorman's eyes narrowed. Jorge shook his head: the signal.

Reporters were outside.

I whirled in place and headed back to the elevator. I took it to the basement, walked through the damp underground garage, and went out the service door to the street.

On 3rd Avenue, I slipped on sunglasses and headed for the Korean's. Though I hadn't shaved in days and wore shades, people recognized me. Some stared; others sneaked looks. My face had been plastered on the local TV news channels and all over the *Post* and *Daily News*, too.

One headline in the *Post* was, "Will the Writer of Crime Do Time?"

A young couple stared at me.

I trudged on, thinking I should wear a hat. Yes, a baseball cap would help.

As I passed a coffee shop, my peripheral vision caught something. It was a brief, head-turning flash. I stopped and swiveled.

It was Nora.

Yes, there she was, sitting at the counter, sipping a cup of coffee.

But no, it was an illusion, fleeting, gone in a second. It happened nearly every day: a heart-stopping moment of recognition—seeing Nora for an electrified instant, walking out of Starbucks, leaving the Food Emporium, or carrying a bag out of Trader Joe's, rushing, moving quickly and gracefully, vital, radiating energy and life.

Then she'd be gone.

It happened whenever I saw a tall, dark-haired woman. That delicious glance, that shock of cognizance, was thrilling, yet seared me with yearning, pain, and disappointment. It was pregnant with loss, with expectancy—with a deep, insatiable craving.

At the deli's salad bar, I grabbed a plastic container and began scooping some oil-covered tomato slices and mozzarella cheese, dropping them into the box. I added a mixture of Greek olives, potato salad, and coleslaw. It didn't matter that it would all flow together: olive oil, oregano, mayonnaise, vinegar, cheese, tomato seeds. It would all slip down the same piehole and taste like cardboard. I snapped the cover shut, poured coffee into a Styrofoam cup, and headed toward the cash register.

"Who made *you* God?"

I was so startled, I flinched.

An owlish-looking woman with narrowed eyes stared at me.

"Who are *you* to decide who lives or dies?"

Heat rose in my face; blood pooled in my cheeks. Rage bubbled within me. For an insane second, I felt the urge to punch her in the face. My hands shook as I moved to the checkout counter.

"That's right. *Walk away*," she called. "But you won't walk once the trial's over."

Ben's voice sounded in my head. *"Don't respond to anyone, Bill. The media will pick your bones clean."*

The proprietor was a bespectacled Korean-born man with jet-black hair and a wide, friendly face. Before the indictment and publicity, the guy always had a world-class smile for me, but now his face was blank. He said nothing, just slipped my items into a plastic bag.

I was a pariah.

The apartment seemed like a mausoleum. It smelled musty, like death.

The telephone rang—a harsh trilling that sent a fearful pulse through me. I screened calls, taking only those from Ben, my brother, Charlie, and my sister-in-law, Lee.

Hearing Lee's voice, I picked up the receiver.

"Bill, it's Lee. How're you doing?"

"What can I say?"

"I know. I know."

"You back at work yet?" I asked.

"Maybe tomorrow," she said. "Are you writing?"

"I can't."

"Weren't you working on something?"

"Yeah, but not now," I said, thinking of *Assassin's Lullaby.*

Lee sounded tentative. Her voice was quavering. I wondered if she suspected I did something to Nora. Over the years, we'd argued about Nora's treatment. It escalated once in a while, and sometimes we nearly exploded at each other. Nora's illness ruled our lives and changed my relationship with Lee.

"Bill, I just had a visit from that ADA, Sean Olson."

My heart dropped in my chest.

"He was with his assistant, Ann Pierce. He asked questions about how you took care of Nora."

"Lee, Ben said that if you're called as a prosecution witness, we can't talk."

"I told him you were a great husband."

"I did my best," I said, as an ache filled me.

"I know, but he kept pumping me."

"Anything specific?"

"Oh, your financial arrangements. Whether you'd been seeing another woman."

Lee's breathing sounded through the receiver. She was on the verge of tears.

"Just so you know, Bill, I told them that without you, Nora would've died long ago." She cleared her throat. Phlegm rattled deep in her chest. "I just want to say . . . I sometimes got much too involved with Nora, and if I ever offended you, I'm so sorry."

"Lee, your heart was always in the right place."

"Now we have only her memory," she said with a catch in her voice; she then began sobbing.

After the call ended, I poured myself another scotch. I was alone, upended, with no future, except the horror of a murder trial.

And then what would happen?

It barely mattered. Conviction or acquittal, I was finished.

I'd be better off dead.

Chapter 11

Ben Abrams entered the Woolworth Building. He'd never tire of gazing at the neo-Gothic structure's vaulted lobby ceiling. Its cathedral-like aura always made him think of the distance he'd traveled in his fifty-two years.

Ben's father, a pattern cutter in Manhattan's Garment District, earned next to nothing. Ben had gone to Columbus High School in the Bronx. He'd been captain of the wrestling team and had graduated with honors. At City University of New York, he was a straight-A student and star collegiate wrestler. The family couldn't afford to send Ben to law school, so he worked as a clerk in the police department during the day and attended New York Law School at night.

As an assistant DA, Ben had prosecuted criminal cases in Manhattan. He had his own street-smart style in the courtroom—colleagues called it *Ben's Bronx Justice.* Jurors loved how he tore into witnesses, frayed judges' nerves, and drilled to the core truths at trial. After seven years, Ben had earned a stellar conviction rate: over 90 percent. His track record, coupled with his courtroom demeanor, earned him the moniker *Bulldog.*

One day, years ago, while Ben was sitting in his cramped ADA's office, John Rankin, the senior partner of a well-known personal injury law firm, appeared at his door.

Rankin was a distinguished-looking man with silver hair and a pencil mustache.

"Ben, I'd like you to consider joining our firm as a litigator," Rankin said.

"John, you guys do *civil* work. I'm into criminal."

"I know, Ben. But let me explain."

Ben glanced at his watch, knowing he was meeting his friend, Bill Shaw, for lunch.

"We've filed lawsuits against New York State," Rankin said. "These were cases involving malicious prosecution of drug-related murder charges, some going back more than twenty years ago. After years in prison, these men were found to be not guilty. The DA's office had withheld exculpatory evidence."

"I've been with the DA's office for ten years."

"We know. And we'd only want you involved in cases going back before then, so there'd be no possibility of conflict of interest on your part."

Ben nodded.

"Ben, can you imagine the horror an innocent man suffers spending years in prison? We need a top-flight trial attorney to try these cases in civil court: someone who's been inside the DA's office, and who's a killer in the courtroom. Ben, *you're* that guy."

"John, I'm flattered, but I've never done civil work."

"C'mon. You'll read the *Redbook Guide to Civil Procedure Laws and Rules* and know it in a heartbeat. Actually, you already know it—rules of evidence, filings, crap like that."

"Lemme think about it."

"Hear me out, Ben. Our fee is one-third of any award or settlement. In a malicious prosecution case resulting in prison time, the demand for a jury award is usually in the millions."

"Sure . . ."

"Ben, your salary's public knowledge. If you join us, you become a full partner—*immediately*—with profit sharing."

Ben's pulse bounded.

"You're guaranteed a first-year salary of seven hundred

fifty thousand dollars—paid up front, before profit sharing. The check'll be written when you sign on."

Ben nearly fell out of his chair.

So here he was, sitting at his huge cherrywood desk in this book-lined, elaborately furnished office, in a multimillion-dollar law firm. His thoughts reeled through the arc of his life.

He and Elaine met at a Hunter College mixer. The sound system was playing Billy Joel's "Just the Way You Are." Ben was entranced by Elaine's delicate features. He kept sneaking looks, and during the melancholic interlude when the saxophone crooned, he walked over and asked her to dance. By the evening's end, they felt as though they'd always known each other.

They were married six months later. After graduating with a degree in art history, Elaine worked at a Madison Avenue gallery and took graduate courses at NYU. When she earned her MFA, she became an art appraiser specializing in impressionist paintings.

Now they had all the money they could ever want. Their older daughter, Melissa, was a medical student at Johns Hopkins, and Donna was prelaw at Yale.

The irony of life: all these years later, Bill Shaw would be arriving at any moment—the same guy he was meeting for lunch the day John Rankin showed up and changed his life forever.

Bill Shaw, his closest friend, other than Elaine, was now a defendant in a murder case.

Life could be so damned strange.

I always admired the decor of Ben's waiting room. The reception area of Rankin, Abrams & Romano was paneled in rich Honduran mahogany. Three earphone-wearing receptionists sat behind a massive, marble-topped desk. The plush leather couches and chairs could swallow you up, and the carpet was deeply piled.

Elaine spent tons of the firm's money acquiring abstract impressionist works by Rothko and de Kooning. The place was a mini museum.

The firm provided no-holds-barred representation. Laminated newspaper articles touting their multimillion-dollar jury awards covered two walls of the reception area. Recessed in another wall was a huge tank of brilliantly colored saltwater fish. Ben always described this shimmering display as "living art."

I met Ben years ago, when he was a young prosecutor. As a crime reporter for the *Post*, I was referred to him by a colleague who said, "You gotta talk to Bulldog Ben Abrams if you want the truth about the DA's office." At the time, I was writing an article about prosecutorial misconduct.

"How would I know about prosecutorial misconduct?" Ben asked. His eyes narrowed. With his wide shoulders and bull neck, leaning forward across this desk, he looked intimidating.

"I hear you're a no-bullshit guy," I said.

"I can only speak for the way *I* prosecute cases, not the other ADAs."

"That's what I need . . . a straight shooter."

The tip I'd received was right on the money. Ben was blunt, brutally direct.

After we'd spoken for nearly an hour, Ben said, "Fuck this. Let's go for lunch. Ever been to Sam's Grill on Duane Street?"

We became close friends. When I left the newspaper trade and began writing crime novels, Ben gave me CliffsNotes tutorials on trial tactics and procedures. To a crime novelist, they were pure gold ore. With his help, I learned to write realistic courtroom scenes, which added a tension-ridden panache to my novels. And Ben always vetted my work for legal inconsistencies. I always listed Ben in the Acknowledgments, right after mentioning Nora's editorial skills.

Ben and I grew so close that if not for my brother, Charlie,

Ben would've been my best man when Nora and I were married. As couples, Ben, Elaine, Nora, and I dined all over town. We vacationed together in Spain, Portugal, and Italy's Amalfi Coast. We were like family.

That was then.

Now I was sitting in his reception area—a defendant accused of murdering my wife.

Ben's office was right off the reception area. He was managing partner—head honcho and the firm's rainmaker. His inner sanctum was a huge space with cherrywood-paneled walls lined with rows of law volumes. Gold-plated trophies from Ben's wrestling days bedecked the shelves set inside glass cabinets. Glossy eight-by-ten photos adorned the walls. There was Ben with the mayor, another with Bill and Hillary along with a bevy of politicians and celebrities. The wall was a testament to Ben's stellar connections, his political tentacles.

I sat in a creamy soft, beige leather chair facing Ben's desk. For the first time ever with Ben, I felt freakishly uncomfortable, not knowing where to begin. I was navigating uncharted and very choppy waters. As upset and dazed as I was, I wanted to deal with something important before we tackled anything else. "Ben, I don't know how I'm gonna pay for this," I said, as a squeamish feeling leached through me.

"There's no fee, Bill," he said, raising his hands.

I blinked. Was I hearing him correctly?

"But your practice . . . your partn—"

"I've made my bones. My partners agree: this case is pro bono."

"Ben—"

"This case cries out for justice."

"But you do *civil* work. My fucking *life's* on the line here."

"I was an ADA for seven years. I know the criminal justice

system like the back of my hand."

"Do you feel comfortable defending a *friend*?"

"Our relationship won't color my judgment. I'll give this case my all."

"You're sure? The time, the effort . . . the money . . . to mount a criminal defense—"

"How could I *not* represent you?" he said, getting out of his chair and leaning toward me with his palms on the desktop.

Did I have a choice? I needed a savvy gunslinger, a shark who really knew the courtroom waters. A top-shelf criminal defense guy would bill at a rate close to $800 an hour. The meter would be running for prep time, pretrial motions, court appearances, and meetings with the DA—all the time-consuming, money-sapping bullshit a trial would inevitably entail. Every telephone conversation would be written up at tenth-of-an-hour billing charges—six minutes a pop, all billed with obsessive accuracy. That would be thirteen bucks a minute for yakking on the goddamned phone. It could cost a hundred bucks for the attorney to talk briefly with an investigator, who would also be billing for time and expenses. I knew all this from a hundred earlier discussions with Ben over the years. In litigation lane, every minute was billed—no exceptions. Defense attorneys charged for reading or drafting e-mails. They charged for photocopying—they billed for time and materials. Nothing was for nothing. Win or lose, you pay.

After the last few years, I was left with next to nothing in the way of assets—I was tapped out, drained dry. Paying for a high-powered criminal defense attorney would leave me broke.

Acquittal or conviction—hiring an attorney would be financial suicide. Nora's illness had been a deep-pockets money pit. I was in a world of trouble—legally and financially.

"I—I don't know what to say."

"Say nothing, Bill. We'll work this out."

My mouth must have been hanging open.

"Are we in this together?"

I nodded, feeling a baseball-sized lump fill my throat. "Jesus. Who'd have thought all those years ago . . . that day we went for lunch . . ."

"Sam's Grill . . ." Ben said with a nod. "I remember it like it was yesterday."

I wanted to wrap my arms around him and cry my heart out—just sob like a baby. A cascade of feelings washed over me: sorrow for the loss of Nora, anguish for her suffering, relief that her pain and misery were finally over, regret that the life I'd known had come to an end, fear of the trial to come, and a rush of gratitude for Ben—a great friend. But this was above and beyond.

"So let's get to work," Ben said.

I swallowed hard—a loud gulp—and held back my tears.

"You okay?"

"Yeah . . . I just need a minute," I said, pressing my palms to my face.

He waited as I collected myself. A soothing calm came over me.

"It's the same routine in every murder trial," Ben said, sitting down, leaning back in his chair. "The prosecutor always shoots for the Triple Crown."

"Yeah, the trifecta," I muttered.

"You remember the mantra?"

I nodded.

The trifecta—now latching on to me.

Ben swiveled his chair. "Olson wants to show you had *motive, means,* and *opportunity.*"

Ben plopped his feet on his helicopter-pad-sized desk. "What does Olson see as motive?" he asked. "First, there's money. I looked at your financials. They're bad. You lost lots of dough in the crash of '08, and were under the gun. The insurance company dropped Nora's medical coverage when she got sick, right?"

I nodded as my stomach looped.

Nora . . . sick, paralyzed, withering away to a shriveled remnant of what she'd once been.

"You spent tons of cash for the last few years."

"Right."

"Secondly, you haven't completed a novel in how long . . . ? Three, four years?"

I nodded.

"Okay, some residual royalties came in, but not enough to take care of expenses."

I could see Olson's trifecta forming.

"There were doctor bills, medicines, equipment, hundreds of thousands over nearly three years. And the home aide—fifteen bucks an hour, twelve hours a day, right?"

I already saw how this could be made to look by a dogged prosecutor. In front of a jury—twelve people with one-tenth the resources of a successful writer.

"You've been in financial quicksand, and to a jury, it'll look bad."

"You always said a trial is showmanship," I said as dread gnawed at me. I felt the case—as well as what little was left of my life—sliding toward a cataclysmic ending.

"In many criminal cases, money is motive. Olson's gonna shoot for the money angle."

"Understood."

"Lemme ask you something . . ."

"Ask."

"Any other expenditures I don't know about?"

"No, not a thing."

"No trips to Atlantic City? Online betting? Point spreads on the NFL, baseball bets?"

I shook my head.

"When people are strapped, they get desperate," Ben said.

"Any money dropped on drugs or hookers? I know. I *know*," he said, palms raised. "But Olson's gonna look, so I gotta ask."

Yes, this was gonna be seedy. No, it would be more than that: it'd be a mud fight, and no matter what the verdict, I'd come out of it smelling like pig shit. Every moment of my life over the years would come under the DA's scrutiny.

"*Jesus*. There's nothing like that."

"Okay. Just tons of after-tax dollars spent on Nora. So money's gonna be Olson's first motive. Let's get to motive number two."

"And that is . . .?"

"A sick wife. Olson's gonna feed the jury the story that you got fed up with the drain on your time and energy, in addition to hemorrhaging money. So, you decided to get rid of her."

"How absurd."

"Olson'll push any button he thinks'll work with a jury." Ben slipped his feet off the desk, got up, and began pacing. "Let's get to motive number *three*," he said. "There's the Kevorkian thing."

"A mercy killing?"

"To relieve Nora's suffering. Forgive me, Bill, but we have to talk frankly here. After all, the rest of your life's at stake."

"I understand." My face muscles went into spasm.

"We know hospitals hustle people's deaths along with morphine drips. Happens every day of the week." Ben paused. "But in this case, Olson has a bonus."

"Which is?"

"If your name weren't Bill Shaw, he wouldn't be so hot for this case."

"So he's looking for *publicity*?"

"Have you seen the papers?"

"I can't look."

"The words *best-selling author* always precede your name."

"I haven't written a thing in . . . what is it . . . ? Four years."

"Yeah, but Olson's got that thing called irony. Imagine, a

best-selling crime writer going on trial for murder. After all, you were living—as you used to call it— the New York life."

A best-selling author, the media, the New York life.

The New York life was the hype that went with writing best-selling books and doing teleplays for *Law & Order*. It meant a cameo appearance as a detective, yelling back and forth with Jerry Orbach—Detective Lennie Briscoe. It was face time on *Entertainment Tonight* and an interview with Charlie Rose.

The New York life meant dinners out with Pete Hamill; being wined and dined by Spike Lee, Martin Scorsese, and Robert DeNiro; and lecturing at the New School. It meant an interview in *Esquire*, another in *New York Magazine*; it was publishing parties, book signings, and weekends at star-studded gatherings in the Hamptons.

It meant a complimentary bottle of high-end wine ferried to the table by the restaurateur when Nora and I dined out. It was being asked for book blurbs and nominations for an Edgar Award. But that was a lifetime ago.

Ancient history. A life long gone.

"The New York life . . . all bullshit," I murmured. "I've been living like a hermit."

"Look, this case puts Olson in the spotlight as a righteous defender of the sick, and he'll milk it like a Manhattan-sized udder."

I'm just ammo for his future.

"We've got three so-called motives: money, mercy, and ridding yourself of a burden. And for Olson, it's career-changing publicity. So he's gonna throw spaghetti on the wall and see what sticks."

I closed my eyes, feeling sick to my stomach.

"Okay. Let's look at item number two—the *means.*"

"Warfarin."

"Exactly. And the last part of the trifecta is *opportunity.*"

"I gave Nora the warfarin every morning."

"Alone. Unsupervised—IV toward the end, right?"

The thought of intravenous warfarin brought me back to Nora's last day of life.

The edges of the room darkened.

"Olson's going for second-degree murder, not first-degree homicide. He claims you acted with intent, but not in a premeditated way."

"Meaning?"

"With a second-degree murder charge, there can be an affirmative defense. You admit doing it but claim emotional duress."

"You mean cop a plea?"

"We can probably plead it down to manslaughter."

"Which means admitting I killed Nora." My pulse ramped up, throbbing mercilessly through my neck.

"I'm just saying we have some bargaining options."

"Admit I murdered my wife? No way."

Ben stopped pacing.

For a moment, my thoughts seemed frozen.

Then I said, "I've noticed something."

"What?"

"You haven't asked me if I did it."

"C'mon, Bill. You were a crime reporter. You know a defense attorney never asks a client that question."

"Yeah, but you're not just an attorney. You're a friend . . . my *best* friend."

"Friend or no friend, my job is to give you the best defense you're entitled to. I don't decide guilt or innocence."

"I'm not asking you to decide anything. I just wanna know what you think."

"What I think is irrelevant."

"Not to me."

"C'mon, Bill . . ."

"Let's cut the bullshit. I need to know if you believe me."

Ben's mouth opened, but he said nothing. He looked down for a moment and then peered into my eyes. "I know you more years than I even wanna think about," he said in a voice that began cracking. "And I knew Nora, too. I knew you as a couple, and so did Elaine. We went everywhere together. I knew the two of you better than anyone except Elaine. So I'm gonna do something no defense attorney does with a client, *ever*. I'm gonna tell you I believe you *one hundred percent*. I know you didn't hurt Nora."

"That's what I need to hear."

Ben's eyes shimmered with tears. He reached out to me with those huge arms. I stood and sank into them like a kid. I sobbed as if my soul poured from my eyes. Ben's thick hands slapped my back.

I pulled away. "I needed you to say that. I just needed to know you believe me."

"I believe you, Bill. I do."

I nodded, feeling as much affection—even love—for Ben as I'd ever felt in all the years we'd known each other.

He walked behind his desk, peered out the window, and turned to me. "I just want you to see the case Olson'll build against you." He sighed. "One thing's for sure . . . he'll be looking for prison time."

"What are we talking about here?"

"Mandatory fifteen to life. With a conviction, the best-case scenario would be a minimum of ten years."

Could this be the final chapter of a crime writer's life? Serving time in some hellhole like Sing Sing, Fishkill, or Attica? Condemned to live in an eight-by-ten-foot cell with the scum of the earth—tattooed psychos, killers, child molesters, and rapists? How would I ever survive?

Muffled traffic noise from lower Broadway seeped in through the windows.

"Jesus, Ben, it just hit me like a sledgehammer. This looks bad."

"Most circumstantial cases look bad," Ben said. "But we'll explain the circumstances."

"Will I testify?"

A siren screamed its way downtown.

Ben's eyes rose and he peered at the ceiling. "Juries don't like when a defendant doesn't take the stand. But testifying can backfire, big-time. I've seen defendants get slaughtered on cross-examination. Totally screwed, even convicted, simply because of what happened on cross. We'll get their witness list and then plan our strategy."

"But right now it looks bad, doesn't it?"

"I don't want to discourage you."

"But it doesn't look good, does it?"

"It looks tough."

Chapter 12

Tramping along a trail behind Charlie in Yorktown Heights, I inhaled the resin-scented air. The madness of the city seemed a galaxy away.

At forty-four, my brother still looked like the athlete he once was. His short-lived baseball career with a Yankee farm team ended years earlier, when a shoulder injury crushed his dream. Now, instead of a Yankee uniform he once hoped to don, he wore khaki cargo shorts and hiking boots. His calf muscles looked like balloons.

At the edge of a craggy promontory, we sat on a weather-worn log. The Croton Reservoir glittered far below, offset by a dark line of spruce trees at the basin's perimeter.

"You know, Charlie, if I get through this trial, maybe I'll leave the city."

"The trial's a travesty," he said. "Forgive me, Bill, but Nora's finally at peace. And I know you've been through hell. You looked really bad at Mom's funeral."

"Yeah, we'd just learned Nora had MS."

"I could've been a better brother to you, Bill . . ."

"You're a great brother, Chaz. You took Mom in after you got married."

"I was trying to get close to her. Honestly, I always felt she favored you."

"Ah, c'mon. It's just that I was older."

"Remember how I tried to compete with you?"

"Yeah . . . always trying to beat the shit out of me, little brother."

I felt a twinge of pleasure calling Charlie *little brother*. At six four, Charlie towered over me, but I'd learned long ago size never conferred status.

"Remember the cheapest suit contest?"

We laughed. I was thirty-one; Charlie was thirty. Admiring my herringbone suit, he'd asked, "What'd you pay for that?"

"Next to nothing. I don't spend money on clothes."

"Bet I can buy a cheaper suit than you."

It was one of Charlie's ludicrous challenges—always fun. So we made a bet: whoever bought the cheapest suit won. We'd meet the following Saturday night, each in a new suit—along with a store receipt as proof of purchase.

P.J. Clarke's was jam-packed the night we met to compare threads. Charlie wore an ill-fitting blue suit that bulged over his massive chest and shoulders. Elated, he produced a receipt. The price for the rag: $99.95 before tax.

"Not bad," I said, whipping out my receipt. Charlie stared disbelieving: $89.99. No tax.

"I paid cash, so he dropped the tax," I said, grinning. "You owe me dinner, little brother."

Amid the barroom babble, we guzzled mugs of Guinness Stout, then decimated the P.J. Clarke's special: Cadillac Burgers—slabs of juicy beef with bacon, cheddar cheese, onions, chili, béarnaise sauce, and mushrooms—along with a pile of P.J. French fries.

Charlie ceremoniously paid the tab.

We were on 3rd Avenue when the night sky opened. Sheets of rain fell as we ran through the downpour until we caught a taxi.

When the cab dropped us off in the Village, Charlie roared with laughter. My winning suit had shrunk by two sizes. I tossed the shriveled jacket into a trash basket. We walked to a nearby bar, where we continued drinking.

Now, as we sat overlooking the reservoir, I said, "I have a confession to make, little brother. That eighty-nine-dollar suit? It really cost a hundred and twenty-nine bucks. The guy wrote me a fake receipt for eighty-nine dollars."

"You lying bastard. I *won*," Charlie cried with a fist-pump in the air.

"I just wanted to set that right."

After we laughed together, silence fell as we stared over the water.

"You writing again?"

"I can't."

"After the trial, you'll get your life back."

"Did Mom ever get her life back after Pop disappeared?"

"You still think about that?"

"Don't you?"

"What's there to say? Pop was always hustling up cash for the shylocks. Most likely he was clipped and then dumped in Mill Basin when he fell too far behind."

Charlie was probably right. Pop was always in debt and trying to lie his way out of it. After he disappeared, Mom's arthritis flared up. She became crippled. I went to NYU—became a subway student so I could help her at home. Charlie went away to college on a baseball scholarship.

"You ever resent staying home to live with Mom?"

"It was the right thing to do," I said, peering at the reservoir.

Crows began a raucous round of cawing. Their clamor echoed off the water's surface far below.

"You know, Bill, I think you became a writer because of Dad. Remember how he told stories?"

"He lied about everything."

"You inherited his storytelling talent."

"Well, a writer lies," I said, thinking how Nora and I brainstormed together and dreamed up plot twists for the novels—*our* novels. God, we were such a team, always wanting to keep the reader guessing. We were incredible fabulists.

"Lying? What do you mean?" Charlie said.

"I mislead the reader. I hold something back 'til the end."

"Is that really lying?"

"Maybe not. But it's devious."

"You *are* a devious bastard. I can't get over that fucking suit," Charlie said with a snort.

"Fooled you, didn't I?"

"Maybe you write about crime because of the rubout . . . after what happened to Pop."

I thought of my novels—gut-wrenching thrillers about murderers, stalkers, hoods—bloody, violent tales, with death imminent or being played out. Like what probably happened to Pop at the hands of some mob goons.

"Maybe it's because I have murder in my heart," I said.

"What're you talking about?"

"My books . . . so filled with killing. Maybe there's something evil inside me. I really don't know."

Chapter 13

"A trial is really a performance."

"You mean it's not a search for the truth?" I said, smothering a smile. I'd sat in on enough trials to know what they really were—verbal jousts, attempts to score points by distorting and, if necessary, dissembling in front of a jury.

"It's performance art for those twelve souls who'd rather be doing anything but sitting in the jury box."

"I've written about it."

"But this isn't fiction. You'll be on display every second in the courtroom. And the jury'll be watching you. You'll have to show grief, innocence, outrage, and dignity, all at the same time. You gotta play a very tough part."

"I don't belong to the Screen Actors Guild, Ben."

"Speaking of acting, you need to gain some weight. You look like death warmed over, though, on second thought, maybe it isn't so bad. The jury'll see how miserable you've been with Nora gone."

An ache filled me as I pictured Nora wasting away during her last days—her face drawn and pale, sinking in on itself. Her eyes hollow, her voice dropping to a hoarse whisper, and then gone.

"Now, lemme answer your question about trying this in front of a judge," Ben said. "A bench trial's fine if there're complicated forensic issues and you don't wanna snow a jury with technical or scientific mumbo-jumbo. But, frankly, I think we're better off with twelve good people in the jury box."

"Why?"

"I like juries. Actually, I *love* 'em. You gotta seduce a jury. It's like wooing a lover. During voir dire, you ask the right questions. You listen to what they say and to what they *don't* say; you get a sense of their politics, their prejudices, their social and religious feelings; you consider their ethics, the work they do, whether they're married, divorced, single, old, young, black, white, Hispanic, their cultural hang-ups . . . everything. You use your gut, but you also use what you know about life."

Ben began pacing.

"Of course, in this case, we'll have to know how jurors feel about having a sick spouse. We want older jurors, people who've had illness, or who've had sick husbands, wives, or partners. People who'll understand your situation with Nora. If I had my way, I'd go for a jury of twelve women."

"The seduction angle?"

"Partly. There's always an undercurrent of sexual tension with female jurors. But to bottom line it: women are more empathic than men, more into family and emotional issues. They're better bets in a case like this."

"Why not a woman judge?"

"All judges—men and women—can come under political pressure. We wanna avoid judicial ambition. No matter how lofty the notion of the law is, it's a system of human beings. And like anything else in life, there are pressures, biases, and other considerations. You know the criminal defense bar actually keeps a list—a judicial rap sheet—on every judge in each county. They know which ones tend to favor defendants, and they know the hang-'em-high types, too. We have no control over the judge we get. But, if we can select enough jurors with even half a soul, we'll be in a reasonable position."

"How about a jury consultant?"

"Not worth a buck up a bum's ass. I *love* picking a jury; I love the probing, slicing, and dicing. Actually, it's not a matter of selecting the right jurors; it's eliminating—really, deselecting—the wrong ones. So I recommend a jury trial . . . where we have a say in the selection process. Not a judge—not some political hack—sitting on high."

"Ben, my life's in your hands. You sure?"

"I'm very sure. We're in this together. And we're gonna prep like crazy, so when crunch time comes, we'll be ready." Ben peered into my eyes. "You gotta trust my instincts and experience."

I nodded, yet I couldn't stop worrying about what a trial could become: a seedy drama with a bevy of salacious implications. Olson would throw everything he could possibly find at me—and what would he unearth? Was there a person alive who didn't have *something* to hide?

"One more thing," Ben said, pacing the office floor.

I waited, thinking Ben might drop some momentous bomb in my lap.

"Ordinarily, in a criminal defense, you try mounting an alternative theory about the victim's death."

"*Victim?*"

"Sorry, Bill. Too many years spent as a prosecutor back in the day. Let me rephrase. Usually, you propose another theory of how someone died; something to deflect the jury and plant seeds of doubt in their minds. Because that's the gold—the paydirt for a defendant—reasonable doubt. But we can't go that way here. There's no one else to point a finger at . . . unless you wanna propose that Roberta, the aide, or Lee gave Nora an OD."

"That'd be absurd. They never went near Nora's warfarin."

"I know. Just giving you an idea of how nuts any alternative theory would look. So we're left with this: instead of another theory about Nora's death, the bulk of our defense is built around destroying Olson's case; and ninety-nine percent of that's gonna be accomplished on cross-examination. That's why I wanna get their witness list as soon as possible—especially their expert toxicologist. I have an idea about who they'll use, but we'll wait and see.

"Meanwhile, I have tons of reading to do about warfarin. And I'll be consulting with an expert, someone to give me the lowdown on how to counter their expert. We're gonna tear Olson's case apart, bit by bit. It'll be death by a thousand little cuts.

"If we can do that effectively, you won't need to testify. After all, the burden of proof's on the prosecution, not us. We just gotta create reasonable doubt in the jury's mind."

Ben plopped down in his high-backed leather seat and looked at me for what seemed a very long time. His brow furrowed; then his eyes narrowed. He tilted his head.

"Meanwhile, I think you could use some Prozac to bring you back to the land of the living."

What the hell is the land of the living? And why is Nora in the land of the dead?

"Prozac won't bring Nora back."

Ben nodded and sighed. "Weren't you writing something before she passed?"

"Yeah, some crap called *Assassin's Lullaby.*"

It all came back to me in a moment. Nora lying in the hospital bed—in our living room—a few months before she died. The MS had progressed quickly; her muscles were paralyzed. Her voice was so weak she could only whisper. She couldn't swallow and she was being fed through a tube. The prednisone increased the effects of warfarin, so she had frequent nosebleeds and bled into her skin. Purple blotches covered her body.

"Nora," I said, "we have to figure out how to communicate when your voice goes."

"I'll use my eyes."

Sitting on the bed, I stroked her hair. The fragrance of talc filled my nostrils.

"Bill," she whispered weakly.

"Yes, my love . . ."

"Will you begin writing again?"

"I want to, but—"

"Bill," she whispered, paused, tried to swallow. "The books were our children."

She was so right. I'd never looked at it that way. The books had come from both of us—they were something we'd breathed life into, together. Yes, in their own way, they were our children.

I watched her throat go up and down, could see her neck muscles struggling. The sight tore at my heart.

"Please write again. As a gift to me."

"Everything I've written has been for you."

"Dedicated to me, yes, but write this one as a *gift* for me."

The harshness of it was like a blow to the gut: Nora would die, and this was her last wish—a gift from me.

Her eyelids fluttered.

"So, you'll write another one for me?"

I nodded, but didn't know if I could enter that white-hot zone again—the frenzied creative haze in which a novel would pour from some deeply hidden recess inside me.

"Please sing to me," she whispered. "You know the song . . ."

"You mean 'Alfie'?"

She tried to nod her head.

The melody and words came through the thickness of my throat. Nora's lips moved as I warbled.

Hearing a sob, I looked up.

Roberta, the aide, stood with tears pooling in her eyes.

I hummed the tune as Nora's eyes closed. I thought she was sleeping. Suddenly her eyes opened. "Please write it for me," she whispered.

Then she was asleep.

The ache was so deep, I felt I was dying. Gazing at Nora, I knew the horror that lay ahead, and with our lives together draining away, I realized the terrible finality of death.

I began trying to write *Assassin's Lullaby*.

Chapter 14

"Who the *fuck* is Constance?" Ben shouted, three days later. His nostrils flared and his eyes looked like they'd pop from their sockets.

A bolt of white light shot through me. My thoughts tumbled furiously. This would be more of a nightmare than I'd imagined.

"Constance Manning? I—I met her a few weeks before Nora died. I didn't even—"

"*Shit.* I asked if there's anything you haven't told me." Ben's chest heaved.

"Ben, I—"

"And I learn about this woman *now*?" he shouted, getting up from behind his desk. "From Olson's witness list? Jesus, this is an attorney's worst nightmare. Who *is* she? And why didn't you tell me about her?"

"Because she has nothing to do with the case. She's—"

"*Bill!*" Ben cried, his face turning crimson. "Let *me* decide what's relevant. *I'm* the attorney, not you. You can't feed me selective information. We'll go down the tubes."

Feeling weak, I plopped into a chair.

"Okay," Ben said, holding his hands up, palms out. He was trying to calm himself but his hands shook. "Tell me everything. Otherwise, Olson's gonna pull a snake outta the bag, and we'll get bitten, right on the ass."

"She's not really part of my life."

"Not *really* part of your life? Goddammit, Bill. You worked the crime beat. You know the game." He shook his head, sucking in his breath. "Okay, lemme ask you some questions, because one thing's certain, Olson's gonna ask 'em." Ben's eyes were on fire.

"You telephone her?"

Something sank in my chest. I nodded.

"How often?"

"I don't know . . . maybe ten times."

"Any e-mails?"

"Yes . . ."

"You text each other?"

I shook my head.

"How about visits?"

"Yeah . . ."

"Her apartment?"

"Yeah."

I was withering.

"How many times?"

"Two . . . maybe three . . ."

The office was unbearably quiet. The air seemed heavy.

Ben's chest heaved. "Okay, Bill. Lemme paint you a picture. A judge grants a subpoena and Olson snatches your phone records. He's got your computer. He sends a detective to her building. Guy talks to her doorman, the neighbors, to anyone who knows anything about her. They build a timeline. You know what a timeline is? Huh?"

I was suffocating.

Ben looked at me with those penetrating eyes.

"Getting the picture?"

I nodded.

"And it all goes in front of a jury—the calls, the e-mails, the visits, and everything on your computer's hard drive." Ben's neck veins bulged. "Now, tell me. Who is she?"

"We met at Starbucks."

"*Starbucks?*" Ben's eyes widened. "Fucking *Starbucks?* A coffee shop liaison? Olson's gotta be drooling."

"Ben, listen to me."

"I'm listening." Ben sank into his chair. His eyes narrowed to skeptical slits.

"Nora made me promise to start writing. I began this novel a few months before she died. I couldn't write in the apartment, so I'd go to Starbucks, write on the laptop. When the library opened, I'd go there."

"So, you're at Starbucks. How does this Manning woman fit in?"

"Her husband was at the DeWitt Nursing Home across the street, and she'd visit. So, we were both at the coffee shop; she was there a couple of mornings a week and we fell into conversation."

"Conversation?" Ben's eyebrows seemed to meet his hairline.

"Her husband had Parkinson's disease."

"Yeah?"

"He died a few weeks before Nora did."

"And *then* what? C'mon. Don't hold back on me."

"We were talking at Starbucks . . . commiserating . . ."

"And at her apartment? Give it to me straight. Were you intimate?"

"*No.*"

"No sexual relations?"

"Not at all."

"Kissing? Petting? C'mon, Bill. I gotta know."

"A kiss on the cheek. Nothing more."

Ben's arms folded across his chest. "You're leveling with me?"

"Yes."

"Lemme tell ya . . . you better not be bullshitting your own lawyer."

"It's not bullshit, Ben. We never had sex."

More quiet. Ben assessing what I said. My heart was leaping out my throat.

"How 'bout a love trail?"

"What do you mean?"

"Any restaurants, bars?"

"No. A few store-bought meals at her place, that's all."

"And the doormen saw you?"

"Sure."

"You stayed how long?"

"An hour or two . . . maybe a bit longer one time."

"A bit longer? How long?"

"I don't remember. Maybe a few hours . . . three . . ."

"Three hours? And there was no sex?"

"None."

"How often were you there?"

"Once a week for maybe three, four weeks."

"Any all-nighters?"

"No. Never."

Yes, I'd been tempted, and so had she. What else could I possibly say? I could tell Ben was skeptical, even disbelieving. His eyes were a giveaway—and his lips, a thin, grim line, bloodless. Incredulity was etched on his face.

"Did the detectives ask about her?"

"I think Kaufman asked if I met anyone at Starbucks."

"And you said?"

"I was so tired. It was late. Nora's funeral was still on my mind. I was all screwed up and I'd been drinking. And that interrogation room was stifling. I was—"

"What the fuck did you say, Bill? I haven't looked at the recording yet."

"That I didn't."

"You denied meeting anyone at Starbucks?"

"Yes."

Then it came back to me in a rush.

"They also asked if I had a girlfriend. I said I didn't, and it's true. I went to Starbucks to *write*, not to—"

"But you said you didn't meet anyone; it's untrue. It's Interrogation 101. Ask a question the answer to which you already know. They didn't confront you, did they?"

"No."

"Because they wanted to trap you. It'll come up at trial." Ben let out a leaden sigh. "How do you think this'll look to a jury? In the pretrial conference, the judge decided to let the interrogation recording in as demonstrative evidence. It'll look like you lied, especially after this Manning woman testifies."

"But Constance has nothing to do with—"

"Doesn't matter. Olson's gonna make it look like the two of you were having an affair."

"So he'll distort things?"

"*Distort*? He won't have to. I guarantee you Olson's subpoenaed your phone records. He has a printout of every call. And he's got Constance Manning's records, too. And every e-mail. We gotta go over everything—*every-fucking-thing*. No more surprises."

Something cold gnawed at me. I was getting a taste of the hell this would be.

"You gotta realize something: a trial's a *show* for the jury. Olson'll show two people—you and this Manning woman—betraying your marriages. She had a vegetable for a husband, and Nora was paralyzed, dying. He'll milk it. He'll squeeze every ounce out of it, and make it look like you were sneaks, cheats, liars. He'll make you look like a guy who's cheating on his dying wife, a sleazebag. That's the game."

Feeling like I was sinking through the floor, I was suddenly aware of the very things I'd portrayed so many times in my fiction: the protagonist's feeling of being trapped in the jaws of something far larger than himself. But not some prehistoric monster out of *Jurassic Park* or *Jaws*; something man-made and brutal, even lethal. It was the power of the State, the law—a cyclopean creature, relentless—ready to devour me. About to chew me up and spit me out.

"This is being blown out of proportion," I murmured.

"You think Olson gives a shit? He only cares how this looks to a jury. He'll showcase it as a torrid affair—a love nest, some sultry liaison between two unfaithful people. With the money drain on you, with Nora paralyzed, and this Manning woman in the wings—just waiting for her husband to curl up and die—he'll peddle his story to the jury. He'll convince them you gave Nora a lethal dose so you could go on with your life . . . with Constance Manning. This is the sex angle Olson was looking for . . . the *other woman*. And you gave it to him."

I was drowning in an ocean of distortions and outright lies. Ben was right. Olson would use Constance to put me away in some upstate shithole, for a decade, or more. And I was so stupid to have kept her from Ben. But how could I have ever explained what really happened with Constance? God, the shame of it all. I couldn't bear it.

"And, Olson's bringing in a computer geek," Ben said. "The guy's going through your laptop. He'll describe everything on the hard drive. And that novel you were writing, *Assassin's Lullaby*? I just finished reading what you'd written. It's about a hit man hired to whack some woman? Gimme a goddamned break. It'll look great to a jury. A man murdering a woman. What else'll they find on your hard drive?"

"I was researching a novel . . . a *novel*."

"What kinda research?"

"I went to dozens of websites."

"What kinda sites?"

"About the Russian Mafia. About hit men. How a hit man

kills . . . poisons, drugs, guns, crap like that."

"How a hit man operates? Poisons? *Drugs*? Fucking *drugs*?"

Ben's huge hands slapped against his forehead. The sound made me jump.

"*Jesus Christ*. And it's all in the manuscript. I couldn't believe it when I read it." Ben's eyes looked bloodshot. "Holy shit. Olson's gonna feed it all to the jury."

"You mean my manuscript's coming in? A piece of fiction can be used as evidence against me?"

"It goes to motive. Olson's gonna claim you had murder on your mind."

"But it's fiction. How's that evidence?"

Ben stared at me. His eyes seemed like pockets of ice. "Anything on the laptop about warfarin?"

"Nora was on it for years. I read all—"

"Olson's gonna make a ton of hay with it. He'll highlight your computer history to show how you used warfarin to kill her."

"Because I tried to learn about Nora's medications?"

"We gotta think like a prosecutor. Olson's gonna build it up for the jury. It's a construction, a stage play, a goddamned story."

"A story? Now, *that's* fiction."

"A trial *is* a story. It's storytelling time in court. It's show-and-tell, like when you were a kid in school. And the jury's like a bunch of kids. *Tell me more* is what they want. Forget that bullshit about the law being about fairness and justice. That's a crock of shit. What counts is what a jury believes. Nothing else."

"So Olson's fiction counts . . . even if he uses *my* fiction to write his own fiction?"

"Now you're getting the picture."

My hands clutched the chair's armrests.

You're going down for the count.

"Okay. I've already got a printout of everything on the computer, and I gotta go through it. All the websites you surfed; and I gotta reread the whole manuscript. I'm gonna have to memorize the thing," Ben said. "Two other things. Dr. David Russell's on Olson's witness list. Who's he?"

"A psychiatrist Nora and I saw after the MS was diagnosed."

My hands began shaking.

"Olson may call him."

"Isn't that privileged . . . the doctor-patient relationship?"

"The privilege ends when the patient dies."

"We both saw Russell. Doesn't that make it privileged? After all, I'm not dead."

"What's admissible is an issue of law. But a prosecutor may put a name on the witness list just to throw the other side off balance. And then doesn't use that witness. We'll see. *We* might want to call Russell. I'll talk with him."

"What's the other thing?"

"Who's Gina Scott? She sounds familiar. Didn't I meet her years ago at some party? She was Nora's friend, right?"

My chest tightened. It felt like a vise was squeezing my heart.

"Gina Scott? She's an acquaintance from Nora's soap opera days."

"She's on Olson's witness list. Tell me why."

"You got a few hours . . . ?"

Chapter 15

Sean Olson peered into the kitchen of his and Lauren's 1931 Tudor-style home, located in the posh Fieldston section of Riverdale. He surveyed the Sub-Zero refrigerator, the six-burner Viking stove, and the brushed-nickel sink fixtures. The kitchen alone was a $120,000 renovation, courtesy of his parents. Not that his in-laws, the Andersons, hadn't pitched in: basically, they'd gifted Sean and Lauren the house.

Lauren's trust money was substantial. And by the time her dad retired, his stock options and golden parachute had dovetailed into a net worth of millions. Sean knew he and Lauren could never live so lavishly on his measly salary.

At thirty-five, Sean had been an ADA for eight years. After graduating from Harvard Law, he did a clerkship for a federal judge in New York's Southern District and then joined the Manhattan district attorney's office.

With a few breaks, Sean might eventually become the Manhattan district attorney. And then? The future could be limitless. But they would have to live in Manhattan, closer to the epicenter of political action, not in the sanitized environs of Riverdale. His friend and squash buddy, Henry Woodruff—now a partner at Polk, Davis & Wardwell—said last week, "Sean, you've got the confidence of a man who knows his destiny."

Yes, he's had a life of privilege and chose a direction in keeping with his family's expectations: law and, eventually, politics.

And the Shaw case could be the passport for his breakthrough.

Lauren, wearing shorts and a cotton shirt, padded into the kitchen. Sean hated looking at her cottage-cheese thighs. And her breasts drooped like narrow yams—no doubt from the ravages of time and from breast-feeding two babies. And their goddamned sex life . . . totally gone.

"Sean, I'm *not* moving to Manhattan," Lauren said, fiddling with the espresso machine.

"Look, honey, this Tribeca place is fabulous. It's a three-bedroom condo with a swimming pool, squash courts, and a sunroof."

"But think of the price we'll pay."

"Three point four million. Lauren, your parents'll foot the bill."

"I mean the *emotional* price. Mommy and Daddy won't get to see the kids if we live in Manhattan."

"Honey, they'll see the kids every week or so. And the money's not—"

"Oh, Sean, it's time we made it on our own."

"On an ADA's salary?"

"I hate Manhattan. It's dirty and crowded. And, they're not our kind of people."

The condo would be ideal. Sean was absolutely certain of it. No more commuting on Metro North from the Spuyten Duyvil station to Grand Central. He could walk from the Tribeca apartment to his office at Hogan Place. And with the condo's gym, Lauren would have no excuses about not getting back into shape. And he'd be a quick walk away from the Downtown Athletic Club, where he'd play squash and use the dining room to mingle with the power brokers he'd need to cultivate.

"Besides, we'll never get a nanny like Agnes," Lauren said, filling her coffee cup.

Her position was hardening. His political plans could be

derailed.

"I'm not moving." Lauren said, as she sat down and stirred her coffee. "I've made enough concessions already, Sean. I never wanted to leave Greenwich and move here. But I did it so you could be a DA in the Manhattan office. I'm not moving again."

"But my future . . . *our* future . . ."

"Is tonight your late night?" Lauren asked.

He just hated when she changed the subject.

"Yeah."

"You and Henry? Squash, then dinner?"

"Right. Me and Henry . . . squash."

Sean peered about his cubbyhole of an office. Lauren thought like a spoiled Greenwich brat, and wouldn't budge an inch for him or his career.

But the Shaw case could propel Sean out of the starting blocks. The story made three magazines this week, including *People* and *New York Magazine*.

"We have to make the most of the news coverage right now," Sean said to Ann Pierce. "As soon as a judge is assigned the case, he'll slap a gag order on us."

"Be careful, Sean," she'd reminded him. "If we stoke the media too much, Ben Abrams will move for a change in venue." Then Ann shot him that seductive smile.

Ann Pierce, his assistant, was light-years away from Fieldston, with its prewar mansions and suburban feel. Ann was a savvy, city-bred attorney. And what's more, she was single and damned good-looking. She had a great body—lovely, full breasts, a fully packed yet slim figure, and great legs. At twenty-eight, she hadn't begun the downward droop claiming Lauren. He'd imagined fucking Ann a thousand times.

The door opened and Ann walked in—sexy, blond, wearing sharkskin, straight-leg pants, a two-button jacket accentuating her hips, and a split-neck silk shirt. She removed her jacket, set it on a chair, and sat facing Sean.

"Ann, I've been waiting for you." He tried not staring at her breasts.

As Ann bent forward to pull a pad from her purse, Sean glimpsed her left breast—white, full, luscious.

"What do you hear from the shrink?" he asked.

"Russell claims doctor-patient confidentiality," Ann said, swiping at a stray lock of hair near her eyes.

"Did you tell him the privilege dies with the patient?"

"Sure. But he said Bill Shaw's not dead; he was a patient, too."

Sean laced his fingers behind his head and leaned back in the chair. "He may have a point when it comes to *Bill* Shaw, but not Nora. So we'll subpoena Russell's progress notes and subpoena him as a witness."

"What if he doesn't have much?"

"Then we won't use him. We lose nothing by looking."

Sean could imagine the warmth of Ann's body. He was about to launch into an erotic fantasy when Ann said, "The Manning woman was very interesting."

"Tell me."

"She said it was just coffee at Starbucks, a few visits, but nothing more. There's no proof of anything."

"Who needs proof? The implication alone can tilt the case."

"Even if he *was* having an affair, Sean, some jurors might understand—a man in his circumstances? After all, a man has needs."

"So you think a jury'll give him a pass?"

"He was living under pretty grim circumstances."

"That's the *point* . . . his grim circumstances. The money's draining and his life's narrowed down to nothing. It could go to motive."

"But there's no evidence of an affair."

"Evidence? Kaufman and Cirillo've been all over this. The phone records and the doormen paint the picture. The jurors can fill in the blanks. They were seeing each other, right?"

"Yes . . ."

Sean unclasped his hands and leaned forward. "Tell me, Ann, what does *seeing* each other mean?"

Ann shot that provocative smirk at him. Tingling began in Sean's groin. He was already at half-mast.

"She swears they weren't lovers."

"She *swore* that to you?" Sean feigned surprise. "Did she raise her right hand with her left on the Bible?" He snorted.

"Oh, c'mon, big guy. She wasn't under oath."

Big guy? Oh, yes . . .

"They were seeing each other?" Sean said, his voice rising. "A euphemism if ever I heard one. Let's not kid ourselves. It was an affair. And don't forget Gina Scott."

"She's some piece of work."

"More icing on the cake."

"You want to question Constance Manning?" Ann asked.

"She'd be more willing to talk with you—woman to woman." Sean swiveled his chair and regarded Ann closely. "Tell me, did Constance Manning feel he was interested in her?"

"She said he wasn't ready for something like that."

"Yeah, I know." Olson tried not to sound too cynical. "He just wasn't *up* for it, right?" Sean refrained from smirking. "As far as Constance Manning goes, slap her with a subpoena."

Ann slipped her notepad back in her purse. Sean caught another glimpse of that creamy breast. His legs tightened.

"Ann, I just had a thought. Why don't you join me for dinner tonight?"

"That's so kind of you, Sean. You've never offered before." A knowing smile formed on her lips as she brushed back that stubborn lock of hair.

"You're a tremendous asset. I really appreciate it. Have you ever been to Bouley?"

"I hear it's *fantastic*." Her eyes widened.

"The tasting menu's incredible. Why don't we head over at seven?"

"That's great, but isn't this your night for squash?"

"Henry Woodruff canceled."

"My good luck."

Ann headed for the door. Olson stared at the fullness of her ass. Tingling began in his chest and moved downward.

When Ann was gone, Olson slipped out his cell phone and pressed the speed-dial number.

"Bouley. Claude speaking."

"Claude, it's Sean Olson."

"Monsieur Olson. How are you, sir?"

Thankfully, I've got this safe place—a lovely restaurant—since Lauren never wants to budge from Fieldston, except to drive thirty minutes to Greenwich so she can be with her parents.

"I'm fine, Claude. I need a favor. Can you slip me in at seven this evening; dinner for two?"

"*Oui*, Monsieur Olson. It would be my pleasure."

"An intimate table . . ."

"*Oui, monsieur*. For two . . ."

"Thanks, buddy."

Sean pressed End Call, pulled up his contacts, found the number, and hit the speed-dial button. He listened to Henry Woodruff's outgoing message.

"Hey, Henry, it's Sean. I can't make it tonight. Something's come up at the office. I'll call to reschedule. Thanks, buddy."

Chapter 16

The Criminal Court building was a foreboding edifice with decades of city grime and pigeon shit encrusted on its facade. I'd been here a hundred times as a reporter, and the building was a frequent venue in my novels, but now I was a goddamned *defendant*. It seemed unreal. With everything that happened over the last few months, I existed in a toxic haze.

Satellite trucks from *Eyewitness News* and *NY1* were parked out front. The local press and tabloids couldn't get enough of the cheap drama, the salacious sizzle. Ben and I hustled up the stairs, brushing past a cadre of shouting reporters. We made it to the courthouse doors. In the lobby, I passed through the metal detectors, was wanded, and walked with Ben down a hallway to the elevators.

As we entered the courtroom, the eerie reality of it all was stunning. This was no TV drama or movie. Nor was it my imagination working overtime writing a scene in a novel.

This was the real thing—a powerhouse punch to my gut.

The government of the People—with its unlimited resources—was doing its best to convict me of killing my wife. There was a terrifying tangibility to it, and whether acquitted or convicted, I'd already been irreparably smeared—damaged beyond repair—by the press coverage alone. In the minds of many, I was nothing more than a sewer rat.

Trying to gain some control over myself, I focused on the

surroundings. The courtroom walls were paneled with dark oak; art-deco chandeliers hung from the high ceiling. The place smelled of wood dating back decades. With the gallery empty, sounds echoed through the space. The first group of potential jurors was seated for voir dire—jury selection. Some panel members stared at me.

One woman's forehead furrowed as I felt her eyes roaming over me. *Did she abhor me? See me as a wife-killer? Or was I imagining it?* Recalling that crazed woman in the Korean deli, I felt naked, vulnerable.

"They'll be gauging everything about you," Ben had said during prep sessions. "So be careful. Everything counts in court. I want your hair short, but not too clipped—and nothing too stylish. Yeah, yeah . . . it's all bullshit, but your appearance matters.

"And, Bill, I know you write at home and usually wear jeans and sneakers, but for court, you gotta dress right. Wear a tweed jacket and slacks. No dark blue suits, like some sleazy-assed Wall Street banker. And buy a decent tie. Nothing flashy. And no winged-tip shoes either. Too goddamned lawyerly."

As I sat at the defense table, I knew I was being judged by how I sat and stood, by my hairstyle and clothing. Every detail about my appearance was subliminally registering with the potential jurors, helping to inform their final judgment about my fate.

A middle-aged man with salt-and-pepper hair looked bored, like he wanted to get home, maybe watch a ballgame on TV. *Jesus. What if he got on the jury? Would he even listen to the evidence?*

I looked up at the judge's desk—the bench. From that high wooden construction with knurled molding, the judge—with his enormous power—would make rulings, influencing where I'd spend every second of the next decade or more of my life.

The Honorable J. J. Marin, dressed in a black robe, presided over jury selection. He'd be the trial judge, as well. He was a tall, thin man with a well-combed mane of white hair. His bushy eyebrows sprouted riotously above clear blue eyes sitting placidly behind gold-rimmed glasses. Never looking at me or the prospective jurors, he wrote on a pad as jury selection proceeded.

"We lucked out," Ben had said. "Marin tolerates no bullshit. There're no politics allowed in his courtroom."

Ben's "book" on the sixty-two-year-old judge revealed that after cross-endorsement by both political party machines in New York County, Marin had been elected four years earlier to his second fourteen-year term on the bench. His law degree was from Fordham; he'd worked in the Manhattan DA's office; and then he did criminal defense work. Ben speculated Marin might lean—ever so slightly—toward a defendant, but at best, that was a flimsy guess.

"Marin knows how to control the courtroom," Ben said during one prep session. "He knows how the game's played."

Ben's analogy about gamesmanship was accurate. For the lawyers, the trial would be a competition, a no-holds-barred contest, and the jury's verdict would be a notch in the belt for one, a sore defeat for the other.

But for me, this was no game. The rest of my life was at stake.

I tried calming myself once again by focusing on the physical setup of the room.

The witness chair sat on a platform below and to the left of the judge's bench. The jury box was about ten feet away, to the left.

The gallery had long, pew-style wooden benches. An aisle ran down the middle, dividing it into two sections, and aisles ran along each side of the courtroom.

I sat at the defense table. The prosecution's table—where Sean Olson and Ann Pierce sat—was to my right.

Surreptitiously, I studied Olson. Watching his confident strut, I felt a bubble of rage simmer within me. This man was trying to ruin what pathetic shred was left of my miserable life. And, according to Ben, Olson's fervor was all in the service of his ambition.

Olson, well over six feet tall, was good-looking in a bland, patrician way: his light brown hair, perfectly barbered, already showed signs of receding, revealing a high forehead. He wore a dark blue suit with a solid gray silk tie—Hermès, no doubt. His tapered shirt looked custom-made, and gold cuff links offset French cuffs. When he moved his left arm, I caught a glimpse of his Rolex watch. Olson sported more money on his body than I'd spent on clothing in five years.

He looked like he'd stepped right out of *The Great Gatsby*. He reminded me of a white-bread actor—Clark Hunter—who'd had his erotic sights set on Nora when she was still acting in the soap. I'd seen an episode of *The Burning World* in which he and Nora kissed passionately. I'd felt sickened, filled with rage as I watched their deep kiss.

"What's going on between you and Clark?" I demanded the moment Nora got home.

"Me and Clark?" she asked, wide-eyed. "What are you talking about?"

"The way you kissed . . ."

"For God's sake, Bill, not again. I *act* for a living. What's the matter with you? I resent the accusation. It's clear you don't trust me anymore."

Rushing to the bedroom, she slammed the door.

When we made love that night, I couldn't erase the image of that kiss with Clark, of her moaning with pleasure, and I wondered if Nora was acting with me.

I'd been such a fool to think that way. But jealously trumps sound judgment and trust. Always.

Ben and Olson stood side by side, handing out questionnaires to the prospective jurors. I wondered how the jurors would view me. Did they harbor some bias against me for my success as a best-selling author? How would they respond to Nora's illness, and the demands it made on my life? Would they be sympathetic, or would they see me as a self-serving, manipulative husband who wanted his wife dead?

After reviewing the jurors' written responses, Ben and Olson began their questioning.

"Thank you for taking the time to be here," Olson intoned. His voice was high pitched, reedy. "The People appreciate your commitment and applaud you for taking your civic responsibilities so seriously."

To me, he sounded condescending.

"Mr. Boyce," he said, turning to the first potential juror. "Have you ever read any of the defendant's novels?"

"No."

"Have you seen the film *Fire and Ice*, based on the defendant's book?"

"Yes, I did."

"Would the film influence your view of the case?"

"I don't think so."

"What did you think of the film?"

"It was a good thriller."

"He could be influenced by the movie," Olson said to the judge, asking that Mr. Boyce be dismissed from the jury pool.

Olson never once looked at me. I was mere fodder for his mill of prosecutorial ambition. Instead he focused on each potential juror like a laser beam.

The questions caromed back and forth—Ben, then Olson, then Ben.

"Have you ever before been a juror in a criminal case?" Ben asked an older black man.

"Yes, I have."

"Thank you, sir."

Ben and Olson approached Marin and a brief discussion followed. The judge nodded and excused the man from service.

"I don't want any juror who's sat on a criminal case," Ben whispered to me at the defense table. "They're jaded; they've heard it all."

Voir dire continued with each new group of potential jurors. On his legal pad, Ben drew a diagram of each new panel, noting the name and occupation of each person, as well as making handwritten notes. He slipped colored Post-it notes over each juror's name; one color for those he felt could be defense-oriented and another for the ones he would dismiss, either summarily or for cause.

With each group, Ben summarized the law governing murder. "I need to know, if you personally didn't agree with the law, would that influence you?"

Olson asked many of the same questions, but he and Ben hit from different angles. It was push-pull, veer left, shift right. It was a jousting contest, each side jostling for jurors who would share its slanted point of view.

Fairness didn't seem to be a consideration.

"Have you or a loved one ever been arrested?" Olson asked one man.

"Yes, for a domestic disturbance."

"What was that like?"

"I was treated like a criminal."

Olson walked to the bench and whispered to the judge.

"Mr. Gomez, you're excused from jury service," Marin said.

Olson deselected that potential juror for cause.

"Are you familiar with the actress Gina Scott, who will be a witness in this trial?" Ben asked a middle-aged woman with oddly colored dyed blond hair.

"Yes. She's in my favorite soap opera."

"Your Honor, I ask that this juror be dismissed for cause," Ben said.

The judge nodded.

"Do you watch TV crime shows like *CSI, Cold Case Files,* or any of the *Law & Order* shows?" Ben asked a young man.

"*Law & Order SVU* is my favorite show," he said.

Ben asked the judge to dismiss him.

Later, Ben questioned a construction worker. "Mr. Wallace, does your car have any bumper stickers?"

"A couple."

"What do they say?"

"*Support Our Troops* and *USA: Love It or Leave It.*"

"Law and order type," Ben whispered.

Mr. Wallace was dismissed.

Sitting at the defense table, I was about to pick up a pen and begin calculating the number of summary dismissals for each side, but recalled Ben's instructions.

"Don't write on a legal pad. Just look directly at each witness. During testimony, don't frown, smirk, or sigh. Keep your expression neutral. Check your feelings at the door. Leave the drama to me. And remember, no matter how outrageous or insulting Olson may be, stay calm."

"I know, Ben. I know . . ."

"For Olson, you're just a stepping-stone. Remember the line from Julius Caesar? *Yond Cassius has a lean and hungry look.*"

"Yeah . . ."

"That's Olson. He'll hang you from the highest tree if he gets the chance. He'll try to strip you naked and roast you over an open fire."

Chapter 17

Though Ben had warned me not to, I snuck a glance at my jury—twelve conscripted souls, along with four alternates. Nine women, seven men. I wondered if the excessive number of alternates reflected Judge Marin's concerns about the jury's staying power—my experience as a reporter was there were usually two, sometimes three alternates, not four.

The jury was a hodgepodge of humanity ranging in age from their late twenties to midsixties. One guy was so grotesquely obese he could hardly fit into his seat. A woman in the first row looked like she'd been under the plastic surgeon's knife a few times too many, her face assuming a masklike appearance. She kept running her pinky tip over her lips, then licking them, as though her lipstick were more important than the trial.

Some jurors were casually, even sloppily, dressed; others were meticulously attired. A few looked tired and bored, while others appeared alert, interested. The group reflected Manhattan's disparity: ten whites, two Hispanics, two blacks, and two Asians. I wondered if race or ethnicity would influence their take on the case—on me.

And on where I'd spend the next ten or more years of my life.

"Ladies and gentlemen, a man is about to go on trial for allegedly committing murder," said the judge. As Marin leaned toward the jury box, his expression and tone conveyed the seriousness of the charges against me. After describing the roles of the prosecutor and defense attorney, he told the jurors, "*You* will be the decider of the facts, and *you* will dispense justice."

I was about to be judged either guilty or not by twelve strangers—people who could never imagine the circumstances in which I lived and Nora died.

"A jury of my peers?" I'd yelled in Ben's office two days earlier. "Tell me, Ben, how does a black guy from some shithole in Harlem understand a white guy living on the most expensive chunk of real estate on earth? He's gonna understand *my* pain?

"And how 'bout some Dominican woman from Washington Heights whose husband works for the Transit Authority while she babysits for seven bucks an hour? *She's* gonna relate to some candy-assed white schmuck of a writer who made more royalty money in a month than she and her husband'll earn in five years?"

"Bill, your case isn't about privilege. It's about basic human emotions."

"Emotions? That's just what that bastard Olson's using. Pure emotion. He's trying to stoke the jury's envy of my success."

It seemed otherworldly hearing Marin tell the jury, "You are to presume the defendant innocent until and unless the State proves beyond a reasonable doubt that he is guilty of homicide."

How could I process what was happening?

The day before, I'd been on the verge of a breakdown in Ben's office. "I'm losing it, Ben," I said, nearly in tears. "I've been thinking of my father, poor guy. He died a horrible death, and my mother's gone, too. And Nora. Everybody's dead. My career's down the tubes. I'm flat broke, busted, and facing a murder rap."

"Bill, you have to find enough meaning to go on."

"And then what do I have?"

"You have me and Elaine. And Charlie loves you."

Events were suffocating what little remained of my sense of

worth. Nora's death already taught me that life wasn't orderly or predictable. Wasn't losing her enough? How much more could I bear? Now, I was being sucked down the deepest and darkest hole I could have imagined.

"Ladies and gentlemen," Marin said, "the burden of proof rests with the State to prove Mr. Shaw's guilt. It does not rest with the defendant to prove his innocence."

I'd heard these concepts of constitutional law before—I'd written about them as a crime reporter and novelist—but they'd never applied to *me*.

Judge Marin told the jurors not to discuss the case—*my* case, my trial—with anyone, not even with one another.

"You are to consider the evidence, and only the evidence, before you arrive at any conclusion about the defendant."

He was talking about *me*.

"You must keep an open mind, not form opinions until all the evidence has been presented. After all," he said, "if you were accused of a crime, wouldn't you want the same fairness for yourself?"

Then it happened. Peering across the courtroom, I saw her.

Nora was sitting in the jury box.

The room swayed. My heart felt like it began to spasm. My scalp dampened.

She was in the second row, third seat from the end. Every nerve ending in my body fired; my skin tingled.

I closed my eyes.

Another glance: of course, it wasn't Nora. She was a dark-haired, Spanish woman—alternate juror number two. She had Nora's nose with those gorgeous, flared nostrils, but was less graceful-looking, less fine-featured than Nora had been.

God, I was still seeing Nora everywhere—even in the courtroom.

"Now, there's been a great deal of publicity about this case," Marin continued. "I'm instructing you to put aside anything you may have read or heard about it. And you must not read *anything* in the newspapers about this case. Nor are you to watch any TV broadcast, listen to any radio program, or look at any Internet article about the case. You must focus on the evidence in this courtroom and nothing else. Do you understand?"

The jurors nodded in unison.

"Only what emerges in this courtroom is evidence. Is that clear?"

There were more earnest nods.

But the jurors were already forming impressions of me, favorable or not. They'd eventually come to a verdict—a strange and telling word—from the Latin, *veredictum*—meaning *something said truly*.

The verdict: their truth determining how I would spend the rest of my life.

Chapter 18

It was Saturday afternoon. Testimony would begin Monday morning.

I stood at the picture window of Cindy Armor's East End Avenue penthouse apartment. Tempestuous and twice-divorced, Cindy had the panache of being one of New York's super literary agents who negotiated megadeals for her top-tier clients. But for me, that was relegated to the past, might as well have been a century earlier.

I stared out the window at the scene fifteen stories below. My eyes took in a clutter of drab-colored warehouses, situated across the East River in Queens. A garbage scow chaperoned by a tugboat churned through the roiling waters toward the red arch of Hell Gate Bridge. Squadrons of seagulls feasting on sewage scraps swooped and fluttered around the barge. The sky was steel-wool gray. The raw ugliness of the scene heightened my sense of desolation. Many times over the years, I'd looked from this window and been envious of what struck me as Cindy's two-million-dollar view—but no longer.

"When did I last see you, Bill?" Cindy said, handing me a martini while placing a sterling-silver mini pitcher holding a refill on the coffee table.

"I guess it's been a long time," I said.

"It's been at least three years."

Decades of cigarettes and single-malt scotch had left Cindy

with a sultry voice.

I turned and watched her settle her lithe frame into the Malaga Italian leather sofa. She was a beautiful woman—of indeterminate age, maybe fifty. Her elongated face with its sloping nose and chestnut hair reminded me of John Singer Sargent's painting, *Portrait of Madame X.* Her endlessly long legs were accentuated by a pencil skirt and crimson peep-toe stiletto heels. I thought of Nora's sensuous tango the night we met so many years earlier.

I settled into an Eames chair, swiveled around, and stared at the Andy Warhol etching on the far wall.

Sipping the perfectly dry martini, I felt fuzzy. Was I now an alcoholic? If so, who cared? A booze-borne haze was better than the needle-sharp reality of my life. I fully understood why people sought an alternate universe—why they found refuge in booze or drugs—why they resorted to any medley of substances to dull their daily agonies. God, I was such a mess.

For sure, Cindy wanted to discuss my career. I felt like a schoolboy in the principal's office—exquisitely uncomfortable. But then, Cindy was so adroit with people, so confident and worldly, she could make the most mature, seasoned person feel like a kid.

"So, Bill, are you working on that project?"

"It's belly-up." I took another sip of the martini.

"Nothing creative dies."

"Cindy, right now, I have . . ." I shook my head. I'd run out of words.

"The trial, of course," she said in a near whisper. She leaned forward and touched my arm.

The word *trial* sent a pang of fear through me. I gulped down the martini, grabbed the pitcher, and poured a refill. I tried to keep steady, but my hand shook.

"It must be terrible," she said.

"It's been hell for years, but especially since Nora died." I brought the martini glass to my lips, and sipped.

"Poor Nora . . ."

"You know, Cindy, along with admiring you, Nora was always a little envious of you." Sadness seared through me.

"And I was a bit jealous of *her*. She was so beautiful, and so very talented. She was an incredible editor and a fine actor."

"She was my muse," I heard myself say through a boozy dullness. "She was the best part of me."

Cindy's eyebrows arched. "The best part of you? Meaning what?"

"You know, when people asked about my career, I'd say, 'It's not *my* career. It's *ours.*' We worked together, and were a perfect duo."

My toes were numb. My face felt frozen. The martini was blasting me. Was I slurring my words?

"Working with Nora was magic," I heard myself say. "We'd brainstorm and the ideas would flow. We'd bounce things around, bang them off each other, and before we knew it, a novel would veer into an entirely new direction. It would morph, like it was organic, living a life of its own. You know, this last project was the first one in years I was writing without Nora's input."

"What exactly was this project—the one you say is *belly-up*?"

"Something called *Assassin's Lullaby*."

"Sounds interesting . . ."

"The DA's gonna use it as evidence against me."

"You're kidding. They're going to use a novel as *evidence*? My God, how utterly absurd," Cindy said, shaking her head. "It sounds like it could be a novel itself."

"They're gonna try to use my fiction to convict me of killing Nora."

"That's utterly obscene. What's it about?"

"An assassin—a hit man for the Russian mob."

I downed the second martini in two gulps. It burned its way

to my belly.

"Is there a love interest?"

"It wasn't settled."

"*Wasn't*? Why're you talking in the past tense?"

"Because it's over."

Silence. I heard a tugboat's horn in the distance.

"You think you'll ever get back to it?"

"Cindy, I could go to prison for ten years."

"Let me make a suggestion, Bill," she said, crushing out her cigarette.

The martini's heat soaked through me. The room blurred as Cindy's voice seemed to come from very far away. I could no longer feel my toes.

"As your agent, I obviously have an interest in your career."

"And you've nurtured it. I've always been grateful to you." My voice sounded to me like I was talking in slow motion, slurring my words.

"Okay, that being said, let me suggest something. Your life's turned to hell and you haven't published a thing in years," she said, leaning back. She hesitated and then looked deeply into my eyes. I had the feeling she was gauging me, trying to assess how I'd react to her suggestion, whatever it might be. I knew she'd propose something, but I could barely consider anything beyond opening statements on Monday.

"Forgive me for sounding insensitive, but you have to begin moving on."

"*Assassin's Lullaby*'s dead."

"Let me suggest something else. When you feel ready . . ."

"And that is?"

"It struck me when you were indicted, and it makes even more sense now, especially if they're going to use your fiction as evidence in the trial."

"I don't follow."

"You were once a journalist." Cindy leaned forward and peered earnestly into my eyes. "Why not write a memoir about the trial? It could be a nonfiction blockbuster. A crime writer accused of murder—and his own work-in-progress being used against him. It could be a powerful exposé of the criminal justice system. It's *better* than fiction."

"Cindy, even if I *could* do it—emotionally—you can't make money from a crime for which you've been convicted."

"My God, Bill, you've already got yourself convicted and sent away. I don't mean to sound insensitive, but I'm convinced of one thing. You have to think about an acquittal. I'm talking as a friend, not as your agent. You've got to see yourself as having a life down the road, a future. It's the only way you'll survive."

"So you think this is just fodder for a memoir?" My words shot forth, slipped by my lips, and I knew in an instant, Cindy felt chastened, even wounded.

"No, it's much more than that," she said, biting her lower lip. "I know it is. But you have to force yourself to see the day when you can write about the injustice done to you."

"I've always respected your opinion, Cindy, but I can't write a memoir about this. It would be too much. I couldn't do it. And I don't know if there's any getting beyond it . . . ever."

"Then you might as well roll over and die."

Chapter 19

Our eyes met for a moment and then darted away. Charlie sat in the third row.

"Don't make eye contact with a juror or anyone in the gallery," Ben had warned me. "This is like a play and you're an actor in it; you don't look at the audience."

But for the few seconds my brother's eyes met mine, a wave of calm washed over me.

The gallery was crammed with spectators. Every seat was taken. People stood packed into the space between the rear benches and the courtroom doors.

A sketch artist scribbled on a pad—presumably drawing me. These would be the only pictorial representations of the trial. I was thankful cameras or recording devices weren't allowed in court. The New York law had changed, and no televised trials were permitted.

"All rise," cried the court officer.

The Honorable J. J. Marin entered the courtroom from chambers. I thought he looked fatherly, even kind—though perhaps my wish for a benign father figure colored my perception. Being on trial reduced me to feeling as powerless as a child. And the same way a child feels about a parent, I was harshly aware that Judge Marin could determine my fate. His decisions—whenever he sustained or overruled an objection, or his tone of voice when addressing my lawyer—could affect the rest of my days on earth.

From this moment on, my life was completely out of my hands.

Marin greeted the attorneys, asked if there was any unfinished business, and then turned to the court officer. "Bring in the jury and let's get going."

The life-altering process of my trial would begin. My pulse drubbed like a jackhammer.

The court officer disappeared behind a door and reappeared moments later. "All rise," he barked.

Ben and I stood behind the defense table. Olson and Pierce: behind the prosecution table. Everyone except Marin stood in deference to the triers of fact—the jurors—the citizens who'd sit in judgment.

Of me.

They entered the courtroom in single file, stepped into the two-tiered jury box, and took their assigned seats. Silence prevailed.

There were eight jurors in each row. They were somber-looking and stone-faced. I sat at the defense table, aware the chair caused my ass to ache. Maybe it was easier to focus on some minor discomfort rather than on those deciding my fate. The jurors became a massive blur in my peripheral vision, a looming presence in the courtroom.

After greeting the jurors, Marin repeated his instructions from the previous week and then said, "We'll begin with opening statements."

After receiving a nod from Marin, Olson rose, walked to the lectern, set down his notes, and turned toward the jury box. The jurors looked expectant, like they wanted to hear Olson's storyline about the murder I'd allegedly committed.

"Ladies and gentlemen, I'm Sean Olson and I represent the People of the State of New York. I'm the People's attorney," Olson said in that reedy voice.

He described how his role was to protect all citizens, no matter their status—old, sick, poor or wealthy, famous or unknown. Everyone was guaranteed the right to life, as expressed in the Constitution.

Something about Olson nettled me. He was too goddamned folksy in an insincere, calculated way, too damned righteous, overly moralizing—far too perfect. To me, he was a snobbish Ivy League frat boy, an overprivileged coxcomb strutting like a preening peacock. I was certain he truly believed his shit didn't stink.

Despite his sometimes-pitchy voice, Olson was smooth; I could tell he'd done this before—many times. He continued, saying, "Murder is the ultimate violation of the sanctity of life, of what we hold most sacred—the right to live one's life to its natural end. Only God has the right to end life.

"*Murder,* the act of snuffing out life—the horror of stealing away the breath and heartbeat of another person—is why we're here today, ladies and gentlemen. We're here because William Shaw took it upon himself to take the precious breath of life away from Nora Shaw. He took her life, violated the law of civilized people, and committed this crime against the woman he'd vowed to love and honor in sickness as well as health, for as long as they shared this precious thing we call life."

As Olson spoke, the room began tilting. I sat unmoving, staring ahead at nothing.

"Ladies and gentlemen," Olson went on, "the defendant acted unseen by anyone; he had the motive, the means, and the opportunity to take Nora Shaw's life. Nora's life was compromised, but she wanted to live, as you will hear during this trial.

"The People will present compelling proof of her murder. And when the evidence unfolds, you'll be convinced that the defendant murdered Nora Shaw."

My armpits were soaked. A trickle of sweat dribbled down my back. How would I endure this assault, one that was only just beginning?

Olson moved to the prosecution table and picked up a glossy, eight-by-ten, black-and-white head-shot photo of Nora from her soap opera days.

He paraded the picture before the jurors. I glanced to my right. Every juror's eyes were locked onto the photograph.

I did my best to show no emotion, but could scarcely control my agony. That photo, marked *Exhibit #1*, telescoped all our years together, collapsing them back to that magical night of Nora's tango at the West Village party. A deep ache filled me and I thought I heard that *canción*. My chin began trembling.

"*This,* ladies and gentlemen, was Nora Shaw," Olson cried, holding the photo aloft. "This beautiful woman, whose disease rendered her helpless, was the victim of the defendant's crime—murder."

Some jurors shook their heads. Was it pity for Nora? Or was it astonishment at the treachery of life? Was it implicit disapproval of me, the accused? A barely audible *tsk* came from someone in the jury box—condemnation? Could it possibly be hatred of me? Or was it acknowledging the randomness of fate?

After what seemed an eternity, Olson moved back to the prosecution table and set the photo down. He returned to the panel and stood before the jurors.

"The evidence will show that William Shaw purposely gave Nora an overdose of warfarin, a potent blood thinner. Warfarin, ladies and gentlemen, is the main ingredient in *rat poison.* It makes blood less able to clot, and if given in the dose Nora received, causes massive internal hemorrhaging."

Olson paused to let his words marinate with the jury.

A stifling silence filled the courtroom. A radiator at the rear began hissing. My hands felt weak; blood drained from my head.

Olson was good. He'd memorized his lines, presenting them well.

"What possessed the defendant on March second of this year to give Nora a dose of warfarin so large that she bled from her nose, her eyes, her mouth, her liver, her spleen, her vagina, and caused her death?"

Olson paused theatrically.

I tried my best to block out his words, but they seared through me like a cauterizing knife.

"Ladies and gentlemen, you will learn that Nora Shaw had rapidly advancing multiple sclerosis. This wasting disease ravaged her body, made her an invalid. It progressed very quickly over two years, to the point where she was paralyzed. She couldn't move her eyes, her arms, or her legs. She was unable to talk and couldn't even swallow food.

"She required an array of expensive medications, an intravenous line, a feeding tube, a hospital bed, and a home health aide. The defendant had no health insurance. Nora's illness was a constant burden on his entire life—financially and emotionally, in every way you can imagine. In fact, she required so much care, the defendant, once a successful writer, stopped writing and had no sustainable income. Ladies and gentlemen, Nora's illness consumed his life.

"You will also learn that Nora had a heart condition for which she took this blood thinner—warfarin—so she wouldn't develop blood clots that could cause a stroke.

"And when Nora's MS advanced too far, when the expenses mounted and money was rapidly running out, things changed drastically."

Tears welled in my eyes and were about to dribble down my cheeks. I blinked repeatedly, trying to hold them back. The courtroom became a blur. Keeping my eyes open felt like staring into a lashing sandstorm.

I stole another glance at the jury: three women jurors looked directly into Olson's eyes. They followed his every movement, nodding with each vocal inflection. Olson had snared them in his drama. A buzz of fear rampaged through me as a man in the second row nodded, and then to my horror, cast a searing look at me. His forehead furrowed.

I averted my eyes.

"And, ladies and gentlemen," Olson continued, "the defendant's life changed when he met *another woman*."

One woman, in the front row, shot a glance at me. Her lips were drawn thin; the corners were downturned. Her head shook back and forth in a barely perceptible way. My skin felt like it was shredding. A man in the jury box nodded, and the woman who'd been fussing with her lipstick stifled a gasp by covering her mouth with her hand.

"And when the defendant became involved with this other woman, he murdered Nora with rat poison."

Olson stood motionless, letting his words penetrate the jury's consciousness.

I felt so light-headed; the room looked bleached, then swayed.

"This other woman—Constance Manning—will testify that she became part of the defendant's life. There were meetings at a coffee shop and at her apartment."

Murmuring came from the gallery.

"Now, some might call this a mercy killing, but it wasn't out of mercy that the defendant killed Nora." Olson's head shook from side to side. "Rather, his motivation was selfish: he decided to end his *own* misery."

I could almost feel Ben seething beside me. Yet he sat like an unmoving boulder.

"The defendant researched methods to kill Nora. He planned it. Oh, yes. He planned it down to the last milliliter of warfarin. And on March second of this year, the defendant prepared the warfarin—as he did each morning—and he sucked extra warfarin into the syringe. It was enough to kill her. Then he injected Nora through her IV line.

"Ladies and gentlemen, at six o'clock in the morning of March second, the defendant knowingly and willfully gave Nora an IV injection of warfarin that exceeded her usual dose by *fifty percent*. We will present ironclad scientific evidence to prove it."

Olson's accusations were raw, dripped with certainty. He was going for my throat, intent on landing a killing blow.

Olson whirled suddenly and faced me. It was the first time he ever acknowledged my presence. I watched as his long, tapered index finger floated upward, pointing directly at me. The jurors' eyes bored into me. Olson's finger seemed huge, menacing, as though it would puncture me with its accusation.

"Yes. *He* did it, ladies and gentlemen!" Olson shouted. "*That* man, sitting there. The defendant. *He* shot the warfarin into Nora's bloodstream to end her life."

My chest tightened and my face felt like a furnace.

"The defendant knew full well—as evidence retrieved from his computer will show—that if given in excess, warfarin would cause massive internal bleeding."

Olson approached the prosecution table. I struggled to stare straight ahead—to focus my gaze on the American flag behind the judge—but could see Olson peripherally. I kept my hands clasped tightly on the defense table to keep from trembling.

"Ladies and gentlemen," Olson intoned, "I want to show you a picture of Nora Shaw as she looked in the medical examiner's office. I know it's graphic, but you must see the horror the defendant visited upon his wife."

There were gasps as the jurors' eyes fixed on the autopsy photograph. Nausea flowed through me as I recalled finding Nora in bed that day. Runnels of crusted blood streamed from her nostrils. Dried, reddish stains had leaked from her eyes. Her face was pale, bloodless, gaunt. Death had taken her.

"*This,* ladies and gentlemen, was what the defendant did to Nora."

Olson was using photographic incrimination—before and after head shots of Nora—in life and in death. He was pitching his theory, and the jury was buying it.

After what seemed torturous minutes, Olson returned the photo to the table.

Back at the jury box, he clutched the wood panel in front of the first row.

"And what did the defendant do after giving Nora what he knew was a lethal dose of rat poison? He went for coffee and then to the library to write his novel. He left her to die."

More jurors' heads shook disapprovingly.

I did my best to keep my hands from shaking.

"And what is this novel called?" Olson cried. "It's called *Assassin's Lullaby.*" He paused. "And what's this novel about? It's about a cold-blooded hit man hired to *kill a beautiful woman.*"

Fear and regret gripped me as I thought back to Nora asking me to write the novel for her, and now hearing Olson's grotesque distortion of the truth.

Olson's eyes locked on each member of the jury in turn. He made contact with each one, creating a bond. "In short, ladies and gentlemen, the defendant killed *this* beautiful woman, Nora Shaw. And during the course of this trial, we will show you why and how he did it."

A juror's cough echoed through the room. The courtroom was stifling. I could barely breathe as sweat sheeted down my torso.

"Now, His Honor, Judge Marin, has instructed you to decide this case on the evidence. I want to tell you briefly about the evidence.

"Ladies and gentlemen, the defendant will claim that no one *saw* him kill Nora. And that's true, because like most crimes, he didn't commit it in public. The defendant will claim that the

People have only *circumstantial* evidence of his crime."

Olson explained circumstantial evidence. He asked the jurors to imagine looking out their windows one morning and seeing snow on the ground. And there are tracks in the snow—made by a man and a dog. Though the jurors didn't see it, they could reasonably conclude that it snowed during the night and a man walked his dog in the snow that morning. "Ladies and gentlemen, *that's* circumstantial evidence; and we all use it every day of our lives," Olson said.

It was the old tracks-in-the-snow routine, the standard and well-worn description of circumstantial evidence given by every prosecutor in the country. I'd written about it many times. As stale as it sounded to me, the jurors had probably never heard it before: they appeared transfixed. Their eyes were locked on the prosecutor.

"So, ladies and gentlemen," Olson continued, "circumstantial evidence tells you exactly what happened, even though you didn't see it."

Olson had honed his act to a scalpel's keenness. The jurors were eating up his theatrics, his narrative of my life.

"Ladies and gentlemen, the People will prove with compelling circumstantial evidence—and with uncontestable *scientific* proof—that the defendant intentionally killed Nora. It will be shown beyond a reasonable doubt. And on the basis of the evidence, we will ask you to convict him of murder."

With my hands clasped in front of me, I felt like a corpse. The notion of murder—the willful taking of a human life—was sickening. And the accusation that I'd killed Nora was repugnant.

I'm going down for the count. No matter what Ben does, it's all heading south.

Olson sat down next to Ann Pierce.

Judge Marin then looked over at Ben.

How the hell would Ben undo the damage Olson had done?

Ben had been away from this arena for so long, he was rusty. How foolish was I, thinking Ben could possibly be my salvation?

Chapter 20

"Mr. Abrams, opening statement."

Ben moved to the lectern. In stark contrast to Olson's patrician appearance, Ben looked like the wrestler he once was— a seasoned pit bull, with his crew-cut silver hair, flattened nose, broad, sloping shoulders, and tapered waist.

His dark blue suit looked off-the-rack from Men's Wearhouse, but it fit him well. He had no notes. No props. He was Bulldog Ben, a battle-hardened veteran, a war dog of the legal trenches. Standing at the lectern, he made eye contact with each juror, one after another. His imposing presence brought an eerie silence to the courtroom.

And even before he uttered a word, I felt myself growing calmer; his powerful demeanor was restoring my confidence in his ability to save me from this hell.

I reminded myself to clasp my hands and keep calm. "The time'll come for emotion—when it counts," Ben said during one prep session. "Stay focused on the witnesses or whoever's talking. Look interested, but neutral. It's a tough act, but you gotta do it. Just remember, Bill, it's theater of the most serious kind."

"Ladies and gentlemen, I'm Ben Abrams. I represent Bill Shaw," Ben said, moving gradually from the lectern to the front of the jury box. "I'll be brief. I won't waste your time.

"First let me tell you about Bill and Nora. They were married nearly fifteen years ago. During their marriage, they were the closest thing to a true partnership you can imagine. Nora helped Bill with his writing, used her acting experience to help with his novels. In fact, they acted out every spoken word in each novel, as though they were reading a play. She suggested plot turns, edited everything, and polished his manuscripts. They were a true team. Bill dedicated every novel he wrote to Nora."

A grief-ridden twinge seized me. Why was I alive while she was dead? Why couldn't it have been me with MS instead of Nora?

Sitting at the defense table, I felt tears collect in my eyes. I fought the pinched watery sensation in my sinuses.

"Bill loved Nora the way any human being would want to be loved and would want to love another. Everyone who knew Bill and Nora felt their connection. And *you* will come to know their bond as you see and hear the evidence.

"Ladies and gentlemen," Ben said, his tone turning severe, "you've heard Mr. Olson's allegations. Simply put: they're *not true*."

Ben paused, let his words sink in, and then folded his arms across his chest.

"Now, one of the first things any trial lawyer learns is never to promise something that can't be delivered. Well, let me say this for the record. I'm promising you, right here and now, that Mr. Olson's evidence will shatter like a pane of glass hitting the floor."

The jurors were wide-eyed. Was it possible? Could Ben actually deliver on such a bold promise? True, he'd been doing his due diligence, but could he torpedo Olson's allegations, his so-called proof? I tried blinking away the tears brimming in my eyes.

"When you've heard all the evidence," Ben said, "you'll conclude that Bill was a devoted husband who loved and cared for Nora. And he never harmed her—*ever*.

"You'll learn that he took her to doctors, asked questions, and became intimately involved in every aspect of her treatment.

Bill's devotion to and love for Nora never wavered, not for a second. Bill did everything humanly possible for Nora, including on the day she died."

Two women on the jury looked sternly at Ben. They appeared skeptical. A young man in the second row gazed at the ceiling. Was he uncaring? Bored? Had he already decided to convict me? Had Olson's oratory poisoned him? Especially Olson's promise of uncontestable scientific proof that Nora was overdosed. Was that juror already beyond Ben's reach?

"We will show you that Nora died from the effects of her conditions combined with the medications used to treat those conditions, not from anything Bill did."

Ben's brazen promise to the jury bolstered me—but only for a few moments—and I feared my resolve would wither as the trial went on. How much could I stand? Olson's accusations of a financial motive, that I'd wanted Nora dead to unburden myself, along with allegations of another woman—it was all unbearable.

"Now," Ben said, "Mr. Olson mentioned circumstantial evidence. He said you can make certain inferences based on snow and footprints. Well, this kind of evidence has severe shortcomings that Mr. Olson failed to describe."

The jurors' eyes were locked on Ben. His arms were spread like a preacher's at a pulpit.

"When you look out your window on that snowy morning, and see those footprints in the snow, yes, it's obvious that it snowed. That cannot be contested. It's also clear that a person and an animal left tracks in the snow. In that regard, Mr. Olson's right.

"But what *doesn't* that circumstantial evidence prove? What's missing in Mr. Olson's little story?"

Another dramatic pause.

The jurors waited. Some leaned forward in their seats.

Hissing began in my ears.

"Well, for one, the prints don't tell you if it was a *man* or a *woman* who passed by. Let's assume it was a man. Do the prints tell you how tall he was? What he looked like? Whether he was white, black, Asian, or Hispanic? Who *was* this person?

"And that dog . . . was it brown or gray? Was it a German shepherd or a collie? How do you know the dog and the man were even together?"

Two jurors nodded. Ben's counterpoints to Olson's theatrics might resonate with them. Maybe I'd stand a chance.

"The man might have walked by, and the dog *followed*. Maybe it wasn't even a *dog*." Ben waited a beat. "It could've been a *coyote*. After all, some years ago, as I'm sure you recall, a coyote was captured in Central Park.

"What it boils down to, ladies and gentlemen, is this: you can actually tell very little about either the man or the dog, or the coyote—if that's what it was—by those prints in the snow."

Ben set a thick hand on the jury box rail.

Two jurors nodded their heads. A man in the second row glanced in my direction.

"Ladies and gentlemen," Ben went on, "circumstantial evidence can be very misleading. My point is really very simple: things aren't always what they seem. You must examine circumstantial evidence very carefully before you draw any conclusion from what it appears to show.

"Because Mr. Olson's so-called evidence doesn't answer the questions that flood this case like a hurricane surge. These questions can't be answered by footprints in the snow. Because there are other crucial factors to consider, and we will point them out during this trial.

"So I say to you, be very wary of circumstantial evidence, which can be misleading and doesn't tell the whole truth. And, ladies and gentlemen, that's what we're here for—the *truth*."

Ben's words filled me with hope. Lightness filled my chest.

"Now, nobody's disputing that Nora died because of warfarin.

The lab tests were conclusive. But circumstantial evidence doesn't begin to answer the question you're being asked to consider: Did Nora Shaw die because Bill Shaw *did* something to her? Or did she die because of other things having nothing to do with Bill?"

Ben paused and stood stock-still. The jurors looked engrossed.

"We will show you that in fact Bill had nothing to do with Nora's death. We will show you that Mr. Olson's imagined motives are utterly without foundation. The evidence will show that Bill loved Nora. He spared nothing, neither time nor energy nor money, to keep Nora alive and comfortable. The evidence will show Bill was a loving, caring, giving husband who devoted his entire life to Nora. Neither money, nor achievement, nor fame counted for him in comparison to his feelings for his wife. The evidence will show that Bill never harmed Nora—*ever.*"

My eyes felt like they were popping from their sockets. The courtroom became a swaying blur as my eyelids brimmed; then tears snaked down my cheeks. It took every ounce of inner strength to keep from dropping my head onto the table and sobbing like a child. It would take far more emotional resilience than I could summon to survive this trial. Did I even want to live through such torment?

"Ladies and gentlemen," Ben said in a rising voice, "just as Mr. Olson's example of the man and the dog could be misinterpreted, so too can all of Mr. Olson's evidence. And please, remember my promise: I will shatter the prosecution's evidence right before your eyes. And when you've evaluated all the evidence according to Judge Marin's instructions, you will conclude beyond any reasonable doubt—actually, you will know with absolute certainty, one simple thing: Bill Shaw is *not guilty* of Mr. Olson's grotesque allegations. Thank you."

The judge called for a half-hour recess.

Chapter 21

Ben always viewed Dugan as a grave dancer. The guy was in his midseventies and still dancing the courtroom waltz. His cheeks looked hollow and his hair was wispy white. His skin appeared paper-thin and yellowish, and the gray suit he wore hung from his cadaverous frame. Dr. Peter Dugan was well known in the legal community. Ben couldn't help but think this renowned pathologist resembled the bodies he encountered each day on the autopsy table.

Dugan was as comfortable in a courtroom as he was in the morgue. Ben's research showed the guy had testified nearly a thousand times over the decades—telling juries the cause of death in both criminal and civil cases. Above all, Ben knew the coroner was a straight shooter and told the pathological truth, never gilding the lily.

Ben knew Bill had visited that meat locker known as the autopsy room, when researching his novels. But the ME's testimony would now refer to Nora: the Y-shaped incision, the removal of her heart, lungs, liver—every organ—examined, weighed, and sliced. Nora—beautiful, vibrant, the center of Bill's life—was, for Dugan, just another cold cadaver who'd been bagged and tagged and then wheeled on a gurney to the ME's office.

For Dugan, it was impersonal—nothing more than the reality of his trade: tissues, stains, slides, and lab reports. It was the business of death.

But Dugan's testimony would refer to the love of Bill's life.

After Dugan was sworn in, Olson took him through his education and training—qualified him as an expert. He was a board-certified pathologist, and as state medical examiner had done thousands of autopsies.

"Doctor, please tell the jury what a medical examiner does," Olson said.

"We perform autopsies when there's a question about the cause of death."

"And what was the situation regarding Nora Shaw?"

"There was a question if her death was caused by excess warfarin."

"And what were your duties in this case?"

"I performed the autopsy and prepared a report."

"And would you tell the jury your findings on autopsy?"

Dugan launched into a detailed description of the flood of internal bleeding that took place throughout Nora's body. Ben could virtually feel Bill cringing beside him. The testimony droned on. Through Dugan's words, it was as if Nora were being split open right in the courtroom.

About twenty minutes into Dugan's testimony, Ben felt a vibration—as though a subway train on the line that ran west of the courthouse was now rumbling beneath the building. He'd been in this courthouse countless times and never felt it before.

Yet the defense table was vibrating.

And then Ben saw it: Bill's hands were clenched, bloodless, his fingers clamped in a bone-crushing knot.

Bill's internal quivering sent waves of tremors through the defense table.

Feeling a surge of pity for Bill, Ben slipped his left hand onto Bill's forearm, pressing gently, trying to offer some modicum of solace. But the shaking—almost like a vibrating tuning fork—continued.

"And in your opinion, Doctor, what caused this internal bleeding?" Olson asked.

"It was caused by warfarin."

"How do you know that?"

"In all autopsy cases, we draw blood for a toxicology screen."

"And what does such a screen do?"

"It measures various substances in the blood, urine, and bodily fluids. It's designed to detect signs of drugs, poisons, or toxins."

"And when it comes to poison, or toxins, you could be referring to methods of murder, correct?"

Ben was about to rise and lodge an objection.

"Murder is a *legal* term, Mr. Olson." Dugan's caterpillar-like eyebrows rose. "We don't use such terminology when doing an autopsy. We determine the physical mechanism of death. Whether by trauma, a drug overdose, poison, or natural causes. It's a *medical* determination, not a legal one."

Yes, Dugan's a stickler for accuracy; but Olson's pretty shrewd, too. He purposely used the loaded word murder, *knowing it would register, if only subliminally, in the jurors' minds.*

Olson was a worthy adversary.

Ben focused his attention on the testimony.

"And, Doctor, as a board-certified pathologist, did you conclude with a reasonable degree of medical and scientific certainty that warfarin caused Nora Shaw's death?"

"Yes. The autopsy findings and toxicology report were consistent with warfarin causing her death."

"And what did you do when you arrived at this conclusion?"

"We notified the police department's Homicide Division."

"Thank you, Doctor. I have no further questions."

"**M**r. Abrams, cross-examination."

Proceeding to the lectern, Ben knew a venerable old guy like

Dugan was something of a father figure, both for jurors and for himself. Ben would moderate his approach with a parental presence and not take too aggressive a stance with a witness like Dugan. But he needed to blend deference with his own authority as an officer of the court. And besides, Dugan's testimony proved nothing.

"Dr. Dugan, assuming we all agree that Nora died as a result of warfarin, you can't say that someone injected *excess* warfarin into her, can you?"

"No, I can't say that."

"In other words, Dr. Dugan, all you can say is that Nora Shaw's death was caused by warfarin, correct?"

"That's correct."

"So, assuming there may be a number of reasons for the warfarin level being high, you can't say whether or not she was given too large a dose of warfarin, can you?"

"No. I can only say that warfarin was responsible for the *mechanism* of death. As for the cause of that amount of warfarin in her blood, it would only be speculation on my part."

"In other words, Dr. Dugan, from a pathologic point of view, there's no evidence that Bill gave Nora Shaw an overdose of the medication, correct?"

"That's correct. From a pathologist's perspective, there could be a number of reasons for the amount of warfarin in her system."

"Can you please tell the jury what they might be?"

"Objection, Your Honor," Olson called, bolting up behind the prosecution table. "It's pure speculation and goes far beyond the scope of direct examination."

"Sustained."

"Well, Doctor," Ben went on, "we won't go into the other reasons right now, but is it safe to say that the bottom line of your testimony is you have no idea whether or not Bill Shaw injected an overdose of warfarin into Nora Shaw on the day of her death?"

"That's correct."

"Thank you, Doctor. I have no further questions."

Chapter 22

"The People call Dr. Daniel Radin."

When Dr. Radin took the stand, my heart began fluttering. I was reminded of the times—hundreds, it seemed—Nora and I were at his office. He looked just as he had each time we'd been there—trim, narrow-faced, with neatly clipped brown hair—except in court, he wore a dark suit and tie instead of a white lab coat.

Olson questioned Radin about medical school, his internship and residency at Yale, followed by a cardiology fellowship at Johns Hopkins.

"Doctor, when did you begin treating Nora Shaw?"

"About nine years ago," Radin said, referring to his records.

"What was her problem at that time?"

"She was thirty-five years old. One evening, she was brought to Lenox Hill Hospital, where they diagnosed an irregular heartbeat."

"Can you please tell the jury the significance of this irregular heartbeat?"

"It's called atrial fibrillation," Radin said. "The heart beats erratically. A patient with A-fib—atrial fibrillation—runs the risk of a stroke because with the uneven heartbeat, blood can pool in the heart and form a clot. That clot can be pumped to the brain, where it blocks an artery, which is a stroke."

"How is A-fib treated?"

"By keeping the blood from clotting, by thinning it."

"Doctor, will you please tell the jury how that's done?"

Radin described how warfarin kept blood from clotting. He told them about putting Nora on Lopressor to lower her blood pressure and slow down her heart rate, also reducing the chance of a stroke.

"Dr. Radin, were there any problems with Nora using the warfarin?"

"Yes, there were."

"Please tell the jury about them."

"Nora tolerated the warfarin poorly. It made her blood *too* thin. She would bleed very easily. Sometimes there was blood in her urine. She also bled into her skin and had frequent nosebleeds."

A rush of tormenting memories overwhelmed me. Purple blotches cropped up frequently where Nora bled into her skin; blood dripped from her nose onto the pillowcase. On two different occasions over the years, she'd bled internally and was hospitalized.

"Doctor," Olson said, "if Nora tolerated the warfarin poorly, didn't that mean she was vulnerable to even a little bit of extra warfarin given?"

"Objection to form. It's a leading question," Ben called, rocketing to his feet.

"Sustained."

Olson will use any tactic to implicate me, any inference or innuendo.

Olson paused, letting his improper question linger in the air. He then asked, "How did you control Nora's warfarin level?"

"I adjusted the dose frequently. But when multiple sclerosis was diagnosed, things got worse."

"When was the multiple sclerosis diagnosed?"

"About two and a half years ago."

"And how did things get worse when the MS was diagnosed?"

"Dr. Braun, her neurologist, prescribed prednisone, a steroid, to try to keep the MS from progressing too fast. Prednisone interacted with the warfarin and increased its blood-thinning effect. It got to be even trickier to control."

The jurors were nodding their heads. They seemed to understand how volatile the medical situation became. Prednisone and warfarin in combination made for a huge challenge—one that ruled our lives.

"So once the MS was diagnosed, how was Nora's treatment affected?"

"The prednisone made Nora bleed frequently and her warfarin levels jumped up and down even more erratically."

"Now, I would like to ask a few other questions about Nora's treatment. To refresh your recollection, you can refer to your office records, which the subpoena required you to bring."

Judge Marin interjected, "Mr. Olson, we're approaching noon. We'll break for lunch. Let's be back by two o'clock, when we'll continue with the doctor's testimony."

"But, Your Honor, I've only begun my direct exami—"

"I don't want a hungry jury," the judge said.

A few titters came from the jury box.

Olson's face turned chalk white. He returned to the prosecution table.

The judge reminded the jury not to discuss the case and to keep an open mind.

Olson, Pierce, Ben, and I stood as the court officer led the jury from the courtroom.

Leaving the courthouse through a rear exit to avoid the clot of reporters on the front steps, I donned sunglasses partly to cut down on the noontime glare, but really for the anonymity I hoped the glasses might provide. I stood amid the Foley Square crowd, as hordes of people rushed by. It was midday madness on an October Monday in lower Manhattan.

Unable to push from my mind Radin's reminders of Nora's illness, I ambled aimlessly east, to Park Row. I turned onto Mott Street, the heart of Chinatown, where crowds swarmed into shops and a dense warren of restaurants. I found myself standing in front of an awning-covered stairway leading down to a narrow restaurant, Hop Kee.

Of all places, I'd walked in a trance and ended up at Hop Kee, where I'd gone frequently during my student days at NYU. This subterranean Cantonese joint served standard-issue dishes: chicken with cashews, vegetable lo mein, and terrific seafood. Living subsistence-level lives, my college friends and I had loved the BYOB policy, which meant lugging in six-packs of Budweiser on Friday nights.

The restaurant was jam-packed with a lunchtime crowd. The noise level was stupendous. Hop Kee had the same faux-wood paneling and red vinyl booths I recalled from years earlier. I grabbed a small booth at the rear and kept my shades on. Ben warned me about having lunch near the courthouse, saying, "You might run into a juror." But I recognized no one.

Two young women sat at a nearby table. One, a pale-skinned blonde with a ponytail, glanced at me. She looked again, so I buried my face in the menu.

The rail-thin waiter approached to take my order.

He looked surprised at my request for an off-menu item—beef with bitter lemon—usually ordered only by Chinese customers.

"No good for you," he said in staccato English.

"I love it."

"Too bitter. Not for you."

"I know what I want. Beef with bitter lemon. And wonton soup to start, please."

He scribbled on his pad, grabbed the menu, and then made

his way to the kitchen.

The women cast furtive glances my way. A few other people were peering, too. There was no menu to hide behind. I'd brought no newspaper to read and had nothing to shield me from curious stares. I'd left my smart phone at home. Nothing to do, no way to look busy. I felt like slithering down in my seat.

The soup came. I was thankful for the steaming bowl; it distracted me from my surroundings. Aromatic mist redolent of shredded ginger and watercress rose to my nostrils. As I slurped the broth, my thoughts tumbled back through time.

I was last at Hop Kee as an NYU senior. Writing was in my blood. I was a compulsive scribbler. I pounded away on an old Coronamatic, whose letters slammed against the platen. Those days were filled with hope and youthful excess. Writing fiction seemed a vaguely distant dream. It was long before my first novel, and ages before meeting Nora and the incredible changes she ushered into my life.

As students, our crowd of wannabe writers frequented the Village Vanguard and the Village Gate and got blasted on cheap booze at the White Horse Tavern, home of Dylan Thomas's drinking bouts. Bellied up to the bar, we'd role-play the alcoholic artist who'd someday write the great American novel.

We quoted Faulkner, Joyce, and Hemingway. We smoked pot bought from the cadre of low-level dealers loitering in Washington Square Park. When weed-induced hunger overtook us, we'd head downtown to Hop Kee and feast on the cheap.

As I sat in the same place where I'd sat countless times years ago, the extent to which my life had changed hit me like a punch to the gut.

I couldn't take a single bite of the beef with bitter lemon.

"Doctor Radin, you informed the Shaws about the danger of internal bleeding, didn't you?" Olson asked.

"Yes, I did."

"Now, Doctor, we know that warfarin is a dangerous drug," Olson said. "And we know Nora was extremely sensitive to it. Furthermore, we know the defendant learned everything there was to know about warfarin, and he—"

"Objection, Your Honor. Is there a *question* here?" Ben called. "Mr. Olson's *testifying*. This is a monologue without a question."

"The objection is sustained." Marin turned to the jury. "Ladies and gentlemen, this is a good time to give you another instruction. The attorneys' roles are to ask proper questions. Those questions are *not* evidence. The witnesses' answers are evidence, not the attorneys' questions." Marin turned to the prosecutor. "Ask your next question, Mr. Olson."

Olson peered at his notes. He fumbled with a few pages, looking distracted, off center. Ben's interruption made him lose his rhythm.

"Doctor . . ." Olson resumed. "Given Nora's sensitivity to warfarin, would an increase in the IV dose be dangerous?"

"Yes."

"Even a slight increase?"

"Probably."

"Now, Doctor, was Mr. Shaw familiar with warfarin and its side effects?"

"Oh, yes. He would ask—"

"And, Doctor, was Mr. Shaw—"

"Objection, Your Honor!" Ben shouted, rising to his feet. "Mr. Olson's interrupting the witness."

"Mr. Olson, let the witness finish answering the question," Marin said, shaking his head. "If you think his answer exceeds the bounds of the question, you can object and I'll rule on it."

"Yes, Your Honor." Olson looked crestfallen. I knew from my reporting days no lawyer wanted to be chastised in front of a jury.

"Doctor," Marin said, turning to Radin, "did you finish your answer?"

"I was going to say that Bill asked frequently about warfarin. He wanted to know about it to ensure that it was safe for Nora, Your Honor."

Radin sounded like he was advocating for me. I knew from my years covering trials, if the prosecutor pointed out the doctor's bias, he could be declared a hostile witness. That would allow Olson to box Radin in, forcing him to answer questions with only yes or no responses. The direct examination would, in effect, become a cross-examination. It could turn into a nightmare. I waited for Olson to jump on this opening, but he continued on. The guy seemed off his game. Maybe Marin's censuring him had thrown him a curveball.

"Now, Dr. Radin, did there come a time when Nora's symptoms changed?"

"Yes."

"And what were those changes?"

"About three years ago, she began feeling weakness and fatigue, and complained of blurred vision. She became lethargic, began dropping things."

"And did you know what caused these problems?"

"At first I thought it was psychological—depression mixed with anxiety. But eventually, I referred her to a neurologist."

"Psychological? What made you think that?" Olson asked.

"Nora was very nervous at the time. Her role in the soap opera had been dropped years earlier. She found it difficult to get other roles and was only doing cosmetic commercials. She was also helping Bill with his novels. Actually, that became her full-time job, working on the novels. But dropping things and losing her coordination made her nervous."

"What happened then?"

"When the symptoms got worse, an MRI was done. It showed lesions in the brain."

The day we learned the diagnosis was etched in my mind. Radin's office was so quiet, I could hear my own heart beating.

"Nora, Bill," Radin said, sitting behind his desk. "I'm afraid I have bad news. Based on the MRI, the neurologist's diagnosis is multiple sclerosis."

Nora turned white as milk.

"That explains the weakness and fatigue, the dropping things."

"What's the prognosis?" Nora asked as I grasped her hand.

"I assume you want the truth," Radin said.

"I *need* the truth."

"Dr. Radin," Olson continued. "Will you kindly tell the jury what you discussed with the Shaws?"

"I told them MS is a disease of the central nervous system . . . the brain and spinal cord. It causes a breakdown of the insulation, the sheath surrounding the body's nerves, so they can no longer conduct electrical impulses properly.

"There are two forms of the disease. The more benign kind has an early onset, usually when the patient is about twenty, even younger. But as I explained to the Shaws, Nora's was the more lethal form, the type beginning in the early forties. The first symptoms are usually fatigue and weakness followed by blurred vision and then rapid progression to problems with swallowing, talking, and finally paralysis and urinary and bowel incontinence."

Sitting at the defense table, I recalled the gut-churning shock of the diagnosis. I was overcome by a sudden realization of life's fragility, of how ephemeral it all was. The disease was like a cyclone rampaging through our lives.

"And Dr. Radin," Olson said. "Please tell the jury what you told the Shaws about the medications you would be prescribing for Nora."

"I told Nora and Bill I'd confer with the neurologist, and we'd use prednisone to reduce inflammation. I said it would be very tricky because prednisone would increase the warfarin's blood-thinning effect."

"And are you confident the Shaws understood the increased danger with the addition of prednisone?"

"Yes. We discussed it frequently throughout the course of Nora's illness."

While Olson shuffled through his notes, my mind replayed every moment of that horror-filled day when we learned the diagnosis. As we stepped from Radin's office into the brilliant sunlight, the sidewalk's gleaming mica specks taunted us with their radiance in contrast to our inner darkness.

"Oh, Bill, I'm glad we never had children."

"Nora . . ."

"Just think of what I'd leave them. They'd be motherless, and if we'd had a daughter, I'd be passing on a legacy of breast cancer and this monster."

I was at a loss for words with which to comfort her. I felt so small and helpless.

I held her in my arms as cars and taxis hurtled by on Park Avenue. People walked past us, unknowing and uncaring. I was frightened to my core.

Turning from his papers, Olson continued. "Dr. Radin, what happened with Nora's condition after the MS was diagnosed?"

"She deteriorated rapidly. She was totally paralyzed in less than two years. She also developed painful burning sensations—neuropathic pain—throughout her body, but especially in her legs."

Those legs, I thought, those lovely legs that once danced that magnificent tango. The image of Nora crying out in excruciating pain as searing sensations coursed through her limbs brought a flood of tears to my eyes. Despite Ben's warnings about showing emotion in the jury's presence, I buried my face in my hands. Ben's palm rested on my back.

"So, Dr. Radin," Olson intoned. "Your notes indicate she

was unable to swallow properly. She would waste away without proper nourishment. And how would she be given medication?"

"She would need an IV line to deliver the medications, and a feeding tube for nourishment."

"Doctor, about the feeding tube, did you discuss it with Nora?"

"Yes, it was important that she had a choice in this."

"So it was *her* choice to make?"

"Yes. The feeding tube would nourish her . . . keep her alive."

"So by choosing the tube, Doctor, she chose to go on living?"

"Yes, I think so."

"And, Doctor, when did Nora make this life-affirming decision?"

"About three months before she died. Though she had trouble speaking, I did manage to have a telephone conversation with her and Bill."

"How long would Nora have lived with the MS?"

"It's hard to say. Once patients reach Nora's stage, some die quickly; others live for a year or even longer."

Olson winnowed through his copy of Radin's office notes. "Dr. Radin, will you please turn to an entry in your notes dated December fifteenth of 2012."

Radin sifted through his notes, then looked up at Olson.

"Will you please read that entry to the jury?"

Radin looked at his notes and read them slowly. "'Patient confides she's afraid Bill will abandon her. She remembers how frustrated he was and lost patience with her before the MS was diagnosed when she complained of dizziness and fatigue, and was dropping things.'"

"I have no further questions, Your Honor."

"**M**r. Abrams, cross-examination."

Ben moved to the lectern. "Doctor, Mr. Olson had you read from an entry in your office notes, the one you just read dated

December fifteenth, 2012. Let me ask you about that entry. Can you please tell the jury what you and Nora discussed that day?"

Radin cleared his throat. "Nora said things I've heard over and over during my years of practice with chronically ill patients. She was worried Bill would abandon her because of her condition."

"Let me stop you there, Doctor. You said you hear this frequently. Is this kind of concern commonly expressed by patients with a chronic illness, even when it's terminal?"

"Yes, it is. I pointed out to Nora that both Bill and I had been frustrated by her symptoms. At first, they seemed to be neurotic. But when the MS was diagnosed, it explained why she was so tired and clumsy. As I saw it, there was no evidence that Bill would leave her, or was unsupportive in any way."

"Thank you. Now, Dr. Radin, how often did you see Nora over those nine years you treated her?"

"About once a month."

"And was Bill with her virtually every time?"

"Yes."

"Did he ask questions about Nora's A-fib and then about the MS?"

"Yes. He was very well informed about her conditions."

"Was that important?"

"Absolutely," Radin said, casting a look at the jurors. "With a tricky medication like warfarin, it's very important. Especially once prednisone was added. It was even more important once everything had to be given via IV, when Nora couldn't swallow."

"How did Bill learn to give the warfarin intravenously?"

"I taught him how to do it."

"Speaking of the warfarin, Doctor, did there come a time, before the MS was diagnosed, when Bill bought a testing device so they could test Nora's blood—monitor her warfarin level—at home?"

"Yes."

"And how much does that home device cost?"

"About fifteen hundred dollars."

"And did Bill buy supplies, medicine, testing strips, things like that?"

"Yes."

"Did he ever complain about the cost of these things?"

"Not to me."

"What about the doctor bills and the cost of medical equipment after the diagnosis of MS? Did Bill pay for them?"

"Yes. Once the MS was diagnosed, the insurance company dropped Nora. They couldn't get coverage for her."

"Did Bill ever complain to you about having to spend money on Nora's care?"

"No."

Images of the apartment looking like an ICU invaded my thoughts. It was nauseating to picture all the medical equipment.

"Dr. Radin, at some point, did you suggest to Bill that Nora might be better off in a nursing home?"

"After he hired the home aide, I brought it up."

"Why?"

"Because Nora was bedridden. She had to be toileted. She needed medication and massages, and had to be turned frequently to avoid getting bedsores. There was bathing, nail clipping, and bodily and oral hygiene. Then there was the IV. It could all go on for another year or even longer."

My stomach clenched as Radin described the sickbed rituals.

"How did Bill react when you suggested a nursing home?"

"He said he'd care for Nora at home."

It all swarmed through my mind: Nora lying there paralyzed, speechless, either Roberta or I lubricating her lips, massaging her back, legs, arms, and neck. I could almost see the misting machine, the lotions, the powdered warfarin, having to mix it each morning.

Ben walked to the edge of the jury box. "Now, Doctor, Mr. Olson asked about Bill's familiarity with warfarin. Is it a good thing to be familiar with a spouse's medications?"

"Yes, of course."

"And Bill learned everything he could about Nora's conditions?"

"Yes. I think Nora did well for a long time because of Bill."

"Objection, Your Honor," Olson called. "Speculative."

"Sustained. The jury will disregard that statement."

"Thank you, Doctor," Ben said. "I have no further questions, Your Honor." Ben turned away from the lectern.

"Any redirect, Mr. Olson?" asked the judge.

"No, Your Honor."

"Okay. We're through with testimony for today," Marin said, turning to the jury.

He gave them the usual warning about not discussing the case and keeping an open mind.

I couldn't help but wonder if some jurors had already made up their minds—had decided on no more than opening statements and testimony from two witnesses—that I was guilty of murder.

Chapter 23

James Sinclair could have kicked himself for opening his big mouth when the detectives came to interview him. Since he was forced into early retirement at the bank by that bastard Stockton who used cutbacks as the excuse to get rid of him, he spent way too much time at home feeling angry and bored. He'd talk to anyone who'd listen.

At sixty-four, he was living an idle life. He'd never married. No big deal—just missed out on a lot of henpecking. He spent his days reading the *Post*, picking up a few items at the Food Emporium, and shooting the breeze with any doorman on duty.

When the detectives came to his apartment, he shot his mouth off. Now he's been subpoenaed and is waiting to testify in this damned courtroom way downtown.

Why the hell did I get involved in this high profile murder case?

When Sinclair's name appeared on Olson's witness list, Ben sent his investigator—a former detective—to interview my neighbors and the building's employees.

The doormen called Sinclair a *lobby sitter*, and merely tolerated his presence. The residents saw him as a chronic complainer, always bitching about something.

I watched James Sinclair, my downstairs neighbor, take the stand. He looked as he always did: overweight, bald with a sloppy fringe of gray hair at the sides. His fleshy face was fixed with its usual sour expression.

After Sinclair was sworn in, Olson began by asking him what he did for a living.

"I'm a retired loan officer at Apple Bank," he said, bringing a cup of water to his lips.

"How long have you lived in the same building as the defendant?"

"About ten years."

Sinclair set the cup down. His hand was shaking.

I know exactly where Sinclair's testimony will go.

"And where is your apartment in relation to the defendant's?"

"Right below his."

I closed my eyes and kept myself from shaking my head. The jury could be watching.

"Mr. Sinclair, was there a day when something drew your attention to the Shaw apartment?"

"Yes." Sinclair cleared his throat and sipped more water.

"Please tell the jury what it was."

My heart thrashed in my chest. How over-the-top would his recounting be?

"One morning, a little more than three years ago, I heard a thump through my ceiling."

I recalled that day. It was the first time Nora fell. She hadn't yet been diagnosed with MS but was dropping things. I found her lying on the bedroom floor; her arms and face were badly bruised.

"Mr. Sinclair, what did you do?"

"I went up there and rang their bell. I asked if everything was okay."

"And what happened then?"

"Shaw said his wife fell."

"And what, if anything, did you see?"

"I saw Mrs. Shaw in her nightgown." Sinclair shifted in the

witness chair.

"Did you observe anything else about her?"

"Her arm and face were black-and-blue, like she'd been beaten up and—"

"*Objection!*" Ben roared, jumping to his feet.

"Sustained," said the judge.

Rage scorched through me. I felt like leaping from my chair and ripping out Sinclair's throat. My hands curled into clenched fists. I slid them beneath the defense table. How could such drivel be presented to a jury? Speculation, rank inference, nothing more. This was a legal lynching.

"Your Honor," Ben called, "this witness has made a prejudicial inference to the jury. I'm asking for a curative instruction."

The judge nodded and turned to the panel. "Ladies and gentlemen, you must disregard any statement about what a witness *thought* when seeing or hearing something. A witness may describe what was *seen* or *heard* but cannot draw conclusions or make inferences about it. The witness must stick with the facts only, not with conjecture, speculation, or opinions."

Two jurors nodded, but the others stared blankly. It wasn't clear they were processing Marin's words. My stomach lurched.

Marin nodded to the prosecutor.

Olson continued. "Mr. Sinclair, did you see or hear anything else?"

"Yes. Things were always banging up there."

When Nora's hands grew weak, she'd drop a jar of mayonnaise or a bottle of ketchup on the kitchen floor. There was no reasonable explanation for her clumsiness and it drove me crazy. I didn't know what to do. That's when I thought it was all psychological. Radin did, too.

"Now, Mr. Sinclair, did there come another time when you went upstairs?"

"Yes."

"When was that?"

"A few weeks after that first time."

"What made you go there?"

"Shaw was yelling and cursing. I'd never heard anything like that in my life."

"*Objection*," Ben shouted.

"Sustained," Marin said. "The witness will relate the facts only. Nothing else. No comparisons or impressions. Is that understood, Mr. Sinclair?"

Sinclair nodded. Beads of sweat popped onto his upper lip.

A bolt of panic pierced my chest. I'd be pilloried by this bastard.

"What was the defendant saying?" Olson asked.

"I can't repeat the curses, sir."

My scalp tightened.

"Well, other than the curses, please tell the jury what you heard."

"Shaw was yelling 'I can't take this anymore. You're driving me crazy.' I heard Mrs. Shaw screaming and crying. Then there was a loud thump of some sort. The wall of my foyer actually shook, and then their front door slammed."

Sitting with my eyes closed, I recalled that day.

I was at the breaking point, so fed up with Nora's helplessness, her clumsiness, fatigue, and moodiness, I couldn't take it anymore. She was no longer the woman I'd married. She'd become a clinging remnant of her former self. Thinking back on it, I hated myself for what I did. I roared at her, snarled, said I was leaving. She stumbled after me, begging me to stay between sob-filled gasps. I kept cursing at the top of my lungs, rushing toward the apartment door. As she closed in on me, I whirled around and shoved her—violently—bashing her into the foyer wall. Then I left, slamming the door behind me. Before I even reached the elevator, I felt like the world's most callous bastard.

"What happened then?" Olson asked Sinclair.

"I went upstairs and rang their bell."

"What did you observe?"

"Mrs. Shaw was crying and said, 'It's not locked.'"

"And what did you do?"

"I opened the door and looked inside. She was sitting on the floor with her back against the wall. She was wearing a nightgown. Her arms and shoulders were black-and-blue."

"What happened then?"

"I asked if she was all right. She said her husband had left her."

"Did she explain why?"

"No, not really."

"Was anything else said?"

"I asked if he'd hit her, but she just asked me to leave. So I did."

"I have nothing further, Your Honor," Olson said.

Judge Marin looked over at Ben.

Ben stood. "May we approach, Your Honor?" he asked.

As Ben and Olson walked to the bench, I felt the jurors' eyes on me. I stared straight ahead, tried to look unruffled but was seething inside, boiling with fury. It was so unjust.

The attorneys conferred with the judge. Although their voices were muffled, a heated exchange was taking place.

"This is a good time for a brief recess," Marin said, turning to the jury. "Let's have the courtroom cleared. Mr. Sinclair, please step down and have a seat outside."

I stood at the defense table as everyone filed out of the courtroom, but my thoughts never left that horrible day when I pushed Nora. I couldn't get it out of my mind. I recalled coming home an emotional wreck. I never knew such rage smoldered within me. Even though I apologized profusely and Nora forgave me, I couldn't absolve myself for what I'd done in that moment of near-insanity. Even in the courtroom, the thought of that day sent a dark tide of remorse through me.

When the courtroom was empty, Marin said, "Mr. Abrams?"

"Your Honor, I move to strike this witness's testimony as prejudicial and irrelevant. It has no probative value. Its sole purpose is to poison the jury with insinuations that Bill Shaw abused his wife."

"Mr. Olson, I assume you oppose Mr. Abrams's motion."

"I do, Your Honor. The purpose of Mr. Sinclair's testimony is to establish the atmosphere in the Shaw household—one of anger, frustration, illness, and abuse."

"That's outrageous, Your Honor," Ben cried. "I ask that the witness be excused and the jury be instructed to ignore his testimony."

"Mr. Abrams," said Marin, "I'm going to deny your motion. I understand your concern, but you have ample opportunity to cross-examine the witness. I think the jurors can make up their minds about the witness's testimony without my intervention."

"Yes, Your Honor, but please note my objection for the record."

"So noted. Now, let's bring the jury back."

Ben lumbered to the lectern. "Tell me, Mr. Sinclair, how many times did you complain about noise coming from the Shaw apartment?"

"Maybe two or three . . ."

"If the doorman said you complained seven times over the year before Nora Shaw died, would that be wrong?"

"That would be wrong, sir."

"Mr. Sinclair, I have a copy of the doormen's logbook. It's been entered into evidence. Is the book wrong?"

"I don't know. I never saw it."

"Did you complain about *other* neighbors making noise?"

"Occasionally." Sinclair's shoulders rose. His eyes narrowed.

"And if the log says that you complained about three other neighbors, would they be telling the truth?"

"I have no way of knowing," Sinclair said with a scowl. More sweat beads popped out on his forehead.

"Well, let's get down to specifics, Mr. Sinclair," Ben said, flipping pages on the lectern. "The logbook says you complained about Mr. Carleton? True?"

"Yes," responded Sinclair, his tongue flicking over his lower lip.

"How many times?"

"I don't recall."

"The logbook says it's three times this year. Is that true?"

"I doubt it."

"And Miss Clarke?"

"Once, maybe twice."

"If the logbook says it was four times this year, would it be wrong?"

"It's an exaggeration."

"Are you saying that the doormen make incorrect entries in the logbook?"

"I'm not saying anything, sir. Just that the entries about Miss Clarke are wrong."

Sinclair's face was soaked with sweat.

Ben read aloud the exact dates and complaints about Miss Clarke and two other neighbors.

Yes, Ben was undoing some of the damage of Sinclair's direct testimony, but the jury heard about the time I completely lost it with Nora.

"And you've complained about dogs in the elevator, true?" Ben asked.

"The owners are supposed to take them in the service elevator."

"Mr. Sinclair? Did you complain about that?"

"Yes," he said, blinking rapidly. His tongue kept flicking from his lips, like a serpent's.

One juror, a middle-aged woman in the front row—juror

number four—appeared to be stifling a frown. Maybe I stood a chance.

"Let's change the subject," Ben said. "Do you know what Mrs. Shaw was suffering from?"

"Someone said she had MS," Sinclair said, pawing his brow.

"Did you learn that the MS made her weak and she couldn't hold on to things?"

"No, I didn't."

"I'm going to ask you to assume, sir, that her physician, Dr. Radin, was here yesterday and testified about that. He told the jury that Nora was weak, and she began dropping things because of her neurological condition. If she dropped things—a bottle of juice or dishes—could that account for the banging you said you heard upstairs?"

"It could."

"Mr. Sinclair, did you know Nora Shaw took a medication called warfarin . . . Coumadin?"

"No." Sinclair's tone was sullen, peevish.

"Then you didn't know the warfarin caused bleeding into her skin, did you?"

"No. Of *course* not."

"Then you couldn't know that the black-and-blue blotches on her skin—the ones you testified to Mr. Olson about—were caused by the warfarin, could you?"

"No."

Ben paused, letting Sinclair's concession marinate with the jury.

"I have no more questions for this witness, Your Honor," Ben said, turning dismissively from Sinclair. He walked back to the defense table and sat down.

"Any redirect, Mr. Olson?" asked the judge.

"Briefly, Your Honor," Olson said, and proceeded to the lectern. "Mr. Sinclair, going back to that incident, you said that you saw Mrs. Shaw on the floor with her back against the wall, and she told you the defendant had left her?"

"Yes, sir."

"I have nothing more, Your Honor."

I felt as though a hand grenade with a pulled pin was lodged inside my guts.

Marin peered at Ben.

"I have nothing further for this witness, Your Honor."

"You may step down," Judge Marin said to Sinclair.

A watery sensation filled my nose. It took every ounce of inner reserve to keep from sobbing.

Just stay calm, but don't look unconcerned. Don't even look at Sinclair, and for the love of God, don't let yourself cry. You can't be a wuss, but you can't be a hard-ass, either. What a balancing act. Ben was right. It's an impossible role.

Olson would drag me through a shit field. He'd portray me as a wife beater, a raging bastard who'd left his sick wife, and of course, in the end, a murderer.

If I'd ever had a shred of belief that justice was the goal of a trial, it was eradicated. This would never be a search for the truth.

And besides, I asked myself, exactly what on earth constitutes truth?

Chapter 24

Lee's dark eyes wandered over the courtroom as she sat in the witness chair. I feared they would come to rest on me, which would taint anything she might say in my favor. It was difficult to believe Olson had called my sister-in-law as a prosecution witness. I felt violated.

Seeing Lee's sisterly resemblance to Nora sent a sickening pang of sadness through me.

"Ms. Walsh, what was your relationship to Nora Shaw?" Olson asked.

"She was my sister." Lee's eyes narrowed.

"Can you describe the relationship?"

"Well, we had our disagreements, as sisters often do. But we were very close."

Ben sighed.

"Lee's too garrulous," he'd said earlier that morning. "She'll overanswer Olson's questions. And since she's Olson's witness, I can't prep her to keep her answers short and to the point. She'll wander all over the place, and Olson'll dive right in."

"Did anything make for a special closeness between you and Nora?" Olson asked.

"Well, Papa died when we were young. Mama died when I was nineteen and Nora was seventeen. After that, Nora and I lived together. We had no one else. And it was—"

"So, Ms. Walsh—"

"I always felt Nora was scarred because she was so young when these things happened. And—"

"Okay, Ms. Walsh. It was a close relationship and—"

"Very close. Maybe I was overprotective of Nora, and I—"

"Understood, Ms. Walsh. If we can move on."

Seeing Lee on the stand reminded me of that night she introduced me to Nora at that West Village party. An image of Nora's sensuous tango flashed through my mind. I momentarily heard the lush music of Carlos Gardel.

"Now, Ms. Walsh," Olson went on, "after Nora got sick, what was her relationship like with the defendant?"

"You have no idea how beautiful and talented Nora was. She turned down offers to go to Hollywood. I always thought she should've taken them." Lee turned to the jury. "Bill and Nora were very supportive of each other. Nora went on book tours with Bill; she went to every city with him. She edited all his manuscripts. And Bill dedicated every book—"

"Ms. Walsh?"

"Yes, sir?"

"Do you remember my question?"

"Why . . . I think so, but . . . no," Lee said, her eyes widening. "Not really," she finally said.

"If you'll just listen to my question, Ms. Walsh, we'll get through this a lot more quickly." Olson paused. "What was their relationship like after Nora got sick?"

"Oh, when he learned Nora had MS, Bill took care of everything."

Why on earth did Olson subpoena Lee? What could she have told him that he wants the jury to hear?

"Now, Ms. Walsh, the defendant was—"

"Taking care of Nora. He even stopped writing."

"Why did he stop writing?"

"He took her to doctors and did everything. It went on for

nearly three years."

"How did that go?"

"How did what go, sir?"

"The visits to the doctors."

"Well, Nora was weak and dizzy, and she would get very tired. But the tests were all negative. Everyone thought it was psychological. That is, until the MS was diagnosed."

"Ms. Walsh, did you and the defendant have differences of opinion about Nora?"

So this was where Olson would take his charade—my arguments with Lee. Yes, Ben was right; Lee talked much too much when Olson visited her. She opened the door, and he'd drive an 18-wheeler right through it.

"I wouldn't call them differences."

"Did you and the defendant have different *opinions* about Nora's care?"

"I suppose so." Lee leaned back in the witness chair and crossed her arms.

"Will you please tell the jury about that?"

"Well, these things happen in any family."

Ben sighed. I could only imagine his frustration.

"Please tell us about these different opinions," Olson said.

"They were mainly about treating the symptoms before we learned it was MS."

I recalled the never-ending telephone calls from Lee.

"Bill, I've found a homeopathic doctor. An herbal approach might help."

"It could interfere with the warfarin. Nora could bleed out."

"You've tried everything else."

"I'd have to run this by Dr. Radin."

"My God, you and Radin are joined at the hip."

"Ms. Walsh," Olson said. "What differences did you and the defendant have?"

"I don't really recall."

"Ms. Walsh, let me remind you that you're under oath."

Lee's face grew pale. Her lower lip trembled.

"Ms. Walsh, what differences of opinion were there about Nora's care?"

"Well, I thought she had a virus, or some vitamin deficiency, or maybe chronic fatigue."

"So what happened?"

"I called Bill pretty often."

"And what happened then?"

"He discounted my suggestions. He thought they were silly."

"And what else, if anything, did he say?"

"That it was crazy."

"Did he say why?"

Lee hesitated and then committed the cardinal courtroom sin: she glanced at me. The jurors *had* to notice it.

"Ms. Walsh? Did the defendant say why he thought it was crazy?"

"He thought it was quackery, especially yoga and acupuncture. Nora agreed with him. I even got into arguments with her."

"But getting back to the defendant, Ms. Walsh, he—"

"Bill wouldn't let Nora go for things like that or—"

"He wouldn't let her go?"

"He thought the doctor shopping was feeding into Nora's problems. He thought it was all in her head. He was at his wit's end, and—" Lee stopped herself.

"He was at his *wit's* end?" Olson paused dramatically. "What happened then?"

"Bill and I had some discussions."

Olson came out from behind the lectern. "Discussions?"

"Okay, arguments." Lee pursed her lips. "It wasn't a big thing."

"What was said?"

"Bill told me to stop butting in. And I think I was *way* too pushy."

"Did he lose his temper?"

"We both did."

"What did he say?"

"That he had enough on his hands taking care of Nora."

"So what happened?"

"You have to understand, Mr. Olson. It was a very difficult time in their lives, in mine, too. I was divorced and living alone; and my son was . . . oh, forget that. The only doctor Bill wanted Nora to see besides Dr. Radin was a psychiatrist. He said Nora was driving him crazy," Lee said in a quavering voice.

"Nora was driving him crazy?"

"It's just an expression, Mr. Olson."

"What happened then?"

"What do you mean, sir?"

"What happened after these arguments?"

My mouth was parched. Lee was giving Olson everything he wanted.

"I'm not sure I understand," Lee said.

"What did you tell me when I interviewed you?"

"Oh, you mean the separation?"

"*Yes.* What about the separation?"

"Nora's illness was the center of their lives. Even Dr. Radin thought she should see a psychiatrist."

"And what happened?" Olson moved closer to the witness stand.

"Bill was fed up."

"He was *fed up*?"

"Yes."

"And then what?"

"He walked out. He took a sublet nearby. But when the MS was—"

"The defendant *left* Nora?"

"But when he realized—"

"Ms. Walsh, please answer my questions. Are you saying the defendant moved out because Nora was driving him crazy?"

Lee stared blankly at Olson.

Blood thrummed behind my eyes. My head was pulsing.

"Ms. Walsh, did you hear my question?" Olson asked. "You said that the defendant moved out because Nora was driving him *crazy.*"

"It was just for a few weeks and—"

"Now, Ms. Walsh, moving on to what happened after the MS was diagnosed, what happened to Nora's health insurance?"

"They canceled it, but—"

"When I interviewed you, didn't you tell me that after the insurance was canceled, the Shaws were hemorrhaging money?"

"*Please,* sir. I'd like to finish my answer about Bill moving out."

"Ms. Walsh," Judge Marin interjected. "I'm sure that when Mr. Abrams questions you, you'll be able to give details. Right now, just answer Mr. Olson's questions, okay?"

Lee nodded and turned back to Olson. Her chin was quivering. Sinclair's testimony now made more sense. Olson wanted to extract the testimony about my not only walking out, but eventually *moving* out, however briefly. I'd left Nora for two horrific weeks, during which I'd felt guilt-ridden and miserable. I didn't know if I could ever make it up to her.

Sinclair's and Lee's testimony fit together perfectly.

"Ms. Walsh, when I interviewed you, you said that Bill was hemorrhaging money, correct?"

"Yes, I said that."

"And you also mentioned your family's finances, didn't you?"

"Yes . . ."

"When your parents died, what was your financial situation?"

"Nora and I had trust money."

"How much was in Nora's trust fund when she and the

defendant got married?"

"I believe it was about six hundred thousand, but Bill was very—"

"And a few moments ago, you told us the defendant was *hemorrhaging* money. Was that how you put it?"

"Look, sir. Bill was very successful. He—"

"Isn't that what you said? He was hemorrhaging money?"

Lee sighed. "Yes. I said that."

She was caving in, but I felt a gush of affection for Lee. She was trying to protect me. The downside was obvious: the jury could see she was a reluctant witness, admitted things only when Olson squeezed, prodded, and pushed.

"And you said the defendant stopped writing, correct?"

"Yes. He was taking care of Nora. He—"

"And what were Nora and the defendant living on when he stopped writing?"

"Savings, I guess."

"Was Nora's trust fund being depleted?"

"I don't really know, sir."

"Didn't Nora ever tell you about her trust fund and their living off it?"

"Not that I recall, sir." Lee again glanced at me. I felt like sliding down the chair to the floor.

As grateful as I was for Lee's loyalty, she was hurting far more than helping me.

"When I interviewed you, didn't you tell me they were depleting Nora's trust fund? Didn't you say that?"

"Yes," Lee replied in a near whisper.

"Please repeat that, Ms. Walsh. I don't think the jury heard you."

"Yes," Lee said, closing her eyes.

"Now, Ms. Walsh, do you recall when Ms. Pierce and I came to your apartment to interview you?"

"Yes."

"Do you remember telling us that you went to the Shaws' apartment on the morning Nora died?"

"Yes . . ." Lee's eyes widened. The whites were visible above her irises.

"And were you alone with her?"

"Yes."

"What about Roberta, the aide?"

"If I recall, she was in the kitchen cleaning up."

"So you and Roberta were the last two people to see Nora alive?"

"Yes, I guess so."

"Would you please tell the jury what you observed about Nora that morning, only a few hours before her death?"

"If I recall, Nora was awake and alert."

Olson's eyebrows rose. He moved back to the lectern and shook his head. "Is that what you told me and Ms. Pierce when we interviewed you?"

"I—I don't recall." The skin around Lee's eyes tightened.

"Do you recall us asking permission to record our conversation with you?"

"I think so."

"Would you like me to play that recording?"

"You do whatever you think is proper, Mr. Olson."

"When we met, didn't you say Nora was sleeping more soundly than you'd ever seen her?"

"I don't recall, sir."

"You don't *recall*?"

"Objection, Your Honor. Argumentative," Ben called.

"Sustained."

"Is something preventing you from remembering what you said to us that day, Ms. Walsh?"

"I—I was so nervous when you showed up, asking all those

questions about Nora. I can't remember what I said."

"Well, let's refresh your recollection, Ms. Walsh. I'm going to play a portion of the recording."

Olson moved to the defense table. He and Pierce pushed a few buttons on a recording device. After a few indecipherable snippets, they located the portion of the recording they wanted. Olson placed the device on the lectern, facing the jury. Though the sound was tinny, the voices were audible.

"When you saw Nora that morning, what did she look like?"

"She was sound asleep."

"Sound asleep?"

"Yes, very deeply. More so than I'd ever seen her."

Olson switched the device off and moved closer to Lee.

"Ms. Walsh, those are your words, aren't they?"

"Yes." Lee's eyelids fluttered.

"So Nora was sleeping more soundly than you'd *ever* seen her, correct?"

"I guess so."

Olson waited, letting Lee's concession sink in with the jury. He'd made Lee look like a liar. Her support for me looked like blatant advocacy. I was shriveling.

"Ms. Walsh, after my office contacted you and you knew you could be called as a witness, did you speak to the defendant?"

Lee hesitated, then shot another glance at me. "I called him."

"When was that?"

"When you and your assistant left my apartment."

"And what did you and the defendant talk about?"

"Bill said if I was going to be a witness, we couldn't talk about the case."

"But you called him the *very day* my office contacted you?"

"Yes."

"Only a short while after Ms. Pierce and I left, correct?"

"Yes."

"Why did you do that?"

"Just to let him know."

"To warn him?"

"There was nothing to warn him about, sir."

"Thank you, Ms. Walsh. I have nothing further, Your Honor."

"Mr. Abrams, cross-examination."

How on earth would Ben undo the damage Lee had inadvertently done?

"Ms. Walsh," Ben said at the lectern, "did you tell us that Nora and Bill *both* thought your ideas about acupuncture, yoga, and supplements were silly?"

"Yes, that's correct." She straightened up in the witness chair.

"So not only Bill discounted these things; Nora did too?"

"Yes."

"And during the last few years of Nora's life, were you as protective of her as you'd been when she was a kid?"

"I guess so," Lee said with a catch in her throat.

"Still, there were arguments between you and Nora?"

"I suggested other treatments, and yes, we argued about that."

"Ms. Walsh, did Bill ever tell you he resented the money spent on Nora?"

"No, he did *not.*"

"And earlier, when Mr. Olson was asking you questions, you wanted to say something about Bill earning money, correct?"

"Yes."

"What were you going to say?"

"I don't want to give the wrong impression," Lee said, turning to the jurors. "Bill was very successful. He didn't live off Nora. It was anything *but* that."

Some jurors nodded. Were the implications of Olson's direct examination being reversed, however slightly?

"Yet, Ms. Walsh, there came a time when Bill stopped writing. Bill and Nora began to spend—draw down—Nora's trust money.

What can you say about that?"

"Bill didn't *want* to write. Once the MS was diagnosed, Nora became his whole life. So, if they were spending that money, it was their decision."

"If Bill resented those expenses, Nora would have told you that, yes?"

"Objection, Your Honor. Speculative," called Olson.

"Sustained."

"Ms. Walsh, you and Nora were close, correct?"

"*Very* close."

"Were you close enough that she would tell you her troubles?"

"Oh, yes."

"And did she ever tell you Bill resented the money spent on her illness?"

"No. Never."

"Did Bill try to skimp on medical expenses for Nora—things like doctor visits, medicines, blood tests, equipment, the home health aide?"

"No, never." Lee shook her head.

"So the only things he didn't want to pay for were things he thought, whether rightly or not, were treatments he and Nora considered quackery?"

"Yes."

"Now, Ms. Walsh, for how long did Bill move out?"

"A week or two. And he was a block away."

"Did he keep in contact with Nora during that time?"

"Yes. He called her every day, a few times a day."

"Was there talk of divorce?"

"Not that I know of."

"And Bill moved back in with Nora?"

"Yes. And then a few weeks later, they got the terrible news."

I recalled holding Nora outside Radin's office the day we learned about the MS.

"Nora, I'm so sorry. Please forgive me . . ."

Radin's words crushed me. Nora, too. We were buried in an avalanche of pessimism.

"Bill felt guilty about doubting her," Lee said. "He felt terrible because he'd walked out in a moment of anger."

"Objection, Your Honor," Olson called out. "Speculative. No question was asked of this witness. She's offering opinions and speculation to protect her brother-in-law."

"Sustained. Proceed, Mr. Abrams."

"Ms. Walsh, once the MS was diagnosed, did Bill neglect Nora?"

"Never."

"Did he ever indicate he wanted her to *die* so he could go on with his life?"

Lee blanched. "Never."

"Ms. Walsh, when did you first meet Bill Shaw?"

"About seventeen years ago. At a party. In fact, I introduced him and Nora."

"So you've known Bill during their entire marriage?"

"Yes."

"Did Bill *ever*, either before or after Nora got sick, say he wanted to end the marriage?"

"No. Believe me, Mr. Abrams, when it came to taking care of Nora, Bill was the best."

"Objection, Your Honor," Olson cried, jumping up. His hands went to his hips. "Speculative and assuming facts not in evidence."

"Sustained."

"Thank you, Ms. Walsh. I have no more questions for this witness, Your Honor."

"Mr. Olson, any redirect?"

"Only one question, Your Honor."

"Proceed."

"Ms. Walsh," Olson said, standing at the prosecution table.

"Isn't it true that the defendant felt Nora was driving him crazy and he took a separate apartment?"

"You have to understand, sir—"

"Didn't you say that a little while ago?"

"Yes."

"Thank you. I have nothing more, Your Honor."

Lee's loyalty was crystal clear. I doubted the jury would believe her.

Chapter 25

At two a.m. Ben sat on the living room sofa, sipping a tumbler of scotch. Its comforting warmth and smoky flavor brought a moment's peace to his racing mind, as Ben thought about the day ahead. Constance Manning was scheduled to testify—under subpoena. It was worrisome. When it came to relations between men and women, you could never know the whole truth. And as well as he knew Bill, in this strange thing called life, you never know anyone's deepest secrets. Would Constance Manning's testimony rip apart their defense?

Ben could never remember a time when Bill didn't attract women. It grew more obvious when he gained notoriety with *Fire and Ice*. His fame, coupled with clear, blue eyes, rugged features, and an athletic build made Bill the envy of every man in a room. Women flocked to him—it was pure instinct—and maybe Constance Manning had been drawn to him, too.

Whenever Ben and Bill met for a drink—at any bar in the city—women always eyed Bill, never Ben.

There was that time after Nora got sick—maybe six months after the diagnosis of MS—when he and Bill were out together. Though he seemed subdued, even gloomy, Bill suggested they go—of all places—to the Blue Note, a jazz club on West 3rd in the Village. Ben understood why: it was the place where Bill and Nora went to hear great music soon after they first met.

After a few tall, cool ones at the bar, Ben and Bill took a corner table and ordered burgers and fries.

Within moments of being seated, Ben noticed two women at a nearby table eyeing Bill. They continued glancing in Bill's direction throughout their meal. When the women were leaving, one of them—a tall, auburn-haired beauty wearing a revealing blouse and skin-tight jeans—casually dropped a business card next to Bill's drink as she passed their table. Then she was gone.

Ben laughed, knowing he envied Bill's allure. Amazed at the woman's brazen approach, Ben fixated on the redhead's incredible ass as she sauntered away.

When Ben turned back, the card was gone. Bill had pocketed it.

Ben never knew if Bill had lovers. As close as he and Bill were, some topics were strictly off-limits. And with Nora's MS, Ben couldn't blame Bill if he had women on the side. There could be no doubt the disease ravaged the marriage as well as Nora's body.

Was Bill too ashamed to tell him the truth about Constance Manning? Was their friendship getting in the way of Bill making that admission to Ben? Or were Bill and Constance just two poor souls sharing the pain of their sad lives over a cup of coffee?

Ben ran through the possible variations of Olson's direct examination of Constance Manning. He tried to imagine every pathway Olson might take. He'd pored through trial transcripts of earlier witnesses, reviewed those from other trials, looked for patterns in Olson's questions, trying to presage his trajectory with the Manning woman.

Ben had interviewed Constance Manning as the law allows—with Ann Pierce taking notes. He'd given proper notice to the prosecutor, asked no leading questions, and had no off-the-record conversations with her. Constance Manning's pain was etched on her face, in her voice, in her entire being. You didn't have to be Dr. Phil to see—to actually feel—her anguish. And it was difficult to imagine Bill—or any man for that matter—not being sucked in by Constance Manning's elegance, beauty, and misfortune.

Exactly what would she say on the witness stand? As Ben had learned over the years, the pressures of the courtroom could force *any* witness to unleash a bombshell.

Look what happened with Lee's testimony—Nora driving Bill crazy, arguments, hemorrhaging money, Bill leaving Nora—facts and inferences, all negative. And all registering with the jury in a not-so-subliminal way. The erosive effect of innuendo could be devastating to a case.

And what would Constance Manning's testimony bring to the surface? What unexpected traps might it open up?

Elaine padded into the living room and settled herself next to him on the sofa.

"Again no sleep, Ben?"

"I'm thinking about Constance Manning taking the stand."

"Listen, honey," Elaine said, reaching for his hand. "You know that a few months before she died, Nora told me she wouldn't blame Bill if he *was* seeing someone, as she put it. Because she couldn't meet his sexual needs anymore."

"I believe Bill when he says he didn't have a girlfriend," Ben heard himself say.

"Okay, Ben, for the sake of argument, let's say Bill *was* having an affair. How does that pan out to murder?"

"Honey, it's the jury that counts, not you or me. If he *was* having an affair, it could make the jury lean toward Olson's theory of the case—that Bill wanted Nora dead so he could be with this other woman."

"Any reasonable juror would understand if he *did* have a relationship."

"But, honey—"

"Ben, I've never seen you this uptight about a trial." Elaine's hand went to his head and stroked his hair. She edged closer to him with a pleading look in her eyes.

"Honey, it's *Bill* I'm defending," Ben said, grasping her hand.

"That's precisely my point. You're not being objective."

"But Bill's life's on the line."

"Ben, haven't you always said your job is to give your client the best representation possible? That it's not your job to live the client's life or suffer his fate, whatever that may be? When the trial's over, you accept the jury's verdict and move on to the next case, knowing you did the best job you could? Isn't that your outlook on any trial?"

"This isn't just any trial, honey. I can't be that way about Bill." Ben's throat constricted.

"Then you shouldn't be representing him."

"Oh, honey . . ."

"Ben, you made a mistake taking this case."

Chapter 26

Constance Manning sat in a small antechamber near the courtroom. Her heart drummed a tattoo beat in her chest.

Olson's subpoena would force her to talk about her life. In front of strangers. God, the public spectacle of it—her entire existence being ripped open and examined. It would be humiliating. Constance had read the muckraking *Post* articles about Bill, and she'd watched the local TV channels. It was heartbreaking.

How on earth did things get so complicated? When she married Louis, her world was filled with promise. But when it turned out she couldn't have a baby, he left her and they were divorced.

Knowing alimony would take her just so far, Constance set out on a career in advertising. As an account executive with McGann & Bartlett, she now earned three hundred thousand a year. Not bad for a forty-four-year-old woman who began as an administrative assistant. She dealt with the sexist innuendos and the jealous backstabbing, and handled the high-octane politics of the Madison Avenue ad world. *Mad Men* showed only a thimbleful of what really went on—and it wasn't confined to the sixties.

With her second husband Alfred's encouragement, she took investment courses and was a quick study. Her mutual fund portfolio did spectacularly, especially during the booming nineties. She became independently well off—didn't rely on a nickel of Alfred's money to get where she is.

Alfred Manning was twenty-five years her senior, wealthy,

and long divorced, with two grown sons. Though she signed a prenup, Alfred's kids viewed her as a money-grubbing intruder, a sponge.

When Alfred developed Parkinson's disease and eventually needed round-the-clock nursing care, his sons demanded to be Alfred's health-care proxies. Constance refused.

"They want him to die quickly so they can get their hands on the money," her lawyer said. "You're holding up their plans."

Constance prevailed in court and retained the medical proxy. She kept Alfred comfortable until his last day.

Waiting to testify, Constance thought, Poor Bill. Poor Alfred. Poor Nora. It's all too much.

It made her heart ache.

Watching Constance push through the swinging door and walk across the well, I was stupefied by the insanity of my existence. My life would be shredded and strewn on the courtroom floor. Low-level murmuring rose from the gallery. Voltage seemed to fill the courtroom.

As the court clerk swore Constance in, my hands began shaking. Constance's testimony would leave me naked. The world would be fingering my guts, my heart. It would be an autopsy on a still-living man.

Ben said repeatedly, "Look neutral while Constance testifies. The jury'll be looking for signals. They'll wanna see if there's sexual static in the air."

The jurors' eyes shifted from Constance to me, and back to her. Yes, they were on the lookout for a glimmer of sexual tension between us—some subtle but discernible erotic energy floating in the air. I'd always known every human being is a bit of a voyeur who feels titillated at the prospect of looking into another person's life. Especially if it's a salacious peek into the forbidden, a glimpse into the bedroom. But this was going to be in public, complete exposure.

And Olson had promised he'd paint me as a man who, in his frustration with Nora's condition, moved on to another woman, desperate to devour the promise of another life. As Charlie said that day at the Croton Reservoir, the trial was a travesty. It was a seedy courtroom drama promising to titillate.

As Olson moved to the lectern, Constance sat very still in the witness chair. She held her head erect and stared straight ahead. Mournfulness showed in her eyes, in the grim set of her lips and the downturn at the corners of her mouth. She was a classically beautiful woman. It was difficult to imagine any man not being attracted to her—and Olson knew it. He would play that angle with the jury. I glanced to my right: the men on the panel were transfixed.

Constance's fine features, prominent cheekbones, pale skin, and chestnut hair were offset by a pearl-gray wool pantsuit. Her face was a lovely oval set on a long, graceful neck. She wore a silver choker.

I recalled the evening shortly before her husband died. Constance called me and we agreed to meet that evening for coffee. It was maybe the third time we'd spoken. I walked her back to her apartment from Starbucks.

"Alfred's been in a nursing home for three years," she said, standing beneath the building's hunter-green awning. The streetlight cast a pinkish glow through the indigo evening air. I could smell the dampness of the East River at the end of 79th Street. "We're each in a terrible place," Constance said. "But I think I've made peace with it."

A twinge of sadness shuddered through me as I thought of Nora, paralyzed in bed.

"I have no illusions about anything," she said.

I nodded, knowing exactly what she meant. "The worst part about all this," I said, "is sometimes I wish Nora would die. I don't know how much longer I can stand this."

"I know the feeling," Constance whispered. She moved closer. I smelled her skin.

"And part of me is dying along with Nora."

"I'm here, Bill," she murmured.

Tears trickled down my face.

Her lips touched my cheek as we held each other tightly.

And then it began. My heart pumped wildly. I inhaled the fragrance of her hair, felt the smoothness of her skin, and my groin tingled. There was a surge of excitement, a swell of blood. I was getting hard. God, it had been ages since I'd been with Nora, and suddenly, a rush of sexual hunger overtook me. I trembled—with desire, fear, and guilt.

"Ms. Manning," Olson said from the lectern, "you're in court today because my office issued a subpoena, isn't that true?"

"Yes," she replied softly.

"Ms. Manning, please speak up so the jury and court reporter can hear you."

"Yes," Constance said more forcefully. She reached for the plastic cup at the witness stand, sipped water, and cleared her throat.

"Now, I'm going to ask you some questions about your relationship with William Shaw," Olson said. He waited a beat. "Is that okay?"

I couldn't believe it: the prosecutor asking a subpoenaed witness if it was permissible to ask questions. What a theatrical crock of shit.

Constance nodded and blinked a few times.

"Ms. Manning, you have to answer verbally so the court reporter can take your answer down for the record."

Unctuous turd. Putting Constance on display, stroking her with buttery bullshit, as though she's a child. Is it okay to ask questions? As if she had a choice about being here.

"Ms. Manning, when did you meet the defendant?"

"About nine or ten months ago." Her voice quavered.

"Before Nora Shaw died?"

"Yes, maybe four or five weeks before."

"How did you meet?"

"We were both at Starbucks. He was writing. I was having coffee."

"In other words, Ms. Manning, it was a casual thing?"

"Yes."

"You kind of picked each other up?"

"Objection, Your Honor," Ben called.

"Sustained," Marin said. "Mr. Olson, please dispense with the color commentary."

"Yes, Your Honor," Olson said, blanching.

Juror number four, a middle-aged woman with short reddish hair, shook her head.

I felt a momentary surge of elation at Olson being admonished by the judge. Murmuring rose from the gallery. *The spectators must love this*, I thought. The sketch artist was scribbling away—capturing Constance's features. I tried imagining the drawing in the next day's *Post*. I felt like flinching, or better, sinking beneath the defense table. No matter how much Ben prepped me, nothing could have readied me for this agony.

"Ms. Manning, did you and the defendant eventually become more than friends?"

Constance stared at Olson. Her eyes seemed to flicker.

My thoughts raced. *Would Constance perjure herself? Or would she break down, cave under questioning? Would she reveal what happened that night? Would she tell the jury we'd gone up to her place for a drink, and after a few awkward moments, began kissing—tenderly at first—and soon our mouths opened, our hands roamed over each other, and we were tearing hungrily at each other's clothing? Would she describe how we tumbled onto the bed in naked disarray, breathless and trembling? How we pawed at each other, and, as tears poured from my eyes, how I'd begun shaking, from desire, from fear, from anguish, and from guilt? Would she describe how we pressed our bodies together, how I sobbed from the deepest reaches of my soul, how I shuddered, and then . . . ?*

At that moment, sitting at the defense table, I could see and hear, could actually *feel* myself after leaving Constance's apartment, as though I'd returned to that place and time. I recalled walking, nearly stumbling, through a misty night drizzle, walking uptown on 3rd Avenue. I stood for a while beneath a dripping ailanthus tree and watched the hazy pink coronas of streetlamps. Tears welled in my eyes as I trudged slowly back to the apartment, under the crushing weight of guilt so heavy, I felt like dying. I sensed Roberta knew I'd been with another woman but would never say a thing, or even cast a look at me that said, *You've been unfaithful.*

"Ms. Manning. Did you hear the question? I asked if you and the defendant became more than friends."

The jurors' eyes were cast downward.

"Can you answer the question?" Olson pressed, leaning over the lectern.

"I don't quite know what you mean, sir."

"What don't you understand?"

"What are you trying to imply?"

Olson's eyes locked onto Constance. She stared back at him.

"Do you not understand what I mean by *more than friends*?"

"I fully understand your implication, sir."

"Well, then, Ms. Manning, what is my *implication*?"

"You're asking me if we became intimate."

"Did you?"

"No, not in the way you're implying."

"So you and the defendant never became intimate?"

"That's correct."

My heart slammed so heavily, my body pulsed.

"You never had sexual relations?"

"Objection, Your Honor. Asked and answered," Ben called.

"Sustained."

"That's right. We never had sexual relations." Constance stared fixedly at Olson.

"Ms. Manning," Judge Marin said, "I sustained Mr. Abrams's objection. You didn't have to answer the question."

"Sorry, Your Honor."

The judge nodded at Olson.

"Ms. Manning," said Olson, "did you and the defendant touch each other?"

Ben's chair scraped on the floor as he stood but said nothing.

"Not that way."

"Not *what* way?"

"The way you're implying."

"You mean sexually?"

"No, sir. *You* mean sexually."

Laughter exploded in the courtroom. It seemed like a thunderclap coming from the gallery. Juror number four covered her mouth. Even Marin stifled a smile. Ben sat down, shook his head, and sighed. Maybe Olson's smarmy innuendos would backfire, make him look prurient. I felt a surge of admiration mixed with gratitude for Constance. She could take care of Olson's wiseass insinuations. And, it was clear the jury liked her.

Olson's face turned scarlet. "Well, Ms. Manning," he said, "didn't you and the defendant see each other frequently—aside from meeting at Starbucks every morning?"

"It depends on what you mean by *frequently*, Mr. Olson."

"Well, how often did you see each other?"

"And it wasn't *every* morning," she added. "It was two mornings a week."

"And the defendant visited you at your apartment in the

evenings?"

"Yes. I think three times, maybe four, over those four or five weeks."

"Did you cook dinners for him?"

"I bought takeout."

"And you spent the evenings together?"

"*Part* of those evenings, yes."

"And during that part of the evening, what did you do?"

"We talked about his wife and my husband. Alfred was in a nursing home and—"

"You *talked?*"

"Objection, Your Honor. Argumentative."

"Sustained."

"So you talked," Olson said. "You never had sexual relations?"

"Objection, Your Honor. Asked and answered!"

"Sustained."

"Is there a reason you never had relations?"

Constance sighed. "It wasn't that kind of relationship."

"Wasn't there one evening, Ms. Manning, when the defendant stayed at your apartment for nearly four hours?"

"I don't know, sir. I wasn't timing anything."

"If I tell you the doorman's log says he was at your apartment for four hours, would that be accurate?"

"I have no way of knowing."

"And you were just talking during that entire time?"

"We talked about our situations."

"And none of this was sexual?"

Ben stood and peered questioningly at Marin.

Juror number four's lips twisted. She shook her head. I wanted to jump into the jury box and hug her.

"No, it wasn't sexual."

"Did you and the defendant ever touch each other?"

"I'm not sure what you mean, Mr. Olson."

"Fair enough, Ms. Manning. I'll be more specific. Did you ever touch any part of each other's body?"

"No, not really."

"You never kissed?"

"On the cheek. A friendly kind of thing between two friends."

"No other kissing . . . on the lips?"

"No. It wasn't that kind of relationship. We were in terrible situations. Bill with his wife, and me with my husband. We commiserated."

"Did you want this to become a sexual relationship?"

Constance paused and closed her eyes. She opened them and said, "Eventually, maybe, but not under those circumstances. No."

Olson glanced at the jurors—no doubt, to assess how his theatrics were playing. I felt a swell of hatred for him even greater than earlier in the trial.

Olson paused and then said, "Okay, Ms. Manning. So you claim that you and the defendant never had sexual relations. You claim that—"

"Objection, Your Honor. Argumentative."

"Sustained."

Olson looked down at his papers and then peered up at Constance. He paused for a beat, and said, "Ms. Manning, didn't I just see you look at the defendant?"

Constance hadn't looked at me. It was bullshit.

I remained stone-faced but felt like my skull would explode. I wanted to knee Olson in his groin—hear him gasp in pain, watch him double over and slump to the floor.

Ben's chair nearly toppled as he sprang to his feet. "*Objection,* Your Honor. Objection! Objection!" he shouted. "If Mr. Olson wants to testify about what he thinks *he* saw, let him take the stand."

"The objection is sustained." Marin's eyes bulged as he glared at Olson.

"Your Honor, this is outrageous," Ben roared. "I intend to issue a subpoena to Mr. Olson. I want him to take the stand to testify about what he *thinks* he saw."

"That's absurd, Your Honor," retorted Olson. "He can't—"

"Mr. Abrams—" Marin interrupted.

"Your Honor!" Ben shouted. "Mr. Olson's injected himself as a witness into this case. His behavior is intolerable. He talks about what *he* saw? He's made himself a witness. I demand he take the stand to be cross-examined under oath. It's only fair."

"Mr. Abrams, I'm losing patience. Your objection's been sustained; now *sit* down."

"Your Honor, it's my right to request a curative instruction to the jury. I *insist*."

"Mr. Abrams, I've already told the jury about—"

"Your Honor," Ben interrupted. "Mr. Olson's statement was highly prejudicial, and moreover, it was improper. I demand he be sanctioned. If not that, I need a curative instruction."

"All right, Mr. Abrams," Marin said, turning toward the jury box. "Ladies and gentlemen, Mr. Olson's comment about what he thinks he may have seen is not evidence. You are to disregard it. As I've told you before, the attorneys' questions or statements are not evidence. Only statements from witnesses are considered evidence." Marin turned back to Ben and Olson. His eyes lasered in on Ben.

"Your Honor, may we have a sidebar?" Ben said.

Marin's lips tightened. He closed his eyes. His shoulders rose and then fell as he sighed. He swiveled his chair toward to the jury. "This is a good time for a recess. Please clear the courtroom. I want the stenographer and the parties here, no one else. Ms. Manning," he said, bending toward her, "please wait outside."

Constance nodded and stepped down from the witness stand.

The jurors filed out to the jury room. Juror number four cast a testy glance at Olson. Maybe I had an ally. Did I have any others on the jury? The other panel members were unknowable, but number four seemed to be on my side. The gallery emptied amid a chorus of whispers and murmurs.

Ben, Olson, Pierce, and I stood behind our respective tables. The court stenographer sat at her little desk, the stenographic machine resting between her knees. The courtroom felt overheated, stifling. The radiator at the rear began clanking.

When the jury room door closed, I sat down.

"Mr. Abrams," Marin said, "I'm losing patience with you . . . and you, too, Mr. Olson. I want each of you to act in a lawyerly fashion. I don't like what's going on in this courtroom, and punitive measures will be taken if this keeps up. Is that clear?"

"Yes, Your Honor," both attorneys said in unison.

"Now, I anticipate a motion from Mr. Abrams," Marin said. "We're on the record."

The stenographer's fingers began moving over her machine.

"Your Honor," Ben said. "Mr. Olson's tactics are highly prejudicial. He's trying this case by innuendo and insinuation. He's asking questions without any foundation for the implications he's feeding the jury. He's arguing with this witness, and moreover, he's assuming facts not in evidence. He's even commenting about what he thinks *he* may have seen, as though he's a sworn witness in this trial. This is unheard of. His questions have no probative value. His game is obvious; he's trying to smear my client. He's attempting to paint him as a cheating lothario. It's unfair; it's prejudicial and has no relevance to the issue in question. Your Honor, Mr. Olson's violating my client's right to a fair trial."

"Mr. Olson," Marin said, turning to the prosecutor.

"Your Honor, I'm questioning this witness about her relationship with—"

"He's trying to impugn her and my client, Your Honor," Ben interrupted.

"That's ridiculous, Your Honor," Olson rejoined. "Frankly, the witness's description of their relationship lacks credibility."

"That's for the jury to decide, Mr. Olson," Marin said.

"Yes, Your Honor."

"Besides that, Mr. Olson, she's *your* witness," Marin added. "You subpoenaed her."

"I understand, Your Honor."

"Mr. Abrams," Marin said, turning to Ben.

"Your Honor, Mr. Olson's forcing this bereaved witness to testify for the sole purpose of maligning my client. Mr. Olson's making implication after insinuation, followed by innuendo. It's nothing more than character assassination of my client. I can't, in good conscience, tolerate it, Your Honor. Mr. Olson's tone to the witness is derisive and salacious."

"How dare you comment about my tone!" Olson snapped.

"Mr. *Olson*," Marin shouted, his face reddening, "you will *not* address opposing counsel. All comments are directed to the court, not to each other. No colloquy in my courtroom. Is that clear?"

"Yes, Your Honor."

"Your Honor, if I may," Ben said softly.

My chest felt so tight, I thought my ribs would crush my heart. The trial was heating up—spinning out of control—and my life was on the line.

"Go ahead, Mr. Abrams."

"Your Honor, the Sixth Amendment guarantees a trial by an impartial jury. Mr. Olson's tainted the jury with the force-fed nonsense he's used to smear this witness and my client, and he's probably succeeded with some jurors. I have no doubt that after hearing these innuendos, the jury's no longer impartial."

"Do you think it could lead to a conviction?" Marin's eyebrows rose.

"Yes, Your Honor, I do."

"For *murder*?"

"Mr. Olson's poisoning the jury, Your Honor. My client's being deprived of his constitutional right to a fair trial. This is prosecutorial misconduct."

Olson snorted and shook his head. His hands were clasped in front of him. Ann Pierce's face looked pale.

Hissing began in my ears.

"Mr. Abrams, do you think it rises to that level? Prosecutorial misconduct?"

"Yes, Your Honor. I do."

"Mr. Olson?"

"Your Honor, Mr. Abrams is laying the groundwork for an appeal. And, he's setting the foundation for a lawsuit against the State in the event of a conviction. It's his firm's way of doing business."

"How *dare* you," Ben shouted.

"Mr. *Abrams*," Marin cut in, his eyes flashing. He pressed his hands to the desk and looked like he'd jump to his feet. "I'm giving you the same warning I gave Mr. Olson. No colloquy. You do *not* address each other, only the court. Any more of this nonsense and you'll both be sanctioned. Heavily." Marin's eyes bulged like golf balls. He whipped off his glasses.

"Your Honor," Olson said.

"I've heard *enough*," the judge virtually shouted, raising his palm—a judicial stop sign.

"But, Your Honor, this needs to be said in my own defense."

"Go ahead, Mr. Olson. But make it quick."

"I'm merely trying to establish that despite the defendant's so-called grief, he was seeing another woman, and it's hard to believe this was nonsexual. After all, it's not 1904 and—"

"That's *your* opinion, Mr. Olson," Marin cut in. "The jury doesn't need to hear your moral judgments—about this witness or the defendant. So keep them to yourself. Is that clear?"

Olson said nothing, bowed his head.

"Is that *clear*, Mr. Olson?"

"Yes, Your Honor."

Marin turned to Ben. "Mr. Abrams, Mr. Olson's behavior hasn't risen to the level of prosecutorial misconduct. That's a gross exaggeration, and I won't buy it. I don't like it when lawyers pile on the drama and try to pull the wool over my eyes. If Mr. Olson's behavior constituted misconduct, I'd declare a mistrial. Are you making a motion for a mistrial?"

"Yes, Your Honor."

"The motion's denied."

Marin turned to Olson. His face was still red and his eyes brimmed with anger. "Mr. Olson, I think you're treading close to the line Mr. Abrams is drawing. You're asking this jury to assume facts not in evidence. And your tone of voice leaves much to be desired. And your questioning the witness about what *you* may have seen is out of line. Completely. That kind of drama is uncalled for. Mr. Abrams's assertion that you're impugning this witness is correct, and I might remind you this is a court of *law*—not a daytime talk show or some third-rate movie on the Lifetime network. I'm advising you right now—before this gets out of hand—be careful if you don't want this to escalate to the point where I *will* declare a mistrial. Do you understand?"

"Yes, Your Honor."

"As for the witness's credibility, Mr. Olson, the *jury* will make that determination. I dislike it when lawyers underestimate a jury's collective intelligence. Is that understood?"

"Yes, Your Honor." Olson averted his eyes.

Marin inhaled deeply and slipped on his glasses.

"Now, I want you both to conduct yourselves like professionals. This isn't a boxing match. And don't try to turn my court into a three-ring circus. I won't tolerate it. Don't let the media influence how you try this case. I want you both to act like experienced trial lawyers. Is that clear?"

"Yes, Your Honor," Ben and Olson said.

"Bring the jury back in," Marin said to the court officer. "Let's finish this witness's testimony."

Ben and Olson sat down.

"Did you think there was a chance for a mistrial?" I whispered.

"Like an iceberg's chances in Aruba."

"Then why ask for one?"

"To throw Olson off balance. Remember, Bill. We're at war."

Ms. Manning," Olson said, "when you and the defendant met, you were married, correct?"

"Yes, I was."

The jurors were stone-faced, noncommittal. Juror number four sighed heavily. Yes, she was in my corner.

"And you knew about Mrs. Shaw's condition—the MS, the warfarin, and the steroids."

"Oh, yes."

"Was it your impression that Nora Shaw didn't have long to live?"

"Objection about the witness's impression, and he's leading the witness, Your Honor," Ben said.

"Sustained."

Olson cleared his throat, tapping his pen on the lectern. "Ms. Manning, what was your understanding of Nora's situation?"

"That the MS had been going on for nearly three years. She probably wouldn't live very long."

"Did you see yourself as having a future with the defendant?"

"I don't know. Our lives were up in the air. My husband was in a nursing home with Parkinson's disease. He didn't even recognize me," she added as phlegm collected in her throat.

"Ms. Manning, are you and the defendant seeing each other now?"

"No."

"Why is that?"

"Because of Nora's death, my husband's death . . . and this trial."

"Ms. Manning, did Mr. Shaw ever say he loved you?"

"We weren't involved in that way."

"And he never told you he felt very close to you?"

"I don't recall that."

"You don't *recall* whether or not a man told you he felt close to you?"

"Objection, Your Honor."

"Sustained. Argumentative. Move on, Mr. Olson."

"Ms. Manning, is there any future for you and the defendant?"

"You have no . . ." Constance replied, dabbing her eyes with a finger. "I don't think you have any understanding of the situation, Mr. Olson."

"An understanding of what, Ms. Manning?" Olson moved toward Constance.

Is he trying to torture her? This ruthless bastard's ripping out her heart.

"You have no idea what it's like to love someone who's dying slowly, right before your eyes," Constance said. Her lips began quivering.

Olson crossed his arms. "Why don't you tell us what it's like, Ms. Manning?"

The jurors sat rigidly, some focused on Constance; others peered down at their hands.

My shoulders ached with tension. I didn't know how much longer I could sit through this.

Constance looked directly at the jury. "It's not living. It's merely existing. You watch someone you love waste away and suffer. It's excruciating," she said, softly.

My heart beat erratically. My insides trembled.

Olson waited, standing halfway between the lectern and the

witness box.

"You know they're going to die," Constance went on, "but you don't know when. It happens day by day, hour by hour. Every day is a step closer to death. And your life together will be over." Tears formed at the corners of her eyes.

Some jurors sniffled. Juror number four dabbed at her eyes.

"It's not the same as a heart attack or an accident. That's a shock, and your world changes suddenly. But with Parkinson's or MS, it's like water dripping. It's torture. And it does something to you. Something changes . . ." Her voice trailed off. Tears ran down her cheeks.

"What changes, Ms. Manning?" Olson asked. His voice softened.

"It's as though some part of you dies but another part wants to live."

Constance pulled a tissue from her purse and pressed it to her eyes. "You begin making peace with it . . . watching someone you love wither away," she said, her voice nasal. "You even begin to welcome it, just to relieve the suffering. I guess the mind has a way of coming to terms with it. You have to go on living."

"So, Ms. Manning, in coming to terms with it, to let life go on, are you saying you hope for the loved one to die?"

"In a way, yes, you do."

"Did Mr. Shaw tell you he felt that way?"

"I'm speaking for myself, Mr. Olson. I can't speak for him."

"Did he say he could see himself going on after Nora died?"

"I don't know if he'd made peace with Nora's situation."

"Meaning what, Ms. Manning?"

"Oh, Mr. Olson, these are difficult things to sort out," Constance looked like she was shivering.

My blood hummed.

"Sure, they're difficult. But didn't you think there would be a future for you together?"

"Objection, Your Honor."

"Your Honor, I'm establishing motive for the defendant," Olson said. "This woman is waiting in the wings, and I'm asking if—"

"*Objection!*" Ben cried, shooting to his feet. "This is outrageous, Your Honor. This is absolutely—"

"Sit *down,* Mr. Abrams!" Marin glared at the prosecutor. "Mr. Olson, no speechifying. No preambles."

"Yes, Your Honor." Olson turned to Constance. "Ms. Manning, how did you envision your future?"

"I don't know," she said as she sniffled.

Marin stared down from the bench at Olson. His eyes were on fire. The judicial message was clear: no more questions would be put to this witness.

Someone in the gallery coughed. A juror cleared her throat. The radiator hissed.

"Do you have any more questions for this witness, Mr. Olson?" asked Marin.

"No, Your Honor."

"We'll take a fifteen-minute recess."

"**Y**our witness, Mr. Abrams," Judge Marin intoned.

"Ms. Manning, did Bill ever express his feelings about his situation?"

"Yes, many times," she replied, nodding.

"What did he say?"

"Well, he was in terrible shape, emotionally."

"Objection, Your Honor. She's not a psychiatrist," said Olson.

"I'll allow it," Marin said. "Obviously, it's from a layperson's viewpoint."

"How was he in terrible shape?" Ben asked.

"He was surrounded by illness twenty-four hours a day. He needed to talk to someone about his situation. He was thinking about seeing a psychiatrist. Someone he and Nora once saw together."

"What else did he tell you?"

If only they would bury me next to Nora. At least this would end. It would all be over. There would be darkness, nothingness.

"He felt devastated. We talked about how terribly sad we felt. We were both trapped in horrible situations."

I swallowed hard. *Trapped? A bad word to use in this trial.*

Ben paused for what seemed a long time. I wondered how he would handle Constance's using that word.

"Ms. Manning, you said you felt trapped in a horrible situation. Just so the jury understands it, what do you mean by *trapped*?"

"There's no cure for these diseases. There was no hope that Alfred or Nora would ever get better. It would only go downhill," Constance said as her voice cracked.

"Ms. Manning, do you need a moment to compose yourself?"

"No," she said, sniffling. "I'm okay."

Ben waited a beat.

"So, Ms. Manning, was love an issue between you and Bill Shaw?"

"No. It would've been misplaced."

"Thank you, Ms. Manning. I have no further questions, Your Honor."

"**M**r. Olson, any redirect?"

Olson was at the lectern. "But, Ms. Manning, despite all these feelings, the defendant kept seeing you?"

"We were clinging to each other."

"We understand, Ms. Manning. You said the defendant felt devastated. Correct?"

"Yes." Constance's shoulders were bunched with tension.

"And you both felt trapped. The word you used was *trapped,* correct?"

"Yes. I know I felt—"

"And, Ms. Manning, while you discussed feeling *trapped*, did you and the defendant agree it would be better if your husband and Nora both died?"

Constance blanched. Her chest heaved, and she closed her eyes.

"Ms. Manning? Did you hear the question?"

She nodded.

"Well?"

"It's a perfectly normal feeling, sir."

"What's a perfectly normal feeling, Ms. Manning?"

"To wish it would end."

"Is that what you felt in relation to your husband?"

"Sometimes, yes."

"And Mr. Shaw?"

"What about him?"

"Did he say it would be better if Nora died?"

My body felt like steel cables were stretching it.

"Ms. Manning?"

She remained silent. I closed my eyes, waiting.

"Remember, Ms. Manning, you're under oath."

She swallowed and kept silent.

"Ms. Manning, I'll ask you again. While he was feeling trapped and devastated, did the defendant ever say it would be better if Nora died?"

Constance looked down and nodded—or maybe it was simply her head shaking from the agony of the moment—and a second later, her head drooped to her chest. Something inside her collapsed inward as though she'd been stabbed in the chest.

"Ms. Manning, please answer the question. Did Mr. Shaw ever say it would be better if Nora died?"

My chest felt like a python was coiled around me.

"Yes, he did," she mumbled.

"He said it would be better if Nora died?"

She nodded.

I felt the moment sliding quickly toward catastrophe.

"Please note for the record that the witness nodded an affirmative response," Olson said.

Murmuring surged through the courtroom. It sounded like a sea swell. I tried staring straight ahead but felt the jurors' eyes on me.

"No further questions, Your Honor," Olson said. He turned and walked back to the prosecution table.

Constance sat in the witness chair. She looked frozen in place.

A jangling sensation coursed through me, shock-like in intensity. The room looked bleached; it swirled and the chandeliers seemed to sway.

An insect-like drone in the gallery continued.

Judge Marin pounded his gavel, trying to regain control of the proceedings.

Ben was at the lectern before Olson took his seat at the prosecution table. "Ms. Manning, did Bill actually say he wanted Nora to die?"

"No," she half whispered. "We just . . . We both knew what would happen, and I guess . . . I think we just wanted it to be over. That's all."

"Wanted it to be over? Meaning what?"

"It was inevitable. Alfred and Nora were at death's doorstep. It was just terrible waiting for the hammer to drop. It was unbearable."

"Thank you. I have nothing more, Your Honor."

Ben, Charlie, and I sat at the conference room table.

"I wish the jury hadn't heard Constance say that," Ben murmured, toying with a pen. "This thing about feeling *trapped* and *devastated . . .* and saying it would be better if Nora died."

"You think it sounded like I'd commit murder?" I asked, my hands going weak.

"Who knows what the jury'll conclude?" Ben said, shaking his head.

"She looked like she was trying to protect me."

"My guess is the jury understood what she was saying," Charlie offered.

Ben seemed distracted. He pinched the bridge of his nose. "I'm still wondering why Olson pushed her about your saying you loved her. Olson's got a strategy."

"Ben, I don't see how I get out of this if I don't take the stand."

"It can be very dangerous."

"But if I don't testify, it'll look like I'm hiding something. That's what *I'd* think if I were on the jury."

"You don't have to prove your innocence. Olson's got to prove your guilt—beyond a reasonable doubt. It's his burden, not yours."

"*Reasonable doubt?* What the hell is that anyway?"

"It's your constitutional right not to testify."

"Yeah, sure, hide behind the Fifth Amendment and look guilty as hell."

"We can't structure a defense on worry."

"How do I *not* take the stand?"

"We'll talk about it later, not now. Olson's waiting to pounce on something. I don't know what it is, but if you take the stand, we might find out. And if there's one thing any trial attorney hates, it's a surprise."

"What can he pull? I *have* to testify."

"Olson would love that. He'd get to cross you. Believe me, Bill. I know the danger. I was a prosecutor, and it's a DA's dream to have a defendant on the stand. Olson'll pepper you with a million questions. He'll needle you, get under your skin, and get you to say things you shouldn't. He'll ask unanswerable questions—crap designed to trap you. He'll ask closed-ended questions that can only be answered with a yes or a no. You won't get a chance to explain anything. He'll bring up everything—any little glitch in your life. Now or in the past. And believe me, he has book on you. Plenty of book. And he'll keep you there for hours—for a day or two—just to wear you down and get you to say things you'd never want in front of a jury. It'll be pure character assassination."

"I have to testify."

"C'mon. You know that's a bad move. How many trials did you cover for the *Post*? You'll be like a duck at a shooting gallery. The truth doesn't necessarily win in court."

"If I don't testify, the jury'll think I killed Nora."

My heart felt like a vise was squeezing it. I realized how Olson had me cornered.

"We have time to decide," Ben said. "Meanwhile, I've gotta figure out what Olson's up to."

Chapter 27

"How long have you known the defendant, Ms. Scott?" Olson asked.

"We met years ago, while Nora and I were on *The Burning World*," Gina replied with a dewy-eyed glance at the jurors. "I knew Nora even before she met Bill."

I was certain Gina's being on the soaps gave her a certain cachet with the jury. After all, she was attractive and well known, and this was her forte—acting in front of an audience. And this one—a group of conscripted jurors—seemed very receptive.

How much of our sickly tangled history together would Gina divulge?

There was that time at a party—a few months before Nora was diagnosed with MS. I'd had far too much to drink. I'd staggered—nearly poured myself—into the bedroom to retrieve our coats before Nora and I went home.

In the darkened room, searching for our jackets while half-clobbered on scotch, I noticed a woman's silhouette at the door. It barely registered as I fumbled drunkenly through the pile of clothing. Someone approached. Before I could turn, the woman encircled my waist and began kissing the nape of my neck. Still in her embrace, I turned. It was Gina. There was only a moment's hesitation before I was totally aroused. We began to kiss, passionately. My hands massaged her breasts and then worked their way down to her hips. I lifted her skirt. She wasn't wearing panties.

My fingers began exploring the warm wetness between her legs. Gina moaned deeply as she unzipped my jeans.

I can't know how far it would have gone, but a chorus of voices snapped us back from the brink. We pulled apart, trying to appear as if nothing had happened. A group of partygoers entered the darkened bedroom, searching for their coats.

Though I'd like to deny it, I craved Gina's body. I was shocked by the rush of arousal, the pure lust I'd felt in those moments. Something primal had surfaced, and I'd acted on it. Later that night, lying in bed as Nora slept, I knew I'd betrayed her. I conceded to myself that a seedy and atavistic being lurked within me. Was I no more than an animal—instinctual, driven by ugly impulses and hormonal surges? I knew the only way to avoid succumbing to temptation was to distance myself from Gina.

Sitting at the defense table, I felt my body begin to pulse. What damning secrets had Olson unearthed to present to the jury?

Gina wore a soft jersey knit dress with cap sleeves and a swingy, angled hem. As she walked to the stand, heat radiated through my face. Ben sat rigidly to my right.

I'd first met Gina and her then-husband, Martin, years earlier, at Monte's Trattoria on MacDougal Street in the Village. It was clear at the very first encounter: some strange static streamed between Gina and me.

"How do you dream up these characters in your novels?" Gina asked.

"In a way, I have to feel *I'm* the character."

"Do you actually *imagine* you're a stalker, a murderer?"

"I try seeing things through their eyes."

"Well, as actors, we *become* that person. Right, Nora?"

"I guess that's why it's called *acting*," I said. "You have to *act* the part and *make* it happen. I create the part."

"Are you saying acting's an *inferior* art?" Gina asked, her voice edgy, shrill.

"Not at all . . ."

I'd been snared in a social bear trap.

"*Yes*, you are. *I create the part.* You're putting acting down by inference."

"I—"

"No. There's something smugly superior in your false modesty."

"Gina," Nora interjected, "I think you're reading far too much into Bill's words."

"Am I? You know, Nora, Bill's success depends on you. Don't you resent what he said?"

As I sat in the restaurant that evening, I had the feeling Gina's animosity might someday come back to bite me. Yet, all the while, I'd been aroused by her raw sexuality.

Now, that day was at hand; and despite everything, I felt a visceral stirring, as she sat before me in the witness box.

"Can you tell us what you observed about the defendant and Nora?" Olson asked.

"They were very close," Gina said. "When Nora stopped acting, she did cosmetic commercials, but her primary job was working on Bill's manuscripts."

"Over time, what, if any, changes did you notice?"

"Beginning a few years ago, Bill became angry with Nora. When she felt weak or dizzy—before they diagnosed the MS—he thought it was all in her mind. Once, we were at a restaurant in SoHo and Nora spilled some wine. Bill stormed out of the place."

It was at the lowest point of our marriage, only weeks before the separation. And now this: Gina rehashing a brutishly insensitive moment in my life—one I've always regretted. The night in that restaurant will always be with me. But, my God, you could selectively take a moment from anyone's life and paint that person as an insensitive lout, a boor, an ogre. My teeth clenched with rage. I was being pilloried.

"And, as Nora's condition worsened?" Olson asked.

"When I'd visit Nora, Bill was never at home."

"Did you know where he was?"

After that episode in the bedroom—except for one other time—I made myself scarce whenever Gina visited Nora. She'd begun calling me on my cell phone. She was secretive—never used the landline—and would leave voice mail messages boiling down to the mantra: "Bill, why not start seeing someone? Your life's circling the drain."

Listening to those messages filled me with revulsion mixed with arousal. I wanted desperately to avoid her; yet, the very sound of Gina's voice could get me hard.

There was that other time, just before Nora's MS diagnosis. We were at a gathering in an apartment on Riverside Drive. Nora stumbled, nearly fell. She clutched my arm. "I feel dizzy," she murmured. She looked pale and leaned against the wall. "Oh, Bill, please help me to the bathroom."

Standing near the closed bathroom door, I heard Nora retching. I retrieved our coats from the bedroom and returned to the hallway. Standing there, feeling sorry for myself because another good time was being cut short by what I thought was Nora's neurotic behavior, I heard that familiar, sultry voice say "Leaving now?" Gina suddenly appeared at my side.

My heart felt like it would burst through my chest.

"Nora's not feeling well." My body tightened.

"Again?" Gina's eyes widened.

She pressed against me. "Put her in a taxi and stay a while," she whispered.

"I—I don't think so," I stammered. My head swam from too much wine. I was sinking into a swamp of remorse and confusion about Nora and our life together.

In the semidarkened foyer between the bedroom and

bathroom doors, with the sound of Rosemary Clooney crooning "Tenderly" on the sound system, Gina's face became a blur as our lips met. We kissed hungrily. The taste of wine on her tongue mixed intoxicatingly with a deep, private scent she exuded.

A stab of arousal pierced me like white heat. My heart pounded through my breastbone, and my sexual craving for Gina was volcanic. I could no longer fool myself into believing I was such a loyal and good husband. I wanted to fuck Gina. I'd wanted to for a long time. I didn't like her one bit. She was mean-spirited and manipulative, but her raw sexuality tugged powerfully at me, and there in the hallway, it overpowered me once more.

Gina withdrew quickly and then looked up at me—wide-eyed, her gamin face frozen in anticipation. I was stunned, and so aroused, my knees went weak. I wanted to make love to her—to sink into her flesh and forget everything.

"Call me," Gina whispered, and then was gone, leaving me guilt-ridden with desire.

And all the while, Nora retched behind the closed door.

Olson asked Gina, "What did Nora tell you about the defendant when you visited her?"

"That Bill was having dinner with a friend."

"Did Nora say anything about that?"

"She thought Bill had a girlfriend, someone on the faculty at the New School."

Ben stood as though he was about to object, but instead, shook his head and said nothing.

I couldn't believe Nora said that. After the diagnosis, I'd wanted to spend every moment I could with her. I ran straight home from the New School any night I was teaching, other than when I knew Gina would be visiting. On those evenings, I'd pay Roberta extra to stay late. I'd call Roberta to make sure Gina was gone before I returned. God, this bitch was crucifying me. She and Olson must have prepped for hours. They were making me look like a self-centered bastard with no scruples.

"But you had to know the kind of person Nora was," Gina said, glancing at the jury.

"Know what?" Olson asked.

"She was very understanding. She said she could accept Bill's having a girlfriend since she no longer could meet his needs. Which was very striking . . ."

"What was striking about it?"

"Because he wasn't sympathetic to her."

"*Objection*," Ben called. "Speculation."

"Sustained."

Olson paused and sifted through his notes.

"Ms. Scott, when you visited with Nora, what did you notice?"

"She could still enjoy things. I brought her audiobooks. And she listened to music."

"And what did she tell you?"

"She wanted to live."

"Ms. Scott, you said the defendant taught at the New School. What did he teach?"

"A course called Creating Characters in Fiction."

"And what did he tell you about creating characters in his novels?"

"That when he creates characters—either a stalker or a serial killer—he gets inside the character's head. He would assume the character's identity, enter into his mind. He'd tell his students to use their imaginations, temporarily lose their identities. *Become the character*. That's what he'd say."

"Did he say anything else?"

"He compared writing to acting. He said the art of acting and the art of writing are similar. Both demand that we lose ourselves in the characters."

"Ms. Scott, are you saying he would assume the identity of a killer?"

"*Objection!*" Ben shouted.

"I'll allow it," Marin said. "We understand the witness is talking about creating fiction, not fact."

"Yes," answered Gina. "Bill would assume that identity." Gina's lips curled into a semismile. She was enjoying her stint on the witness stand. It was pure performance.

"Thank you, Ms. Scott. I have nothing further."

Disgust buzzed through my bloodstream. It was so powerful, for the first time in my life I knew what it was to feel complete hatred for another person. Enough hatred to want to kill.

"**M**s. Scott, how did you become involved in this case?" Ben asked.

"When I heard about the indictment, I called the DA's office."

Murmuring rose from the gallery. Marin looked up sternly; the courtroom quieted.

"Why did you come forward?"

"I felt I owed it to Nora," she said in a honeyed voice.

Nausea sloshed through me.

"What did you owe her?"

"I felt it was important to put Bill and Nora's relationship in context."

"You mean Bill's frustration with her before the diagnosis of MS?"

"Yes. I guess so."

I wondered how the jurors perceived Gina. She had an actor's ability to suck an audience into her drama. But glancing at the jurors told me nothing; they were poker-faced, a deadpan group.

"Now, Ms. Scott, you talked about Bill's fictional characters— that he enters into the characters, correct?"

"Yes."

"Are you implying that Bill *becomes* those characters?"

"No."

"So, you were talking about Bill Shaw's use of *imagination,* correct?"

"Yes."

"Now, Ms. Scott, you're an actor, correct?" Ben stepped toward the witness stand.

"Yes."

"And when you're playing a part, don't you in essence *become* that character?"

"Yes. I enter into the role," Gina said, suffocating a smirk.

"And in playing that part, do you actually *become* that person?"

"Of course not."

"So, does Bill's losing himself in the creative process make him a *killer*?"

"No, of course not," she said with pseudo-earnestness.

"And by telling the jury about Mr. Shaw's entering into his characters' minds, Ms. Scott, what *debt* to Nora Shaw did you feel you were satisfying?"

"I don't understand your question, sir."

"Well, you said you came forward because you felt you owed it to Nora. Yes?"

"Yes."

"And what was it that you *owed* Nora by describing Bill's creating fictional characters?"

"I still don't understand your question." She blinked repeatedly. *How fucking disingenuous can you get, Gina?*

The courtroom was eerily quiet. My hands were clasped so tightly on the defense table my knuckles felt like they would snap.

Ben shook his head, signaling to the jury he found Gina's response duplicitous.

"Okay, Ms. Scott, let's go on to something else. Nora told you that she thought Bill had a girlfriend, right?"

"Yes."

"Did she say she had proof of that?"

"No."

"Did she share anything that would lend credence to such a belief?"

"No."

Ben nodded and began pacing back and forth in front of the jury box.

"Now, you visited Nora in the evenings?"

"Yes."

"And Bill was never there, correct?"

"Yes."

"Ever wonder why?"

"I thought about it."

"What did you think?"

"It seemed strange. He was always out."

"You mean on the nights *you* visited, right?"

"Yes. I don't know about other evenings."

"Did you think he was avoiding *you*?"

"I suppose it's possible." Gina canted her head.

"Ever wonder why?"

"No. Not really."

"And how late did you stay?"

"Usually till around ten."

Some jurors leaned forward. They were listening intently, especially juror number four.

"Why so late?"

"No particular reason," she said with an indifferent shrug.

"Were you waiting for Bill to get home?"

"Of course not." A V-shaped crease formed between her eyebrows.

Ben opened a manila folder at the lectern.

Gina's eyes narrowed.

Blood coursed in my ears. I thought back to the two episodes at the parties and the phone calls.

Please, Ben, don't go too far with her. She's a viper.

"Now, Ms. Scott, did you ever call Bill on his cell phone?"

"I'm sure I did."

"Why not on the landline?"

"It would disturb Nora's sleep. So I called Bill's cell to make arrangements to visit."

"Did you call him more than once?"

"Oh, I'm sure I did."

"Didn't you always call Bill in the evenings?"

She peered toward the ceiling as though trying to recall.

"I may have."

"Ms. Scott, isn't it true you told Bill that he had too much going for him to waste his life taking care of Nora?"

Olson stood up as though he would object.

"Mr. Abrams," Gina said in a cloying voice, "My life was very busy then. I'd just gone through a divorce. I don't remember every call I made. But I would *never* say anything like that."

"Divorce, Ms. Scott? So you were going to be single and available?"

"Objection. Speculation," Olson called.

"Sustained."

Ben peered down at the folder again.

Gina blinked repeatedly.

"Ms. Scott, I have Bill's cell phone records. We can go through the dates and times of every call you made over the year before Nora died."

"The People will stipulate the record speaks for itself," Olson said.

"Thank you, Mr. Olson," Ben said. "Now, Ms. Scott, the record shows you called Bill *seventeen* times over the ten months before Nora died. Do you agree?"

I closed my eyes, hoping Ben would nail her. His investigator had looked deeply into her life. There was a riptide of information: her three divorces, her many affairs, her showing up on the set drunk or hungover, her tumultuous relationships with other cast members—men and women. But Ben couldn't chance being viewed as badgering or belittling the witness.

"The telephone record says whatever it does," Gina replied. "I've already explained that I didn't want to disturb Nora, so I called Bill's cell to arrange visits. I don't think it requires any further explanation, Mr. Abrams."

"Ms. Scott, didn't you tell Bill that life was too short for him to spend it taking care of an invalid?"

Olson sat down and sighed.

"Ms. Scott? Didn't you tell Bill that?"

"I would *never* refer to Nora that way," she said as her face reddened. "And I never did. That's a gross mistruth."

"How *did* you refer to her?"

Gina shook her head. "Nora was my friend. We worked together. Nora was a dear friend who'd become sick and was probably dying. That's all, Mr. Abrams."

"Ms. Scott, didn't you tell Bill his life was 'circling the drain'?"

"That's not true."

Juror number four's eyes narrowed.

"Weren't those your exact words, Ms. Scott—'circling the drain'?"

"That's utterly false."

Olson looked like he'd spring to his feet.

"Ms. Scott, isn't it true that at a party, you kissed Bill and asked him to call you?"

I held my breath, terrified of what Gina might say. Ben was opening the door. It was a huge mistake not to have told him the whole truth about that night in the bedroom.

"Objection," Olson called. "No foundation, Your Honor."

"Sustained."

"I withdraw the question, Your Honor."

"Move on, Mr. Abrams," Marin said, scowling.

I waited for the next question. What might Ben ask that could unleash a torrent of revelations?

"Now, Ms. Scott, you said you came forward because you wanted to put Bill and Nora's relationship into 'context,' didn't you?"

"Yes," Gina said, rearranging herself in the witness chair.

"How did mentioning Bill's New School course and talking about his imagination put Bill and Nora's relationship into its context?"

"I'm not sure I understand your question."

"Fine, Ms. Scott. I'll rephrase it. What does Bill's method of creating fictional characters have to do with his relationship with Nora?"

"I—I don't really know how to answer that."

That's right, Gina, play dumb. Just pretend you're the innocent little ingénue you play so well.

"It has nothing to do with their relationship, correct?"

"I guess . . . I don't really know."

"Does it have anything to do with Nora's death?"

"I—I don't know. I can't answer that either, sir."

"That's fine, Ms. Scott. One more question."

The jurors' eyes flitted between Ben and Gina. Juror number four glared at Gina.

"Isn't it true, Ms. Scott, that you have a personal vendetta against Bill because he spurned your advances one night at a party and then avoided you completely?"

Without knowing it, Ben threw Gina the payoff pitch. Yes, Ben wanted to plant that seed, but if Gina told the jury about what really happened in the bedroom, it would be a home run for Olson.

"Objection, Your Honor," Olson cried.

"Sustained."

Thank you, Olson. And thank you, Marin.

"Thank you, Ms. Scott. I have nothing further."

Marin turned to the prosecutor. "Any redirect, Mr. Olson?"

"No, Your Honor."

Olson obviously decided nothing else from Gina would benefit his case.

As Gina passed by the defense table on her way out of the courtroom, I breathed deeply, hoping to inhale her essence.

Chapter 28

Sitting at my desk, I thought about Gina's testimony. I was the luckiest bastard alive that she never got the chance to crucify me. But, did any of the jurors believe her bullshit that I was capable of murdering my wife because I wrote about fictional killers? Juror number four could barely disguise her distaste for Gina, but what about the rest of them?

And, Olson's strategy was becoming very clear: he was using a legal trowel—setting one block on top of another, cementing them in place . . . Sinclair, Lee, Constance, and then Gina.

He would try for a conviction by any means possible: misdirection, insinuation, character assassination, and even using my fiction to paint a villainous picture to sway the jury.

Olson's next witness would be the IT guy who'd gone through my computer and read my half-completed novel, *Assassin's Lullaby,* which would be an exhibit.

Ben's words rang chillingly true: a trial is a *story*—a goal-directed narration—in this case, a dramatic tale told by the prosecutor.

Feeling half-slammed by a few Johnnie Blacks, I decided to look at *Assassin's Lullaby.* My God, my own words—fictional creations—were going to be used against me.

The cops had never taken my laptop. They'd simply extracted the information using some sort of device—right in the apartment.

I realized I'd last looked at *Assassin's Lullaby* when Nora was alive. It had been more than six months since I buried her.

As Nora lay dying, I tried keeping my promise: I'd written each morning, trying to enter some hazy zone of fantasy, to immerse myself in the realm of imagination. The story seemed to have materialized from some strange realm outside myself.

I can't even go back and re-create the moment the story began forming.

Somehow, Killian, my main character, began taking shape. I remembered feeling like an observer, not his creator. And by some strange process, the story took on a life of its own.

After booting up the laptop, I opened the script and scrolled down the pages.

> Killian is escorted to the fat man's table. The fat man is part of the Odessa Gang out of Brooklyn, a murderous sect of the Russian Bratva.
>
> "I understand you have a job," Killian says.
>
> "This one . . . different. Her name—Irena. Her brother—dead now—was doing laundry with money." The fat man chortles. "He maybe told sister. So we took care of him. This Irena, she could know too much. Maybe she have accident, too . . . Mr. Green."
>
> "If she's innocent, I won't do it . . ."
>
> "If she knows laundry business, you make accident. Here is information on Irena Sakarov." A pause. "You take job?"
>
> "I'll call you."

Nora's vision was too blurred for her to read. We could no longer act out the dialogue. And I'd never read a single word of *Assassin's Lullaby* to her. That realization tore at my heart, and looking at the script, my eyes brimmed with tears.

I scrolled down, forty pages ahead.

Killian was a highly trained former Army Ranger. He'd left the reservation—gone rogue. He'd learned dozens of killing techniques in Special Forces.

When it came to love, Killian's life was far different from mine: no intimacy, no attachments. Killian lived life alone in the shadows.

As for meeting Irena: the fat man had set it up. It would happen at a party.

Killian agonized over whether to take the job. Though he was an assassin, he had a heart. But Killian sensed Irena's death was inevitable.

My novels were populated with beautiful women. They were always variations of Nora: exquisite ethnic types—Spanish, Ukrainian, or Swedish—all some version of Nora blended with fantasy.

In the novels, the women were fiction playing off life.

My life. And, Nora's, too.

After all, Killian met Irena at a party.

Now I could see it: Irena was part Nora—the Polish half. She had Slavic features: high cheekbones and incredibly deep eyes. She laughed just as Nora had the night we met. I'd used half of Nora's bloodlines in describing Irena.

Irena was a hairdresser from Russia who had been in New York only one year. She mentioned her brother getting her an apartment. I recalled Lee getting the apartment for Nora and me.

It was strange how fiction and life could blend. I knew sometimes one could step through the creative mirror so the line between fiction and fact disappeared.

Would Killian take the job? Would he dally with the target and risk exposure?

The story had veered in an unplanned direction. That often happened in my novels. Just the way events occur in life.

Soon after meeting at the party, Killian and Irena got together in a coffee shop. She told him that in Russia—or was it Poland?—she'd acted in a soap opera. But in America, her English was too poor for an acting career.

Her nearness is exhilarating. Her smile and the sheen of her lips kindle Killian's excitement. "Is there a man in your life?" he asks.

"There was only brother," she replies, near tears.

"Was?" he asks, hating his own deception.

"Maxim work at bank. For crazy boss. Maxim call me, very upset. I run to see him. When I get there, Maxim is on ground with blanket. Police say he jump from window." She's trembling.

So . . . the mob launched him from a window . . . Killian thinks, reaching for her hand.

For the first time in his life, Killian wants to be part of something outside himself. He wants to love Irena.

On the street, she opens her purse and hands him a card: "Effie's Hair Salon." Where she works.

A sedan pulls up.

"Hello, Sasha," Irena calls to the woman driver.

"My boss . . . is like mother to me." Irena turns to Killian, kisses his lips, and then slips into the car.

He closes the door, savoring her taste.

Killian's story had been dormant since Nora's death. It was nothing more than a string of words coming from somewhere deep within me. It had stopped flowing, was suspended.

My gift to Nora was never completed.

It was stillborn.

Chapter 29

"The People call Cedric Chang."

Chang was a slim Chinese-American man in his early thirties. He wore plastic-rimmed glasses, a blue suit with a white shirt, and a narrow, black cloth tie. His short black hair glistened with gel.

By the time Olson went through Chang's background, it was clear that as an IT specialist for Data-Pursuit, Chang was an expert in identifying, extracting, and preserving computer data. He could reconstruct a computer's digital trail even after it had been defragmented or reformatted. He was an Internet bloodhound.

I felt resigned to what was coming—a digital indictment based on my research and writings.

"Now, Mr. Chang, am I correct," Olson asked, "you went with the police to the defendant's apartment and extracted the data from his laptop?"

"Yes."

"Why didn't you seize the computer?"

"There was no need to. I used a Computer Online Forensic Evidence Extractor."

"Please tell the jury what that is."

"We call it COFEE. It's a modified flash drive for the extraction of data from any computer. You just plug it into a USB port and gather all the digital evidence. It lets us decrypt passwords, search a computer's Internet activity, and analyze the data. Since it's inserted while the computer's still connected to the Internet, we can get anything stored in volatile memory, which could be lost if the computer's shut down and taken to a lab."

"And after you inserted the COFEE device into the defendant's computer, what was done with it?"

"It was brought directly to police headquarters."

"And then?"

"It was turned over to the detectives. They signed for it and stored it in the evidence room."

Ben stood. "The defense stipulates that the chain of evidence is intact."

"So stipulated," said Marin.

"Mr. Chang," Olson continued, "Please direct your attention to the printout of files extracted from the defendant's computer."

At Olson's request, Chang began reading the file to the jury. It listed the websites I'd visited over the year before Nora's death. I'd surfed hundreds of sites, including the most mundane— *Newsweek*, the *New York Post,* eBay, *Roget's Thesaurus, Refdesk,* and others. The reading took twenty minutes.

"Mr. Chang," Olson asked, "what other sites did the defendant visit?"

"There were sites about the Mafia and the Russian mob," Chang said. "There were sites about crime. There was one called 'How to Commit a Contract Killing' and another called 'Ten Tips to Committing the Perfect Murder.'"

It was heart-stopping testimony. I could feel the jurors' eyes on me.

Murmuring from the gallery sounded poisonous to my ears. Yes, sitting either in Starbucks or at the library, I'd gone to plenty of websites to research the novel. Olson had obviously spent plenty of time with Chang, going over the computer files. God, it looked bad.

The jurors were statue-still. It was clear Chang was an honest witness: he had no dog in the fight but was merely recounting what he'd found on my computer.

"What did this site about committing the perfect murder describe?" Olson asked.

"It told how murder can be made to look like a medical condition—a heart attack or stroke—so it looks like the victim died from natural causes. It would be hard to detect as a killing."

I had a sinking feeling. Two jurors glanced at me, juror number eleven shook her head, and another looked appalled. I was chin-deep in trouble; my research was nudging me toward conviction.

"Mr. Chang, what other websites were visited?"

"There were some dealing with poisons."

In a moment of chilling clarity, I realized Chang had scanned every single file, and Olson would waltz him through my digital trail. Chang spoke about one site that described using succinylcholine—SUX, as it was termed—to paralyze the victim's muscles. "It leaves only minute traces in the victim's blood and would be difficult to find at autopsy," said Chang. "Another method described giving an overdose of potassium chloride to stop the heart."

I'd surfed through these websites only a few months before Nora died. All to provide Killian with ways to commit murder. I was sliding toward conviction—step by damning step. Olson was cherry-picking—selectively dipping into a palette of evidence, painting the picture he wanted the jury to see.

And now, this horrifying distortion: my novel-in-progress was being used to convict me of murdering Nora. Killian—my hit man, my antihero—was pointing his fictional finger at me. He was being used to assassinate—not Irena, but my own character in a court of law.

Killian's story and my life were merging. The creator and his creation were coming together, like Dr. Jekyll and Mr. Hyde.

Olson's strategy was chillingly clear: persuade the jury to see me as a fiendish, unfaithful husband who used his imagination to kill his wife. Now, the earlier testimony from Sinclair, Lee, Constance, and Gina made perfect demonstrative sense. They were the building blocks, stepping-stones.

All leading to Chang's testimony and ultimately, to the inevitable conclusion that I was a wife beater and killer—a cold-blooded assassin. All confirmed by my computer's surfing history.

More circumstantial evidence . . . negative inferences—using the known to divine the unknown—to confirm murder. Tracks in the snow.

"What other poisons were researched by the defendant?" Olson asked, glancing at the jurors, gauging the impact of Chang's testimony.

"They were mostly organic poisons."

"What are *organic* poisons? According to the websites?"

"Objection, Your Honor," Ben called. "The witness is not a chemist or toxicologist."

"I'm only asking him to describe what the sites said," Olson shot back. "I'm not asking for his opinion. Just what he saw and read."

"The objection is overruled."

"Please, Mr. Chang, describe what the sites said about organic poisons," Olson repeated.

"They're described as poisons that blend with the body's natural substances, making them very hard to detect at autopsy."

"Did the sites give examples of this kind of poisoning?"

"There's a description of using shellfish toxin as a way of killing."

"What does it describe?"

"Objection. Irrelevant," called Ben.

"Overruled."

My stomach jumped up to my chest. This could be it: I'd slide quickly down the chute—straight to Attica, Fishkill, or Sing Sing, the hellhole in Ossining, New York.

"Please go on, Mr. Chang," Olson said. "What did the site describe about shellfish toxin?"

"It shuts down the nervous system. It can be slipped into seafood. It's undetectable. An autopsy will conclude the victim died of food poisoning after eating tainted shellfish."

Yes, Killian used that method on two Bronx-based Albanian mobsters who were into human trafficking, bringing in Eastern European girls, enslaving them as prostitutes. The Albanians had to be eliminated because they were competing with the Bratva.

A juror in the back row—alternate juror one—glared at me. My scalp tightened as my heart pounded, ramping up to warp speed.

"Now, Mr. Chang, did the defendant go to websites about things other than poisons?"

"Yes, there were websites dealing with drugs."

"Which ones were visited most extensively?"

"There were sites about warfarin, digitalis, prednisone, Lopressor, and intravenous warfarin."

The jurors looked frozen; some nodded their heads. One guy's eyes swiveled toward me and then darted back to Chang.

"What, if anything, did the websites say about using prescription medication to kill?"

"There were descriptions of using insulin to make a killing look like an accidental overdose in a diabetic. There was another about digitalis, a heart medicine. It can be used to make a death look like an accidental overdose."

Killian used it on a seventy-four-year-old Russian syndicate boss, a leader of a sect competing against the one that hired him. The old man's heart gave out while he was swimming in a Brighton Beach bathhouse.

The courtroom was so silent, my ears hissed.

Ben jotted notes on his legal pad.

"You mentioned sites about warfarin?" Olson went on.

"Yes."

"Did these sites describe the danger of hemorrhaging?"

"Yes. According to the sites, that's the biggest danger with the drug."

Olson paused, letting Chang's words resonate with the jury.

"Did the defendant visit other kinds of websites as well?" he continued.

"There were sites about money laundering and offshore bank accounts," Chang said, turning a page. "There were others about listening devices, night-vision goggles, things like that."

After forty-five minutes of testimony, it was clear: I'd gone to Web pages detailing nearly every conceivable killing method— especially by poisoning. I'd researched compounds designed to stop the heart, cause paralysis, shut down the nervous system, or cause the victim to bleed out. The killings could be made to look like accidental ODs. All were lethal; all were prescriptions for murder.

Injected, swallowed, or inhaled.

Odorless, colorless, tasteless—completely undetectable.

Deadly.

All part of an assassin's armamentarium.

I was being fed through a legal meat grinder—right into the cutting blades, being ground and then squeezed into wormlike strings of raw meat.

A galvanic series of shocks thrummed through me. The implications of Chang's testimony were toxic.

Could Ben put Chang's testimony into another context? Could he make clear to the jury that my research was strictly for *Assassin's Lullaby*? It was in the service of fiction, not anything in my life.

And to learn more about Nora's illness and medications so I could keep her alive.

Could Ben undo the damage Olson had done?

But with Chang's testimony reeking of deadly implications, the door leading to a Not Guilty verdict was slamming shut. Very fast.

Ben set the printout of website pages on the lectern. Another sheaf of papers an inch thick sat on the defense table. "Mr. Chang," Ben said, "you can tell if someone's deleted their surfing history, can't you?"

"Yes. We specialize in retrieving lost or deleted data."

"And you examined Mr. Shaw's laptop thoroughly?"

"Yes."

"In fact, you have nearly seven hundred pages of printouts from the sites he visited, correct?"

"Yes."

"Any deletions?"

"No."

"So the browsing history was intact. All the cookies from the temporary Internet files were there?"

"Yes, they were."

"Now, Mr. Chang, you examined *all* the computer files, didn't you?"

"Yes."

"Including the contents of 'My Documents'?"

"Yes, sir."

Ben retrieved the sheaf of paper from the defense table. "Did you see a double-spaced printed file that was two hundred pages long?"

"Yes."

"And what is that file . . . that document?"

"It's an unfinished novel."

"You say it's unfinished. But did you get the gist of the story?"

"Oh, yes."

"And what's the name of the novel?"

"It's called *Assassin's Lullaby*."

"*Assassin's Lullaby*," Ben mused. "Now, Mr. Olson didn't ask you about that file, did he?"

"No."

The jurors leaned forward, listening intently. Juror number four nodded her head. So did juror number six.

Ben momentarily turned away, glancing at the jury. It seemed he was giving them time to ponder his next question.

"Do you know why he didn't ask about it?"

"No, sir."

"Did you read what was written of *Assassin's Lullaby*?"

"Yes, I did."

"All of it?"

"Yes, sir."

I knew at that moment, Chang was neither an advocate nor an adversary. He was a straight-shooter.

"And being a novel, means, of course, that it's fiction, correct?"

"Yes."

"Will you tell the jury, Mr. Chang, what *Assassin's Lullaby* is about?"

"Objection," Olson called, standing to his full height.

Marin peered at Olson. The judge's glasses reflected the courtroom's lighting. "Let's give the jury a ten-minute break," he said. "Clear the courtroom."

My heart began rampaging in my chest.

Marin asked Chang to step down from the witness stand and wait outside.

The courtroom emptied. Ben, Olson, Pierce, and I stood bchind our respective tables. My legs were taut and my breathing turned shallow.

When the courtroom was empty, Marin regarded the attorneys. "We're on the record. Mr. Olson, state your objection."

"The novel's *contents* are irrelevant, Your Honor."

"Mr. Abrams . . ."

"Your Honor, Mr. Olson opened the door by having the witness describe the contents of the computer, especially sites about methods of murder. And he knows the novel is *completely* relevant. It's every bit as relevant as the websites about drugs and poisons. At first blush, this looks very damning because Mr. Olson cherry-picked the computer's contents to be read to the jury. But those websites are explained by referring to the novel—the *fiction*—my client was writing. Because the websites visited were in the service of my client's writing that novel, Your Honor. The novel's relevancy will be crystal clear once the jurors hear a bit about it."

"Mr. Olson . . ."

"Your Honor, as Mr. Abrams said, it's a work of *fiction*." Olson waved his hands in the air as he spoke. "This isn't a creative writing class. We're not here to dissect Mr. Shaw's work in progress."

"Your Honor," Ben jumped in. "All the websites Bill Shaw surfed—about poisons, toxins, and methods of murder—will be completely understandable if we look at the manuscript, if we take it all in the proper context. And I don't intend to *dissect* the novel. I intend to set the websites he visited in their proper perspective so the jury isn't misled. The jury needs to hear about the novel for the trial to be fair."

"I'll allow it for its relevance concerning the direct examination about websites the defendant visited."

"But, Your Honor, it's a dissection of a piece of *fiction*."

"The witness will not *dissect* the manuscript," Marin said. "Mr. Abrams is right: you opened the door by referring to the websites. It's a matter of basic fairness. I'll allow testimony concerning the novel for any light it sheds on the websites visited by the defendant. The objection is overruled."

"**M**r. Chang, before the break, I asked you to tell the jury what the novel *Assassin's Lullaby* is about. Will you please do that?"

"It's about a man named Killian, a contract killer."

"Who does he work for?"

"He's basically a freelancer."

"Now, Mr. Chang, can you describe this assassin, Killian, to the jury?"

"Objection, Your Honor," Olson whined. "This wasn't addressed on direct examination."

"Overruled."

"Please continue, Mr. Chang," said Ben.

"He was trained in the military," said Chang. "He had a background in weapons, martial arts, and Army Ranger operations. He was an assassin for the CIA. Then he goes out on his own and becomes a consultant under an assumed identity. He contracts out to mob syndicates."

"With the understanding, Mr. Chang, that the novel's not finished, so far as you could tell, who did he work for?"

"For some Russian mobsters called the *Bratva*—the Brotherhood. He and the people who hire him never really know each other."

"So the novel mentions the Russian Mafia?"

"Yes."

"And some of the websites extracted from Bill's computer are about this Bratva?"

"Yes."

"Can you tell us a little more about this hit man, Killian?"

"Objection, Your Honor," Olson called out.

"Overruled."

"Please tell us about Killian," Ben said.

"By keeping his identity secret, he stays safe," Chang said. "He contacts clients with disposable cell phones, electronic bulletin boards, or anonymous e-mails. He's very skilled with high-tech equipment."

"So that's consistent with Bill's research into high-tech equipment, methods of surveillance, and the websites Mr. Olson questioned you about, correct?"

"Yes."

"What else can you tell us about Killian?"

"He always meets a client in a public place, where he'll be safe. And he gets there early to scope the place out, to make sure it's not a setup."

"Again, consistent with the websites about surveillance equipment, yes?"

"Yes."

"What else does the novel say about Killian?"

"He works for gangsters, even corporations like Blackwater if the money's right."

"Will he do *anything* for money?"

"No. He's made lots of money and doesn't just take *any* job. He's never killed a woman, and he won't touch kids. He calls them *noncombatants*. The target has to be 'dirty,' as he calls it."

"And he makes a living this way?"

"Yes. He has a computer consulting business as a front."

Both Ben and Chang really read the manuscript.

"So there's plenty in the novel about computers? Using the Internet? Surfing websites and that kind of thing?"

"Oh, yes . . ."

"Which fits with many websites Bill Shaw visited?"

"Yes."

"Does the story mention guns?"

"Yes."

"Were a Walther P22, an Uzi submachine gun, and an AK-47 mentioned?"

"Yes, I recall that."

"So even though Mr. Olson didn't ask you about them, *many* ways of killing are described . . . not *just* poisoning and drugs, correct?"

"Yes."

"And Killian's an expert with these weapons?"

"Yes. He's an expert in military tactics, surveillance, and evasion."

"All consistent with the websites visited, Mr. Chang?"

Glancing at the jury, I saw some of them nodding.

"Yes."

"Does the novel mention methods of killing besides poisoning?"

"Yes."

"What are they?"

"Oh, garroting, shooting, using martial arts, things like that. It's pretty graphic."

"Graphic, how?"

"About how a hit man can make a death look like it was from natural causes or accidental so there's no suspicion it was a mob hit."

"Which is consistent with the website 'Ten Tips to Committing the Perfect Murder'?"

"Yes."

"Can you give the jury an example from the novel?"

"Oh, there's snapping a victim's neck and then dragging the body down a stairway so carpet fibers are on it. When forensic experts examine the body, it looks like it was a fall."

"How about shellfish toxin?"

"Yes. It's in the novel."

"The method you described to Mr. Olson a little while ago?"

"Yes. He killed some Bronx gangsters that way."

"And does the novel describe *other* poisons that Mr. Olson

didn't ask you about . . . things like cyanide and strychnine?"

"Yes."

"Does the manuscript mention prescription medications for killing?"

"Yes, those, too."

"And is there a scene in the novel where Killian does that?"

"Yes. He killed a Russian mobster with digitalis."

"So then, keeping in mind that Bill was writing this novel, *Assassin's Lullaby,* about a contract killer using these methods of killing—either poison or drugs, accidental falls, shooting, garroting, and other means—the computer sites are consistent with the novel Bill was writing, aren't they?"

"Yes, it looks that way."

"So this manuscript would explain Bill going to these sites, wouldn't it?"

"Objection, Your Honor. Calls for a conclusion," Olson called.

"Sustained. The jury will disregard the question."

Ben paused and let his disallowed question sink in with the jurors.

A quick glance told me the jurors got the point.

"Would visiting those sites be consistent with Bill's research for the novel?"

"Yes, it appears consistent."

"Mr. Chang, you mentioned that Bill went to sites like Drugs .com, PDR.net, and other medical pages, didn't you?"

"Yes."

"Researching these sites could have been for the novel. Is that right?"

"Yes. I suppose so."

"Or it could have been for something personal in Mr. Shaw's life, correct?"

"Yes."

Ben moved toward the witness stand. "I'm going to ask you

to assume, Mr. Chang, that Dr. Radin, a physician, testified that Bill's wife had multiple sclerosis and a heart condition and was taking warfarin, Lopressor, prednisone, and morphine. Given that testimony, would websites—such as PDR.net or WebMD—that Bill searched be consistent with such a situation?"

"It could be."

"And you said the sites Bill visited most often were those about warfarin and prednisone, right?"

"Yes."

"And his wife was taking those medications, right?"

"I don't know, sir."

"I'm going to ask you to assume there was medical testimony that Nora *was* taking them. Would Bill's going to those sites be consistent with his wife's medications?"

"Yes."

"Now, Mr. Olson asked about sites about money laundering and offshore bank accounts. Are these things mentioned in *Assassin's Lullaby*?"

"Yes."

"How?"

"The Russian gang strong-armed a guy who'd worked in a bank to siphon funds to offshore bank accounts. They killed him. They were worried he might've told his sister, Irena, and she could expose them. And Killian's been asked to kill the sister if she knows anything about it."

"So, that would be consistent with Bill visiting websites about money laundering and offshore accounts, wouldn't it?"

"Yes."

"And isn't it true, sir, that every website Mr. Olson had you mention to the jury is consistent with research for the novel *Assassin's Lullaby*?"

"It looks that way."

"Thank you, Mr. Chang. I have no further questions, Your

Honor."

"Mr. Olson, any redirect?" Marin asked.

"Mr. Chang," Olson said, standing at the prosecution table, "what was the most frequent site surfed by the defendant?"

"Probably sites about warfarin and prednisone."

"I have no further questions, Your Honor." Olson sat down.

"Mr. Abrams, any recross?"

"Briefly, Your Honor."

Ben got up and went to the lectern. "Mr. Chang, there's been medical testimony that Bill's wife, Nora, was taking warfarin for years. Please assume that Bill and Nora saw the doctor frequently for medication adjustments, and assume also that the warfarin caused Nora to have nosebleeds and bleed into her skin along with other problems. Assume also that she was put on prednisone, which worsened the problems with warfarin. Would that situation be consistent with Bill going to websites about these drugs?"

"Yes, I think it would."

"Thank you, Mr. Chang."

I thought fleetingly there might be some hope I wouldn't be convicted by my own computer searches.

Chapter 30

Charlie pulled the car over to the curb on 3rd Avenue. We'd been with Ben at his office for a strategy session after Chang's testimony.

"Chaz, I can't thank you enough . . . coming into the city every day." My throat tightened as I choked back tears.

"Forget it, big brother. It was a good day. I think Ben's cross-examination of Chang undid the bullshit Olson threw at the jury."

I nodded, wondering if it mattered at all.

Charlie was dropping me off half a block from my apartment building. At that hour, the sidewalks were pretty empty, except for the clot of reporters we spied outside my building. "Look at the reporters," Charlie said, peering at the crowd lingering in front of my building.

"Goddamned leeches. I'll go for a drink. They disappear by ten."

Charlie would be heading back home to Scarsdale. I felt thankful for the silence as we watched a stream of taillights snake uptown.

"So I'll see you Monday," Charlie said.

"Yup." As my hand went to the door handle, I turned to him. "Hey, Charlie . . ."

"Yeah?"

"I can't tell you how much your being here means to me."

"Don't be a dick, Bill. I owe you—big-time."

"What're you talking about?" I let go of the door handle.

"Man, you're *all* fucked up. Don't you remember when I came to you?"

"Oh, *that*?"

It seemed a millennium ago. Charlie's career in the minors was over. Nursing a bad shoulder, he returned to New York. Disillusioned, he couldn't find work but finally got a job with a contractor.

Soon after I'd hit a home run with *Fire and Ice*—Charlie came to see me.

It was a frigid winter night; the streets were snow-draped, silent. We met at Chez Ma Tante Claire, a cozy spot on MacDougal Street in the Village.

We had window seats at my preferred table. My favorite waitress waited on us and often comped me glasses of the house wine. Charlie fidgeted with the utensils and barely touched the chateaubriand we were sharing. He polished off the better part of a bottle of Médoc while I was still on my first glass. It was torture watching him squirm, trying to find the words to begin.

"Whaddaya wanna talk about?" I finally said.

Color drained from my brother's face. "Bill, I have an opportunity. Sal, the owner of the company's retiring. I can buy him out, but I don't have the cash."

"How much you need, Chaz?"

"Fifty thousand . . ."

"You got it."

Charlie's eyes widened. "Fifty Gs? Just like that?"

"Of course, dickhead. You're my brother."

Lunging across the table, Charlie wrapped his massive arms around me. "I can't thank you enough, big brother."

"Forget it. Just make it work."

And Charlie did. He made damned good money; he built a bigger house and persuaded Mom to move in with his family when her arthritis became crippling. I was always thankful for Charlie's taking care of Mom, especially after Nora became ill.

"I could never pay you back for what you did," Charlie said as shafts of light slanted through the car. "That money helped me make a new life."

"Yeah, tell me, Chaz, how the fuck do *I* get a new life?"

Jesus, I sounded like a puling kid. How had I become so self-pitying, so whiny, lamenting my lot to my kid brother?

"Nora's gone, and you can never have what you did with her again," Charlie said. "You need time to put this horror behind you . . . to heal. Maybe, down the road you'll find someone else to share your life. You can't know the future."

In that moment, looking at Charlie's face, I realized he was the last link to everything I'd ever known. Everyone else was gone. I leaned toward him and we hugged. I felt like crying but held it in.

"See you Monday, big brother," he said with a catch in his voice.

Getting out of the car, I turned back. Charlie had begun pulling away from the curb.

Standing in the night air amid the drubbing of the 18-wheelers pounding uptown on 3rd Avenue, I called, "I love you, little brother."

I didn't know if he heard me.

Gromann's Tavern was dimly lit and seedy-looking. It had a vintage tin ceiling, an oak-slatted floor, and vinyl-covered bar stools from Paleolithic times. No flat screen TV in this joint. A muted, cathode-tube television cast an aqueous hue over the bar. No music either. Dust was everywhere.

The place had that dark, boozy aura—a friendly, malt-smelling atmosphere I'd grown to crave these last few months. It almost made me forget the fear and dread that brought me there. A faint hint of nicotine hung in the air even though the city had long ago outlawed smoking in bars and restaurants. I figured there was at least a century's worth of smoky residue seeping from the walls, beams, and joists. I walked to the rear of the bar and plopped wearily onto a worn, round-topped stool. A brass foot rail ran the length of the old oak bar.

The tavern catered to old-timers, hangers-on left over from when the area was known as Yorkville. Back then, residents were lower-middle-class Eastern Europeans—Poles, Hungarians, Ukrainians, and an enclave of Germans on 86th Street. Nearly all the old tenement row houses had been converted into condos or co-ops. Gentrification's relentless march had wiped out all but a few of the old-time gin mills.

The guys in this souse house were old. No California chardonnays or Malbecs were served here. The place didn't cater to the Absolut or Stoly crowd. These dinosaurs guzzled Four Roses and Miller on tap, idling away what little was left of their desolated lives. They sucked down the juice to dull arthritic pain and quell loneliness. I was the only guy in the place under sixty. It was seedy, utterly depressing. Here, I had anonymity mixed with misery: the perfect cocktail for my mood.

The bartender, a huge bald guy, recognized me and knew my poison. He set an ice-filled glass onto the bar, poured a generous shot of Johnnie Black, and ambled away. I dropped a twenty onto the pockmarked bar, knowing I'd easily drink up the Andrew Jackson. Maybe I'd add a Hamilton to cover more booze. I was in no rush to leave.

I inhaled the scotch's smoky aroma, put it to my lips, heard the ice cubes clink in the glass, and sipped. The booze felt cool on my tongue, brought on a slight sting, and then slipped back and down. The whiskey burned my gullet. Heat mushroomed though my stomach and then soaked through my chest. Warmth leached through me. As it did each night since Nora's death, the dulling embrace of Johnnie Black soothed me. If I was lucky, it would soon take me to that precious point—the half-embalmed nether-world of the walking dead.

The gloom of the tavern with its aged, flickering neon signs in the window, the dust-covered snake plants on the sill, the cohort of old men at the bar—all heightened my sense of loss. My thoughts drifted to the time soon after we got the diagnosis of Nora's MS. We were suddenly aware of the brief window of time we would have before the disease ravaged her.

Though Nora had forgiven me for the terribly insensitive things I'd said and done in the past, I couldn't absolve myself from the guilt I felt for having treated her so badly.

But Nora insisted there would be no recriminations, no looking back. She made me promise not to let dread cast its pall over the little time we'd have together.

"Do you want to go to Argentina and visit the town where your father grew up?" I proposed.

"No, my love. I want to be here with you."

So, we lived in the moment, taking pleasure from simple things. Walking to Carl Schurz Park, then my pushing her in the wheelchair when walking became impossible. Dancing the tango, then listening to its music when her body grew too weak to dance. Enjoying romantic dinners at our favorite little haunts, or later, those I prepared at home when going to restaurants became too difficult for her to manage.

We were together nearly every hour of each day.

As Nora's condition worsened, a sense of acceptance bordering on resignation came over us. The disease was seizing her, and we knew the inevitable outcome.

"I'll always be here for you," I whispered to her.

"I know that, Bill. I never doubted it."

"I wish this was happening to me, not you."

"It's happening to both of us," she whispered. "And your pain is worse than mine because when I'm at peace, you'll still be suffering."

The bartender knew not to start a conversation as he poured me another scotch. He'd worked behind this bar, and, no doubt, others like it, long enough to see the "Do Not Disturb" look in my eyes.

My thoughts drifted back to that magical night when I saw Nora tango and Lee introduced us at that West Village party. After dinner at El Charro, we went back to my Charles Street apartment.

"And you've never been married?" I asked.

"No."

"How can that be, a woman so beautiful, so smart, so alive?"

"Oh, Bill, let's not talk about regrets. Let me teach you the tango," she said, moving closer. "Can you feel me now . . . close to you?"

Heat radiated from her body and flowed into mine. My flesh hummed. I quivered with anticipation. "I feel every part of you," I whispered.

"The tango is a dance of intimacy and seduction," Nora murmured. "It's a dance of passion, of things to come. Above all, the tango is a promise. Can you feel it?"

"I'm hungry for whatever's coming," I whispered.

And then, she was in my arms. Her breath was on my neck. When our lips met, her mouth opened, her tongue slid over mine, soft and delicious. I could barely believe this gorgeous, vivacious, intelligent woman was kissing me with such abandon.

In the bedroom, she unzipped her skirt—the crimson garment in which she'd tangoed. When it fell to the floor, I stared at her, barely able to absorb the sensuous beauty before me.

We consumed each other with our eyes, naked, free of restraint. Her breasts were lush, full, with deep red nipples like rosebuds. There was the luscious curve of her belly, the delicate slope of her flanks, her sculpted shoulders and arms, her incredibly long legs, and the beckoning gleam in her eyes.

On the bed, my mouth roamed over her lips, breasts, thighs, between her legs. She moaned, and I realized I'd never felt such joy in giving pleasure; she tasted as sweet as I knew she would. Sinking into her, I felt her hot soak, and as we made love—though I was lost in the depth of those moments, I knew I would crave having her with me for as long as we would live.

Later, wrapped in each other's arms, I tried to reanimate the moment we met—only hours earlier—feeling stunned by the kindness of the night.

"I have this feeling," she whispered.

"What?"

"That my life is about to change."

"*Our* lives."

"Because I've always felt marked," she murmured.

"Marked?"

"Yes, marked for tragedy. Does that sound dramatic?"

"It sounds sad. Tell me."

"I will, but not now."

Tears formed at the corners of her eyes. I dabbed them away.

I held her so close, it seemed we could melt into each other. "Nora, I'll be here for you, always," I whispered.

"I already know that." Then, she sighed.

So, with Johnnie Walker invading my brain, I sat at the bar with the grizzled old men—the stale, besotted leftovers of the world—in a gloomy, depressive, and soon-to-be-demolished tavern. I belonged with these booze-guzzling dregs of humanity whose time had come and gone.

And as I finished the last of the scotch remaining in my glass, I knew no matter what the trial's outcome, I'd be better off dead.

Chapter 31

Dr. Leopold Pauling sat on a toilet in the courthouse men's room.

His bowels were acting up. Nerves, gut-wrenching nerves did it every time. After twenty-five years of testifying, you'd think it would get easier. "Maybe I'm getting too old for this game," Leo said to his wife, Hilda, this morning. "Hell, I turn sixty-three next month."

"Why not retire, Leo? We could move down to Boca. How much more money do we need?" Hilda asked.

Yes, courtroom testimony was a shock to the system. It was hell on earth to endure a blistering cross-examination, especially by a lawyer like Ben Abrams. That's what he tried to explain to Sean Olson yesterday at their prep meeting.

"Look, Leo," Sean said. "I know you wrote the book on toxicology, but just give the pertinent facts about warfarin."

"I'm not a medical prostitute, Sean."

"I know," Olson said in that smarmy way of his. "But, the jury doesn't know warfarin from Pepto-Bismol. That son of a bitch, Shaw, overdosed his wife. The toxicology report is definitive. You don't have to teach the jury everything. Abrams will just try to deflect the evidence."

"Okay, Sean. You choreograph it and I'll dance."

Fuck You was scratched into the toilet's metal stall door. Below that, was etched *Fuck the Lawyers*.

Yes, fuck the lawyers. A pack of weasels with nothing but disdain for the truth. Fuck the judges, too, political hacks. And fuck the jurors—losers who couldn't wiggle out of jury duty. And fuck the expert witnesses—a hodgepodge of high-paid whores.

Frau Hilda was right. They could move to Florida, become snowbirds. No more lawyers, judges, court dates, no stress, just the sun, beach, breeze, and water.

Leo glanced at his Rolex. Soon he would testify.

As I watched Dr. Leopold Pauling take the witness stand, dread gnawed at my guts.

He was a portly sixty-something guy wearing wire-rimmed glasses. His neatly trimmed, graying beard was accompanied by a mottled, push-broom mustache. He had a full head of closely cropped, salt-and-pepper hair. Wearing a double-breasted, gray tweed suit with a blue bow tie, he looked like the professor he was. He exuded scholarly authority.

"Pauling's their finisher, the guy the prosecutor calls in to pitch the last inning," Ben said. "They always save the science for last. It's what they want the jury to remember, and anything with the ring of science impresses juries."

Olson established Pauling's credentials, asking the toxicologist about his education and training. The doctor's responses sounded as polished and professional as his background was impressive.

He rattled off the prestigious schools and hospitals where he trained: a medical degree from Yale and a PhD in pharmacology from Harvard. A full professorship at NYU's Langone Medical Center. Ben mentioned Pauling had appeared in hundreds of trials all over the country. "The guy earns over a million bucks a year," Ben added.

Listening to Pauling's background made my skin crawl: why wasn't he on my team?

"Your Honor," Olson said, "I respectfully request that Dr. Pauling be qualified by the court as an expert in toxicology and pharmacology."

"The witness is so qualified," Judge Marin replied. "As such, he may give his opinions in the area of toxicology."

"Dr. Pauling, did there come a time when you were contacted by the district attorney's office and asked to review records in this case?"

In an even, clear voice, Pauling testified about reviewing Dr. Radin's records, the autopsy report, the interrogation tape of me with Kaufman and Cirillo, and the postmortem toxicology report.

"Please, Doctor, tell the jury what the autopsy report and records said about Nora Shaw's death."

"She died of massive internal bleeding from many organs in her body."

His words reinforced those of Dr. Dugan, the medical examiner, uttered only a few days earlier. I shuddered, thinking of what would come next.

"And as an expert in toxicology, as well as being a medical doctor, would you please describe to the jury what warfarin is and how it works?"

Pauling launched into an avalanche of verbiage about warfarin: how it slowed the blood's ability to clot, how the drug acted at various doses, and how it acted when given orally compared to intravenously. He explained warfarin's osmotic gradient, its half-life, and its rate of decomposition by the liver. He even presented a chart demonstrating warfarin's degradation rate in the human body over the hours after it was given. Pauling's exposition exuded pharmacologic authority.

But after forty minutes of testimony, some jurors seemed to be drowning in a scientific tsunami. Though Pauling was knowledgeable, he was overwhelming them with detail. A few panel members seemed bored, especially juror number four and two others. I began to rethink wanting him in my corner.

Even Judge Marin's eyes appeared glazed. He removed his glasses, held them up to the light, exhaled on the lenses, and wiped them on his robe's sleeve. A surefire sign of boredom, I thought.

Ben scribbled on a yellow legal pad as Pauling droned on.

And then Olson, in a surprisingly resonant voice as compared to his usual reedy tone, delivered the crucial question. The jurors seemed to snap to attention as he asked, "Doctor, what caused the massive bleeding from every organ in Nora Shaw's body?"

The entire courtroom seemed to hold its collective breath as Pauling paused, and then said, "Nora Shaw's hemorrhaging was caused by the sudden infusion of a larger-than-usual dose of warfarin given intravenously at six in the morning on the day of her death."

Olson moved closer to Pauling. "Doctor, you said 'A larger-than-usual dose of warfarin.' How do you know the dose that morning was *larger* than usual?"

"My conclusion is based on the amount of warfarin left in her body when blood was drawn for a toxicology screen at eleven that morning."

"And how do you know there was an overdose?"

"As I've explained, warfarin is broken down at a certain fixed rate. It has a predictable degradation curve. It's scientifically *impossible* for so much warfarin to be in a patient's system five hours later without an overdose having been given at six a.m."

"And, Doctor, did I hear you correctly? Did you say it is *scientifically impossible* she *wasn't* given an overdose?"

"That is correct."

Silence saturated the courtroom. My brain felt like it was pulsing.

"So, Dr. Pauling," Olson went on, "what have you concluded

about Nora Shaw's death?"

The jurors looked mesmerized. Even Marin leaned forward and looked expectant.

"According to my calculation, Nora Shaw received a *fifty percent increase* over her usual dose at six a.m. That overdose led directly to her death."

It was a punch to the gut. Shivering began inside my torso.

"How do you know she received the dose at *six* that morning?"

"In the interrogation tape, the defendant said that was when he gave her the warfarin."

"So you're saying the defendant himself acknowledged giving Nora the injection of warfarin at six a.m.?"

"Yes."

"And, Doctor, this overdose of fifty percent at six o'clock that morning meant how much warfarin was given?"

"About a milligram more than the two milligrams prescribed. She received three milligrams instead of two. That's a fifty percent increase, a substantial overdose."

"And what did this overdose do to Nora Shaw?"

"The overdose of warfarin led directly to her death."

"And is your statement here in court today based on scientific knowledge and calculation?"

"Absolutely. Knowing the degradation rate of warfarin, knowing the time the warfarin was given, and knowing how much was left in her system five hours later made the calculation easy."

"Dr. Pauling, based on your training, education, and experience as a physician, a pharmacologist, and a toxicologist, is it your testimony that Nora Shaw died from this fifty percent overdose?"

"Yes, it is."

"And has your testimony been given with a reasonable degree of medical and scientific certainty?"

"Yes. It's hard-core science."

"Thank you, Dr. Pauling. I have no further questions."

The courtroom was silent. That radiator began clanking. Blood pulsed through my veins, throbbing in my temples.

"You may step down, Doctor," Marin said. "We'll take a brief recess and resume with cross-examination."

The court officer held the door to the jury room open as the jurors filed out. Two jurors cast sidelong glances in my direction. I felt like shriveling. Olson had choreographed the trial masterfully. He'd set the stage, strategically placed the scenery, directed the players, and defined their roles. He'd moved seamlessly from one act to another. The story took shape slowly in a step-by-step fashion; it prepared the way, ultimately, to Pauling's testimony.

Olson had established motive, means, and opportunity. And then, he dipped into pure science, the finale—Pauling's damning testimony.

And my defense?

We had no toxicologist.

No pathologist.

No computer expert.

No scientific expert to counter Pauling's testimony.

Yes, the curtain was coming down on my life.

Ten years—minimum—of hard time would await me.

And my defense?

Who did I have?

Ben Abrams.

What could he do?

Who did he have?

Only me.

"Isn't it true, Doctor," Ben began on cross-examination, "that some patients are very susceptible to bleeding from warfarin?"

"Yes," Pauling said, settling back in the witness chair.

"And don't some patients clear warfarin slowly or poorly?"

"Yes . . ." Pauling sounded tentative, wary.

The jurors didn't look drowsy or bored. Not then. A tug-of-war was unfolding before them, and their eyes darted from Ben to Pauling and back again. Judge Marin leaned forward, obviously listening intently. Voltage streamed through my body as the thrusting and parrying began.

"And didn't Nora Shaw have poor ability to clear warfarin?"

"I don't know that to be so."

Temporizing—a disingenuous answer if ever there was one.

"Didn't she *always* run high warfarin levels?"

"Yes, for the most part," Pauling said, nodding his head slowly.

"And *why* did she run high levels of warfarin?"

"It might have been her genetics."

"Fair enough, Doctor. Her genetics. Could *other* things have caused Nora to run high levels of warfarin in addition to her genes?"

"Yes, it's conceivable."

"What other factors could *conceivably* play a role?" Ben's eyebrows rose toward his hairline.

"The dose, for one."

"But didn't her warfarin spike even when she was on the *same* dose?"

"Occasionally it did." Sheen began forming on Pauling's cheeks. He crossed his arms in front of his chest.

"In fact," Ben said, his eyes boring into Pauling's, "she had so many spikes, Bill bought a device to monitor her warfarin level at home, didn't he?"

"That's in Dr. Radin's records."

"Now, you mentioned the dose as *one* factor. Couldn't *other* factors cause Nora to bleed internally, even at the prescribed dose of warfarin?"

"Yes. There can be other variables."

"Can diet affect warfarin levels?"

"Yes," Pauling said, caution permeating his voice.

"If a patient ate food with lots of vitamin K—let's say, dark, leafy greens like spinach—couldn't that make the blood thicker, making it less prone to bleed?"

"Yes, but not in Nora Shaw's case. She was being fed through a feeding tube and received the same canned alimentation every day."

"Now," Ben said, shifting gears, "are there any other variables that could make Nora bleed, even when she was kept on the prescribed dose of warfarin?"

"Her general health could have had an effect."

"And her general health was what, good or bad?"

"It wasn't very good." Pauling's lips twitched.

Ben waited at the lectern, again letting Pauling's acknowledgment sink in with the jury.

I glanced at the panel; they looked focused. No, it was more than focused: they seemed wired.

"Are there any other variables that could have made Nora bleed excessively?"

"None that I can think of."

"Maybe I can help you out, Doctor."

Juror number four was paying rapt attention. She leaned forward, her forearms resting on the rail in front of the jury box.

"Are previous GI bleeds one of the *known* risk factors for excessive bleeding in a patient taking warfarin?"

"Yes. They can be." Pauling seemed to be hugging himself.

Ben sure knows plenty about warfarin.

"Thank you, Doctor. And did Nora have a history of GI bleeding?"

"I believe she did."

Pauling's tongue flicked across his lower lip.

"Didn't you tell this jury you read Nora's medical records?"

"Yes."

"Do you recall reading that she had episodes of GI bleeding?"

"Yes. There were a few times."

"Well, let's see," Ben said. "May I approach the witness, Your Honor?"

"You may approach."

Pauling's glasses slid down his nose. He pushed them back up.

Ben set some papers in front of Pauling and then returned to the lectern. "I've highlighted in yellow a paragraph in Dr. Radin's notes. The ones you *said* you read. Will you kindly read that part aloud to the jury?"

Squinting, fiddling with his glasses, Pauling began reading in a soft voice.

"Please, Doctor, read the entry in a loud and clear voice so the jury can hear you," Ben said.

Pauling cleared his throat, coughed softly, and then began reading aloud. "October eighteenth, 2011. Patient reports black stools. Likely lower GI bleeding caused by warfarin. Cut dose back to one milligram."

"Doctor," Ben said, "to save time, if I tell you there are seven more entries over nine years that reference significant GI bleeding, with two bleeding episodes requiring hospital stays, would you take my word for it?"

"Yes."

"Is what I just said an accurate representation of the record?"

"Yes, I believe it is."

"And you read the record, yes?"

"I did."

"And it references two hospitalizations for GI bleeding, doesn't it?"

"Yes."

"Thank you, Doctor."

Olson scribbled on a yellow legal pad. His jaw muscles were bunched and his brow was deeply furrowed. Looking at the prosecutor, I felt a surge of hope; I sensed Ben was undoing some of the damage Olson had created.

"So we've now established that Nora had a number of important risk factors for bleeding while she was taking warfarin." Ben counted them off. "We have genetics, the dose, her general health, and a *history of previous GI bleeding*. Four separate factors, right?"

"Yes."

"Now, Doctor, what's the *PDR*?"

"It's the *Physicians' Desk Reference*."

Pauling's eyes suddenly narrowed. He nearly grimaced as he shifted his bulk in the witness chair. Something about Ben's question clearly disturbed him.

"What's the *PDR* used for?"

"It describes all medications prescribed by physicians."

"Is it used by physicians to get information about medications?"

"Occasionally, it is."

"And it contains scientific descriptions of the medications, doesn't it?"

"Yes, but—"

"So the *PDR* would be authoritative, wouldn't it?"

"I'm not sure it's authoritative."

"But have you ever referred to the *PDR* to look up a medication?"

"Yes, but it's not the only—"

"And you relied on what the *PDR* said, didn't you?"

"Well, I guess so."

Ben yanked a copy of the *PDR* from his briefcase and plopped it on the lectern.

"Objection, Your Honor," Olson called. "The doctor didn't acknowledge the *PDR* as authoritative. Mr. Abrams can't read from it."

"The doctor acknowledged having *relied* on the *PDR*," Marin said. "That's as good as recognizing it as authoritative. The objection is overruled. For the purposes of this trial, the *PDR* is recognized as an authoritative text."

Yes. Ben would be allowed to read from the *PDR*. He might make headway with Pauling. My stomach began doing somersaults.

"Thank you, Your Honor," Ben said, flipping the tome to a page he'd marked off with a green Post-it.

"Now, Doctor, I'm on page 993 of this year's *PDR*—the scientific description of warfarin."

Pauling reached for a water-filled plastic cup and sipped from it. He swiped at sweat beads on his forehead.

"The *PDR* lists side effects and drug interactions of each medication listed, doesn't it?"

"Yes."

"Scientifically validated by the drug manufacturers themselves?"

"Yes." Pauling's eyes darted toward the prosecution table, then back to Ben.

"And it lists warnings about the medications, correct?"

"Yes."

"Well, it says right here in the *PDR*—about *warfarin*—that there's an increased risk of bleeding if the patient has had highly variable blood level readings of warfarin while taking the drug. Did Nora Shaw have highly variable blood levels over the years?"

"Yes." Pauling repositioned himself in the witness chair.

"In fact, Dr. Radin testified to that fact. Are you aware of that?"

"Yes, I am."

"So that's another risk factor Nora had, wasn't it? Highly variable readings?"

"Yes. It could have been."

"And it also says in the *PDR* that there's a higher risk of bleeding with warfarin for any patient with a history of hypertension—high blood pressure. Did Nora Shaw have hypertension?"

"I recall her pressure tended to run high."

"We can go back to Dr. Radin's records just to make sure, if you'd like."

"I'll take your word for it." Pauling blinked rapidly.

"Thank you, Doctor." Ben turned the page. "And the *PDR* also says the bleeding risk is much higher with 'concomitant use of other drugs.' Is that true?"

"Yes."

"And what *other* drugs increase bleeding risk for a patient taking warfarin?"

"Let's see . . . vitamin E, Ultram, and some others. I can't think of them at this moment."

"How about Lopressor?"

"Yes," Pauling said, nodding his head.

"And you didn't mention *prednisone*, did you?"

"That's one," Pauling offered.

"And prednisone dramatically increases the risk of bleeding when it's mixed with warfarin, doesn't it?"

"It can . . ."

"And Nora Shaw was taking both prednisone and Lopressor along with warfarin, wasn't she?"

"Yes."

"So we have a combination of *three* medications interacting and increasing Nora's tendency to bleed internally, don't we?"

"Yes."

Pauling's tongue again slid across his lower lip.

Juror number four nodded. So did a few other jurors.

I felt a surge of elation. Ben was making headway with Pauling—pushing against his mound of molecular computations. But still, there was the calculation of residual warfarin five hours later. Scientific numbers could impress a jury like nothing else.

"Now," Ben said, "I'm going to page 995 of the *PDR*, where

it says an important factor for increased risk of serious bleeding with warfarin is the 'duration of therapy with warfarin.' I'm quoting directly from the *PDR*. '*The duration of therapy with warfarin.*' Is that correct, Dr. Pauling?"

"Yes."

"Tell me, how long was Nora Shaw taking warfarin?"

"I believe it was nine years."

"Yes, Nora was on warfarin for nine years. Isn't it true, then, that she would therefore have an increased tendency to bleed?"

"Yes. That could happen."

Another concession by this respected toxicologist. My skin tingled.

The courtroom was tomb-like. There were no shuffling feet, no coughing, or throat clearing.

"So, Dr. Pauling, you've come to court today and you've told this jury that Bill Shaw injected his wife with an extra dose of warfarin—fifty percent more—on the morning she died, didn't you?"

Pauling's head moved in a barely discernible nod.

"Didn't you tell that to this jury?"

"I said nothing about Mr. Shaw. I said the *dose* was excessive, given the—"

"Oh, yes, I stand corrected. You said it was likely the *dose* was increased by fifty percent, didn't you?"

"Yes."

"Meaning that in your opinion, Bill Shaw injected a milligram *extra* into his wife, and it killed her, right?"

"It was a lethal dose."

A lethal dose. Pauling tried to bottom-line it with that statement.

Hearing those words, I felt my shoulders hunch.

"So let's see if we're getting this straight, Doctor," Ben said, closing the *PDR* and moving toward the witness stand. "You've told these jurors—these people who're deciding Bill Shaw's future—that Bill gave his wife an overdose of warfarin. That it's scientifically *impossible* that he *didn't* give her an overdose of warfarin, correct?"

"The numbers don't lie, Mr. Abrams. They're scientifically objective."

"That's not what I asked you, Dr. Pauling. Please listen to the question."

"Mr. Abrams," Pauling said, "you can try to deflect the findings with other possibilities to explain the elevation of warfarin in Nora Shaw's body, but the toxicology screen tells the story. She was overdo—"

"Dr. Pauling, that's not the question before you."

"But, sir, the numbers are very clear. They're—"

"Objection, Your Honor!" Ben shouted, turning to Marin. "The witness isn't answering my question. He's pontificating, but avoiding my question." The veins on Ben's neck bulged. He looked like he would explode. "Please admonish the witness, Your Honor."

"Doctor," Marin said, leaning toward Pauling. "Just answer the attorney's questions as they're put to you. Please don't speechify."

There was a moment of silence. My heart thudded in my ears.

"Now, listen carefully to my question," Ben said, moving closer to Pauling. He reminded me of a panther crouched, stalking, ready for the kill. "You acknowledged—you *conceded*—only a little while ago that there are many other possibilities that could be responsible for Nora's excessive bleeding, correct?"

"Yes."

"And I listed them for the jury, correct?"

"Yes."

"And you agreed they could make Nora bleed easily, yes?"

"Correct."

"And *before* that, when Mr. Olson was questioning you, you told this jury that it's scientifically *impossible* that Bill *didn't* give

Nora an overdose of warfarin, didn't you?"

"Absolutely, sir. And I stand by that statement."

"You said this even though Nora's nine years on warfarin increased her chances of bleeding. Dramatically. You said this even though her warfarin level zigzagged wildly on the same dose over the course of those nine years. You said what you did even though Nora bled frequently over the years—bled into her bowels, her skin, from her nose, and into her urine. Even though she'd been taking prednisone and Lopressor, which interacted with warfarin and made her bleed more easily on the warfarin. Even though she'd been in poor health and was exquisitely sensitive to the effects of warfarin and had high blood pressure."

Ben stopped—red-faced—and glared at Pauling.

"Despite *all* these very potent factors that would cause excessive bleeding, you told this jury Nora was overdosed, didn't you? That she was given a lethal injection. Isn't that what you said? *Yes* or *no?*"

"These same issues had been going on for years and hadn't caused her death—"

"Your Honor," Ben cried, turning to Marin, "please instruct the witness to answer my question."

"Doctor, I'm directing you to answer the question," Marin said.

"I'll repeat the question for you, Doctor. You said that Bill Shaw is a murderer despite *all these other* variables, these many other things that could easily have caused Nora Shaw to bleed out, didn't you?"

"The amount left in her system tells the story."

"You told this jury that Bill Shaw *killed* her?"

My hands were clasped so tightly, my knuckles turned white.

"Doctor, didn't you say—in effect—that Bill killed Nora?"

"Yes, I did."

"And didn't you say it was scientifically *impossible* that Bill *didn't* overdose Nora?"

"What I meant was—"

"I'm not asking what you *meant*, sir. I'm asking you what you *said*. Didn't you say it was impossible that Bill didn't overdose Nora?"

"Yes. I said that."

"Now I'll ask you *this*: in light of all the important variables I've read to you and the jury, will you amend the statement that it's *scientifically impossible*?"

"I would say it was scientifically improbable."

"Improbable?"

"Yes. It's highly improbable."

"Thank you, Doctor," Ben said with a nod. "*Improbable*. Now, that's an interesting word. And, it's a very important word. *Improbable*," Ben repeated, and then paused, still staring coldly at Pauling. "So now you're talking about *probability*. It's *probable*. Doesn't the word *probability* have a very specific meaning in the scientific, medical, and legal communities?"

"Yes, but—"

"You've answered my question, Doctor. It's *probable*."

Murmuring came from the gallery.

"Doctor, this is very important. In fact, it's *crucial*, so let's not skip over this. I don't want to make light of this, and I don't want any kind of backtracking, so please bear with me." Ben waited for a beat and then closed in on Pauling. "Will you define the word *probable* as it's used in medicine and in the law?"

"Well . . ." Pauling cleared his throat and clasped his hands on the ledge in front of him. "Something's probable if there's a fifty-one percent or greater chance it could occur."

"So, something's probable if there's a fifty-one percent or greater chance of it happening?"

"Yes."

"And that leaves a forty-nine percent chance that it *would not*, *could not, or did not* occur, right?"

"Mr. Abrams, it's a sliding scale. The lesser probability begins at forty-nine percent and then drops—"

"Yes or no?" Ben cut in. "There's a forty-nine percent chance, or maybe less, that Bill did *not* kill Nora with an overdose. *Yes or no?*"

"I—I don't think—"

"Yes or no?" Ben pushed.

"Yes."

"Thank you for answering my question, Dr. Pauling."

Ben paused, again letting Pauling's words soak into the jury's collective awareness. He shuffled some papers on the lectern. It was clearly a delaying tactic to let Pauling's admission sink in.

Ben looked up at Pauling.

"Just so we all understand this, Dr. Pauling, you're now saying there's a forty-nine percent chance that Bill did *not* do that, yes or no?"

"I can't answer that question with a yes or no."

"Please answer my question, Dr. Pauling. The question is this: based on the toxicology report, isn't there a forty-nine percent chance that Bill did *not* overdose Nora?"

"As I just said, I can't answer that question yes or no."

"Fair enough, Doctor. Let me rephrase it. Based on the toxicology report, isn't there a forty-nine percent or less chance that Bill did *not* overdose Nora?"

"Yes . . ."

"Thank you."

Ben tapped his pen on the *PDR*. He waited, letting silence punctuate Pauling's concession about probability.

The jury waited expectantly for Ben's next question. Every member of the panel leaned forward. My pulse bounded in my wrists and throbbed in my throat.

Ben moved in front of the lectern and glared at Pauling. "Now,

Dr. Pauling, you don't actually *practice* medicine, do you?"

"No. I'm a researcher and a consultant."

"For whom do you consult?"

"Attorneys. When there are legal questions about drugs and toxins."

"So you're a professional witness?"

"*Objection*," Olson bellowed, crimson-faced.

"Withdrawn, Your Honor," Ben said.

"The jury will disregard that question," Marin said. He swiped off his glasses. His eyebrows formed a bushy scowl. "Watch yourself, Mr. Abrams."

"Yes, Your Honor."

Pauling folded his arms across his chest once again. He leaned back in the witness chair.

"Doctor, isn't it true that you derive your entire non-university income by reviewing cases in litigation—for either prosecution or defense attorneys—and then testifying in court?"

"Yes."

"Now, you were paid for the work you did in this case—the records review and preparing your report, weren't you?"

"Yes."

"And how much did you charge Mr. Olson's office?"

"The fee was three thousand dollars."

"On what basis did you charge?"

"I bill at five hundred dollars an hour."

"Are you being paid for your testimony today?"

"I'm not paid for my *testimony*, sir. I'm paid for my *time* in court."

"Of course. You would never be paid for your testimony. Forgive me. You're being paid for your *time*. And how much are you being paid for your time here, which according to my watch is nearly three hours? How much are you being paid by Mr. Olson's office?"

"Eight thousand dollars."

"Eight *thousand* dollars." Ben spat out the words for the jury's benefit. "That's for your time on the stand and the time spent traveling to court, and time going back?"

"Yes, and—"

"Where did you come from to get here today?"

"From my office at NYU on 38th Street and 1st Avenue."

"And when you leave court, you'll go back there?"

"Yes."

"So breaking it down, it's about thirty minutes each way, and if we can tack on the time you've been in court today, it comes to a total of four hours, doesn't it?"

"Yes, but—"

"So your rate, then, is really *two thousand dollars* an hour, isn't it?"

Pauling's lips formed a half smile. "Well, there was time preparing for—"

"Did I say something funny, Doctor?"

"No." Pauling's smile evaporated.

"Didn't you just smile?"

Pauling sat like a rotund Buddha.

"Didn't you begin to smile right here in front of us all?"

Pauling's face was frozen, masklike.

Olson stood like a statue behind the prosecution table.

"Do you think this trial is funny, Doctor? Is it funny that Bill Shaw is being accused of murder?" Ben's chest looked like it was expanding, as though he would explode. "Is it *funny* that the scientifically flawed testimony of a professional witness is being used by Mr. Olson to—"

"*Objection!*" Olson shouted.

"*Sustained!*" cried Marin. "That will do, Mr. Abrams." Marin's lips quivered and his eyes bulged in their sockets. "Sit down, Mr. Abrams. Your cross-examination is over."

A hum percolated through the gallery.

"I have no further questions for this witness, Your Honor," Ben said, swiping the *PDR* from the lectern. He turned dismissively from Pauling, proceeded to the defense table, and sat next to me.

The courtroom voices sounded oceanic in my ears.

Judge Marin slammed his gavel down.

The gallery quieted.

"Mr. Olson, any redirect?" Marin asked, looking at the prosecutor.

"Only a few questions, Your Honor."

"Proceed."

Olson was at the lectern, legal pad in hand.

Pauling sat motionless and red-faced.

"Doctor," Olson began, "despite all the variables Mr. Abrams mentioned, the toxicology report indicated excessive warfarin in Nora Shaw's system, didn't it?"

"Yes, it did," Pauling said, straightening up in the witness chair.

"Is a toxicology screen something the medical community relies on?"

"Yes."

"Is it viewed as scientifically accurate?"

"Yes. It reflects the molecular amount of a substance in a person's system when the blood was drawn."

"And it did so in this case?"

"Absolutely."

"And what did the amount left in Nora Shaw's body five hours after the last dose was given indicate?"

"That an overdose had been administered that morning."

"Thank you, Doctor. I have no further questions."

"Mr. Abrams, any recross?" asked Marin.

"Only a few questions, Your Honor."

"Proceed."

Ben stood behind the defense table rather than go to the lectern. "Doctor, Mr. Olson just asked you a question. And he preceded it by saying, 'Despite all the variables.' Do you recall that?"

"Yes."

"What exactly are *variables*?"

"Variables can involve extraneous factors that may cause changes, inaccuracies, or inconsistencies in a laboratory reading."

"So you concede there are potential inaccuracies?"

"No."

Ben nodded, brought a hand to his chin, and rubbed it.

"*Variables* was the word used by Mr. Olson," Ben said. "*Variables*, an interesting word. Like the weather is variable?"

"Yes."

"Or moods can vary or people vary in their reactions to things?"

"Yes." Pauling's eyes narrowed. Ben was cornering him.

"And there were many variables in the situation with Nora Shaw's level of warfarin. The ones I mentioned on cross-examination and the *variables* that Mr. Olson just mentioned?"

"Yes."

"Do all those *variables* affect the toxicology reading on which you relied?"

"It's highly unlikely."

"But they *could*, Doctor?"

"They could—to a very minor extent."

"They *could*," Ben said, nodding his head. "They very well could, perhaps forty-nine percent of the time?"

Pauling stared at Ben and said nothing.

"Again, Doctor, the variables could affect the readings forty-nine percent or less of the time? Yes or no?"

"Possibly."

"Doctor, that's a yes-or-no question."

"It's impossible to answer that question with either yes or no, sir. It's possible. That's all I can say."

"Thank you, Doctor. I have no more questions, Your Honor."

"Mr. Olson, any more questions?" asked Marin.

"Just one, Your Honor." He stood behind the prosecution table. "Doctor, Mr. Abrams asked you about these *variables*. Did they alter the calculation about the amount of warfarin in Nora Shaw's system five hours after the last dose?"

"It's *extremely* unlikely."

"In other words, it's not probable that they affected the calculation."

"It's highly improbable."

"Thank you, Doctor." Olson sat down.

"You may step down, Doctor," said Marin. "Mr. Olson, any more witnesses?"

"No, Your Honor. The People rest."

Marin turned to the jury. "Ladies and gentlemen, the prosecution has concluded its case. This afternoon, we'll begin the defense's case."

Chapter 32

Charlie and I were finishing lunch in a small conference room down the hall from the courtroom. The turkey sandwich felt like sawdust in my mouth. Even the lettuce felt dry. I could barely eat a morsel. I was still reeling from the tug-of-war between Ben and Pauling.

The door popped open. Ben entered, closed the door, and sat across the table from me. "Olson just made an offer."

I nearly choked.

Charlie reached for me and put his hand on my wrist.

"He's willing to reduce the charge from second-degree murder to manslaughter. It's a Class C felony, much less serious."

"*Manslaughter?*"

"It's a straightforward deal."

"A deal?" I asked. "Did your cross of Pauling suck the wind out of Olson's sails?"

"I don't know. Nobody can predict what a jury's gonna conclude. Here's the deal, Bill," Ben said, sitting down. "You acknowledge Nora died because of what you did. But it wasn't willful. It was careless, negligent, a mistake. It's straightforward manslaughter, not homicide."

"Manslaughter?" The word sounded strange—even repugnant.

"But you serve time."

"Don't take the deal," Charlie said, leaning toward me.

I tried to speak, but phlegm filled my throat. "Serve time?"

"It's a mandatory sentence of at least one year and as many as ten. But in the worst case scenario, you'd only do eighteen months at a minimum-security residential facility like Edgecombe or Lincoln Correctional, uptown. Right here in Manhattan. Not Attica or Fishkill or some maximum-security shithole. You'd be with white-collar guys—forgers, embezzlers, Ponzi schemers."

"Don't do it, Bill," Charlie interjected. "You don't belong there."

The table seemed to tilt.

"I—I don't want it. No."

"Bill, you gotta think this through," Ben said, shaking his head.

"I just have to admit to murdering my wife, right?"

Sounds came from the corridor—snatches of conversation approaching, then receding, salvos of laughter, static from a court officer's handheld radio, the tattoo of women's heels on the marble floor.

"Why an offer now?"

"Maybe I made some headway with Pauling."

"Enough to convince the jury?"

"Pauling was Olson's star witness; and even if I extracted some concessions from him, there was a shitload of warfarin in Nora's blood. We can't get around that. I only mitigated some of Pauling's testimony. I got him to admit there were other *possibilities*; that's all. We can make only so much hay with that."

"But, Ben, you made Pauling look like a whore."

"Every expert's a whore. They're in it for the money."

"But he looked like a hack."

"Let's face it, Bill, Nora had a ton of warfarin in her blood."

I was stunned. Did my very best friend of twenty years—my defense attorney—think I killed my wife? If *Ben* thought so, the jury would surely shove me under the bus.

"Jesus, Ben. Do *you* think I overdosed her?"

"Never mind what *I* think, Bill. The only thing that counts is what the *jury* thinks." Ben sucked in some air and exhaled deeply. "Look, I've always had a simple view of this kind of thing. You never settle a case you'd rather *try*, and you never try a case you'd rather *settle*."

"So you'd rather settle my case? Cop a fucking plea?"

"No, but Olson's offer isn't bad. Negligence." Ben shrugged. "We can live with that. It could be plenty worse."

"*We* can live with it? No. *I'll* have to live with it." Something hot coursed through me. My blood hummed.

"Listen, Bill, I—"

"I was watching the jury. Some thought Pauling was full of shit."

"Every jury's an unknown," Ben said, getting up from his chair, pacing. "A complete unknown. You might as well flip a coin. It's a goddamned crapshoot." He stopped pacing, leaned on the table, and then sat down again.

"So, are you telling me to take the deal?"

"I'm just weighing things," he said. "Only you can make the decision. Olson's like any prosecutor; he wants a conviction—on *something*. He just wants a win. It's mileage for his career."

"*Ben*, are you telling me to take the goddamned deal?"

"I'm just advising you to weigh the pros and cons."

"Then let's go over the cons," I said as my thoughts raced.

My brain felt like it was on fire.

"The jury knows I'm familiar with warfarin. Like Pauling said, there was a high level of warfarin in Nora's system. You gave them a dozen reasons why that could happen. Then there was Constance, the trust money, the arguments . . . and the separation."

Ben nodded, got up, and began pacing again. He was jacked— pumped, worried. For the first time, Ben looked completely unnerved about where the trial was going.

"So what're the pros?" I asked.

Ben rehashed the trial testimony from beginning to end. "With Pauling, I managed to blunt his testimony a *bit*. That might be the biggest thing in our favor. But when jurors hear Harvard and Yale and all that academic crap, they're impressed. And let's face it: the guy's top-notch in his field. Jurors put a lot of weight on testimony like his.

"And another thing," Ben said, as he stopped pacing. "We don't have an expert toxicologist. We can't get one because no qualified expert's gonna testify contrary to what Pauling did. Bottom line's this: it's probable Nora was overdosed, by whatever means—her illness, genetics, who the fuck knows? It's plain and simple—she was killed by warfarin that morning."

Ben had just rendered his verdict: guilty.

This was torture. What should I do? Admit guilt? Cop a plea, take a rap? Manslaughter? Do a year and a half in some white-collar warehouse for lessor felons, not lockdown in a snake pit like Attica or Fishkill? Or take a chance, push on with the trial?

"Bill, I gotta ask again—and I hope you're not offended."

"Ask."

"Is there anything you're not telling me, something that'll slam us down the road?"

"Don't you trust me, Ben?"

"I gotta cover all the bases. *Please* . . . understand where I'm coming from."

"No, there's nothing else. Not a thing."

My thoughts were swirling so fast it was dizzying. Was I losing it, just going insane?

"You want some time to think it over?"

"Think about what? A deal like this makes me a wife killer. I'm branded for life."

Charlie stood to his full height. "I don't like this," he said, glaring at Ben. "Copping a plea means my brother admits to killing Nora." He turned to me. "Don't do it, Bill."

"I know it's a bitch," Ben said. "But it's a knowable outcome. You *never* know where a case is going."

"You just told me you never settle a case you'd rather try, and you never try a case you'd rather settle."

"You gotta understand—"

"*I* gotta understand? What do I gotta understand, Ben? My *life's* on the line, and you're telling me you'd rather *settle* this case than send it to the jury."

"I'm just spelling out your options."

"Yeah, Ben, and one option is to admit guilt and be branded a wife killer for the rest of my life."

Ben sighed. "It's my obligation to lay out your options, Bill. I'd be guilty of gross negligence if I didn't do this. I'm asking you to consider it, that's all."

"Don't cop a plea, Bill!" Charlie shouted, red-faced and pacing.

Ben shot a hard look at Charlie. "I think we ought to discuss this alone," he said. "Charlie, will you give us a couple of minutes?"

"No. I want Charlie here."

"Look, Bill, this is too important to—"

"Charlie stays."

We sat silently for a moment.

Then it dawned on me. "Olson's playing me, isn't he?"

"Of *course* he is."

The overhead fluorescent light hummed; it reminded me of the interrogation room.

"Like I said, only *you* can decide, Bill. But I'll tell you what I'd do in your shoes."

Staring at Ben, I suddenly felt paralytic.

"I'd take the deal."

My heart nearly stopped. Here was my best friend, my attorney and confidant, telling me to take a rap. Lesser charges, acknowledge I killed Nora.

"Why? Why take the deal?"

"Because you could do a long stretch if you're convicted."

"Don't you have confidence about where we are?"

"Don't be a schmuck. Do you wanna go to prison for ten years?"

"Of course not. But if I take the deal, I'm screwed for life." Tears flooded my eyes.

"*Fuck* that," Ben shouted. "You wanna go on with your *life*. That's what counts. Eighteen months is a bump in the road. Then your life's your own." The veins on Ben's neck looked like steam pipes.

"No fucking way. No fucking way am I gonna cop a plea."

"Listen, I'm advising you to take the deal. I think it's in your best interest. If you don't, I'll have to do something I never wanna do, especially in this case."

"What's that?" I asked. My heart rate accelerated.

"Put you on the stand."

"So I'll take the stand. I have nothing to hide." I stood, ready to explode.

"It's too risky, Bill. It's a defense attorney's nightmare. Olson'll come at you with his fangs bared. He'd *love* to do it—cross-examine you. He'll pulverize you."

"Let him come."

Ben's eyes narrowed. "Tell me something, Bill, and give it to me straight. No bullshit, okay? Do you *wanna* go to prison? Is that what you're trying to do? Railroad yourself upstate with the dregs of humanity for the next ten years? Is *that* what you want?"

"I wanna win this case."

"It's too fucking *risky*. Don't you see that, for the love of God?"

"Fuck it, Ben. I'll go the distance."

"As your friend and attorney, I'm advising you against it. I'm telling you, you're making a terrible decision. *Take the fucking deal.*" Ben's eyes bulged.

"I just can't."

"Let me propose to the judge that we're willing to take a compromise deal of manslaughter. That way, even if Olson—"

"No fucking way. I won't let you do it."

"Don't box us into a winner-takes-all contest."

"We can always come back for the deal, right?"

"Not necessarily. Olson can take it off the table at any time."

I closed my eyes.

"I'll take my chances."

"*Bill*, don't do it."

"I have to. I just have to."

Chapter 33

"The defense calls Roberta Morgan."

Roberta was a heavyset Jamaican-born woman. Her skin was the color of mocha chocolate. Her lustrous black hair framed her round face like a helmet.

I'd hired Roberta when caring for Nora by myself became impossible.

At the outset, she said she was doing the work God put her on earth to do: caring for suffering souls. The first thing she did was recommend a hospital bed, which made things much easier.

"Mrs. Morgan," Ben asked, "you just swore an oath before God. Is that so?"

"Yes, sir, I did."

"And how do you feel about such an oath?"

"I take it very seriously. I pledged to God I would tell the truth."

"Mrs. Morgan, is it fair to say that even if your testimony would hurt Bill, you would still tell the truth?"

"Yes, sir. I would."

"Now, Mrs. Morgan, when did Bill Shaw hire you?"

"About a year and a half ago, sir."

"And what did the job involve?"

"I worked six days a week, from seven in the morning till seven at night. Sometimes I'd stay longer so Bill could go out for an evening."

"Did you and Bill discuss Nora and her condition?"

"Yes, sir."

"What was your impression of Bill's relationship with Nora?"

"He was very devoted to her. He wanted the best for her."

A dark swirl of sadness enveloped me as Roberta spoke. Her voice was reminiscent of those last months of Nora's life, and images of my wife lying in the hospital bed assaulted me.

"And what did you do for Nora?"

"I cooked meals while she could still eat solid food. I made soft foods when swallowin' got hard for her. I sponge-bathed her and swabbed her lips so they didn't dry out. I gave her the medications. 'Cept toward the end when she was gettin' IV fluids. Bill did that 'cause I'm not trained to do IV meds."

"Anything else, Mrs. Morgan?"

"Bed sores were a big danger. Bill and I turned her and we both massaged her."

"So Bill helped with these chores?"

"Oh, yes."

"Did he ever complain about this?"

"No. Not at all."

"Now, Mrs. Morgan, what was your relationship with Nora like?"

"It was very good. We got to be close. It happens in this kind of work. The patient starts talkin' to you like a friend."

"Understood. Now, Mrs. Morgan, did Nora confide in you? Did she tell you how she was feeling?"

"Oh, yes."

"What did she tell you?"

"How she felt physically. And how she wished she could be more of a wife to Bill. She had regrets about it all, but mostly for Bill and what he was goin' through."

"Did she ever tell you she doubted Bill's devotion to her?"

"No, sir."

"Did she say she thought Bill had a girlfriend, that he was seeing someone?"

"No, sir. She never said a *thing* like that," Roberta said, shaking her head.

I felt like cringing. It sounded rehearsed, canned, as though Ben had prepped the hell out of Roberta.

"Thank you, Mrs. Morgan," Ben said. "Let me turn your attention to something else. Now, on the morning Nora died, what time did you arrive at the apartment?"

"I was in by seven."

"What was Bill's demeanor that morning?"

"It was nothin' special. It was an ordinary mornin."

"And what happened?"

"Bill was gettin' ready to leave, like he did most every mornin'. Nora was asleep, like she usually was when I got there."

"So her sleeping in the mornings wasn't unusual?"

"No, sir. 'Cause of the burnin' pains, she was on morphine."

"What happened then?"

"At ten o'clock, I saw blood at her nostrils."

"Was it unusual for Nora to bleed from her nose?"

"It was happenin' all the time from the warfarin."

"What then?"

"I got a tissue and wiped her nose. But Nora's breathin' got real heavy, sir. I tried to wake her. But I couldn't. So I called Bill on his cell."

"And what did he say?"

"To call 911. And he rushed home."

Ben approached the witness stand. "Mrs. Morgan, how did Bill treat Nora?"

"I never seen a husband so devoted." She turned to the jurors. "Bill sponge-bathed her. And at night, he carried her to the bathroom 'cause she was too embarrassed to use the bedpan." Roberta sniffed, then took a handkerchief to her nose.

Memories of Nora's last few months flooded me.

"He'd help her with the toilet. He went to the pharmacy, the grocery, bought supplies, and everythin' else, too. He loved her so much. I could tell."

I felt a stake puncture my heart.

"Anything else, Mrs. Morgan?"

"Yes." She paused and swallowed hard. "Somethin' I never seen in all my years carin' for people."

"What was that?"

"He sang to her." Roberta's eyes grew wet. "She'd ask him to sing. She loved his voice."

A sob began strangling me.

"He'd sing this beautiful song."

A muffled sob came from one juror. Another cleared his throat. I bowed my head, sinking into a reverie.

"It was from that movie . . . a song called 'Alfie.'"

Nora had always loved Michael Caine's acting. We'd streamed the film and watched it together. The theme song became ours, and she'd ask me to sing it to her. Then, sitting there in court, I heard it—from somewhere in the deepest recesses of my brain— violins. Sweet, elegiac, gorgeous beyond belief, they tugged at me, and then, suddenly changed tempo. I heard a bass, cello, and flute, then two bandoneons, and a tango's melody streamed through the air. The instruments' strains, their tender passion were unbearable; the ache grew so intense, it seemed my heart would burst. I was filled with fear and regret, ravaged by rage and remorse at Nora's fate; I felt loathing and fury at the doctors, the hospital, at myself, and the world.

Though I'd tried a thousand times, I couldn't imagine what Nora felt lying there, unable to swallow, or move, or talk—held prisoner by her failing body, frozen, helpless, and in excruciating pain—and I recalled how she spoke to me with her eyes when she could no longer talk. Those eyes were so expressive, I knew what she was saying by gazing into them, as though I could peer into her soul.

Yes, Nora spoke to me in her way.

My head drooped from the weight of Nora's agony. I barely heard a word in the courtroom as I closed my eyes, shutting out the misery of this world.

Olson said, "Mrs. Morgan, you mentioned nights when the defendant went out?"

"Yes."

"Did he ever tell you who he was with?"

"No, sir. I know there were nights he was teachin' and sometimes he'd go out for dinner."

"How late would he come back home?"

"Oh, it could be nine or ten o'clock."

"And you never saw what went on during the twelve hours you weren't working for the Shaws, right?"

"Yes, sir."

"And you weren't there at six o'clock in the morning on the day Nora died, were you?"

"No, sir."

"So you never saw how much warfarin Mr. Shaw injected into Nora on the day she died, did you?"

"No, sir."

"One more question, Mrs. Morgan. On the morning of Nora's death, when her sister, Lee, visited, was Nora asleep?"

"Yes, sir. She was."

"Was it a deep sleep?"

"It looked that way."

"Thank you, Mrs. Morgan. I have no further questions, Your Honor."

I sat alone at the defense table. Ben, Olson, Ann Pierce, and the judge were in chambers. A procedural issue had come up. Whatever it was, I felt it would push me deeper into the abyss. I could have joined them in chambers but could no longer bear hearing the attorneys' venomous arguments. I was hanging from the edge of a cliff, just clinging by my fingers, about to slip down into a chasm.

The court clerk was reading the *Post*. The jurors were in the jury room; the gallery had been cleared. I stared at the New York State seal and the flags on each side of the bench. For the hundredth time since the trial began, I realized these few days would determine the next decade of my existence. This wasn't fiction. It was true life. A life that now seemed worth very little. I began doubting the wisdom of having turned down Olson's deal.

Ben emerged from Marin's chambers. His brow was furrowed and his eyes looked hollow. He looked as though he'd been beaten with a tire iron.

"We have a problem," he muttered, sitting down. "Juror number four's been excused. Her husband's in the hospital."

It felt like a sledgehammer slammed me in the chest. Juror number four—front row, reddish hair—the one who'd virtually sneered at Gina and who'd been nodding when Ben went at Pauling like a speeding locomotive.

"We've lost our best juror," Ben said.

The edges of the courtroom darkened.

"A fifty-year-old schoolteacher, married, no kids. My paralegal's been in court giving me feedback. Most of the jurors are unreadable, but juror number four was definitely a defense juror."

The steamroller was barreling toward me, and I was lying in its path.

"She's been replaced by alternate number one—a guy Olson fought tooth and nail to get on the panel. His favorite TV show is *Law & Order*. Conservative, votes Republican, reads the *Post* and the *National Review*. Loves Sean Hannity and Rush Limbaugh.

Olson's gloating like a barnyard rooster."

"What do we do now?"

"We have to rethink our strategy. I told you. A trial's a crap-shoot. You never know what's gonna happen." Ben sighed. "You'll have to testify. There's no choice. I'll prep the hell outta you."

"What's that gonna do? I'm ready to toss in the towel."

Would it be hard time at some upstate snake pit surrounded by a chain-link fence and concertina wire, with cinder-block walls and clanging gates like on *Lockup Raw*?

I could see it, hear it, and smell it: holed up for years with mani-acs, skinheads—tattoo-strewn, bench-pressing, hyper-muscular hatemongers. I could imagine the ethnic slurs, the name-calling, the threats, the turf wars, the drugs, the shrieking shit flingers, the groaning masturbators, desperate cornholers, robbers, rap-ists, and murderers—lifers with nothing to lose. I'd be confined with men who'd shank me for a nickel. It'd be like something out of my novels.

I'd be a prisoner for ten or more curse-filled, shut-away, life-wasting years. I'd be a goner. I'd never survive.

"Maybe I should take the plea."

"Olson just took the deal off the table."

Chapter 34

D r. David Russell was a tall man, with longish hair and an angular face. He was dressed in a gray tweed suit, a blue, button-down Oxford shirt, and blue cloth tie.

"Since Olson didn't call him, I decided to have him testify," Ben said. "He had good things to say about you."

On direct examination, Ben established that Russell was an attending psychiatrist at New York-Presbyterian Hospital and a clinical associate professor of psychiatry at Cornell Medical School in New York City.

"Now, Dr. Russell," Ben asked, "is this your first time in court?"

"Yes."

"Are you being paid for your appearance here today?"

"No, I'm not."

Ben was obviously contrasting Russell to Pauling, trying to further paint the toxicologist as a nonpracticing hack.

"Now, Doctor, Bill Shaw waived confidentiality so you could testify here today; is that true?"

"Yes."

"So you're not violating the doctor-patient relationship, are you?"

"No. I have permission to talk about him and Nora."

"Doctor, when did you first see the Shaws?"

"About two and a half years ago, after she was diagnosed with MS. They wanted help dealing with it."

"And you also met with Nora Shaw alone?"

"Yes, four times, and there were two sessions with her husband present. And one meeting alone with Mr. Shaw."

I remembered our first session together. Nora and I sat facing Russell. She shuddered and began crying. "Bill," she said, tears pouring down her face, "I don't know how you can stand it."

I reached for her, but she raised her hands. "No. Let me say this. I've been such a disappointment. I've . . ."

"Oh, Nora—"

"I've caused you only heartache. I couldn't have children. I've been sick for so long."

On my knees in front of her, I clutched her, sobbing. "Nora, please, it's not true . . ." She felt so small in my arms, so fragile.

When I glanced at Russell, his eyes shimmered with tears.

"Doctor," Ben continued, "as a psychiatrist, what do you do when you see someone in consultation?"

"I make an assessment of their emotional state."

"And what assessment did you make of Bill and Nora Shaw?"

"They were a very loving couple trying to cope with this tragedy."

"What assessment did you make of Bill Shaw?"

"That he was very supportive and committed to Nora. It was clear he wanted to hold on to Nora for as long as possible."

"And, Dr. Russell, your clinical view of Bill Shaw is based on what?"

"It's based on my meeting with the Shaws, both together and individually," he said, facing the jury. "And on my training, education, and my years of psychiatric experience."

"You said Bill wanted to hold on to her? What evidence was there of that?"

Russell turned to the jurors. "Actually, it's always a complicated picture. It's quite common for a spouse to have mixed feelings in a situation like this. It's—"

"But, Doctor," Ben cut in, "you said—"

"Objection, Your Honor," Olson called. "Mr. Abrams is interrupting the witness."

"Sustained," said Marin. "Let the witness finish his answer. Go ahead, Doctor."

"When I saw the Shaws," Russell went on, "they were reeling from the shock of the diagnosis. Over time, it's not unusual for a spouse to develop mixed feelings. After all, it's excruciating to watch someone you love suffer."

As the ache in my heart deepened to a drawing pain, I was reminded of Constance's testimony.

"Then, Doctor—"

"In fact," Russell went on, "the healthy spouse often goes through bereavement in *anticipation* of a loved one dying. In essence, grief is a process. It means letting go of a loved one, coming to terms with the loss and, eventually, going on with life. Many people in this situation go through anticipatory grief. Almost by definition, the situation is filled with ambivalence."

Had I been ambivalent about Nora? Had I wanted her to die? Had I gone through anticipatory grief?

Olson was scribbling away.

Ben looked ashen.

"And, Doctor, did you see any evidence of ambivalence in Bill Shaw?"

"No, I didn't."

"Thank you, Doctor. I have no more questions."

"**Dr.** Russell," began Olson, "weren't there marital problems between Nora and the defendant going back some years?"

"That was before the diagnosis of—"

"Yes or no, Doctor?"

"Well, yes, but—"

"Thank you. And isn't it true that the defendant left Nora at one point?"

"I . . . Yes . . ."

"And he once stormed out of a restaurant when she dropped a glass of wine?"

"I was never told that."

"Fair enough. In a few sessions you can't learn everything that goes on in a marriage, can you?"

"No, of course not."

"Which brings us to another point, Doctor. You saw the defendant, Mr. Shaw, only *three* times over three months, yes?"

"That's correct."

"So it was a brief view of the defendant in a narrow window of time?"

"Often a patient reveals lots about himself, even in a narrow context."

"You depend on what someone tells you, yes?"

"Yes, you depend on the history. Every physician does."

"And on the person's demeanor?"

"Yes."

"And it's fair to say that Mr. Shaw could have presented himself to you with the demeanor he *wanted* you to see?"

"I felt his presentation was genuine."

Olson nodded and waited a beat.

"These sessions involved you, Nora, and the defendant talking. Nothing more, correct?"

"Yes."

"Now, Doctor, you saw the Shaws soon after the MS was diagnosed, correct?"

"Yes."

"And you testified that it's not unusual for a spouse to become ambivalent—to develop mixed feelings—as time passes. The spouse begins going through anticipatory grief, correct?"

"Yes, that can happen."

"And you never saw Mr. Shaw again for the nearly two years before Nora died?"

"Correct."

"So, Doctor, you have *no* knowledge of the defendant's feelings during the two years preceding Nora's death, correct?"

"That's true."

"Then you can't know if—*after* meeting with him—he developed ambivalent feelings, and wanted Nora to die. True?"

"I have no way of knowing."

"Thank you, Doctor. I have no more questions, Your Honor."

Olson returned to the prosecution table and sat down next to Ann Pierce.

"Mr. Abrams, any redirect?" asked Marin.

"Briefly, Your Honor," Ben said.

"Doctor, Mr. Olson asked you about ambivalence, right?"

"Yes."

"Is it universal that a spouse develops ambivalent feelings?"

"There's no one-size-fits-all way of dealing with a loved one's impending death. It can vary from person to person."

"In other words, Doctor, many people don't develop such feelings."

"Yes."

"Do some people refuse to accept that a loved one will die?"

"Yes."

"What's that called? When a person refuses to see or accept the obvious?"

"It's called denial."

"Is denial a common reaction to illness, death, and dying?"

"Oh, yes."

"Could denial have happened with Bill Shaw?"

"Yes."

"One other thing, Doctor, Mr. Olson questioned you about marital problems going back a number of years, correct?"

"Yes."

"When did those issues arise—before or after the diagnosis of MS?"

"They were before the diagnosis, when there was no explanation for Nora's problems."

"Thank you, Doctor. No further questions, Your Honor."

"Doctor," Olson said, moving to the lectern, "you have no idea how the defendant reacted to his wife's illness for two years after you saw him briefly, correct?"

"That's true. I don't."

"No further questions, Your Honor."

Chapter 35

My legs felt rubbery as I approached the witness stand. I tried to look controlled, reasonably calm, but knew it would be impossible. Ben and I had prepped for hours the night before, but Ben's flood of instructions seemed impossible to recall.

Walking past the jury box, I glimpsed the woman who reminded me of Nora. Her head dipped down.

What does that mean? I'm latching on to every little thing, thinking it's a signal—how an eyebrow rises or a lip moves. If a juror makes eye contact, nods, or shakes her head, or turns away, it must have meaning. Every gesture is filled with portent. I'll drive myself crazy. Maybe I've already done it, gone mad.

I felt like a mannequin in a store window.

Alternate number one—a burly guy wearing a sport jacket and dress shirt, no tie—sat where juror number four had been. He had hooded eyes, a steady stare, a square face, and pursed lips.

Any signals there? Will he hang me from the nearest tree?

Stepping up to the witness chair, I nearly stumbled. The steps seemed insurmountable as my legs tensed and nearly went into spasm. I glimpsed Judge Marin sitting placidly in his black robe, leaning rearward in his high-backed, padded chair.

I looked out over the courtroom. The gallery was filled to capacity—a sea of people watching, waiting. Silent. Spectators stood at the rear. I couldn't spot Charlie in the crowd.

Ben stood behind the lectern: broad-shouldered, hulking. He

seemed so far away. Had the room elongated? Was it distorted? It was my first view of the courtroom from the perspective of the witness box. It seemed surreal. I noticed a clock on the rear wall. Papers on Marin's desk rustled. Was he looking at me? Did it matter?

I stood stock-still, waiting to be sworn in. The Bible sat on a wide guardrail beside the witness chair. It had a black pebbled cover with gilt edging. A red ribbon protruded from between the pages. It awaited my palm and my sworn word—to God—that I'd be truthful.

Is there any real truth?

The court clerk asked me to place my left hand on the Bible and raise my right. My arm floated upward, weightlessly. My palm hovered near my right ear.

"Do you swear the testimony you are about to give will be the truth, the whole truth, and nothing but the truth, so help you God?"

"I do," said a distant, weak voice. *Was a stranger speaking through me?*

"Please be seated," said the clerk. His voice resounded in my ears—harsh, condemning. "When you speak, use a loud, clear voice."

The chair felt hard, cold; it was wood, no cushion. I clutched the armrests.

Row upon row of people watched me. Faces, more than I could count—watching, looking up expectantly, waiting to hear what I would say. I could *feel* the jury sitting to my left, staring, making judgments. I looked straight ahead at Ben and the mass of faces in the gallery.

"State your name and address for the record," said the clerk.

My voice sounded distant and thin. The words were lifeless, puny.

Is there a tremor in my voice? Am I shaking as I sit here?

My hands—resting on the armrests—looked huge, like they
didn't belong to me. And they were soaked with sweat. A wooden
shelf sat atop the railing in front of me. I recalled Ben's instructions so I set my hands on it and intertwined my fingers.

The clock on the rear wall read ten fifteen. *How long would my
testimony take?*

I waited amid a hellish cloud of anticipation.

"Mr. Abrams, direct examination," Judge Marin said.

Ben began by taking me through that terrible day when Nora
died. Though we'd prepared for hours, it seemed I was hearing
the questions for the very first time.

"And that morning, before Roberta got there, what did you
do for Nora?"

"I gave her the warfarin."

Is my voice coming from far away?

"Was it her usual dose?"

"Yes. Two milligrams."

"Was it the same dose she got each morning?"

"Yes," I heard myself say.

"How long had Nora been on that dose?"

"About four months."

"And before that time?"

"She was able to swallow and took the warfarin by mouth."

"And how did you give her the warfarin when she could no
longer take it orally?"

"It was given by IV. She couldn't take pills anymore; she
couldn't swallow."

"And you followed the same procedure that morning?"

"Yes."

"At what time?"

"At six a.m."

"Why at six?"

"I'd wake up at five," I said, feeling less shaky as I recounted my morning routine. "It's given at the same time so the warfarin keeps a steady level in the body. That's what Dr. Radin said to do."

Please, Ben, let's just finish. I don't know how long I can keep going. This is excruciating.

"And what would you do after giving Nora the warfarin?"

"I'd get dressed, change Nora's position, massage her with lotion, have breakfast, and when Roberta got there, we'd make sure Nora was comfortable. Then I'd take my laptop and leave."

"On the morning Nora died, when did you leave?"

"A little after seven."

"Where'd you go?"

"To the coffee shop . . . Starbucks."

"Did you meet Constance Manning that morning?"

Voltage shot through me at the mention of her name. I knew I'd have to control my voice—keep it from warbling.

"No."

"Why not?"

"She wasn't working that day."

"How often would you meet her there?"

"Usually two mornings a week, only on the days she worked. She was working part-time."

"Now, Bill, do you recall the night the detectives came to your apartment and asked you to accompany them to the police station?"

"Yes."

"They interviewed you, true?"

"Yes."

"And during that interview, they asked you about meeting anyone at Starbucks, yes?"

"Yes, they did."

"And you said you didn't meet anyone there. How come you told them that, when you'd met Ms. Manning there a few times?"

"Starbucks and Constance were the farthest things from my

mind that night. I was tired. I hadn't slept since the funeral, and I was exhausted. I'd been drinking before they showed up. I saw no need to drag Constance into something with the police. She had nothing to do with anything."

"Were you lying when the police asked you about meeting someone at Starbucks?"

"No, I wasn't. I don't think I answered the question the right way, but I wasn't lying. I thought they wanted to know if I was going to the coffee shop specifically to meet someone."

Ben and I had rehearsed my answer, and I worried the jury would find my responses too pat, even canned, lacking in sincerity.

"Why did you go there each morning?" Ben asked.

"To spend time writing until the 79th Street library opened at ten."

"Were you writing the novel Mr. Chang talked about . . . *Assassin's Lullaby?*"

"I was trying to."

"What do you mean, *trying to?*"

"I could barely concentrate with Nora's situation."

"Why were you writing a novel with Nora in such bad shape?"

"She'd asked me to, as a gift to her."

"So the novel was Nora's idea?"

"Yes, she wanted me to get back to writing. She made me promise I would try."

Ben paused, nodded, and then asked, "On the morning Nora died, what happened?"

"I left Starbucks and walked around for a while."

I felt a sudden chill. My voice grew tremulous. I tried to control it. Suddenly, my stomach growled. Could the jurors hear it?

"Then at ten o'clock, I went to the library. I sat at a table and tried to write. At around ten fifteen, my cell phone vibrated. It was Roberta."

Phlegm filled my throat. I coughed, swallowed, and took a sip of water.

Ben waited.

"What did you do when Roberta called?" he asked.

"I told her to call 911 and I rushed home."

"And then?"

"I found Nora . . ."

An image of her lying comatose in bed rushed through my mind. Nausea nearly overcame me.

Stay calm. Stay in control. Just keep going. It'll all be over.

There were more questions, dozens of them: about the dose of warfarin, how it was given, Dr. Radin's instructions, how I massaged Nora and changed her position; it was an avalanche of minutiae. After what seemed hours, the courtroom receded, and the lights dimmed. My head swam.

Runnels of tears dripped from my eyes. I gripped the railing as a vise tightened around my chest.

In a voice coming from far away, Judge Marin called for a recess.

We continued after the break. Despite the prep time with Ben, I'd never imagined it would be so excruciating. And people were judging my credibility, my devotion to Nora.

"Now, Bill, I want to ask a few questions about you and Nora," Ben said.

Ben said he'd humanize me, reveal me as anything but the murderous, selfish husband Olson had portrayed to the jury.

"When you and Nora met, what were you both doing professionally?"

"She was an actor in a TV soap opera. I was a writer."

"And you'd been published by then?"

"Yes," I said, feeling more comfortable. We'd gotten away from Nora's illness, her dying; we were talking about the old days, before everything sank into the pits.

"Did you write the novels before or after meeting Nora?"

"One before and five after we met."

"Were any of them best sellers?"

"Yes. They all were."

"And were there any films?"

"Two were made into movies."

"Did you make a good living as a writer?"

"We were comfortable."

"Did you depend on Nora's work for income?"

"There was no *mine* and *yours*. We were a couple . . . really a team."

We were more than a team. Our lives and minds had fused. We brainstormed about plot twists. We fed off each other and antici-pated each other's thoughts. It was uncanny. Our lives, our bodies, everything—intertwined.

"When you say you and Nora were a team, what do you mean?"

"We worked together. She edited the manuscripts, got them in shape, pointed out plot inconsistencies. She helped with dia-logue. That was her greatest input, the dialogue. We acted out every word in each book. They were *her* books as much as mine. I wanted her to be listed as coauthor, but she didn't want that."

I sipped water. It almost came up on me. I sputtered and coughed.

"And when did Nora stop doing television work and commercials?"

"Almost four years ago."

"Why was that?"

"Because she was getting clumsy, losing her balance, and dropping things, and we didn't know why it was happening."

"Did you suffer financially when she stopped working?"

"No, not from Nora's not working. We lost a lot of money

when the markets collapsed in 2008."

"And why was that?"

"We weren't very good investors. We made some bad mistakes. They were mostly my mistakes." I felt like choking.

"When Nora stopped doing commercials, what were you living on?"

"We had some savings, and royalties were coming in. And we were writing."

"You said *we* were writing?"

"Yes. It was a team effort."

"But that stopped, too, didn't it?"

"Yes. Her condition got worse. It was the MS, though we didn't know it then."

"After she stopped helping with the novels, what was your financial picture?"

"We had some savings and there were still royalties from earlier books."

"What happened then?"

"Nora's heart condition deteriorated, and then came the MS diagnosis," I said, nearly shuddering. "I didn't want to write anymore."

I tried not thinking back to Nora's breathlessness, the fainting spells, her weakness, the dizziness, and fatigue.

"Things just went downhill," I said.

"Meaning what?"

"The MS progressed very fast."

Ben stood between the lectern and the jury box.

"Bill, I want to ask you, over the years of Nora's illnesses, what kind of conflicts, if any, did you two have?"

I swallowed hard. "Before the MS was diagnosed, Lee began interfering, offering a million suggestions about what might be wrong. Lee and I had arguments about what to do for Nora. For a little more than a year—before we knew it was MS—I thought

Nora was just complaining about every little sensation. I lost patience with her and we argued. Looking back on it, I was insensitive and unsympathetic. I—we had no idea what was going on. I was frustrated and angry."

"And at some point, you left Nora . . . took an apartment nearby?"

"Yes."

"And what made you come back in a few weeks?"

"I couldn't stay away. I . . . I just couldn't. It was impossible. And once the MS was diagnosed, I realized Nora's problems weren't imaginary."

Ben went on with dozens of questions—a detailed probing of every aspect of Nora's and my struggle with her illness. As I answered each question, the image of my beautiful Nora flashed through my mind. It felt like I was tumbling through space and time.

"And you heard Gina Scott testify that sometimes you weren't that understanding of Nora's situation?"

"Yes. Before the MS was diagnosed I didn't know what was going on."

"How did you feel when you learned she had MS?"

"Horrible. I didn't know if I could ever make it up to her."

Please, Ben, let's stop. I can't take any more of this.

"I want to ask you a few more questions about the final months of Nora's life."

I swallowed again, but there was no saliva. My mouth was parched. My eyes felt swollen. My ears were clogged.

"Did it become increasingly clear that Nora would never recover?"

"Yes."

"How did that make you feel?"

"I can't describe it. I'm sorry, I just can't . . ."

"Permission, Your Honor, to ask some leading questions?"

"I think we can allow that. Proceed, Counselor."

"Thank you, Your Honor."

Ben approached the witness stand. "During the last year of Nora's life, did you feel sad?"

"Oh, God, yes."

A shiver moved up my spine. Coldness seeped through me.

"Did you feel angry?"

"Yes."

"Who were you angry with?"

"At fate, I guess."

A deep, drawing ache began inside me.

"Angry at fate?"

"Yes. I was angry at the world. Even at God. Angry . . . feelings of . . . I wondered . . . why *Nora?* Why *us?* How could this happen?"

"But it did happen. How did you deal with it?"

"I tried not to let it eat away at me."

"And you began writing *Assassin's Lullaby?*"

"Yes."

"Despite everything, you could do that?"

"I did my best. Nora wanted one more novel as a gift. Looking back, I think the writing kept me sane. It took me away from the horror of our lives. For a few hours every day, I could live in an imaginary world."

"The world Mr. Chang described during his testimony?"

"Yes."

"The imaginary world of the novel . . . of *Assassin's Lullaby?*"

"Yes."

"Now, Bill, we heard Dr. Radin testify that he recommended a nursing home. How did you feel about that?"

"I could never do that."

A nursing home, such a sickening thought. It reminded me of Constance and her husband, Alfred.

"Why not?"

"I'd rather die."

"You'd rather *die?*"

"Yes."

"Did you actually think of suicide?"

"No. But I felt some part of me was dying with Nora."

"Getting back to a nursing home . . . Why couldn't you do that?"

"It would have been giving up on Nora. She'd never want that. Nora's the most . . ." I shook my head. "She was much too courageous for that."

Sniffling came from the jury box. Someone coughed.

Sweat dribbled down my back. My undershirt was soaked, clinging to my body like soaked tissue. The chill seeping through my flesh grew more intense, as though something dead was crawling inside me.

"Bill, just a few more questions."

I nodded and closed my eyes.

"Toward the end, after talking with Dr. Radin, you knew Nora would die, true?"

"Yes."

"Had you given up all hope she might survive?"

"I guess I never completely accepted it . . . emotionally."

"But at some point, *did* you accept that she would die?"

"Yes, I think so." I nearly choked, making that admission.

"Did Dr. Radin make any comment about that?"

"Yes. About a month before Nora died, I went to his office to talk."

"What was said?"

"He didn't think Nora would live much longer."

"Did you think his opinion was correct?"

"Probably," I said, quelling a sob.

"Bill, please forgive me, but I have to ask these questions.

Okay?"

I nodded as I tried to stifle the trembling within me.

"Would you possibly kill Nora to save money?"

"Of *course* not."

"Would you kill her to be with another woman?"

"I wouldn't kill her for anything."

"For anything?"

"Never."

"For mercy?"

"No."

"Now, Bill, just one or two more questions," Ben said, moving closer to the witness stand. "Again, forgive me for asking this . . ."

A cramp began at the back of my thigh.

"Did you kill Nora?"

"No. I did not."

"Did you ever intend to harm or kill her?"

"Never."

It hardly mattered how many times we'd gone over it; this was unbearable. I was about to shatter into a million pieces.

Can the jury see how I'm shaking . . . or is it just my insides?

My trembling hands rose to my face. I felt faint.

The gavel came down as Marin recessed court for lunch.

"You did fine, Bill," Ben said in the conference room. "I think the jury was with you. We may have undone some of the damage that jackass Russell did. You know, I prepped him for three hours, paid him for the prep time, too. I told him to *forget* that shit about anticipatory grief, but he had to open his mouth. Some doctors gotta show the jury how much they know."

"So now Olson takes his shots, right?"

"Just tell the truth, Bill. Don't fudge a thing. Don't argue with him and don't be hostile. He'll try to box you in. The jury may resent it." Ben leaned across the table and stared into my eyes.

"The only weapon you have is the truth."

"The truth?"

"Yes. The truth is on your side."

So, I'd been wrong assuming Ben thought I was guilty when he recommended the plea. He believed me.

A triumph of sorts: my own attorney and best friend believed I didn't kill Nora.

Chapter 36

"Mr. Olson, cross-examination."

My eyes throbbed and my brain was pulsing.

How will I ever get through this?

Judge Marin rustled some papers. The clerk cleared his throat. The stenographer looked up at me expectantly, clutching her little machine between her knees.

Ben warned me the cross would be brutal. If I could zone out, somehow, maybe I'd gut my way through this ordeal.

The clock read one fifteen. *How long could it last? Would he push it to the end of the day, then into tomorrow?*

"I'd like to ask you about giving the warfarin intravenously," Olson said, flipping a page of his notes on the lectern.

My scalp dampened. My cheeks felt hot. Dread ramped through me.

"How did the warfarin come prepared?"

"It was a vial of powder. I had to make up the liquid each morning."

"Why each morning?"

"It had to be made fresh. Once it was mixed in solution, it would lose potency quickly. That's what Dr. Radin said."

"How did you mix the warfarin solution?"

My mouth went dry. My tongue prickled.

Details, endless specifics, minutiae. That's what this'll be.

"It was a kit with one and a half milliliters of sterile water and a premeasured amount of powder," I said. "There was one milligram of warfarin powder for half a milliliter of water. So it made three milligrams of warfarin solution."

"But Nora only needed *two* milligrams, isn't that right?"

"Yes."

"I'd like to focus on the morning of Nora's death. That morning, there were *three* milligrams of warfarin inside the syringe when you made the solution?"

"Yes."

"That's fifty percent more than the prescribed dose, right?"

"I never thought about the percentage, but I guess so."

"Do you agree that three milligrams of warfarin in the syringe that morning would be a *fifty percent* greater dose than the one Nora was supposed to receive?"

"Yes."

"And that fifty percent amount of extra warfarin, if it was injected, would be consistent with the toxicology report prepared by the medical examiner—the one reviewed by Dr. Pauling?"

"Objection, Your Honor," Ben yelled, bounding to his feet.

"Overruled."

"I repeat," Olson went on, "the fifty percent amount of extra warfarin is the exact amount described in the toxicology report, which has been entered into evidence, and about which Dr. Pauling testified in this courtroom. Isn't that correct, Mr. Shaw?"

"Yes, I guess so."

"So," Olson said, "that morning, once you prepared the dose, you had fifty percent more warfarin in the syringe than Nora needed, yes?"

"Yes."

"What did you do with the extra milligram?"

"I discarded it."

"You discarded it?" Olson's forehead furrowed as his eyebrows rose. "How did you do that?"

As I spoke, I visualized our kitchen. "Just like I did every morning, I held the syringe over the sink and pressed the plunger to squeeze out the extra half milliliter. That left one milliliter of solution with two milligrams of warfarin in the syringe."

"And you say you did that on the morning Nora died?"

"Yes."

"You're certain of that?"

"Yes."

"How can you be so certain, so sure about what you did?"

"I looked at the syringe very carefully."

"You did?"

"Objection. Argumentative."

"Sustained."

"Okay, so you say you looked at the syringe carefully. Was it clearly marked?"

"Yes."

"How was it marked?"

"With heavy black lines. Each line was half a milliliter, or one milligram, of warfarin. So two milligrams were left in the syringe after I squeezed out the extra solution."

"Did anyone watch you do this each morning?"

"No. I was alone."

"Each and every morning?"

"Yes."

"Including the morning Nora died?"

"Yes."

I tried staying calm though a taut wire hummed in my chest.

Olson returned to why the warfarin was given at six a.m.

Six o'clock . . . an even hour, easy to remember.

Six o'clock . . . I'd been awake for an hour—if I'd slept at all. I was alert, focused.

Six o'clock *every* morning, to keep a steady twenty-four-hour level of warfarin in Nora's bloodstream, as Radin instructed. No variations, no deviations.

The questions kept coming. It was like an echo chamber. Olson's voice reverberated and then grew soft and distant. Was I zoning out?

Then, Olson switched gears.

"How do you come up with ideas for your novels?"

"It's very hard to say."

"Do you plan them? Plot them out?"

Plan, plot. Loaded words, calculated to register with the jury. Olson's a wordsmith, too.

"I'm not really sure."

"Where do they come from, these stories about stalkers, killers, and criminals?"

"Sometimes a newspaper item sparks a thought, or I'll hear a newscast. But I can't really say."

"Do these ideas come from somewhere inside yourself? From your own mind?"

"Objection. Calls for speculation, Your Honor," called Ben.

"Sustained."

"I want to ask you specifically about that novel Mr. Chang found on your computer, *Assassin's Lullaby*."

I waited as Olson turned pages of his notes. My pulse quickened.

Killian's story seemed a universe away from the trial. It was from a time when Nora was still alive—a lifetime gone.

"How did you arrive at the title for the novel, *Assassin's Lullaby*?"

There was a shuttling rush, a frenzy of images, but nothing coalesced. "I don't know. I never really thought about it."

"It's about a hit man who's asked to eliminate a woman—the sister of a mob associate, yes?"

I imagined Killian, the fat man, then Irena. I could barely recall the details though I'd looked at the manuscript only hours before Chang's testimony two days earlier. The novel—what little there was of it—existed beyond me, with a life of its own. It seemed to have sprung from a place other than my imagination; the one Cindy Armor thought served us both so well. Cindy Armor—who wanted a memoir of the trial, of this torture, of my carrying this cross along my own Via Dolorosa.

Was I in the Garden of Gethsemane? I suddenly had a flash of something I'd read long ago in the Bible; somehow, it stayed with me all through the years. It was from the New Testament, the image was unforgettable—of Luke's saying that in the Garden of Gethsemane, Jesus's anguish was so deep, his sweat was as if it were great drops of blood falling to the ground. Why was I thinking about this now? About Jesus . . . and suffering . . . and blood . . . seeping . . . dripping everywhere . . . My God.

Assassin's Lullaby . . . *From what sick corner of my mind did the title and story emerge? A novel about a remorseless killer asked to eliminate a woman—one with whom he was falling in love.*

"Mr. Shaw, did you hear the question? The novel is about an assassin who's going to kill this woman, right?"

"Yes."

The room began swaying.

"And you always write about crime?"

"I . . . yes . . ."

"About killing, shooting, stabbing, poisoning?"

"I—I've written about crime as a reporter and as a novelist."

"But no book before this one was about killing a woman, right?"

"Objection, Your Honor," Ben cried. "Irrelevant."

"It's *extremely* relevant, Your Honor," Olson countered. "It goes to the defendant's state of mind—"

"Objection. *Objection!*" Ben shouted, leaping to his feet.

The judge called for a sidebar.

The attorneys huddled at the far side of the bench. I heard

snippets of whispering, indistinct garbled words, glottal sounds, some passionate, others beseeching. I closed my eyes, felt removed from it all, and began floating through some strange ether.

Olson returned to the lectern.

"Does Killian agree to take the job and kill this woman?"

"I guess he's still thinking about it."

"You're using the present tense. Why?"

"Present tense? Am I? I guess I am."

"Do you always do that when referring to your novels?"

"I never thought about it."

Do the novels live on in my mind? Is Killian alive inside me?

"But this novel, *Assassin's Lullaby,* is still in your mind, still waiting for completion, for some resolution?"

Is this really happening? I'm being cross-examined in a court of law about words and ideas, about my imaginings—about a partially completed novel?

"Did you hear my question? This issue is still up in the air, undecided?"

"What issue?"

"Whether or not Killian will kill this woman?"

"I haven't thought about it."

Ice water trickled through my chest.

"Does Killian want the job or not?"

"Objection, Your Honor," Ben called. "Irrelevant."

"I'll give Mr. Olson a bit of latitude here," Marin said. "Continue, Mr. Olson, but let's not drag this out."

"Is Killian *ambivalent* about killing her?" Olson asked.

"I—I don't really know." Buzzing began in my ears, an insect-like drone.

"You have no idea, or should I say, *Killian* has no idea yet whether or not he'll murder this woman?"

A jackhammer was pounding through my skull.

"Did you hear my question?"

"Huh?"

"Does Killian—or you—know if he'll murder this woman?"

"I don't know."

Olson's talking about Killian as though he's a living, breathing person. As though he's some kind of alter ego—Jekyll and Hyde. A lover and a monster. It's insane. And Killian . . . falling in love with Irena? How absurd. A hit man falling in love with his target? Impossible.

"But a central conflict in the novel is whether Killian will murder this woman?"

"I—I guess so." The buzzing in my ears grew louder.

"How will he plan to kill her?"

Something snapped in my brain. I was slipping away.

"Mr. Shaw?"

"Huh? Yes?"

"How would he kill her?"

"It—I don't . . . it really hasn't been on my mind."

"But the murder of a woman is central to the story?"

"Objection. Asked and answered," Ben called from far away.

"Sustained."

"I object to this entire line of questioning, Your Honor," Ben shouted so loudly, my head snapped up and I looked at him. His face was crimson, and a vein on his forehead looked like it would pop. "Mr. Olson's asking my client about a work of fiction as though it's reality. This is *absurd*. He's being cross-examined about *fiction*. I object."

"I think the jury knows it's fiction, Mr. Abrams," said Marin. "It's certainly not factual. I'll allow it. Continue, Mr. Olson."

Ben plopped into his seat.

Olson had corralled me into talking about murder—fictional or otherwise—as though it were a burning issue in my life.

"Is this woman—the victim—beautiful?"

"I guess so." It felt like sandpaper was stuck in my throat.

"Did she have any acting experience?"

Olson had virtually memorized the manuscript.

"Yes . . . in Russia."

"What kind of—"

"Objection, Your Honor," Ben roared, standing. "This is all irrelevant."

"Sustained."

"But, Judge—"

"I've given you plenty of latitude, Mr. Olson. You're delving far afield. Move on."

Olson's face reddened. "Your Honor, may we have a sidebar?"

Marin paused; his brow furrowed. He plucked his glasses from his nose. "Okay, let's clear the courtroom. We'll take a ten-minute break."

Within minutes the courtroom was empty. I remained in the witness chair. Motionless, stuck in place, frozen. My legs trembled and my heart pounded. The attorneys stood behind their respective tables.

"I've cleared the courtroom because the jury shouldn't hear this," Marin said. "And I want everything on the record," he said with a glance at the court reporter. "Proceed, Mr. Olson."

"Your Honor, the contents of the novel are crucial to the prosecution's case. This relates to the defendant's state of mind, his *thinking* at the time of his wife's death. The novel is a product of his inner mental life. It involves the murder of a woman, as does this trial. It's entirely relevant."

"Mr. Abrams?"

"Your Honor, the novel is *fiction*. Mr. Olson knows the difference between fact and fiction. This trial is about the facts surrounding the death of Nora Shaw, not a detour into the realm of fiction writing."

"Mr. Olson?"

"How do we separate fact from fiction, Your Honor?" Olson

rasped. "We have a novelist who's writing a book about a man killing a woman, which is exactly what Mr. Shaw is on trial for. The novel and the defendant's life are intimately connected. This goes directly to motive."

"No, Mr. Olson," Judge Marin said softly. "You're asking the jury to speculate about a man's creativity, about some inner spark of inspiration for his writing. We're not here to dissect artistic creativity."

"I'm asking about the defendant's *thinking*, Your Honor."

"Your Honor, it's inflammatory," Ben called, his voice nearly hissing. "My client's not on trial for writing a novel. Any more questions along these lines and I'm going to ask for a mistrial. And furthermore, if there's a conviction, this is grounds for reversal. I'll take it—"

"No, it's not," growled Olson.

"*Enough*," Marin said. "No colloquy."

"Your Honor, you allowed Mr. Abrams to cross-examine Mr. Chang about what was in the novel. I should be accorded the same opportunity."

"Mr. Abrams?"

"Your Honor, you allowed me to cross-examine Mr. Chang about the contents of the novel because it shed light on the computer searches. Not to explore Mr. Shaw's imagination. There's an important distinction, Your Honor."

Ben's eyes were so wide I could see the whites above his irises. Marin looked at Olson.

"Your Honor," Olson said, "this man Killian, his motives, the ways he kills—by strangling, poisons, toxins, shootings—they come from Mr. Shaw, from the inner workings of his mind. These details shed light on his state of mind at the time of Nora Shaw's death. And I would remind the court that even as she lay in bed dying, the defendant was writing the novel in the coffee shop and then the library."

Marin turned to Ben.

"Your Honor, I don't want this to sound patronizing, but I feel forced to remind the court that Mr. Shaw is not on trial for writing fiction. Facts are facts. Fiction is fantasy. This trial is about the truth. Not fiction. I object to this line of questioning, Your Honor."

"Anything else, Mr. Olson?"

"No, Your Honor."

"The objection is sustained, Mr. Olson. You will *not* cross-examine the defendant any further about the contents of his novel. As counsel states, it's fiction, not fact. It has no place here in terms of trying to determine his state of mind. You had ample opportunity to cross-examine Dr. Russell. You could have brought in your own psychiatrist if you'd chosen to do so. I allowed Mr. Abrams to cross-examine the computer expert to explain the sites the defendant visited."

"But, Your Honor—"

"No, Mr. Olson. If we were to use fiction as evidence against its creator, then every author alive could be put on trial for thoughts or imaginings, and we'd be far less than the democracy we are."

Air rushed from my chest. But was it too late? Sitting in the witness chair, I realized the jury had already heard so much about Killian and Irena, it could influence their views. Still, the judge had it right, and maybe the jury would see it that way, too.

"But, Your Honor," Olson warbled, "the novel is—"

"No, Mr. Olson. I've given you plenty of latitude. The contents of the novel are *not* germane to this trial." Marin turned to the court officer. "Okay, let's call the jury back in."

Back at the lectern, Olson shuffled pages and drew a line across some notes. I felt a surge of hope; he'd been forced to drop a bunch of questions.

"Mr. Shaw, isn't it true that as a novelist, you write fiction? You make things up, fabricate stories?"

"*Objection*, Your Honor."

"Sustained. Mr. Olson, I think we all know that novelists make up stories."

"Your Honor, I want a curative instruction to the jury," Ben called.

"I don't think it's necessary, Mr. Abrams. We all know novelists write fiction. It doesn't mean they tell lies in their real lives. Next question, Mr. Olson."

"Mr. Shaw, isn't it true that you taught a course at the New School?"

"Yes."

"And the name of that course was *Fiction and Reality*?"

"Yes. That's correct." My voice was weakening.

"And didn't you say in one of your lectures that a writer must drag his own life experiences onto the page for a novel to come alive for the reader? Onto the page, right?"

"Yes, I'm sure I said that."

"Are any of your experiences found on the pages of your novels?"

"I—I'm sure some are."

"Which ones?"

"I can't really say offhand."

I was withering right there, on the witness stand.

"Especially when you're writing about murder?"

"*Objection*. This is *outrageous*, Your Honor!" Ben shouted. "Mr. Olson is implying that Bill Shaw is guilty of murder because he's *written* about it. I object, Your Honor."

"The objection is sustained. I'm *warning* you, Mr. Olson. Move on."

Olson blinked a few times. Then he closed his eyes and shook his head from side to side. Silence prevailed for what seemed forever. I felt like leaping from the witness stand and racing from the courtroom.

"Next question, Mr. Olson," the judge said with a sharp tone in his voice.

"Mr. Shaw. Did you hope Nora would die?"

My head snapped up. I heard some jurors gasp.

Did I want her to die? Was that a wish I'd had . . . ever? Maybe it was. How can I know? If I had, would I even admit it to myself? Was I ambivalent about her life . . . the way Dr. Russell described many people's reactions to a long illness and the inevitable death of a loved one?

"I'll ask you again, Mr. Shaw. Did you want Nora to die?"

"No. Not at all."

Olson scribbled something in his notes.

"So, Mr. Shaw, you weren't *ambivalent* about your wife's situation? About wanting her to die, to get her suffering—and yours— over with?"

My jaw clenched. I could no longer keep any distance from the questions. I'd have to be made of ice or stone to do that.

"Ambivalent?" I said softly

"Please speak up. The jurors need to hear you," Olson said.

"Ambivalent?" My voice was cracking. "I don't know. I was miserable. I felt like *I* was dying . . . little by little. I felt guilty about being alive. What can I say? My whole life was crumbling. I don't know *what* I felt. I was sad; I was beside myself; I was bereft, confused."

I sat in a feverish reverie, waiting for Olson's next question.

"Mr. Shaw, didn't you tell Ms. Manning you wanted Nora to die? That you wanted Nora to get it over with?"

"I said I was mixed up. It was torture. I didn't know how to deal with it."

"You were mixed up and felt tortured?"

"Yes . . . I . . . I didn't know how I could go on. Or how to deal with it all."

"But you wanted Nora to die, didn't you?"

"No, or maybe . . . maybe for it all to end. Her torture, and mine. I just didn't know . . . and I'll never know how I was able to deal with it all."

"And you did deal with it, didn't you?"

"I don't know. I did the best I could."

"The best you could? Did that include helping Nora die?"

I sat there, dazed, as though a shroud had dropped over me. I shook my head.

"You must answer verbally," Olson said.

"No."

"The morning she died. You're sure you discarded that extra milligram of warfarin?"

"Yes." My vision blurred as tears filled my eyes.

"We'll come back to this in a minute, Mr. Shaw. I want to ask about your finances."

Finances . . . just money . . . printed paper . . . credits and debits . . . meaningless.

Olson pored through some pages on the prosecution table and then returned to the lectern.

"Isn't it true that for long before Nora died, you wrote very little?"

"Only a few magazine articles . . . and I began that novel."

"Were you living on the money you earned from those articles?"

"No."

"Did you receive an advance on *Assassin's Lullaby?*"

"No."

"Couldn't a writer of your reputation get an advance by submitting an outline to your editor or have your agent sell it?"

"I guess so."

"Why didn't you do that?"

"I was just writing, trying to stay alive. I was writing for Nora."

"Getting back to your finances, what were you living on these last three-plus years?"

"Royalties from my earlier books. And savings."

"When you say *savings*, you mean money from Nora's trust, don't you?"

"Yes . . . once our other savings were gone."

"They were gone because of bad investments, correct?"

"Yes."

"And you were drawing that trust money down once you'd stopped writing, true?"

"Yes."

"And how much were you spending on Nora's upkeep?"

"It was probably two hundred thousand a year."

"And what about paying for regular living expenses, things like co-op maintenance, food, telephone, utilities? Were you worried you'd run out of money?"

"It was on my mind, but I didn't dwell on it."

The room seemed to swirl. If this kept up, I'd pass out.

"Considering these huge outlays for Nora, how long would you have been able to cover them with what was left of the trust money?"

"I think there was enough for maybe another year."

"And then what?"

"I don't know. I didn't let myself think about it."

"Isn't it true, Mr. Shaw, that you were behind on your mortgage payments?"

"Yes."

"And you were making only partial payments on your credit card?"

"Yes."

"Paying exorbitant interest rates to the bank as a result?"

"Yes."

"And you were racking up huge bills on medications,

equipment, doctor visits, and the home health aide?"

"Yes."

"And the insurance company dropped Nora once she got sick, correct?"

Can I even remember which one it was, and all the others that turned us down because of Nora's condition?

"Mr. Shaw, the insurance company wasn't paying for any of this, right?"

"Yes."

"It was all out of pocket?"

"Yes."

"Including the bills for two hospital stays?"

"Yes."

"And the IRS said you owed back taxes?"

"That's right."

"Interest and penalties were accruing?"

"Yes."

"And you were paying Roberta Morgan off the books, weren't you?"

"Yes."

"In cash?"

"Yes."

"Why?"

"Because she charged less than an agency."

"Were you paying Social Security for her?"

"No."

"You knew you were breaking the law, didn't you?"

"Yes."

"Is she an illegal alien?"

"I don't know. I—"

"Objection. *Irrelevant,*" Ben cried.

"Sustained. Move on, Mr. Olson."

Olson tapped his pen on the lectern, glanced at the jury, and then said, "And when Nora's trust money ran out, you'd be facing personal bankruptcy, wouldn't you?"

"I guess so. I didn't think about it. I really didn't care," that small voice answered.

"You didn't *care*?"

"Objection, Your Honor. Mr. Olson's arguing with the witness."

"Sustained."

"If you didn't care, Mr. Shaw, why were you doing computer searches about offshore bank accounts?"

"It was for the novel."

"Did you personally ever open up an offshore bank account?"

"No."

"Remember, sir, you're under oath."

"*Objection*, Your Honor," Ben cried, rising to his feet. "Mr. Olson's remark is uncalled for. It implies that my client is lying."

"Sustained." Marin turned to the jurors. "Ladies and gentlemen, you will ignore that last statement." He turned to the prosecutor. "Proceed carefully, Mr. Olson. Ask questions. Don't make statements or give speeches."

Olson waited a beat, flipped a page, and looked at me. "Now, Mr. Shaw, you entered into a relationship with Constance Manning, right?"

"A relationship?"

Jesus, where is he going with this line of questioning?

"Well, what would you call it?"

"She was an acquaintance."

"An acquaintance with whom you spent over four hours in her apartment one evening, correct?"

"I guess so," I said, afraid Olson was trying to trap me.

"Okay, an *acquaintance*. And a few minutes ago you denied feeling ambivalent about your wife's impending death. Is that so?"

"I—I said whatever I did."

"Would you like the court reporter to read it back to you?"

"No, not really."

"It's no trouble, Mr. Shaw. The court reporter can read it back if you'd like."

Olson's sarcasm caused something incendiary to brew inside my skull. White lights flashed before my eyes. I breathed heavily, sucking in stale courtroom air.

"Will you take my word for it that you said you had *no idea* if you were ambivalent about your wife's situation, about whether she lived or died?"

"Yes."

"Mr. Shaw, please tell us all, what does it mean to be ambivalent?"

Patronizing bastard.

"It means to have mixed feelings."

"Meaning *wanting* something to happen and yet being *afraid* it could happen?"

"Yes."

"Mr. Shaw, you recall that Mr. Chang had printouts from your computer?"

"Yes."

"I would like to direct your attention to one printout. With your permission, Your Honor, I would like to approach the witness."

Was this Olson's ace in the hole? Had he found something that would make me look like a liar? He knew I'd be forced to testify. He'd nail me with it. I felt like keeling over, collapsing in the witness chair.

"You may approach," the judge said.

"Before I do, I'd like to ask you, Mr. Shaw, did you send e-mails to Constance?"

"Yes."

"Well, I'm giving your attorney a copy of an e-mail we extracted from your computer. I would like Mr. Abrams to stipulate that this evidence was exchanged as per the rules of evidence."

"So stipulated, Your Honor," Ben said.

"And I'll give the defendant a copy and ask him to read it to himself," Olson said, dropping a paper onto the defense table. Ben's brow furrowed as he read it.

Olson proceeded to the witness stand and slipped another copy onto the ledge before me. "Will you please read that to yourself, Mr. Shaw?"

I peered down through bleary eyes.

The heading read: *w.shawwriter@aol.com.*

"Mr. Shaw, is that an e-mail you sent Constance Manning?"

"Yes."

The e-mail looked so strange. The printed words wavered before my eyes.

"With Your Honor's permission, I would like to read to the jury from People's exhibit three, this communication written by the defendant."

"Go ahead, Mr. Olson."

Olson read slowly, enunciating each word. I heard him through clogged ears.

> Dear Constance. You ask if it's just sharing our tragedies that's brought us close. Yes we're two very desperate people, clinging to each other, but meeting you is the only ray of hope in my life.
>
> I know I love Nora and always will. It's impossible for me to live with myself knowing Nora is dying, and realizing that some terrible part of me waits for her death and wants it to happen.
>
> This is hell, and I don't know how much longer I can bear it. But it would be worse without you.
>
> Bill

The courtroom was silent. Throats cleared. Someone coughed.

Sniffling came from somewhere.

I sat, frozen, staring in unfocused stupefaction. My mind went blank, as though every thought had evaporated.

"Keeping your e-mail in mind, sir," Olson said, "didn't you say you wanted Nora to die, that you were waiting for her death and wanted it to happen?"

"I guess so."

"Then Mr. Shaw, is it still your testimony that you weren't ambivalent about your wife's death?"

"I guess I was," I said.

Something was changing inside me. It was an unforeseen metamorphosis. I no longer cared about the trial. It seemed not to matter if I was sent away to some hellhole to rot. Whether I lived or died or what others thought of me. Nothing mattered.

"Mr. Shaw, is it fair to say that on some level you wanted Nora to die?"

"I guess so," I said, feeling detached.

"Well, sir, without *guessing*, isn't that what your e-mail to Constance said?"

"Yes."

"So you weren't being truthful a few minutes ago when you told this jury you weren't ambivalent about Nora's situation, were you?"

"I've been trying to answer your questions honestly."

"But I'm not asking you *questions* now, sir. I'm asking you this one, single, very important question. It's a very specific question. Please, sir, listen carefully to the question." Olson paused theatrically. "I asked you if you wanted Nora to die. And your answer was—and I'm quoting you exactly—'No, not at all.' We can have the court reporter read it back if you'd prefer. Do you remember answering the question that way?"

"Yes. I think so."

"Thank you. Now—"

"I was mixed up. I can only say I was devastated. I felt sorry for Nora, and for Constance, for her husband, and myself. Everything was so dark, so filled with death and dread, and there was nothing left for me, nothing at all. The whole world was just—"

"There's no question pending, sir."

"I felt guilty for living my life and for—"

"Sir, there's no *question*—"

"I don't know how I got through it all; I just—"

"*Mr. Shaw,* there's no—"

"It was a terrible time for me and for Constance," I rasped. A torrent of words was slipping past my lips. "I couldn't give anything of myself. Not a thing. Not a single thing. Not anymore. I was burned out, wasted. Like . . . like . . . it's the way I feel now. There's nothing, nothing at all left for me. It's all over. I'll never get over Nora's death. My life's meaningless. I might as well be dead."

I stared ahead, seeing nothing. My insides felt poisoned. I was unable to move or care. Everything was over . . . just gone.

Olson fell silent.

I was lost in some mental fog bank.

Finally, I looked up.

Marin stared fixedly down at Olson.

The prosecutor's eyebrows rose; his mouth twisted into a befuddled grimace.

Ben sat silently with his elbows on the defense table. His hands were clasped in front of his mouth.

"And you weren't ambivalent?" Olson asked.

I said nothing. I could barely hear a thing above the oceanic roaring in my ears.

"Sir, can you answer the question? You weren't ambivalent?"

"Ambivalent?" I croaked. "Call it whatever you want, Mr. Olson. It's only a word. I can't describe what I felt, then or now. It's just . . . it's impossible. Words fail me."

"Words fail *William Shaw*? A *writer*?"

"Objection. Argumentative," Ben called.

"Sustained."

The courtroom was quiet. A juror coughed. It went on for a long time, hacking, insistent. The room darkened. I was fading.

"Mr. Shaw, do you want to take a break?" asked Judge Marin.

"No," a strange voice replied.

"Did you kill Nora?" Olson asked.

I stared straight ahead.

"Mr. Shaw. I repeat. Did you kill Nora?"

I stared into the distance—beyond Olson, above the gallery and the throng filling it, and saw the courtroom's swinging doors. It was all so strange, so otherworldly, beyond everything. Something inside me snapped. I got up from the witness chair, moved down the middle aisle, left the courtroom, trudged down the hallway and out the building's front entrance, crossed Foley Square and the next thing I knew, I was traveling through the Queens Midtown Tunnel. Leaving the tunnel, I squinted in blinding sunlight, feeling insensate, uncaring. I trudged along in the vastness of the cemetery with its endless rows of gray headstones and saw people mourning at gravesides. Tears and moans were everywhere. It looked surreal, like a Fellini movie. I watched the walnut-stained coffin lower into the hole, saw people throw roses onto it, watched them shovel soil onto the casket, and saw the earth cover Nora as rocks and loam thumped onto the wood. Choking, I heard people crying, sniffling, heard the preacher utter words, invoking God, and I was about to faint, drop to the ground, when I felt Charlie's arm wrap around me and hold me up, and then Ben hugged me, Elaine, too. Sobs continued in the humid air, the whoosh of traffic from the Long Island Expressway sounded in my ears, and the Manhattan skyline was silhouetted against a glaring white sky.

My life was buried in that dark hole, slipping away with Nora. There would never be her voice, her arms, her gorgeous legs, her love, her passion. There would never be another tango. Nora now lived only in my mind, an image, a memory, a taste, a sight, a lingering sense of her and our life together, nothing more—and while shivering in the witness chair, with tears in my eyes, I heard Olson say something.

I opened my eyes and gazed at the courtroom ceiling with its circular fans and art-deco lights, knowing I'd slipped away from it all.

For how long? Seconds? Minutes? More?

Olson stood behind the lectern. I sat rigidly in the witness chair with the judge to my right, the jury to my left, and a mass of spectators in the gallery.

"Let the record reflect that the witness has not answered the question about whether he killed Nora Shaw," Olson said.

"Objection, Your Honor," called Ben. "Mr. Shaw looks like he's not well. I think he needs a break."

"Do you want to take a break, Mr. Shaw," Marin asked.

I shook my head from side to side.

There was a pause. I don't know how long it lasted.

"Mr. Shaw, I'm going to repeat my question. Did you kill Nora?"

"No, I did not," said that weak voice.

The courtroom remained silent. I stared straight ahead. Everything seemed muted, blurred, unreal.

"Mr. Shaw? Do you hear me?"

"Huh?"

"Are you listening to me?"

"Yes."

"Do you recall the night the police brought you to the precinct?"

"Yes." My thoughts spooled back to that night.

"And the detectives told you they were recording everything, correct?"

"Yes."

A flat-screen video monitor stood before the jury.

I could smell that cork-lined room, the stuffiness, the odor of sweat, damp cement, felt the intolerable closeness, and saw the sickly fluorescent glow.

"Do you recall being asked if you met anyone at Starbucks in the mornings?"

"Yes . . ."

I was lost in a blur of memories: the interrogation room, Ben, Kaufman, Cirillo, the arraignment, grand jury, images of the funeral, the graveyard, sitting in the empty apartment, Johnnie Walker, Gromann's Tavern, the old men guzzling booze—it all fused in an ugly stream of despair, death, and disbelief.

The DVD player was on: an image appeared on the monitor. In the right lower corner was a digital indication of the date and time. An angle shot showed me sitting in a metal chair. Kaufman's voice came from off camera.

"So you'd leave Nora with Roberta, the aide?"

"Yes."

"Did you meet anyone at Starbucks in the mornings?"

"At Starbucks? No."

"Mr. Shaw, are you seeing anyone?"

"Seeing anyone? What do you mean?"

"What do I mean? Romantically, is what I mean."

"No. Not at all."

"You sure about that?"

"Yes, of course."

The DVD player clicked off. The monitor darkened.

Murmuring rose in the courtroom. Music, too—some orchestral strains of melody—mostly violins; was it "Alfie"? Or was it the beginning of Nora's tango? It was so strange. Was it in my mind?

"Mr. Shaw, does that refresh your recollection of your interview with the police?"

"I suppose so."

"And you told the detectives you *didn't* meet anyone at Starbucks in the mornings. Is that correct?"

"That's what I said."

"The question used the plural—*mornings*—didn't it? 'Did you meet anyone at Starbucks in the morning*s*?'" Olson repeated, emphasizing the *s*. "Meaning on *different* mornings, not just one specific morning. Isn't that correct?"

"Yes."

"And you said no, didn't you? You *didn't* meet anyone in the *mornings,* right?"

"Yes."

"So you denied *ever* meeting anyone at Starbucks, correct?"

"I guess so."

"And that wasn't truthful, was it?"

"I didn't—"

"Sir, in fact, you *did* meet Constance Manning at Starbucks, didn't you?"

"Yes."

"But you denied it when the police asked you, didn't you?"

"Yes."

"So you didn't tell them the truth, did you?"

"I didn't think . . . I didn't want to—"

"Mr. Shaw, if it wasn't the truth, then it was a *lie*, correct?"

"I guess so."

"So you were lying to the police?"

"I didn't want to get Constance—"

"The bottom line is you lied to the police, right?"

"Yes."

"So you were lying then, but you're not lying now?"

"No, I'm not."

"So, Mr. Shaw, you've denied killing Nora, correct?"

I nodded.

"You must respond verbally, sir."

"I—I—don't . . . I didn't kill her."

"And today you denied feeling ambivalent, which was not true. Correct?"

"I guess so." I was losing track of his words, of my own, too. Everything was cascading down a dark tunnel.

"And even though you lied to the police and lied in this courtroom, even though you didn't speak *truthfully* today, you're asking this jury to believe you when you deny wanting Nora to die and when you deny having killed her. Is that so?"

"Fate took her from me."

"I have no further questions, Your Honor." Olson shook his head, whirled in place, and walked to the prosecution table.

"Just a couple of questions," said Ben from behind the lectern.

I sat, waiting, an insensate remnant of myself.

"Do you recall Mr. Olson questioning you about feeling ambivalent?"

"Yes."

"Can you explain what you were feeling at the time?"

I tried gathering my thoughts, but they were tumbling out of control. "It's impossible to put into words," I said. "There were so many feelings. It was—I'm trying to think what it was like . . ."

I was an empty vessel—famished for thoughts, devoid of words, utterly defeated. Though I wanted to say more, as I'd always been a wordsmith, nothing would come to me.

Suddenly, the room swayed as panic filled me. I shook violently; my thoughts shredded and I was certain my mind was going.

"I'm sorry . . . . I'm so sorry, but I—I just can't do it. Since Nora died, something inside me dropped away and I can't get it back."

I slid down in the witness chair, lower, collapsing inwardly, ebbing away.

"I have no more questions, Your Honor."

I was gone.

Chapter 37

Olson began his closing argument by thanking the jury for its patience. He again preached about being the People's attorney, and the need for respect of the law and life.

Alternate number one—now juror number four—nodded in assent. He and juror number eleven looked like they were buying Olson's narrative. Sitting at the defense table, I shuddered.

Step by step, Olson reassembled his building blocks, reiterating his theory about Nora's death.

"As you can see," he said, "the defendant had *motive*. He'd made bad investments, and once Nora got sick, was hemorrhaging money. He was on the verge of bankruptcy. He was also seeing Constance Manning. And you will recall the defendant lied to the police about knowing Ms. Manning.

"Ladies and gentlemen, the defendant had the means," Olson said. "It's clear by his Internet searches he had intimate knowledge of warfarin. On the morning of her death, he mixed the lethal solution and injected Nora Shaw. Did she—a woman who chose life, who chose a feeding tube, who listened to music and audiobooks even as she lay in bed—have any choice in the decision to end her life? No, she did not. That choice was made by the defendant.

"Now, the defense conceded that Dr. Pauling is a highly respected physician and pharmacologist. And the defense did *not* produce its own expert to challenge Dr. Pauling's testimony.

"Ladies and gentlemen, Mr. Abrams attacked Dr. Pauling, and tried to deflect your attention away from the truth of the laboratory values. Yes, I call those values the truth, because the numbers don't lie. They're hard-core, scientific fact. And what did Mr. Abrams do? He brought up other remote *possibilities* to explain the sky-high level of warfarin in Nora's blood. And I'm sure you noticed that Mr. Abrams tried to link Nora's death to other possibilities whose chances of causing her death hovered just above zero percent.

"You heard the defendant himself testify that he gave the warfarin at six o'clock that morning. And the lab report unequivocally showed the excessive level remaining in her blood at eleven o'clock that morning, five hours later. You learned the *scientific* facts. It's clear: Nora Shaw was given fifty percent more warfarin than her usual dose. She was overdosed, and because of that, she bled to death.

"And, ladies and gentlemen, please recall the defendant, Mr. Shaw, in his own sworn testimony confirmed that the syringe he used held three milligrams of warfarin when he was preparing it for injection the morning Nora died. It was the amount determined to have been injected into Nora by analysis of her blood postmortem, as described by Dr. Pauling.

"And let's address those other variables Mr. Abrams mentioned. They were present for years, and she never suffered a massive bleed resulting in anything even close to death. The truth is simple: the overload of warfarin that morning killed Nora. And, the defendant gave her that lethal dose."

Olson paused for a beat and moved along the jury box.

"But this case has far greater social implications than Bill Shaw's guilt. I ask you, ladies and gentlemen, what sort of society would we have if we sanctioned such killing? Would we be any different from Mr. Shaw's character Killian, in his novel *Assassin's Lullaby*? Wouldn't we become a society sanctioning murder for money or for some other venal, selfish reason?

"Do we sanction murder because a man has a sick wife? Because his life has narrowed down to that of a hospital attendant? Because he lusts for another woman? Because he's running out of money? Because *he* decides when 'till death do us part' happens?

"Is *that* the precedent we wish to set by this trial?" Olson asked. "Murder for convenience? For money? For lust? For freedom from the obligations of marriage?"

The jurors stared at Olson. A sinking sensation filled me.

"Ladies and gentlemen, the People ask you for justice. *Nora Shaw cries out to you for justice.* The People ask you to weigh the evidence and render a just verdict.

"The People ask you to find William Shaw guilty of murdering his wife, Nora Shaw. Thank you."

Chapter 38

"Ladies and gentlemen," Ben began, "you've been asked to determine Bill Shaw's future. You've accepted an awesome responsibility."

Ben stood directly in front of the jury box with his hands outstretched.

"I'd like to briefly go over the evidence and ask what could possibly lead you to conclude that Bill killed Nora."

Ben redrew the case beginning with Dr. Dugan and went through each witness. He lauded some witnesses' testimony, berated others.

"Now let's look at what Mr. Olson showed you with Mr. Chang's testimony. That Bill surfed websites about murder, poisons, drugs, and money laundering. Mr. Olson fed you *inferences* about Bill based on his Internet searches.

"But the truth came out during cross-examination, when Mr. Chang described a novel in the computer. It was obvious Bill visited those websites for research about the novel, *Assassin's Lullaby*, a piece of fiction.

"Mr. Olson fed you pure fiction when he tried to make it look like Bill was doing research to plan an actual murder. He tried to blur the line between writing a novel and the real lives of Bill and Nora Shaw."

Ben's eyes rested on each jury member.

"Is a trial meant to prosecute a man for writing fiction? Is a trial's purpose to pillory a man for his creativity, his imagination, his art? Mr. Olson would have you believe that's the purpose of this trial."

Ben's finger pointed toward the prosecutor's table. Olson looked unflinchingly at Ben.

"Ladies and gentlemen, there's a higher purpose in our being here," Ben said. "That purpose is to find the *truth*. And Mr. Olson presented anything *but* the truth. He tried to snooker you with fiction.

"Now, you heard Dr. Pauling," Ben said. "This nonpracticing doctor, who earns the bulk of his living appearing in court, testified. And what a flawed and distorted analysis this two-thousand-dollar-an-hour witness gave you."

Ben excoriated Pauling for not factoring the variables that could have caused Nora's bleeding. He enumerated them one by one.

The jurors stared at Ben, just as they had at Olson.

"And this paid witness claimed that Bill overdosed his wife. He said Bill killed Nora!" Ben shouted. "But he didn't share with you—until I dragged them out of him—the many reasons why Nora Shaw bled on the morning she died.

"So I ask you, ladies and gentlemen, how much stock can you put in Dr. Pauling's testimony? All eight thousand dollars of it. Not much.

"Now, Mr. Olson tried to portray Bill as a cheating husband. But you heard Ms. Manning—and Bill—testify. Mr. Olson tried to paint their relationship as something sordid, illicit, ugly, and once again, he fed you misinformation.

"These two bereaved people were trying to deal with the horror in their lives. They were two desperate souls, each with a slowly dying spouse. Can you imagine their anguish, their indescribable suffering? I ask you, ladies and gentlemen: try to put yourself in the situations of Bill and Constance. If you do, I'm certain you'll have some idea of the profound sadness at the core of their times together.

"So, ladies and gentlemen, forget Mr. Olson's ugly insinuations. And that's exactly what they are—vile inferences and innuendos—accusations without evidence. They're insults to Bill Shaw, to Constance Manning, and frankly, they're insults to your intelligence as members of this jury. Please, I ask you to use your sound judgment and compassion in understanding these people and the horror of their days. And ask yourselves this: were Bill and Constance any different from people meeting in a support group? No, they were not."

Ben's eyes roved over the jury members.

"Now, ladies and gentlemen, you heard Mr. Olson talk about a higher purpose to this case—how we cannot undermine our social contract.

"Well, there's an even *higher* purpose to this trial. It involves two pillars of our democracy, the very foundation of our democracy. They're *truth* and *justice.* Yes, truth and justice are why we're here today. And I ask you, ladies and gentlemen, what will best serve truth and what will preserve justice?

"Now, Judge Marin will read you the law," Ben said. "His Honor will define murder in the second degree and ask you to apply the law to the *facts* of this case. He won't ask you to apply the law to fantasy or fiction, or to Mr. Olson's salacious inferences. Judge Marin will ask you to make your determination based on the law, and beyond *a reasonable doubt.*

"Ladies and gentlemen, Mr. Olson's case reeks of doubt," Ben cried. "It's bloated with speculation and fictional implications. Mr. Olson presented fiction and asked you to view it as fact, as evidence. He distorted truth in the service of trying to convict Bill of murder."

Ben paced back and forth. The jurors followed him with their eyes.

"There's not a shred of proof that Bill Shaw committed any crime. None. So, if you weigh the facts and the evidence—not Mr. Olson's insinuations—if you consider the *law*, which derives from the English common law, and above all, should make *common* sense, you will find Bill Shaw is not guilty of anything.

"I'm certain when you consider what makes common sense, and what is just and truthful and right, your verdict will be that Bill Shaw is not guilty."

Ben paused and then said, "I thank you."

A lump formed in my throat as Ben took his seat beside me.

Marin turned to the prosecutor. "Mr. Olson, is there any rebuttal argument?"

Olson stood. "Nothing more, Your Honor. The People have presented credible evidence for a conviction, and there's no need to rebut a thing the defense has offered."

Chapter 39

Judge Marin cleared his throat and turned to the jury. "Before you begin your deliberations, I must instruct you about the law." He began reading a prepared statement detailing how the State claimed it had presented proof of murder, while the defendant claimed the State had not proved its case.

I sat there, transfixed, knowing this was a crucial part of the trial—the judge's charge to the jury, the judge's reading of the law and how it should apply to the testimony and evidence that emerged during the trial.

"Now, let me define exactly what constitutes murder in the second degree," Marin said. "Murder in the second degree is defined as the intentional killing of another person that is not premeditated or planned. It is the killing of another person by direct action."

Marin let the jurors absorb his words. The courtroom was tomb-like.

Marin reiterated that I was entitled to the presumption of innocence, that the State was obligated to prove its case; that I, the defendant, was not required to prove my innocence. He instructed the jurors to consider only the evidence, not media reports or anything else. He reminded them again that attorneys' questions did not constitute evidence. He said that the jurors should not be influenced by the number of witnesses called by either side and that a guilty verdict must be rendered unanimously, and beyond a reasonable doubt.

"Now, please give me your complete attention while I explain the legal meaning of the term *reasonable doubt.*"

I waited fearfully, knowing jurors often had trouble wrestling with this elusive concept—*reasonable doubt*. It could be such a confusing puzzle; I'd never even tried to explain it in my novels. And it could confound jurors to the point of exasperation.

"Reasonable doubt is the uncertainty of a person who is earnestly looking for the truth," Marin said. "It does *not* mean the doubt of a person who is *looking for doubt*. After all, if you're *looking* for doubt, you can always find it, somewhere."

At that juncture, Marin paused and eyed the jury. Each member of the panel looked directly at him. A few looked befuddled, with furrowed brows and narrowed eyes.

"If you have reasonable doubt," Marin went on, "it means a question exists in your mind about the defendant's guilt, after you've made an honest effort to determine the truth."

I felt a swell of hope hearing him utter those words. Yet fear of the jury's verdict clung to me like a chill.

"Beyond a reasonable doubt does not mean beyond all imaginary or possible doubt," Marin said. "I say this because nearly everything in life is open to some possible doubt. The law does not require proof so convincing that it amounts to *absolute* certainty.

"You must understand, ladies and gentlemen, there are no absolute certainties when we deal with human affairs."

The jurors nodded in unison, but I thought some still looked confused.

"I have now completed my instructions regarding the law and your duties as jurors," he said. "I've tried to preside over this trial in a spirit of fairness and impartiality."

Marin paused once again and then leaned toward the panel.

"Ladies and gentlemen, you have a solemn duty to deliberate

honestly, to be fair, to be impartial, to weigh the evidence carefully, and to reflect on it with all the due consideration in your power."

I felt a rush of admiration for Marin. He was a superb jurist.

"I'm instructing you in this way, so when you reach a verdict, it will be in the service of truth and justice."

Chapter 40

Ben and I left the courthouse by way of the rear loading dock and headed toward the river. The jury had been deliberating for hours.

The sky's glare was blinding on this brilliant autumn day.

News vans were parked around Foley Square. Reporters roamed through the lunchtime crowd, asking for opinions about my guilt or innocence. Ben and I slipped away undetected.

A damp breeze wafted in off the harbor. It smelled of brine and engine oil. I wore sunglasses and an old Brooklyn Dodgers baseball cap that had been my father's. I kept my head lowered as we strode toward the water.

Traffic was thick with cars, taxis, and trucks. A city bus revved its engine and roared up the street, leaving a pall of fumes in the air. Horns honked, air brakes whooshed. WALK and DON'T WALK signs flashed. Hordes of pedestrians swarmed in hurried squadrons across streets. Flocks of pigeons strutted about, cooing in sunlight glinting on the sidewalk's mica specks. Food-truck vendors sold hot dogs, pita sandwiches, souvlaki, tortilla wraps, shish kebobs, and falafel amid an outpouring of smoke from chestnuts roasting atop handcarts.

We found an empty bench in a mini park. The Staten Island Ferry's foghorn crooned mournfully in the distance.

"The jury's taking forever," Ben said as we settled on the bench. "I'm worried about that alternate and one or two others.

Jesus, I wish we hadn't lost juror number four."

A gauntlet of memories took me back to Nora. I was lost in reverie.

"I didn't do you a favor by representing you," Ben said.

"Come off it, Ben. Without you, I'd be down the tubes."

"I fucked up. I overlooked that e-mail. If I'd addressed it on direct, it would've taken the wind out of Olson's sails."

"So, I was ambivalent. I think anyone could understand how I felt," I said, trying to sound hopeful, but dreariness seeped through me.

"Elaine was right. I'm too emotionally involved."

"Forget it, Ben." I stared at the harbor.

"I should've gotten you to a top-notch defense lawyer. I'd've put up the money. You'd pay me back down the road."

"Yeah, with what?"

"You see the best-seller list?"

"No."

"You have three books up there right now—paperback and e-books. You don't have money problems anymore."

We sat silently for a few minutes.

"I'm worried about two jurors in the back row," Ben said. "Juror number twelve looked bored during my closing argument."

Nora's words came back to me. *"My fate is written inside me. It's in my genes, and it falls on you. Bill, I'm so sorry."*

Ben said, "You never know with a jury."

My thoughts reeled back to a night shortly before Nora died. She whispered, *"I'm so sorry, Bill. I have to pee."*

I kissed her lips, slid down the bed rails, raised her upright, and slipped one arm behind her back, the other behind her knees. I carried her to the bathroom—she weighed next to nothing—and then sat her on the toilet. She could no longer hold her head up. I pulled a stool in front of her; then we sat knee to knee as I balanced her. She was like a wasted rag doll, and I told her how much I loved her, as urine whished into the bowl. I pulled toilet paper from the roll and wiped her gently.

As I lifted Nora to return her to the bed, she whispered, "Tango."

I thought at first she wanted me to play her favorite *canción*, the one she used to teach me the dance so many years earlier.

But no, with whatever strength she could muster, she whispered again, "One last dance."

And so we did.

I pulled her up, held her close to me, and she collapsed in my arms.

Her head fell softly against my chest. I grasped her right hand and raised her arm straight above our heads, lifted her off the floor, and with the lushness of the music in all its sadness and beauty playing in my head, I carried her to the living room. I moved slowly across the carpet with Nora in my arms.

And so, we danced our tango.

I was glad her eyes were closed so she couldn't see the tears spilling down my cheeks.

The shriek of a siren brought me back to Ben, who was talking about the trial.

"Olson saved that e-mail. He knew you'd *have* to testify after Constance, Lee, and Gina, but especially after we lost juror number four. He knew it and figured he'd catch you big-time. Ah, shit. I hope the jury's smart enough to understand. They can't put much weight on that police interrogation," Ben continued. "Jesus, you didn't want to involve Constance. And you were dead tired.

"It takes more than fantasy about motive, means, and opportunity for a conviction. And it takes more than looking at how a novel's created. It takes *facts* to prove murder. I don't think Olson leaped the reasonable-doubt hurdle, Bill."

Why can't I get Killian out of my mind? Was Olson right? Does Killian live in my heart and in the depths of my poisoned soul?

Even if the jury decides I'm not guilty, it's what I'll always be known for . . . the writer accused of murdering his wife. I might as well be Killian. Fantasy, reality—they've come together for me, finally.

"The jury's been out for ten hours." Ben sighed. "Not a good sign."

We continued waiting in Ben's office. Darkness had fallen. The jury was still at it. Not knowing my fate was excruciating.

I thought of the sultry, beautiful Nora dancing the tango the night we met. I couldn't let that image go—the arch of her back, the perfection of her body, of her legs, the thrust of her lovely chin, and her stunning profile, as the music played and she moved with such grace, with so much passion.

That picture would stay with me forever.

How filled with life she was and how she'd animated my writing—breathed life into it. Her love for me transformed me, made me whole.

"We should've taken the plea," Ben said. "I made a big mistake. I shouldn't have let you pass on it." Ben paced back and forth before a wall of bookshelves.

"Maybe we're headed for a hung jury," he mused. "Olson would love that. He'd push for another trial. It'd be more exposure for him."

I thought of the jury: twelve people—complete strangers—deliberating the course of my life.

And here I was sitting in Ben's office, hearing the cacophony of squealing car tires, the wail of sirens, the blaring of horns, the incessant tumult—the noises of an indifferent city going about its business on the street below.

And then we got the call.

Chapter 41

The jury members filed into the courtroom, snaked into the jury box, and took their seats.

Ben and I stood behind the defense table. My heart faltered and my legs were on the verge of buckling as I watched them. Three jurors cast furtive glances in my direction. What did that mean? I recalled Ben once saying, *"You can't tell a thing by how jurors look at you when they come into the courtroom. I've tried for years . . . just can't do it."*

Olson and Ann Pierce stood behind the prosecution table. Marin sat high above us and looked at the jurors.

Whispering and murmuring came from the gallery.

Reasonable doubt . . . moral certainty . . . truth.

All ambiguous.

The jurors were inscrutable—two rows of blank-faced people, impossible to read.

Once seated, not a single juror glanced our way.

The court officer stood to the side of the judge's bench.

The stenographer sat behind her machine.

"Please come to order," Marin said to the assemblage.

The crowd's hum subsided, becoming a rustling. There was coughing, clearing of throats, and then silence.

"Madame Forewoman, has the jury reached a verdict?" asked Marin.

"Yes, we have, Your Honor." Her voice was neutral, hinting at nothing.

My insides trembled.

"Please give the verdict forms to the court officer."

My jaw ached from clenching. I bit my inner cheek and the ferrous taste of blood filled my mouth. I swallowed hard.

The court officer walked over to the jury forewoman and took the verdict sheets.

He handed them to the judge.

Marin opened the paper, peered down, and said nothing. His expression was unrevealing.

He handed the paper to the court officer, who returned it to the forewoman.

"Will the defendant please rise for the verdict?" Marin said.

I rose on legs of liquid. My heart tumbled in my chest. It seemed a shroud dropped over the room. A shiver rippled through me.

Ben stood at my side.

"Please render the verdict, Madame Forewoman."

She stood and faced the judge.

Numbness gave way to an upsurge of adrenaline—it was pure fear and a sense of doom. Everything seemed distant, removed, surreal.

Looking at the paper, the forewoman said, "We the jurors in the matter of the State of New York against William Shaw find the defendant, William Shaw, not guilty of murder in the second degree."

Air burst from my lungs. Something collapsed inside me. The room swayed and then began spinning. My knees buckled. I was swooning. Sounds came from far away. There was a hollow whooshing as I sank downward, but Ben grabbed my waist and held me up.

"Justice was served," Ben whispered, holding me in a bear hug.

My hands shook and my lips quivered. Leaning over Ben's shoulder, I tried making eye contact with the jurors but could barely see through my tears.

A tumult rose from the gallery.

The words were indistinct, but I heard The Honorable J. J. Marin thank the jurors for their service and commend them for deliberating carefully. He said something about the jury being dismissed, but I'm not sure what I heard. The room stirred in a dizzying swirl. Ben lowered me into the chair.

Ben and Olson approached Marin at the bench.

They all shook hands as Judge J. J. Marin said something. There were nods, more handshakes, and smiles. Charlie bulled his way from the gallery, and his huge arms wrapped around me. My brother sobbed.

Depleted, I wondered if it mattered. There was no elation.

There was only emptiness, desolation.

It was over.

Chapter 42

How strange it seemed. My life was my own.

Cindy Armor called. "Bill, the *Post* and *New York Magazine* want to talk to you. What do you want me to tell them?"

"The buzzards wanna feast on my guts."

"You have four paperbacks on the best-seller list. And you're number one on Amazon. Are you interested in doing some interviews?"

"No way."

"Are you sure? I can get you a publicist. Or the publisher will use its in-house resources."

"Not interested, Cindy."

"Are you working on anything?"

"Not right now."

"How about *Assassin's Lullaby*? The trial alone will make it a huge best seller."

"Maybe when the dust settles."

Ben called.

"How're you doing, Bill?"

"Getting by. How're you, Elaine, and the kids?"

"Great. Elaine wants you over for dinner. How's next Monday evening?"

"Sounds good."

"You hear about Sean Olson?"

"Hear what?"

"He left his wife, and he's living with Ann Pierce somewhere in lower Manhattan."

It didn't take long for the news cycle to move on, as it always does. A few neighbors still stared, but most gave me friendly greetings. The sight of James Sinclair around the building brought back images of the courtroom. The building lobby, mailroom, elevators, and hallways reminded me of Nora's suffering, her death, and the trial.

The neighborhood—all of 3rd Avenue in the 80s—filled me with a mixture of sadness and yearning for times past and things gone. The apartment—the furnishings, our bed, the dishes, knick-knacks, everything in the place—was oppressively reminiscent.

But most especially, the framed photos of us Nora had placed on the walls haunted me with their cruel window-view into a long gone time when our lives were so beautiful, when we were together.

I descended the stairs of the Lexington Avenue line at 86th Street. The downtown 6 train screeched to a stop. I got into the subway car. The train powered through a darkened tunnel.

Climbing the subway stairs, I emerged in brilliant sunlight. I walked to Bleecker Street, passing pyramids of black, plastic garbage bags and trash baskets brimming with refuse, smelling of rotting fruit, burnt pizza crusts, and discarded dog shit—the flotsam and jetsam of Greenwich Village.

Charles Street was quiet. Federal-style row houses and brownstones lined the tranquil street. It was a world removed from the tumult of the Upper East Side.

Standing in front of the brownstone where Nora and I once lived, I was overcome with a draining sadness. I recalled the apartment with the ailanthus tree in the patio, beneath which we'd have late dinners on summer evenings. Back then, we'd listen to the voice of Lidia Borda, or the Calambre Quintet's "Tango Argentino."

And the dance would begin. It was our lovers' tango.

"*Stand closer*," Nora would say.

"*This close?*"

"*Yes, this close. The tango is a prelude, Bill. It's a promise of things to come.*"

How I ached with sadness.

I walked east through the warren of Village streets, past boutiques and restaurants, past what had once been the Village Gate and the Blue Note, where Nora and I had listened to jazz.

I knew I could never live in the Village again.

Jorge, the doorman, and Edgar, the co-op's superintendent, were in the foyer.

"You gonna give us all this?" Edgar asked, his eyes roaming eagerly over the apartment.

"Everything that isn't packed in boxes or plastic bags is yours," I said.

"It's beautiful stuff," Jorge said.

"Mr. Shaw, we can't thank you enough," Edgar added.

"You guys've been good to me. It's all yours."

Two burly guys from the Salvation Army dragged away the black plastic bags stuffed with Nora's clothing. My eyes welled with tears as they hauled out the few pieces of furniture Jorge and Edgar left behind. They packed the dishes and flatware, loaded everything onto a dolly, and wheeled it into the freight elevator and onto a truck.

After renting a place on the Upper West Side, I bought furniture at IKEA, tried to settle in, but felt uprooted.

Some months later, I reread what I'd written of *Assassin's Lullaby*. Knowing Nora never heard or read a word of it filled me with regret.

How could I launch myself into the universe of fiction? Could I still craft a story? Could I create an imagined life? Could I even keep living my own?

Cindy Armor called again. "Bill, people are buying your books not just for the stories; they're looking for hints about what really happened between you and Nora. Your backlist is the hottest thing right now. You won't be having any money problems."

"I'm glad to hear that, Cindy."

"*Assassin's Lullaby* would be a huge best seller, but a memoir of the trial would be over the top."

"It may take a while before I can get back to the writing."

"I know. You need time to decompress."

"Let's stay in touch."

I spoke with Lee once in a while, but the calls grew infrequent. It was just too painful for each of us.

Francesca's was a small, out-of-the-way bistro on East 78th Street. Dimly lit by wall sconces, the place was nearly empty early on a weekday evening.

Sitting at the bar, Constance smiled weakly when I entered. Her hair was done in an elaborate chignon. She sipped a glass of white wine.

"I'll have the same," I said to the bartender.

A glass of Pinot Grigio was set before me. We touched glasses.

"How do you feel?" she asked.

"Not good."

"I so looked forward to seeing you, but I feel the same way . . . not good at all."

I took her hand and looked into her eyes. I felt so many

things: sadness, relief, temptation, and remorse. It was too much to understand or try to explain.

"Constance, do we have a chance?"

"I don't know," she said, looking down. "I realized I couldn't answer Olson's questions. He made me look at things I didn't want to see."

"I can only thank you for not saying anything . . . for . . . well, you know . . ."

"I lied for a reason," she whispered. "There was no need for Olson to destroy you in front of the jury."

"You mean your perjury about that night in your apartment?"

"Of course."

"The night my spirit was willing but the flesh was weak."

"No, Bill," she said, shaking her head. "The spirit was *unwilling*, which is why the flesh was weak. You felt too guilty."

I nodded and sipped the glass of wine.

"Did the trial take something from us?" she asked. "Did it kill all possibility?"

"Maybe," I said, trying not to sound pessimistic.

Her eyes grew wet. "I guess we try to move on."

It was the end of something that had never really begun. It was futile to try imagining a different outcome. There was no way to undo or remake things. I leaned over and planted a kiss on her forehead.

She smiled faintly and nodded. Her eyes glistened with tears.

"My God, Constance, I hope your life goes better than mine."

"I'll find a way," she said.

"We both will."

I dropped some money on the bar, turned, and left.

I tried to return to *Assassin's Lullaby*, but nothing came to me. Staring at the laptop's screen, I heard Nora's words.

"I want you to write again . . . for me. It will be a gift from you

to me, the child we never had. Promise me you'll write it. Just for me."

Just one more novel.

It would be my gift to Nora.

Killian and Irena?

I'd painted them into an impossibly desperate corner. A killer and his intended victim.

In love with each other. Wanting to start a new life—together.

How could they survive if the Bratva wanted her dead? It was an impossible love story.

I started to write.

Somehow, the story's end began to form.

ASSASSIN'S LULLABY

Killian strides into Effie's Salon.

How beautiful Irena looks. He yearns for her more than he's ever wanted any woman.

"Hello, Killian," she says in that husky Russian voice. "I was waiting for you."

"You look amazingly beautiful," he replies.

"Hi, Killian!" says Sasha, her boss. "You're as handsome as Irena says."

These warm feelings of being welcomed have never been part of his life. Has he belonged to some ghoulish clan of dead men? Yes, the walking dead: killers, assassins.

But now, Killian could become part of a family. He feels a deep sense of kinship. There could be something beyond the next kill; and the one after that, perhaps someone to live for.

They sit at a corner banquette. Wall sconces cast peach-colored light.

The restaurant menu is difficult for Irena, so Killian reads it to her.

"You will order for me, no?" Irena asks.

He wants to protect her, care for her, learn her preferences and dislikes. He craves to know everything about her. It's blended with deep desire.

She says that as a child she was ugly. When she was eighteen, she became "looking-good."

She went to beauty school and studied acting. But she followed her brother to New York to begin a new life. Irena reaches for his hand and asks about his past.

He tells her his parents died and then he lived in a succession of foster homes. He says nothing about the beatings, and he doesn't tell her about the foster father who used him for pleasure. He shares nothing of his military experiences, of his connection to the Russian mob. He tells her about his computer repair service.

What he can never tell her—the work he really does— must end now.

Irena is an innocent, a danger to no one. He'll tell the fat man there's no need to kill her. But the fat man will have her killed anyway.

So he'll take her away and begin a new life. He has enough money. There can be a future.

Her cell phone rings. She speaks in Russian. Killian studies her face, knowing he could spend his life gazing at her. Only God could create such beauty, he thinks.

"No, Sasha," she says in English. "*Killian* take me home." Her smile holds such promise. "Yes, Killian is good man . . ."

In the taxi, she snuggles close. The fragrance of her hair is intoxicating. He kisses her forehead and she murmurs. As she curls her body and leans against him, he can't believe he met Irena to kill her.

Her building is newly constructed.

As they enter the lobby, the doorman tips his hat.

Her brother must have lacked Irena's flair. The apartment is furnished in beiges, off-whites, and neutral wall-to-wall carpeting.

She melts in his arms; he's lost in the taste and feel of her.

"Come with me, Killian," she says, pulling him into the darkened bedroom.

He hears her clothes coming off. He undresses and waits on the bed for her to join him.

She's on top of him. Their tongues roll through each other's mouths. She nibbles on his lips; he kisses her, wanting to taste every part of her. Her skin is creamy soft and smooth. He's lost in the pleasure of Irena.

She sits up. Then she straddles him, and he suddenly feels her soaking heat as she slides onto him.

The pleasure is exquisite, intense.

She rides him. Her hands are on his shoulders. Her movements quicken. Her hands go to his face. She rocks and sways, moaning and whispering. Her hands are beside his head, on the bed. Faster and faster. The pleasure is so intense, he whispers how he loves her. He's lost inside her.

Then in an instant, with time now gone, there's a hot cracking and it goes black.

Irena rises from him. Killian slips out of her. She rolls over and stares up in the darkness, finished.

She turns on the lamplight.

Killian remains still, on his back.

Everything is sprayed red. Killian's blood, skull, and brains are everywhere.

Irena unscrews the silencer from the pistol. Then she puts the pillow back. It's where the weapon had been waiting. She slips the pistol into her purse.

After wiping everything down, she gets dressed, goes

through Killian's clothing, and extracts a wad of bills. Killian lies amid a spreading lake of blood. Irena leaves, locks the apartment door, and takes the elevator. *What a surprise awaits the cleaning service when they come to tidy up the model apartment*, she thinks on the ride to the lobby.

A black Lincoln Navigator waits. Irena and the doorman get into the backseat. "It's done," she says.

"Go!" the fat man commands the driver.

"Why the hit?" she asks.

"He knew who we were."

"You have the rest of my money?"

"Spend it well," he says, handing her a briefcase.

She grabs it and holds it tightly.

"Did you learn his name?" the fat man asks.

"Killian. That's all I know."

At Penn Station, she says, "I'm outta here."

"Young woman, your name is what?"

"You'll never know," she says, getting out of the Navigator.

When and how Killian's death crept into my imagination remains clouded for me. It was unplanned until it actually happened.

Or, so I think.

Every love story has a tragic ending: either the lovers grow apart or death takes them from each other.

There are no happily ever afters—least of all, in life.

Chapter 43

It's been two years since Nora's death, a year and a half since the trial.

I still think of Nora every day. It happens in a thousand ways, no matter the circumstances or where I may be.

Looking at the pages of any novel I wrote, I hear Nora's voice reading the dialogue, bringing it alive. She lives on in our books. In my mind, I can still feel the lithe movements of her gorgeous tango as our bodies meld. Her closeness and the intimacy of the dance stay with me. I hear her laughter, and luxuriate in the memory of her smile and the glint of those luminous eyes.

I cherish these images, knowing Nora will always be part of me.

The trial, too, will stay with me always. It's not just the nightmarish dreams that continue to haunt my sleep, but my waking realization that the trial forced me to see so much about myself I preferred to keep hidden.

And I think often of the Honorable J. J. Marin's words when charging the jury:

"You must understand, ladies and gentlemen, there are no absolute certainties when we deal with human affairs."

So very true.

I cannot banish recollections of those dreadful days of Nora's demise, or of when my freedom hung in the balance.

That's why I've written this story, all of it—about Nora and me, about Ben and Olson, Constance, Marin, and the trial.

I first called this novel *Assassin's Lullaby*, the name I gave to Killian's story. But the title changed when I realized it was, above all, a tale of love, promise, and tragedy as embodied by the tango.

To write this story, I took on the personae of every character: of Ben, Lee, Olson, Sinclair, Constance, Dr. Pauling, and the others. I wrote as though I was each of them. I thought their thoughts and felt their feelings.

Much of this story is true; some is embellished, even fabricated—fiction telling facts and truth disguised as fiction. The line is blurred, and sometimes, even I cannot remember what actually took place.

I've written all this because in the courtroom—as in life and in novels—fact and fiction coalesced.

By now you know I cheated on Nora and hated myself for it. I lied to the police and to Ben; and I perjured myself on the stand.

I've written *The Lovers' Tango*—to finally tell the story of what really happened, to tell the whole truth, as I failed to do in the courtroom.

On the morning of March second, I finally fell into a tortured sleep. As often happened, I was startled awake. It was usually the rampant thrashing of my heart, or some horror-filled thought or dreamlike image causing me to bolt up in a state of indescribable dread.

But on that dark morning, I awoke, feeling as though ice had crystallized in my veins.

Nora's groan startled me.

It was her agony. I shot up from the sofa as my heart drubbed heavily. I staggered to the hospital bed where Nora lay.

I turned on the dim lamplight.

The morphine had worn off. Nora was awake. Her groans told

me she was in exquisite pain. I could only imagine the nerve endings sending molten discharges, scorching her flesh.

I could no longer endure her agony. If I could, I'd have willed the pain to leave her body and enter my own. I'd have gladly accepted it.

I stood beside her, watching helplessly as she endured her torment.

The bedside lamp cast a dim glow. Shadows pooled in the hollows behind her collarbones. Though unmoving, Nora was alert and suddenly, her eyes opened. I could tell she was awake, aware, more so than she'd been for weeks. Her face was masklike—frozen by paralysis. She couldn't even whisper; she was rendered mute by pain, by disease, and by morphine-induced languor.

But something was different that morning.

She looked pleadingly at me and then moaned.

That sound—Nora calling—was what woke me.

With tears in my eyes, I took her hand in mine. Then, of all things, she squeezed. Barely perceptible, it was the first movement she'd made in what seemed to have been weeks. Was I imagining it?

Then, it happened.

Her lips moved, and she whispered, "Please . . ."

Was my desperation to comfort her distorting reality?

No. It was real. Nora spoke to me.

"Nora, my love . . . what is it?" I whispered through my tears.

"Please . . . end this," she whispered.

Was this some sick imagining, some grotesque rendering of my own wish?

Nora peered up at me with those soulful eyes and then closed them.

I knew what I heard, saw, and felt, though now—two years later—I wonder if my senses deceived me. The passage of time creates distance, crafts doubt, and can make a mockery of memory.

Time can distort everything—can make one question what was perceived with ironclad certainty.

But I've relived it countless times.

It was no deception. It was real. It happened.

Nora had spoken and squeezed my hand.

Her face had a gaunt, Modigliani look, was so drawn, yet so lovely. The sight of her agony filled me with an ache so intense, I grew weak with sorrow.

My life would be empty without her, but I could no longer bear Nora's pain.

I knew, even then, by staring so intently at her, I was trying to clutch her—to visually capture forever her impossibly beautiful face, as if its lovely contours could be seared forever into my brain. As if she would be preserved indelibly in my memory.

I gazed at her luscious lips, took in her hollowed-out cheeks, her nose with its delicate contours sweeping downward to those exotic nostrils, and felt sadness so profound I still weep from the pain of those moments.

I was flooded by a tide of memories—of our times together, of the things we'd done, the life we'd shared.

I realized Nora *was* my life. And life as I'd known it was ending.

Then she opened her eyes.

Grief and yearning, insufferable fear and desperation overcame me. I managed to whisper, "I love you so much, Nora. I wish we could stay together forever."

Though she could no longer move a muscle, she shook her head.

Was it my imagination? Was I going insane?

But I saw it. I know I did.

I knew what she was saying.

Her eyes, so expressive, spoke to me.

They said, "No, my love. Our time is over. I must go . . ."

I was bursting with love, fear, regret, and sorrow.

"Nora, do you want your medicine?"

"Yes, my love. Give me the medicine this one last time."

"Are you sure, Nora?" I whispered.

"Yes, Bill . . . my love. Give me the medicine once more, because there is too much pain. I cannot go on. And then I'll wait for you . . ."

In the kitchen, with trembling hands, I poured the powdered warfarin into the sterile container. I mixed in the distilled water. I shook the solution and then sucked it into the plastic syringe. I pulled the plunger up, watching the black, double-edged rubber gasket as it rose in the tube. The clear liquid filled the syringe barrel to the third black line.

There was a full milliliter and a half of warfarin—three milligrams. Yes, 50 percent more than her usual dose.

I didn't squeeze out the extra half milliliter into the sink. It stayed in the syringe.

It was the choice I made.

I stood there, paralytic, wondering if I could do it.

It was five thirty in the morning.

At her bedside, I whispered, "Nora, this is three milligrams, not two. Do you really want it, my love?"

My heart throbbed—felt like it was splitting apart—and I trembled with love, fear, futility, rage, and regret.

"Yes, my darling, yes," she pleaded. "Please release me. I know you'll do this because you love me. I must go now. And, Bill, I will wait for you."

I waited for another moment, hoping she would speak again.

"Please give me this last dose," she said. "And know more than anything else that I love you. And, my darling, I know your love for me is greater than life itself."

Those were her last words.

I can no longer recall if she said them with her eyes or

whispered them. But they were her words.

So, with the agony of the damned, I set the syringe into the IV cap and then turned and tightened it. I hesitated, thinking I could never do it. My hands and fingers shook. My heart ached.

I looked into Nora's eyes—open again—and they spoke, *Please, Bill, give me the medicine.*

The plunger sank down in the cylinder, the gasket lowering slowly. The medicine flowed into the catheter, where it would stream gently—with such love—into Nora's blood, into her still breathing, living being, where it would make its way to every part of her.

And then I kissed her lips as she closed her eyes.

My tears splashed onto her face, spreading onto her skin.

Oh, the pain of the good-bye. Good-bye, my love.

I tried to hum that song to her, but my throat was parched.

I sat at the edge of the bed, stupefied, in mortal terror, knowing it was over, that I'd done something terrible yet loving. It was the saddest, most violent, yet gentle and caring thing I'd ever done in my life.

I was uncertain if I knew a thing about life or love, about giving, sharing, or about death itself.

But I knew this: everything left in this life was meaningless for me. I knew, too, that in the end, we must relinquish everything we love.

That's simply how it is.

Nora lay in repose. Soon, she would be at peace.

The digital clock read 6:00 a.m.

Roberta arrived at seven a.m. We must have talked, but I don't recall. I was numb, lost, simply floating through some strange dreamlike state, unthinking, unknowing, and barely alive.

I recall taking my laptop and going to the coffee shop, where I sat in a torpor as people chattered and the espresso machine hissed amid the morning madness and background babble.

I relived how Nora and I had made a life together. The memories washed over me like curling wavelets—sad but joyous, filled with love, nostalgia, regret, and deep yearning.

I tried making sense of it all. But it was impossible.

I vaguely recall walking on 3rd Avenue amid the rush of traffic and the city's voices, its blaring horns, the pall of fumes and frenzied clatter. I saw nothing. The passing crowds were a meaningless blur as I trudged wearily to the library in a tear-filled trance.

And soon Roberta called.

So, Dr. Pauling was correct in his analysis.

Nora died of an overdose of warfarin.

And Sean Patrick Olson, though calculating, arrogant, and ambitious, was a very perceptive man. He saw more clearly than I, the connections between Killian and myself.

It seems that in writing *Assassin's Lullaby*, my own life and Killian's intersected: we merged—became one person. Fact, fiction, perception, memory—they all came together as they have in this story.

I never realized fiction and life could blend so seamlessly, but really, it happens in every novel.

After all, where does fiction come from, if not from life?

When a novelist writes fiction, does it not come from some deeply hidden recess of the writer's mind? From the bank of life experiences merged with the magic of imagination.

Is there truly *any* fiction?

I ask myself so many questions about Nora and myself, about love and death, about right and wrong, about truth and justice, good and evil.

I find myself turning over and over again two questions:

Did Killian love Irena enough *not* to kill her?

And did I love Nora enough *to* kill her, to end her earthly existence?

I cannot answer these questions. They're beyond my limited abilities.

As Judge Marin said, there are no certainties in human affairs.

I know this: just as she loved me, I loved Nora more than life itself. Her illness and its aftermath killed the life I loved. Nora's death brought me to court in a battle for my own life. Ben once compared a trial to gladiatorial combat. He also called it war.

And now I'm left with shrapnel in my heart.

Though I think I did the merciful thing by relieving Nora's suffering, I know it was wrong. And maybe murdering Killian was my attempt at killing off some hateful part of myself. I'll never know.

I should have told the police I overdosed my wife. If I had, I'd surely have gone to prison; but maybe the confession would have set me free from the prison of self-loathing in which I find myself entrapped today.

Of course, I could have told the police I'd injected Nora with 50 percent more warfarin than the usual dose.

But I lied.

If you ever read this, you may very well view it as my confession.

Perhaps it is.

I can't be tried again for murder; that would be double jeopardy.

I haven't yet decided whether or not to give this manuscript to Cindy Armor. She keeps asking about *Assassin's Lullaby* or a memoir of the trial.

So, this manuscript—*The Lovers' Tango*—is fiction and fact, a novel (and a novel within a novel), a memoir and a confession—all fused as one. The lines of distinction between reality and fantasy, fiction and fact, aren't very clear.

Are they ever?

These pages may sit in my desk for years. If I do give them to Cindy, some people reading them will feel I did the right thing.

Others will condemn me.

Still others may feel angry, hurt, or outraged—if this goes public.

So, for the time being, these pages will be read by no one.

The trial is over for everyone except me. I now live in a hell of my own making. I'll subsist here for the rest of my life.

But I'm certain Nora waits for me. Therein lies my salvation.

Perhaps this manuscript will be found after my death—either by Ben or Lee or whoever cleans out my desk. Perhaps it will be published posthumously; so if you're reading this, it could mean I'm dead.

Meaning, I've joined Nora.

I must live with the knowledge that I took Nora's life, but in my heart, I know what I did was an act of love.

William Shaw
New York City

Acknowledgments

M any people's fingerprints are all over this novel.

Deepest thanks to Kristen Weber for showing me the way of the novel. I owe a great deal to Kristen: she was my enthusiastic cheerleader, editor, and patient writer's workshop all wrapped up in one incredibly generous person.

I owe special thanks to the people at Thunder Lake Press. Foremost among them is Sharon Goldinger. Skye Wentworth, Kristen Havens, and Penina Lopez helped enormously.

Friends graciously devoted their time and talent to reading the manuscript and made valuable suggestions. They include Marty Isler and Natalie Isler, Helen Kaufman and Phil (the Man) Kaufman, Arthur (Arturo) Kotch and Jill (Chilly) Kotch, and Barry Nathanson and Susan Nathanson. (Susan reminded me that despite the thriller and suspense elements in the novel, it is, above all, a love story.) Their suggestions, criticisms, and comments vastly improved the novel.

Other people, both living and dead, made their own (many, unknowingly) contributions to my knowledge base and authorial efforts. Psychiatrically, they include Dick Simons, Bill Console, and Warren Tanenbaum.

Others who helped enormously were Bruce Glaser, Melissa Danaczko, Victoria Colotta, and a cadre of historians, artists, physicians, and educators of every stripe.

My forensic background came heavily into play in this novel. It was strengthened by relationships with a stellar group of trial attorneys and judges: Rick Aiken, Hon. William Bellard, Jim Biondo, Howard Borowick, Donald Cousins, Jason Dodge, John Downey, Hon. Leonard Finz, Carl Lustig, Hon. John Mastropietro, Frank May, David Morrissey, Ben Rabinowitz, Ivan Schneider, Leon Segan, Max Toberoff, and Scott Williams.

Writers, journalists, and playwrights with whom I've spoken have been incredible sources of inspiration. Sharing author panels with, corresponding with, or interviewing them has taught me more about the craft of writing than can be described. Included are Kelley Armstrong, Ace Atkins, Joseph Badal, Steve Berry, Grant Blackwood, Michael Connelly, Patricia Cornwell, Catherine Coulter, Barry Eisler, Linda Fairstein, Joseph Finder, Ken Follett, Felix Francis, Alison Gaylin, Anna Godbersen, Elissa Grodin, Andrew Gross, Dianne Harmon, Rosemary Harris, Dorothy Hayes, Conn Iggulden, Peter James, Jan Karon, Faye Kellerman, Jesse Kellerman, Jonathan Kellerman, Raymond Khoury, John Land, David Mamet, Phillip Margolin, Judith Marks-White, Joe Meyers, David Morrell, Todd Moss, Scott Pratt, Ian Rankin, James Wesley Rawles, James Rollins, M. J. Rose, John Sandford, Danny Schechter, Tony Schumacher, E. J. Simon, Jessica Speart, Wendy Corsi Staub, Cathi Stoler, Brad Taylor, Ingrid Thoft, Simon Toyne, Karen Vaughan, Jane Velez-Mitchell, Randy Wayne White, and Stuart Woods.

To all the authors whose novels I have yet to read, thank you, in advance, for the pleasure I will derive, and for the literary insights I know I will gain.

I'm especially grateful to Alex Mead for allowing me to refashion and use his beautiful essay on the Argentine tango as a preface.

My gifted wife, Linda, tirelessly reads, reorganizes, and redirects the disordered peregrinations of my cluttered mind, edits every word of each draft of each novel, and brainstorms with me as I write. She puts up with my fierce penchant for rushing heedlessly through everything; but most of all, she puts up with me. She's a source of incredible courage, inspiration, and the deepest love.

About the Author

MARK RUBINSTEIN graduated from NYU with a degree in business administration. After college, he served in the US Army as a field medic tending to paratroopers of the 82nd Airborne Division. After discharge from the army, he returned to college, studied the premedical sciences, and gained admission to medical school. He became a physician and psychiatrist. He worked as an attending psychiatrist at Kings County Hospital, both on the wards and in the psychiatric emergency room. Maintaining private practices in New York City and Connecticut, he became involved in forensic psychiatry and testified as an expert witness at many hearings and trials.

As an attending psychiatrist at New York-Presbyterian Hospital and a clinical assistant professor of psychiatry at Cornell University Medical School, he taught psychiatric residents, psychologists, and social workers while practicing psychiatry.

Before turning to fiction, he coauthored five nonfiction books. He is a contributor to the *Huffington Post* and *Psychology Today*.

You can contact Mark through his website: http://markrubinstein-author.com.

Or, chat with him via Twitter using @mrubinsteinCT. Mark's e-mail address is author.mark.rubinstein@gmail.com.